Justicar Jhee
and the
Hole in the World

-The Justicar Jhee Mysteries Book 2-

by Trevol Swift

To my mother and sisters for all those books they left laying around the house.

1
____

THE WELCOME

~

The Maid of the Mists

Jhee pointed the viewer at the stately villa where they would holiday for the next long-tides as artisans finished the last bit of construction on their new home on the capital island. She brought the viewer down so Shep, her senior husband, could see her face. "Our ferry arrived without incident, and we are safely at the resort. I wish you were here with us," she said.

Shep frowned. "Non-stop social engagements? I'll pass. You're in Kanto's world now. Allow him to show you around. This will give you more time with him in his element. It'll do you and him good to spend more time together especially in an environment that showcases his talents."

"It won't stop me from missing you anyway."

"Ether crest life never suited me, but it's cut to fit for Kanto. You three need time together without me. Besides, someone needs to oversee the final work on our new home, so it's ready for your arrival. You'll be so busy with balls and parties you won't even notice."

"Don't remind me."

"Jhee, it'll be fine. Between them, I'm confident they'll see you don't make a fool of yourself."

Jhee spun to capture the rest of the private island off the cape's view of Straya, the largest island in the Blessed Isles, even larger than the capital isle. A few buildings from Galleon City towered in the distance. She ended on the magnificence of the ocean and the harbor, a combination of both Makers' and mortal achievements.

Kanto and Mirrei approached. "Is that our absent, boring, old *denme* who'd rather babysit a house than ride the high crests with us?"

"Correction: who'd rather babysit a house than babysit you."

Kanto made the childish gesture of pressing his nose. "Fine. Then every stick of furniture must be precisely where I specified and every possession as I outlined or else I'll blame you."

"A fair turn," Shep said.

This was the first time Jhee recalled Shep not being there to act as a buffer or point of friction.

Kanto had spent days laboring and poring over manuals and catalogs and images of furniture. He would see their new home brightly and gaily and fabulously and opulently appointed.

Jhee had the utmost confidence in his design skills. He would know what every stick of furniture and window treatment would convey about their situation. They had spent their night together going over it extensively. He quizzed her on what impression she wanted their home to communicate to visitors. Jhee did not much care herself, but it made him happy. She wanted him to feel fulfilled and tasks like this delighted him. He vowed to make their new home convey the tone and image she wanted while also remaining stylish and opulent as befitted her rank.

"I've seen images of places like this. In my grandmere's day, this was all the rave. A stay at a posh resort, then you motor up to the capital and stay at your own place or rent a townhouse during festival season."

Jhee tried not to think too hard about what that said about her taste or her age.

Lady Delphine, their host, awaited them atop the sandstone and seashell steps to the entryway. Jhee held out her hands. "Oh, Lady Delphine, thank you again for hosting me and my cohort."

Delphine clasped her forearms, then pressed each temple against Jhee's. "Oh, you old fool. Come here. Come here. Shame on you for thinking to slip through our waters without a visit. So good to see you. It's the least I can do for the help you gave me when we were in the academy together. I couldn't believe it when you told me you had expanded your household. When do I get to meet the rest of your welcome entourage?"

"Momentarily. Shep sends his regards. He's overseeing the final transport of our belongings from the barges to our new home."

"How regretful. He will join us later, I hope."

"He'll do his best. Shep isn't much for the festival scene."

"Ah. I won't press." Lady Delphine linked her arm with Jhee's. "About those other matters we discussed, have you mulled them over?"

"While the situation has been a little hectic, I gave your proposal some thought. Let's see how the stay goes before making any final decisions."

Lady Delphine cleared her throat and glanced from side to side. "And the last matter? The death of the mining supervisor?"

"I had no immediate conclusions to draw from what you told me. I might have a better idea once I've examined the work sites."

"You will be discrete?"

"As much as I can be."

Liveried barbarian porters bustled by them and picked up their trunks and suitcases. Mirrei held Kanto's arm as they ascended the broad stairs of the front of the island resort. Mirrei had a figure slenderer and daintier than her mother at that age. Her gossamer champagne traveling robe hid her delicate steps. She appeared to glide up to meet them. The pale complexion to her fuzzy skin along with her light gown gave her ascent an ethereal quality. It reminded Jhee of the stories of the Maid of the Mists. Right near the top, Mirrei's steps faltered. She coughed and turned red. Kanto held her steady.

Jhee offered her arm and helped Mirrei up the mansion's broad steps. "You should have let me secure a mobility chair or litter for you."

"Nonsense, *denbe*," Kanto said. "Poor Mirrei didn't want all that fuss."

Mirrei cut Kanto a brief look. "My fellow spouse is right, denbe. What would your friend think of me if I can't manage the simple task of walking up the stairs?"

And any situation Jhee might later wish for them. "As you wish, my... dear," Jhee said, trying a less formal term.

Both Kanto and Mirrei pulled a face. Mirrei smiled wanly and gave a slight shake of her head. Jhee agreed. Too much. Jhee had only said it to please. Her affection for her had not become even that deep yet. It was an insult to Mirrei to pretend otherwise. She rushed to amend herself. "As you wish, my wife."

"Thank you, denbe."

"Yes, thank you, denbe," Kanto repeated. He smirked. Those two and their teasing.

"Will I have to separate you two?"

"No," Mirrei said.

The three of them finished their graceful ascent to the landing. Misty rain had replaced the torrential downpour which plagued most of their journey. The island resort rested far enough away from the storm curtain to experience lessened effects from its significant weather disturbances. Once the storm curtain stabilized, even the drizzle might stop.

Hopefully, the drier weather would ease some symptoms from Mirrei's Fresh Lung Sickness. The less saline waters of the inner islands did not agree with many. Mirrei, like Kanto and Jhee, was used to the saltier waters of the Far Reaches. Though, their Fresh Lung Sickness had come and gone rapidly. The damp also did not help. Much like the storms, hopefully, the younger woman's condition would stabilize.

Jhee checked her pockets to see if she had any saline tablets on her. Even if they did not have to manage her saline levels and ensure her diet heavy in rock salt, Mirrei never had the hardiest constitution to begin with, according to her mother.

Miramar, Mirrei's mother, had had a difficult pregnancy. Mirrei had been Miramar's only child. A miracle child, much like Kanto. That may have been why the two spouses had bonded so quickly. Still, it was one more child than she and Shep had managed. Perhaps that would change. Or perhaps that was indicative of what difficulties Jhee might have if their plans for Kanto proceeded.

"Lady Delphine, may I present you Bright Harmony, my second husband."

"A pleasure, Lady Delphine," Kanto said. He gave the most formal of bows before planting a kiss on the back of Lady Delphine's hand.

"Likewise, Bright Harmony," said the Lady Delphine.

"This is Star Mirror, my youngest spouse," Jhee said. Jhee used their outside name because neither had been formally introduced to the Lady Delphine. Once they had stayed under her roof, they would be less formal.

Mirrei curtsied. "Lady Delphine."

"Delighted, Star Mirror."

"Are we the only guests?" Mirrei asked.

"I dare say we have quite the full house. There's a rather crude business-man, a travel writer, an organizer for fishing combines, a free-spirited advocate, and a mining director. We're also hosting an ambassador to the barbarian lands. He is also a man of waves."

"More clergy. My, we'll have to be on our best behavior."

"I don't know about all that now. He seemed a perfectly reasonable sort. Some others though are quite the characters."

"Speaking of waves and devotion," Jhee said. "I'd like to pay my respects to your Makers' Shrine."

"I'll have you brought to it once I've shown you to your rooms and given you a chance to refresh yourselves."

"Much appreciated." Jhee lowered her voice, "A mining director? I see, now, why you wanted my assistance."

"I'd like to put the issue to rest before Styrling sends any more help," Lady Delphine whispered.

Lady Delphine wrapped her arm in Jhee's and bundled them up the stairs to the solar where drinks with ice melon balls in them awaited them. Warm sunny drinks for these overcast times, but Lady Delphine loved them so even when they were first-years together. Lady Delphine had also been assigned to the intelligence pool just as Jhee had. The compulsory military service every citizen had to undergo had better positions than others. The intelligence pool is where the wealthier could get themselves or their offspring stationed and kept off the front lines. Not so much for Jhee and Shep, though. The Path Maker had had different plans.

Jhee shuddered and tried to shake off thoughts of her and Shep's military service.

"We have much to catch up on," Lady Delphine said. "I've put you up in the Observatory suite: one master bedroom with adjoining suites. If that doesn't suit, we can rearrange. I'll have the last bed put away until you need it."

At their rooms, Jhee turned to Kanto and nosed him on his cheek. Kanto pressed his *esca*, the star-shaped Makers' mark that adorned Water Folk's forehead, against hers. "See, here in time for festival season. Just as I promised," Jhee said.

"I had no doubt you would see your promise fulfilled. If anyone could, it would be you, dear wife."

"Thank you for your vote of confidence. You'll be happy to know, Mirrei, besides following Pascoe food protocols, they operate as Blue Waters certified for environmental protection and sustainability."

"Excellent." Mirrei plopped down on the master bed. "Our own beds, again."

The yacht and the detour to the Tranquility Bridge Abbey had them sleeping double and sometimes triple. As denbe, the anchor spouse, Jhee was the only one who ever had the luxury of a bedroom to herself at any point since they left their home in the Far Isles. Though, if propriety would have permitted it, she would have allowed Shep to share it on her nights to herself.

Jhee looked over the invoice from their abbey stay. Now she understood more and more why so many rural Justicars were corrupt. The sum had almost matched the cost of booking the resort stay, due in no small part to purchasing Tranquility Gold at market price.

"Now if you'll excuse me," Kanto said, "I need to ready our outfits. I claim this space right over here for a sewing area and to do design sketches. From now on, it's off-limits to anyone but me."

"Far be it from us to interrupt the Maker at Making."

"Laugh all you wish, but I intend for us to make a splash and be the envy of even the most fashionable houses."

"Live your Make, *denye*, always."

Kanto and Mirrei waggled fingers at each other. "Pure truth."

Kanto pulled out various robes and laid them on the bed. He touched his chin as he pored over them, ever the fashion-conscious one. Jhee had better uses for her mind share. Let him and Mirrei tend to such matters, likely why the Makers had put them in her path.

Jhee cleaned herself up and went looking for the Makers' shrine to perform her devotions and thank the Makers for their safe arrival, as was her duty as the head of household. The shrine occupied a shell grotto off the central atrium. She gave of the elements of air, earth, fire, and water to the First Makers; the sweat of her brow to the water feature; incense shavings for the ever-burning candle; breath and warmth for the plants; a respectful touch of her esca to the ground for the Unknown Maker, so that one would not turn her way. Next, she paid devotion to the Lesser Makers. For Kanto, she jangled Maker geld coins and bounced a few off Futou's drum-like belly. She burned a scented prayer letter and gave an extra measure of laughter to Pascoe and Lashae for Mirrei.

Though now that Kanto had mentioned the subject, the suite provided them much more room than the yacht. Since they had space, setting up a workshop for her and Mirrei while they were here did not sound like such a bad idea. Although constructing a chemistry lab in your hotel room was a far cry from designating a makeshift sewing room. Jhee would have to ask Delphine if she had an area where they could practice.

With a few moments of quiet to contemplate, Jhee thought through the scant details Delphine had given her about the mining supervisor's death and minor acts of vandalism, theft, and a poisoning incident. Most disturbing was the mining supervisor's death. Her fall down the mineshaft had been called an accident, but with all the other happenings Lady Delphine suspected otherwise. She wanted to get ahead of the matter before Styrling Mining stepped in and made matters worse.

Hake Hill

Jhee leaned against the balcony railing to catch a bit of spray and morning suns before Kanto arrived for their walk. Gentle rain patter and crashing surf eased the tension in her shoulders. Two figures yelling and gesturing at each other caught her notice. The strong winds and surf cut off most of their conversation. She had been refining her eavesdropping cypher. A small wind drawing might produce more than a clipped word. She synced herself to the winds. Such a strong presence of the winds here was hard to control. While this might make excellent practice, it made for poor ethics. Jhee allowed the winds to slip through her mental grasp. Unaided, Jhee still caught a word or two.

"You need to leave."

"Why you?"

"I have no answers. Just leave."

One turned to leave. The other grabbed his arm. The first man pushed the second to the ground. "Nowhere near us again."

The first man ran full on down the beach. The second got to his knees. He punched at the ground then clasped his hands into the traditional angle of the Makers where he meditated for some moments. He must have been Delphine's aforementioned ambassador and man of the coif. Jhee stepped back inside. She heard the door of the residence open and slam.

The encounter on the beach stayed with Jhee as she and her spouses went on an excursion. Jhee hung back while Kanto and Mirrei rushed along the Avenue from store to store. She was content to let them have their fun though she wished Shep were here to help her keep herself occupied.

Kanto came to a stop in front of a luxury clothier. "Oh! Let's go in this one."

They dashed inside and wandered the aisles handling bolts and realms of vibrant, high-end cloth.

"Denye, look at this fabric. Have you ever seen anything like it?"

"No, it's got an excellent hand, practically slips through my fingers." Kanto threw the fabric about Mirrei. "It drapes wonderfully."

"This pattern reminds me of our house watermark."

Kanto and Mirrei emerged from the shop sometime later with several bolts of expensive fabric. They walked further along the Avenue. Kanto came to a dead stop. "You want to be bad?"

"Let's be bad," Mirrei said.

"Iced fruit and cream. Let's get iced fruit and cream."

"Yes!"

Kanto and Mirrei ran inside giggling. Jhee smiled and trailed after them. The three of them found a lovely little table overlooking the deep blue water. Jhee kept her gaze focused beyond the immediate drop and further out to the crafts in the water. The two younger spouses gabbed about the latest doings and goings-on at the capital.

"The famous Hake Hill row. I've always dreamed of being able to shop here," Kanto said. "You'll love the capital city with all the finest foods, fashions, and entertainment."

"No, she'll be too busy with courses. The capital boasts some of the finest schools and academies in the inhabited worlds."

Mirrei raised an eyebrow, then shook her head and smiled. "Who needs to plan the rest of their life when I have you to do it for me?"

"My lady Justicar," a voice called. "Look, sibs, aren't those our guests?"

Jhee turned at the greeting. Two young women and a young man, all quite fetching, approached them with a few shopping bags in their hands. The young woman in the lead waved her arm then hurried to greet them.

"What a pleasant surprise. I'm Erma. This is Semele and Vash. We're Lady Delphine's children. How wonderful to meet you."

"Ah," Jhee said. She clasped forearms with each of them. "A pleasure to put faces to the names."

"For us, as well," the young man, Vash, said. Vash was one of those she saw arguing from her window. She now wished she had used that eavesdropping charm. He ended his forearm clasp with a rather forward extra squeeze before his attention immediately turned to Jhee's spouses.

"Allow me to introduce my consorts, Bright Harmony and Star Mirror."

"Pleasure to meet you," Kanto said

Vash's greeting lasted that extra fraction with them too, so she assumed him to be too affectionate. "Such evocative outside name choices."

"We picked them ourselves," said Mirrei. Her gaze lingered on the young man's.

"We didn't give you our outside names. You must think us terribly improper. It's just mumsy told us so much about you. We felt as if we already knew you. Given how close you and mumsy used to be, we didn't feel the need to stand on ceremony."

"Now, correct me if I'm wrong. You were mumsy's society fellow in the Academy days?" Semele asked.

"That is indeed correct."

"Come with us and let us give you the grand tour of the city."

Jhee checked for her junior spouses' reactions. Both bore eager expressions. "Very well then."

The Delphines escorted them to the heart of the city after they finished their treats. Jhee and her spouses stopped dead in their tracks near the monumental Cetus Fountains in the square. A group of Doombringers preached openly and proudly about the Unmaking, and no one, including their escorts, broke their stride. Young Folk protesting drowned out their proselytizing.

"Philosophy Making in the public square, a proud inland tradition," Semele said.

Each fountain hosted a different preacher.

Dusty folk in work aprons fought to out-yell the Doombringers, "The Empire thought nothing of them when it built the wall and submerged their isles. If the Empire didn't want to house or do right by them, it should have thought of that before it destroyed their homes."

"Yeah, put them to work in the mines," yelled someone from the crowd.

"Them and the barbarians," chimed in someone from another.

A group of young folk with crimson and ocher scarves countered, "Where they can get not one lung disease but two? We don't need another drain on Imperial resources. We need to improve the working conditions in the mines."

"A drain on the empire's resources? The empire's the one who destroyed our homes, our livelihood."

A group with a banner depicting the ocean with a giant numeral one on it spoke up next, "But that's the game, isn't it? Keep refugees and the Fire Folk at each other, so the Empire can do as it wills."

"The only true unity is that of the Final Sword and the glorious forces of remaking," the Doombringers said.

"Blast this trenched drizzle," Erma said. "At least it's better than storms. When those rolled through regularly, it was a treat. However, everything is still moist and sodden. It's sinking into the food and draining the flavor. Meals need seasoning with twice as many sea peppers as before."

"I wonder what they are eating at the capital," Semele asked.

"I doubt the capital has all this rain," Jhee answered. She continued to marvel at the manic street preaching. "They are too far from the storm zone."

"Too true."

"What about you, gentlefolk?" Erma asked. "Looks like we had the same idea. I figure as part of your stay here we should get you started on joining the social scene at the capital as soon as possible. That way, you can learn who the players are."

Semele clasped her hands. "If you have time, stop by the street fair this weekend. It involves lots of local businesses. Mumsy, along with Styrling Mining, is one of the co-sponsors. It's to help raise awareness of Miners' Lung Disease."

"That and Fresh Lung Syndrome are causes of mine," Vash said. "I'm a fellow of the Breath of the Deep, a foundation close to my heart."

"Nice to know," Mirrei said. She fluttered her eye color. Vash grinned.

"If you're heading back, we'd be glad to accompany you," Vash said.

Mirrei glanced back at Jhee and Kanto. "No, we still have errands. Hope to see you at the villa later."

"I look forward to it."

2

THE RESORT

~

Weirs

The next morning, the weather turned bright. Jhee sipped her honey and herb tea. Mirrei and Lady Delphine's daughters played in the surf by the small seaside lawn to Lady Delphine's country estate. Vash joined the frolic. They, too, had welcomed relief from the rain. Jhee and Delphine reclined on the east lawn watching the tide roll out. The four waded into the waves ankle-deep crabbing and picking up other exciting finds from the beach with a beach-combing rake.

"Your Mirrei looks so much livelier since she got here. I see a definite improvement in the color of her cheeks since she has arrived."

"She might have acclimated to the climate further inland."

Jhee glanced out at Mirrei basking and frolicking among the waves. The image of Miramar on the shores of their home, which must surely have sunk beneath the waves rolled in then out of her thoughts.

"She might at that."

"It may also be as much to do with the company as the final arrival and subsequent stability of dry land after such a long water voyage."

"Indeed."

Mirrei, Erma, Semele, and Vash returned with a bucket full of crabs. Mirrei had hitched up her skirts, which held more sea crabs. They rushed towards the white table and chairs they had set up on the private beach. Mirrei dumped her catch into a nearby bucket. She leaned over and pecked Jhee on the cheek. Jhee brushed sand from Mirrei's face.

"I see we will probably have sea crabs for lunch," Jhee said.

"We used to roast crabs on skewers when I was growing up," Mirrei said. "I haven't roasted crabs since I left home."

"I'll have the staff set up a bonfire," Lady Delphine said. "We may have enough here to put on the dinner menu tonight."

"And don't forget the skewers," Vash said.

Mirrei smiled and then looked away sheepishly. "Should we invite Kanto, denbe?"

"Whatever you wish."

"We can play weirs while we wait," Erma said.

"That would be lovely," said Semele. "Mirrei, care to come with?"

"Come on. It will be marvelous," Vash said. "You can be on my team. This way, they can't gang up on me."

Mirrei hesitated and glanced at Jhee. Jhee tucked her hands in her robes. "We should continue your lessons."

"Oh, so soon."

"Yes, we only have so much daylight left. The currents will be too weak at night. At least for our current lessons."

"If you insist, denbe."

Mirrei fluttered the tint of her eyes at Jhee. Not fair. Jhee drooped her shoulders then nodded.

Mirrei and Lady Delphine's offspring took off down the beach again, leaving their haul of crabs snapping and crawling in the nearby bucket. Jhee smiled. Yes, this environment seemed to agree with her. It was good for her and Kanto to have friends their own age.

"I must thank you for the use of your boathouse as a workspace."

"No need. No need. To discuss our proposal. Are we still in agreement?"

"Such as it was. She seems to be happy and thriving here. But we shall see. I'll force her into no arrangement she does not want."

"Understood. Understood. I, for one, was never one to give any member of my family such autonomy. But that is part of what makes you such a better woman than I, Jhee."

Jhee tensed under the unearned praise. Better woman. Jhee tried not to scoff. Many on her home islands might have a word or two to say on the subject. Most of all, Miramar had she still inhabited this sphere with them.

Miramar had held her home together against all mundane assaults only to see it done in by the stroke of a finger quill. Not from a natural disaster, but because of some official who did not even know or care her family existed. Bureaucracy, the force of nature no one could stand against.

Yells of alarm carried from the weir court. Jhee and Delphine barely had a moment to look at each before they ran for the courts. Vash cradled a collapsed Mirrei in his arms. They quickly brought her to a lawn chair.

"What happened?"

"We were having a spirited match of weirs. She started coughing, then collapsed," Vash began.

Semele shaded Mirrei from the sun while Vash touched Mirrei's face and neck. "She's clammy and cool to the touch. I've sent for my bag."

They brought Mirrei to a lawn chair. An anxious Kanto arrived on the heels of the servant with the bag. He must have been watching them this whole time.

Vash, the house physician apparently, placed his stethoscope against Mirrei's chest and held her wrists and hands. Kanto hovered while stroking his lacquered nails. Jhee remained poised. Yet, inside her sleeves, where she had hidden her hands, she pressed her palms tight together.

After a few moments, Vash put away the stethoscope, patted Mirrei's leg, and smiled at her.

"So?" Kanto asked.

"Our Mirrei here will be fine."

"What sort of aftercare does she need?"

"She needs some rest."

Vash patted her leg again. Jhee noted the signs of discoloration on his fingers and the wear patterns on his bag. She knew he had attended the medical program at the Imperial Academy and had good marks. What she sought now was additional signifiers of technique and expertise.

Jhee tapped her nose. "You're the house physician. Clinically trained at Tihalmec Imperial Academy. At the capital or Galleon City?"

"TAGC. Galleon City."

"Whole health?"

"Epidemiology."

Kanto ceased fidgeting to position himself beside Jhee. Mirrei appeared mortified.

"You also volunteer at a free clinic."

"You're quite astute. I provide services two long-tides a moon. Mumsy says it's important to give back."

Mirrei's eyes lit up. She seized control of the conversation. "Admirable. I'm considering joining the Imperial Academy of Medicine."

Jhee nodded, satisfied for now.

"You are such a lucky young lady to have such a caring household to look after you."

"She is," Kanto replied. "Denbe, denme, and I see she gets plenty of rest and eats right. We look after her."

"I can tell. Your household gives our Mirrei such excellent care. If I say so myself."

"All this fuss," Mirrei said.

"If you wanted to show mercy to my sisters and give them the match, you could have just resigned."

"Resigned," Erma said. "Tosh. We were winning."

"Hardly. Mirrei here is a fierce weirs player."

"A stinger if ever I saw one," Semele said.

Mirrei blushed.

"You gave us quite the fright," Kanto said. He moved in between Vash and Mirrei. "You should not have exerted yourself so."

"I was just having so much fun."

"I'm afraid it's my fault," Vash said. "If I had known about her condition, I would not have been so active. I would have kept a better eye on her."

"I know. Which is precisely why I didn't tell you."

Mirrei smiled.

Jhee took hold of her hand and kissed it. "You must not frighten us again like that."

"I know. Simply little too much excitement. Please, oh please, don't let this ruin the crab roast. I was so looking forward to it."

"If you insist. You are sure you wish to do this?"

"Yes. Please, a clam bake would be a marvelous way to end this day."

"Only for you."

The Delphines and Jhee's cohort spent the day's remainder roasting crabs by the beach.

Moonlight Reflections

During the crab roast, Jhee slipped away and began to set up their boathouse workshop. It might make a pleasant surprise for Mirrei where she could work on healing sequences in peace.

"I'd wondered where you'd gotten to," Mirrei said.

"I was hoping to have it set up before you noticed."

"Care for a walk along the beach?"

Jhee hesitated. Mirrei twinkled her eyes and pouted. Again, not fair. "How can I deny you, dende?"

As the narrow strip of beach tapered near a quiet little grotto, Jhee reached out and held Mirrei's hand on impulse. They smiled at each other. Mirrei leaned in. Jhee turned away and walked on. Mirrei stopped her, then leaned in for a kiss again. Jhee allowed herself to savor the moment. Then like the roar and sound of the surf, the moment evaporated to be replaced by another.

"I couldn't think of a better end to the day," Mirrei said.

"Seconded."

Though Jhee believed Mirrei the most likely of the two younger spouses to stay, she had kept Mirrei at a respectable remove because of more than allowing her some independence. She was not sure if what she felt for the young woman was only some residual of her feelings for Miramar. If so, it was not fair to encourage an attachment based on false pretenses, not when they were about to settle some place where there were better opportunities for her with those richer or those who would love her for who she was.

Would this ever not be awkward? Would Jhee always be reminded of Miramar and her betrayal of her? Jhee had loved her mother so much. So much she wondered if she could ever separate the two entirely in her mind and soul—which is why she always felt so guilty whenever she and Mirrei were romantic. Were her feelings for Mirrei or the residual of what she felt for Miramar? Perhaps she would never know.

Back in the suite, Jhee raised her head from her notes when Mirrei emerged from the dressing room in her nightgown.

"Will our home in the city have access to the beach?"

"No, but there is one nearby."

Mirrei's shoulders sagged.

"Once we're situated and I'm surer of my position, I might look into acquiring a beachfront vacation estate. And Lady Delphine says we have a standing invite to visit her whenever we wish."

"All right, then I shall speak no more of it."

"It was so good to see you laugh and play today."

"It was great fun. Sorry to have worried you."

"Now, now, go straight to bed. We'll skip the lessons tonight."

Mirrei hopped into bed and pulled aside the covers waiting for Jhee to join her.

"You should rest. I have more ledgers to look over."

Mirrei cocked her head at Jhee. "I won't break. My day. I say what goes on my day."

Consummation had been Mirrei's idea. Jhee understood the nuances involved and that their marriage was primarily one of convenience. It could have been chaste. Jhee had only delicately inquired into whether their match was Mirrei's preference. She supposed her keen interest in Vash had answered her question, another reason Jhee believed their match would not last long. Mirrei might be better off with another situation. She entertained getting another marriage for Mirrei. If their pairing was not Mirrei's preference, she knew they would have to arrange another marriage for her, one she would find more satisfying and passionate. She owed the young woman at least that much. She wanted her junior spouses to be happy. While she was not always the most conscientious denbe, she did not want to be entirely unconcerned with their happiness.

Mirrei attributed Jhee's hesitation to a belief the young woman too frail. Her reluctance had a more bittersweet cause. Too often, when she looked at Mirrei, all she could see was the junior's mother.

Jhee beckoned Mirrei toward her, "You may not be strong enough for Drawing, but I have a lesson to offer you tonight. These right here are the listings of our seabeds and shipping lanes and the deeds to some smaller atolls we owned. We still own them. It's just they are now storm-wracked or many feet underwater."

"I remember."

Mirrei touched the picture of one atoll: Talas island.

"Yes," Jhee said and turned away. Talas island where Mirrei's family home used to be and Jhee's.

"I remember when mamere and I came to stay with you. You two fought like seals and whales."

"Much like when we were young."

Jhee thought about the day when Miramar barged into their highland house with Mirrei in tow. She strode right past the staff and dropped her day bag in the middle of Jhee's entryway. She dared Jhee to kick her out. Jhee hadn't.

"I want to be open about the household finances with you. This may be your job one day. I spend a lot of money on Kanto."

"I understand. He's high maintenance."

"Your expenditures dropped off rapidly after you first got here. I initially thought I'd have two high-spending spouses to account for. Though, I don't mind. I am prepared to spend as much money on your interests and hobbies. I'd up your allowance, but you and Shep barely spend any of it already. And ask for even less little else besides. I initially gave you all the same allowance. Perhaps you can help me come up with a more equitable balance."

"Switch over to gifting and shopping trips. Those are fun, and to be fair, he spends as much of his allowance on us as himself."

"Case made. You have such a quick, detail-oriented mind. Should you change your path, I'd be more than happy to help you get your legal tabard. I still harbor hopes of a joint legal venture."

They walked through her investments. Jhee explained how she tended towards the more practical and old-fashioned. She liked to keep her investments in tangibles like food and shelter and sometimes safety: commodities people always needed. She saw too many prominent families ruined by speculative investments in next-wave, dodgy technologies. While it had paid off spectacularly for some like the Zeloachs, more often it led to ruin.

Mirrei was attentive, but soon, Jhee heard a light snore. Mirrei had fallen asleep on a stack of shipping reports. Jhee slipped them from under her head and coaxed her to bed where Jhee joined her.

Beach Lesson

Kanto accompanied Jhee and Mirrei down to the beach where she had decided that the ocean grotto would be an excellent locale for another lesson in drawing.

"We are sure your element is wind, yes?"

"Yes, teacher," Mirrei said jokingly.

"So, this would be a good place to practice, especially if we want you to expand into other elements for drawing. This is a liminal space where wind and sea meet."

"You sure it's proper I'm here," Kanto said.

"Yes. We will obey the traditional forms, but I will not dignify this no-male-arcana nonsense any longer. You will see what you will see."

"As you wish, denbe."

"Now shall we begin?" Jhee asked.

"Yes, teacher."

Jhee and Mirrei took a stance. They moved and flowed their arms with the wind and the waves. Kanto studiously kept his gaze averted. Jhee's clock wound back to other shores years ago: Miramar and Jhee at their morning practices while Shep watched in an utter flouting of convention. The similarity dashed her concentration. She overextended her reach but caught herself before she lost balance.

Mirrei paused but said nothing. Kanto glanced her way.

"Kanto, why don't you join us?" Jhee motioned for him to take a stance. She reset and dropped back into a neutral position. "Don't think I won't be as hard on you as I am on Mirrei because you haven't been practicing as long as she has. This space has other limnalities: the sand, the soil, the rocks from the grotto. Good for a male to sense. Clear and center your mind. Focus your weight down like an anchor stabilizing your position in the Mechanism."

They moved their arms back and forth.

"This is the place for big movements. Finger arcana is not strong enough to manipulate this amount and strength of winds. No mortal menfolk can draw the seas. No mortal womenfolk can draw the winds. Move the air around some, but you must understand your limitations. That is the lesson. Meet the vast glory that is the sea and the winds and realize your place under heaven, under the Mechanism, under the Makers. Here is a place to truly learn the Makers' magnificence. It is meant to be humbling."

Jhee placed her hands onto Kanto's arms to correct his form. He tensed. He still seemed uncomfortable with arcana. Traditional women who instilled in him the idea of male artificers as evil had raised him. Drawing probably seemed so as well. Though they had loosened the restrictions on male drawing, the cyphering laws were in flux. Cyphering and derivations for men were still in a legal gray area, one where she did not want to lead her spouses astray. As an officer of the court, she had to uphold the law even if she thought it was wrong. Perhaps she should still exclude Kanto from watching the cyphering lessons even if she only intended to teach him to draw until the laws settled.

For their lesson proper, Jhee started with synchronating the area. It would give them a baseline to work from and gauge if they had to fight any other artificers' influence. She applied the prime forces within to the gears of the Divine Mechanism. Another external factor beyond the Shield countered her. She pinpointed a source that emanated from the direction of the grotto. Odd. Perhaps she would check it out later.

While they gave their lesson, they had drawn the attention of the children who greeted the ferries on their arrival, offering to carry bags for coins and treats. Many had swarmed their cohort the day they arrived on the docks. They watched in wide-eyed fascination as the lesson continued. Jhee moved the lesson in full view of the children. She slowed to give the children a chance to follow their movements. She pitched her voice loud as she explained the actions to Mirrei and Kanto.

"Now. Feel the rhythms of the waves and the winds. Feel them moving through you. Feel the sand and the earth. Experience their weight holding you down. Grounding you to the land. These are our lands and our waters. We are the Water Folk. The other barbarian races may have taken over the rest of the world, but these lands and these waters more than any others are ours."

Wind drawing was Jhee's primary ascendant though she had gained secondary dominance in fire drawing because of her service. She commanded the elements which research increasingly tied to the women of their people. Researchers found mastery of elements such as water and earth to be most dominant in men. Hence, why men had become increasingly vital to the Shield project and a dilemma since male arcanists had been banned for almost four generations. In theory, the ban did not prohibit them from learning elementalism. In practice, most dampened that training for men too.

"Water and earth for you, the male. Fire and wind for you, the female. All elements working in concert. That is how achievements like the Shield are Made. Its completion represents the ultimate devotional act."

The Shield, though, needed ever more water and earth drawers. With the focus on training practitioners to build the Shield, fire drawing had fallen back in importance. Since it was also a product of the winds, it needed wind and fire drawers specialized in lightning. Given the papers Jhee had written on the subject, the Shield commission had asked her to consult on the Shield project. Which she would have happily done if not for her duties to the law and the courts.

Again, Jhee's mind went back to the abbey. She regretted that she could not find a less violent way out of that. She prided herself on solving problems with intellect. If she someone called upon her to judge herself, what would have been her finding?

After a while, they had a whole group of children doing their best to follow along or at the very least, mimic their movements.

Jhee made minor corrections to Mirrei's forms, as well. She and Mirrei harmonized and synchronized with the winds and the warm sun above them. They dug their feet into the ground and felt the sand squish between their toes. Water gulls screeched and wheeled around the skies above them. Crack-crack went the shells of the clams on the rocks lining the shore as the gulls dropped them to get to the treasure inside.

The visit with the Delphines had the underlying end to feel out what Mirrei wanted. Kanto had made himself plain frequently that whatever his affectations, Jhee was his choice. Lady Delphine had both eligible daughters and a son; an ideal situation in which Mirrei could find herself and express her needs. It did not have to be either-or. But she needed to give Mirrei an opportunity for another arrangement that better suited her nature. Jhee then could make arrangements everyone found acceptable.

Jhee thought about the situation she sought for Mirrei and Kanto. He had put a full stop on it, and she had finally listened. Mirrei had still voiced little opinion on the matter. Mirrei was young, and she deserved a better situation than to be saddled with two broken and aging anchors such as Jhee and Shep. Jhee figured, though, this was the least she could do. She had made a promise to Miramar, Mirrei's mother, that she would see the young woman to the capital and installed in whatever situation she wished. She owed them and their family that much.

Once the lesson ended, Jhee sent her spouses back to the villa and approached their audience. Some ran away. The rest swarmed her again vying for some change or candy. She pulled out a lace root melon candy and a low denomination shell. "All right, these go to the person who can tell me anything about the mischief happening over at the worksite."

Jhee had an immediate taker. A precocious little girl with a mix of barbarian and Water Folk features, elongated, droplet-shaped esca but golden eyes and pure-toned body hair, grabbed the candy and the money. The barbarians, also known as the Fire Folk, oddly enough had an esca shaped like a droplet, while the Water Folk bore ones shaped like a star. Perhaps there was some irony to that. The next difference was usually to be found in eye color.

"It's nature wisps," the tiny girl said. "I've seen them sometimes. Hovering over the equipment at night."

Jhee produced another bit of candy and money. "Now, these go to the person who can tell me anything about the supervisor that died."

At this, most of the children fled. The little precocious girl stood her ground. She grabbed the candy and money again. "Come with me."

The little girl led Jhee in the direction the Prime Forces had pulled her earlier. Just as during the lesson, Jhee felt a distinct energy shift in the forces within around this location. The Prime Forces were aquiver here. Jhee outpaced the girl as Jhee tracked them to a source, a crude shrine.

Votive offerings had been left for the Mischief Makers and other Lesser Makers by the work crews or locals. Small traces of incense and peppermint lingered. Inscribed shells and remnants of candle wax surrounded a nearby sheltered hollow. The high tide crashed against the rocks behind her. Jhee was mindful to not dwell on her proximity to sea and waves. A litany of cyphers and statutes distracted her from speculation about the dangers the watery vastness held.

In front of depictions of the Singers of the Sea family: the Witch Sisters, the Storm Child and hir pet shell drake, the Lady of the Isles, the Maid of the Mists, Grandmother, Whale Rider, Pearl Diver, Star Stealer, and the Moonwave Runners, had been placed fruit geld. The hair and gown of wispy clouds and rain common to the Maid of the Mists imagery stood out from the other members of her family. A protective hex mark encircled her. The locals must genuinely believe this to be the work of glitch or mist mites. Most modern communities put up a shrine to Maker Supreme when they're being terrorized by criminals.

The girl placed one of her candies on the shrine. "You can feel them can't you? The nature wisps."

"Nature wisps?" Jhee repeated.

"Everybody knows about nature wisps. They also like to hang about the Shield poles. All that mining, it made them restless. That's why they been messing with the site. Company's been digging too deep. They might go down and hit the mother or the root."

"Mother? Root?"

"You really don't know nothing."

"I suppose I don't."

"The mother or the root. All the miners know. That person died messing around the without the wisps' blessing. They offended the Singers of the Sea. That's what got them killed. They didn't do their devotions proper. Not like me. My 'mere showed me how. She was mine folk. Made her sick. She died. Since then, that's why I help people—to get extra money. You need a guide? Me and a few others we can show you around."

"Perhaps later."

"Suit yourself. If you change your mind, just come back to the docks and ask for the Latchers."

"The Latchers? That's what you're called?"

"Yep. You just let me know if you need anything. Me and the others we know where everything is, where all the stuff goes. We can help you out with whatever you need."

"I will at that."

The girl smiled, bobbed her head, and ran off. There were so many orphans. Were there always this many, or was that just the result of the displacement caused by the Shield? Netherwise, Jhee marveled at the resourcefulness of children. While tracing the flow of energy around here produced a resonance within the system, Jhee was not sure what to make of the girl's stories. She doubted haunted mines were the problem. Jhee suspected she had just been scammed out of candy and coin.

3

———

BAD COMPANY

～

Worksite Woes

Jhee met Mirrei at breakfast. "It's your day. What do you want to do? They have a lot of lovely museums and libraries. One local gallery even has a copy of Oandzo's original Grand Design, one of ten in existence. As well as the Orgonne treatises and the Chronicles and The Principles of The Blue Light. And a copy of Selisse's interim bible."

"Oh, I promised the Delphines I'd play weirs with them today. Sorry. I forgot."

"Apology accepted. You've been playing an awful lot of weirs. I would have never figured you to have taken to a sport so well."

"Neither did I. Rain slip?"

"Of course. Of course. It's good to see you out and about with people your own age."

"Glad you understand."

While Mirrei and the younger Delphines played weirs, Jhee used the opportunity to tackle the ongoing trouble at the mines Lady Delphine asked Jhee to investigate. Jhee had Lady Delphine walk her down to the site.

"The mining supervisor's accident was an exception. Mostly, it's been just mischief," Delphine said, "but I'm afraid someone else might get hurt if the equipment breaks at the wrong time. Not to mention the poisoning, lost nearly a dozen miners for a week."

Jhee returned to the beach. The drawing sensation she felt had piqued her curiosity, especially with the work site around the bend from the site of their arcana lessons. Near the grotto's entrance was the mine site. The Delphines' family business used to be mining before outfits like Styrling bought most out. Many families needed to change how they defined themselves nowadays.

The assignment to the capital came at just the right time. Kanto and Mirrei had shown signs of discontentment and boredom in their simple home on the heights. Kanto had redecorated continually, citing how dreary the place was. Yet, every attempt fell short of the idea he had in his mind, and he started over. Sometimes Mirrei helped. She preferred to explore the house finding new nooks to read and the caches of Jhee's books. On her good days, she even walked the grounds. Eventually, Kanto had decorated anew rooms he had finished and Mirrei reread the same books.

Jhee evaluated the damage to the heavy equipment. The electronic control panel on the heavy equipment had been fried. This had to come from a massive electrical overload as if lightning had struck the equipment. The ground and the vegetation showed no fulgurites or evidence of scorching. Whatever phenomenon occurred here had been confined to the equipment. No wonder everyone suspected glitch mites or nature wisps.

A glint on the ground under the generator caught her eye. She found a foil candy wrapper among the dirt. Jhee picked it up. It smelled heavily of cloves. A strong flavor like that had to be an acquired taste. Jhee suspected the only glitch mites afoot to be the little sea urchins who hustled her out of candy and coin. Poisoning, though—even more than the supervisor's fall—hinted at something larger or more sinister.

A loud break whistle pierced the air. Jhee offered a few devotions to the Singers of the Sea, topping off her prayers with a small offering to the Grandmother.

"Oi! Fancy Lady at our shrine." Jhee lifted her head to see an older pale skinned miner emerge from behind a support pillar. "Few folks the likes of you know how to show proper respect for Grandmother Whale Crusher."

"I'm from the Far Isles, the Reaches. You always wanted Grandmother Orcinus's blessing before you headed out into unknown waters. Who might you be?"

The old timer nodded. "Nix. Pod leader."

"So, you're like the Grandmother of the miners?"

"Yes, ma'am. Not sure as I deserve the title at the moment. You some high-crested investigator the lady brought in or are you mine company folk?"

"Lady Delphine's an old friend. She's worried about what's been happening around here lately. Might you part the waters about the subject for me?"

"It ain't us, if that's what you mean," the miner snapped. She eyed Jhee again then hastily bowed and snatched her soft cap off her head. "Begging your pardon m'lady."

"No offense taken. Why don't you just tell me what's been going on?"

Nix spoke with a rapid patter it took Jhee a moment to get. "My family's worked these mines for the Delphines for generations. Ain't seen nothing like it. At least, not since the stories grandmere told of the mining war days. Malfunctioning equipment. Foul tastes and beer that sours overnight. Missing tools. Sure signs we are beglitched. Like our gear and our site have drawn the notice of the Unknown Maker."

"Beer? You drink beer on site?"

"It's hot, thirsty work, m'ladies." The old timer bowed her head to Lady Delphine who waited at a respectable distance while Jhee worked. Delphine, sensing she might still have a chilling effect on the investigation, slipped away.

"So, you have a little something to quench your throats."

"Yes, but not in the mines. I sees it's only after we finish for the day if I can, ma'am. Danger. Dehydration. You got to stay crisp down there. Not just your life, but that of your fellows depends on it."

"Likewise for the mining supervisor?"

Nix squeezed her hat. "Company folk. They take care of their own. We take care of ours."

Miners lined up to drink from various coolers. "I'm keeping you from your break."

"Not at all, m'lady. I like to wait."

The initial rush at the shared coolers subsided. Jhee joined those gathered around one then waited until Nix drank before doing so herself. Some miners seated themselves on the non-working equipment pretending not to notice them conversing, while others were blatant. A few presented geld and libation at the shrine.

Jhee and Nix walked a few feet over with their cups. "What about folks getting sick?" Jhee asked.

Nix shrugged. Another glance at the shared coolers brought back Nix's comment about the soured beverages. Jhee downed the cup of brown liquid lest she contemplate too long about what it might be. The pleasant tang of chilled kolal leaf tea greeted her palate.

A group of miners congregated around a cooler at a remove from the others. The group remained small. If any excess wandered over, they were turned away with a furtive glance or two in Jhee's direction. The two miners staffing the cooler were studious about avoiding eye contact with her.

"Would you it bother you if I mixed a bit?" Jhee asked.

"No, m'lady. You need anything, come direct to me."

"Thank you. I will." Jhee drifted over to the out-of-place cooler and held out her cup. "May I?"

The eyes of one of those manning the cooler went bright umber and wide, making a severe contrast to their grimy, rose dust-streaked face.

The other answered, "You wouldn't like it, m'lady. Weak tea. Us is the only few what could stand it."

"As you wish. Did the mining supervisor like it?"

"Um, yes ma'am."

A few more discreet questions away from Nix confirmed Jhee's suspicions. The mining supervisor and the ill had drank from the same cooler, one known to be spiked with squelch, homemade liquor.

The break whistle sounded again and Jhee found Nix again. "Thank you, Grandmother."

Nix gave a gap-toothed smile as she donned her soft cap again. "Ma'am, about the mining supervisor."

"Any idea why she fell?"

"No, ma'am I just question the timing; off hours."

"Do company folk often go into the mines off shift?"

"Their business ain't none of mine unless it affects the pods. They give us a thorough going over of when we go in the mines and what we take out. Not so, Styrling folks."

"The mining supervisor may have been stealing templarite?"

"Someone had been going in the mine off hours. I just know it won't us. You don't take from the mines without proper devotions to appease the glitch mites and mine sprites. It may be her carelessness what drew Old Unknowable's notice."

Jhee found Delphine on the ridge above just out of sight.

"Anything?" Delphine asked.

"The mining supervisor liked to drink and was prone to visiting the mine after hours. As for your other troubles, there's some indication the mining supervisor may have also been stealing. All the accidents and the sabotage may have been a cover for her activities."

"Employee theft. So, it could have just been an accident? Styrling might accept that. What of the poisoning?"

"I may not have the full solution to your glitch mite problem, but I believe I know what made many ill: spoiled, alcoholic tea coolers."

Tension drained from Lady Delphine's posture. "Styrling suspected a work slowdown. That made them more anxious than the supervisor's death."

"Because they viewed it as a prelude to greater organizing action. I'll keep my eye out for any other answers."

"Homemade liquor." Delphine smirked. "Remember that one time we punched up the punch at that Academy reception?"

Jhee chuckled. "Don't remind me. I was sick for two whole days."

"Me too."

~

On the Town

Jhee stepped out into the hallway. Vash stormed by her. Then turned. "I'm sorry. Good morning, Justicar."

She noted he held a slip of bio-film in his hands. He twisted it and twisted it.

"I had a weirs date with Mirrei. Please, give her my regards and my apologies."

"I will. Is everything all right?"

"No, Justicar. No, they are not. Pardon my abruptness. If you will excuse me, I'm not fit company at the moment. I need to speak with Mumsy."

Erma walked by brandishing her weirs racket. She registered mild concern as Vash stormed by her. "I wonder what that was about."

"It would seem he cannot make your weirs date."

"Well, we will somehow persevere without him. How are you this morning, Justicar?"

"Fine. I was contemplating taking a constitutional."

"Perhaps you would like to join us for weirs. I can only assume Mirrei gets her extraordinary talent at it from your instruction."

"Alas, no such luck. I am quite the horrible player."

"Oh well, suit yourself. We'll go threesies."

Kanto entered the corridor from the adjoining suite.

"Kanto, we're going to play weirs," Erma said. "Would you and Mirrei care to play doubles?"

"No, thank you, I have other matters to attend to," Kanto said.

Jhee leaned over and said, "You should. It will be fun, and it will be good for you to spend more time with those closest to your own age."

"No. Thank you. Besides, if I didn't know any better, I might think you were still trying to get rid of me."

"Of course not. I made you a promise. I would never do such an action or even entertain that idea again."

Once Jhee dressed quickly and plainly, she headed down to breakfast. The ambassador browsed the buffet table while appearing decidedly dour. After she assessed the buffet and picked a few fruits for herself, she also sampled the buffet's new herbal orange tea. She had developed a taste for the beverage. A splash of Tranquility Bridge's nectar would go along with it nicely. She would make a cup for her and Mirrei. Jhee's sinuses had swollen. Not quite in headache territory, but she did not want to let it sneak up on her. The open sea had not agreed with her.

As Jhee went about gathering breakfast, the ambassador approached and spoke before she could politely affect an escape. "Justicar, allow me to introduce myself formally. Ambassador Naiman."

"Ambassador Naiman, how are you this morning?"

"Contemplative." He continued to pick at the buffet listlessly. The cast of the Ambassador's teal colored eyes softened. Teal eyes, but a star-shaped Makers' mark. Either he had spent extensive time in the Scorched lands or.... Faint rosettes dotted his body hair.

"You, Ambassador? Are you a barbarian?"

"Yes. Though, I find that term to be a bit of a misnomer, don't you? Have you visited the other continents?"

Jhee throat went dry. She swallowed.

"Only briefly," Jhee said and left the "during the war" part of the statement unspoken. The Makers' mark along with eye color was one of the more prominent means to distinguish between the various Folk. Water Folk had golden eyes while the barbarians had teal or greenish eyes. Both eyes gave off a slight bit of illumination. That was one of the creepiest things from her service. When you went into a night raid or on one of her missions, all you saw in the darkness was those greenish eyes staring back at you. Was that experience as unnerving for the barbarian soldiers as well? To see a slew of golden eyes in the blackness coming at them. Perhaps the barbarians did not fear Water Folk as much as the Water Folk feared the barbarians. The barbarians and the Other Folk who lived off world had resoundingly thrashed the Water Folk.

"I see. You're from the outer islands? Visit any interesting places on your journey here?"

"We recently spent time at the famous Abbey of Tranquility Bridge."

"With their famous blessed wines and healing waters?"

"The same. I understand you to be a man of the waves, too, Ambassador."

"I trained as a vicar and chaplain before being appointed an ambassador. Though, unlike the monastics, my Path Maker emphasized working with the community at large. Because I drove a water junk during my conscription, I got a water taxi license. I used to help the elderly run errands and transport them to doctors' appointments."

"Ah, the Formalist tenets of outreach and service. You come from a ministry which practices being amongst the populace, unlike Drakists."

"No offense to the seclusionists, but what good does faith do you and your community alone on an island? Faith needs to be put under pressure and challenge, but only enough to temper it. Now, though, how much is too much? How much temptation goes too far? At what point does seeking to test faith weaken it and have the opposite effect of what you were going for?"

"All interesting questions."

Vash entered the dining hall. The two men caught each other's gaze. Vash glared then left.

The ambassador frowned. "Begging the fine lady's pardon, I have other less spiritual matters to contend with."

Mirrei came down the stairs happily chatting with Erma and Semele. She rushed over and slipped her arm into Jhee's.

"For me?" Mirrei purred.

"I have some nectar stashed in our room if you want it."

"Thank you. I've just become a fiend for these orange tea and nectar healing draughts. I think I owe them my improvements these past long-tides."

"My hope is you're right. It is one reason I put aground there. It might have been one of the few things to make what we went through there worth it."

"Also, you and Kanto getting along better, too."

"Yes that too. What are your plans for today? I spoke with Vash, and he told me he had to cancel."

"I know. It's a shame. Semele, Erma, and I will persevere without him. We're going to head into town and perhaps catch some shows."

"Would you do me a favor?"

"Anything."

"Invite Kanto. I've tried to encourage him to do activities on his own, but he doesn't listen to me."

"He doesn't listen to me either. I'll see what he can do, but likely all he will do is sulk, anyway. He's been such a wipeout lately."

Later, Jhee went to the villa pool to find Kanto swimming, Mirrei and the Delphines having long since left. He emerged from the pool lean, sleek, and glistening in the suns. It reminded her of being a quarter jubilant and watching along with Mai, their nickname for Mirrei's mother, as Shep approached them the first time fresh from diving. He dumped a bucket of fresh-caught sea meat before them. Fearless Mai had leaped to her feet first and offered him a towel.

Jhee stood and offered Kanto a robe. He slipped into it, pulled her gently against him, and muzzed her cheek.

"Thanks," he said, in a low voice. He arrayed himself on the beach chair beside hers with a confident smile. By the secluded poolside, she allowed her gaze to linger in a brazen manner she would have been too embarrassed, too scandalized to do only weeks before.

"Didn't you want to go into town with Mirrei and the Delphines? I thought they invited you."

"No, I figured I'd find my own amusement today."

"I have some meet-and-greets to do around town. Would you like to come with?"

"Isn't this your off day?"

"Yes, but since you didn't go into town with them, I thought I'd offer you another outing. Unless you want to lounge around by the pool alone."

"Not at all. While this is your day, I'd very much like to spend it with you if you'll let me. Your day, your say. I'd be delighted so long as you don't consider this me impinging on your personal time."

"Consider this business, not personal. I'm going to chat with the local dignitaries. I need my secret weapon with me."

Kanto grinned. "In that case, I'd be delighted. Let me go get changed. Come with. If you know who'll be meeting ahead of time, I can brief you."

They walked arm and arm back to the observatory suite.

After they returned, Jhee showered. She emerged to find Kanto organizing her papers and ledgers.

"I hope you don't mind. Perhaps we should go over your holdings again. I'm concerned about the water rights dispute you have with those spiteful Brackfins, and now it seems the Foresters are making a claim too."

"Surely you must want to do something other than pore over these musty old ledgers. Mirrei and the younger Delphines will be doing more crabbing and weirs later. You can always join them."

"I much prefer to spend time with you if I may."

"As you wish."

"Please, denbe, I want to understand our holdings. I don't want you to give me anything which will hurt you to give."

"If you insist, my dear husband."

Jhee patted Kanto's hand affectionately. He covered it with his other and stared at her long and intently.

"It is not my day," he said. "Perhaps we could get a bit of an early start to it, anyway."

"Tell me about the new furnishings you got for our new home."

"Well, as it turns out, I got an excellent deal on most of the driftwood pieces. The old master recently died, and his son took over. He is still under apprenticeship, but his work is every bit as good as his father's. So, it's undervalued. However, he wants to get his name out and established and gave us a deal on some sets so he can have his work on display in the capital. I think it will suit your aesthetic very well. We should not just imitate the fashions of the capital but seek to bring aspects of our home districts into the forefront and make a fusion of the various styles. A mind burrower to keep the Far Reaches and outlying islands in their thoughts whenever they see us or our home. A way of showing the capital what the future could be and perhaps how much of a forward thinker you can be."

"That sounds wonderful. I often forget the little nuances, and you never fail to remind me."

"And I always will, my denbe."

4

DIVERGENT STREAMS

~

Street Fair

"Denbe, can we attend the street fair, instead? Please, please, oh please."

"It's your day. I suppose I can indulge you. The museums waited this long. I suppose they can wait longer."

"Thank you." Mirrei gave Jhee a tremendous kiss. Jhee upturned the corners of her mouth to cover her disappointment. The girl had been cooped up so long at home and during their journey. Jhee could let her live some. The capital had bigger, better galleries. Mirrei grabbed Jhee's hand and pulled her to a table selling turquoise and sandstone jewelry. Despite herself, Jhee enjoyed it. The blending of cultures and great food and music. Mirrei danced while Jhee stood on the sideline. Every so often, Mirrei sought to entice Jhee to join in by flashing the golden light of her eyes. Jhee continually declined.

"Yoo-hoo, my lady Justicar," came Erma's voice. She waved excitedly to Jhee from further up the lane. "Kanto, look who we found."

As she continued to wave, Erma and her sister cut through the crowd along with their reluctant companion Kanto.

"Glad you could make it. Having fun, I hope?"

"Oceans of it," Mirrei said.

33

The three chuckled and clasped hands.

"You have got to see this sand painter," Semele said.

She and Erma grabbed Mirrei and dragged her back through the crowd, leaving Jhee and Kanto to studiously avoid interacting. The travel writer had hir conch aimed at what Jhee believed to be another guest from the villa. The man, who operated a table at the fair, grew wide-eyed with Jhee's approach and cracked a huge smile.

"My lady Justicar, you can't imagine what a great pleasure it is to meet you. I'm Lake, the fishing combine rep." The fishing combine representative grabbed for Jhee's hand. Kanto intercepted the gesture with his own outstretched hand. He pumped Kanto's hand vigorously. "Such an honor. Would you like to sign our petition? I'm here trying to recruit people for the fishing combine—a small group of fisherfolk who decide on fishing rules and pool resources for beyond the Shield fishing licenses. The fees are prohibitively expensive for the individual fisherfolk. Together we can accomplish what none of us can alone. The power of the school of fish protects the individual fish contained within. Let me get you some literature."

The travel writer held hir conch closer. "This will make great local color for my piece."

"When will it be published?" Lake asked. "We can really use the exposure."

"Still at it I see, Lake." A jovial woman stuffed the remains of her apple fritter in her mouth and wiped her hands before offering one to Jhee. She sidestepped Kanto's attempt to intercept her. "Sianna, director of company relations for Styrling Mining and Staffing, and this is my associate Inksy. And you are the indefatigable Justicar from the Sixteenth District."

Jhee took Sianna's hand. Inksy hung back and said nothing. "Allow me to introduce—"

"Bright Harmony. My pleasure." The woman clasped her hands behind her back and rocked on her feet. At Jhee's confused look, she said, "I'm staying at the resort with you."

"That's odd. I don't recall—"

"I keep odd hours. Toodles and enjoy the fair."

The pair walked away. Inksy gave a brief look back at them and popped a mint.

"How rude," Kanto said. "I have to catch up to my hosts. Maybe we'll all supper together later."

Jhee encountered other guests at the gaming tables though they had not been introduced. One woman had a large supply of winnings in front of her. She wore a headscarf with an end that dangled down her left side and over her shoulder. This guest at the villa had made no secret of her comings and goings, unlike Sianna and her companion. A heat shimmer around her made it hard for Jhee to focus on her. She picked up the dicing cup and shook it near her ear. "Six, did you say? No, sixteen? You sure?"

"Dumb, rotten luck. That's all it is," grumbled a rough and burly man at the end of the table. She recognized him as another guest, a businessman of some sort. He stroked at his bushy mustaches. "One more throw."

"Perhaps you should be giving more offerings to Lethys and her luck wisps." The woman put down her money and the next person rolled. Sure enough, sixteen came up. Jhee approached. "Hello-o, fellow guest. Advocate Farkhande. I just adore street fairs, don't you?"

"I haven't attended many," Jhee answered.

"What a shame indeed. Just as well you're attending this one then. You are missing quite an experience of culture and atmosphere. It's good to remember ways different from yours exists. The gossip wisps sure are abuzz today. They are having the time of their lives. Keep an eye out for those Mischief Makers. If you see one, make sure you show them proper respect and give them an offering. You'll thank me later and save yourself a lot of trouble in the meantime."

"To the trench with those dice." The mustachioed man tore his promissory stubs into tiny bits and scattered them to the winds. Jhee watched awhile longer. His luck did not change. He pressed his hands together at angles then took a drink and poured one into another glass for the Unknown Makers. "Who are you again?" he asked Jhee.

"One of your fellow guests at the villa, Mister...?"

"Eldjin. Ah, yes. The Justicar. How fitting cause it's a crime how fast my fortunes turned."

"Your name. I feel I've heard it beyond the villa."

Lady Delphine approached the gaming tables in the company of an athletic, younger woman wearing a sporty sailing ensemble.

"Well, if it isn't my favorite guests all in one place," Lady Delphine said. "Allow me to introduce the heritage committee liaison, Oriel. She helped organize all this and convinced me to sign on as a sponsor."

"Not single-handedly," Ms. Oriel said. Her voice was throaty and soothing. "All I did was help an already finely tuned endeavor run smoother."

At some point, the travel writer had wandered over. Advocate Farkhande offered xe the dicing cup. "Care to try your luck?"

"No, I already know it's bad," xe said.

"Justicar, what about you?" Jhee also passed. "Well, I'm going to go spread the love. Hope to see everyone at the fundraiser."

"Will we see you gentle folk there?" Ms. Oriel asked.

Jhee shook her head confused. "What fundraiser?"

Ms. Oriel gave the formal touch of her heart to both Jhee and household to convey she did not know how familiar of a greeting to provide her with. The woman was familiar with court etiquette and from the middle ranks. Jhee inclined her head to show basic familiarity was sufficient.

"You haven't heard about the fundraiser? Well, Justicar, allow me to tell you all about it. On behalf of the Breath of the Deep, I've organized a charity event at the local observatory. The proceeds go towards the local free clinics as well as fighting and researching Fresh Lung Syndrome. We'll also be auctioning a few Mechanist artifacts."

Jhee clasped her hands, and her ears perked up. "Mechanist artifacts?"

"Yes. I'll send you invites and put your names on the list."

"Truly, I am in your debt."

"My pleasure, my lady Justicar." Ms. Oriel gave a quick touch of heart. "Now, I must be going. Waves to damp. Preparations to finish."

Farkhande went to Lake's table and picked up his sign-up board. After she applied her signet with much ceremony and vigor, she flipped the tail of her headscarf over her shoulder.

This confirmed it, Jhee thought. All the other guests were a bunch of weirdos and cranks, not at all the guests Delphine's family hosted in their heyday. Was it due to changing times or changing family fortunes? Another consequence of the vandalism, harassment, and sabotage happening at the resort?

Not long after Lady Delphine left, invites arrived via ether.

"Stall the wall! Stop the squall!"

Out of nowhere a stream of protesters, swept through the fair. If Jhee had eyes on her spouses, she lost them here.

~

Protests

"Stop the wall! All Folx unite!"

After she got cut off from the Delphines, Mirrei wandered the stalls and small tucked away shops of the Furnace District at the edge of the fair. The colors and scents of the Fire Folk fare bore earthier notes than Water Folk food and dress. Both though had a love of spice.

Mirrei stopped at a food cart temporarily turned into a stall which emanated the most wonderful, mouth-watering scent of bay and cape root. "Sea meat stew and a lamb and crab skewer, please."

The woman and man team working the cart served orders fast and furious; the man performing entertaining flourishes with the ladles, spatulas, and spices, while the women displayed various tricks cutting and seasoning the meats. The dishes had Mirrei sweating and wiping her brow. She contemplated not finishing them, but she had no means to save them for later. The marvelous pepper taste and guilt over wasting the fine meal made her persevere. Afterwards, her head and sinuses felt fit to explode as if she had sneezed dozens of times in succession.

A mix of Folk at a sidewalk café nearby cheered. A skinny-framed man with very short, light brown hair and modest clothes watched from the door. He gave a slow clap. "For a moment there, we didn't think you were going to make it."

A protester tried to shove a flier in Mirrei's hand. The cart vendors shooed them away with their utensils. "Trouble Maker! Trouble Makers!"

Xe melted back into the flow of people. Another wave of protesters swept by. A fight broke out.

"Quick, in here." Semele beckoned to Mirrei from the doorway the man had occupied. They watched the fray from the safety of the club.

More chants floated in from outside. "Stop the wall! All Folx unite!"

"What are they protesting?" Mirrei asked.

A woman with messy, reddish hair and a cut over her eye answered, "The wall isn't safe. The effects on the ecosystem and as well as the islands deliberately sunk, the displaced wildlife, and the destruction of coral reefs pose a health hazard. The winds and rains it generates could create a self-sustaining vortex which will be subject to thermal runaway, resulting in a cascade effect that will suck in and destroy all the Blessed Isles."

"My word," Mirrei said.

Erma treated the first woman's cut. "Must you always be so alarmist? Some are protesting for better working conditions in the mines. There's been a spike in Miners' Lung Disease since the last big orders came in."

"Why're you explaining anything to this guppy, Wynne?" the man who had laughed at her earlier asked from a stool at the bar. He knocked back a shot. He swept his gaze over Mirrei. "Hey, guppy. Let me guess. You're here to soak up the exotic, barbarian culture."

"Guppy?" Mirrei asked.

"This is Star," Semele began.

"Star. Just Star," Mirrei interrupted. She did not want him knowing even her veiled name.

The man smirked. "Name's Chappy. I own this and another establishment. Can I get you ladies a drink?"

"No. We should probably be heading back."

"Suit yourself."

~

"Stop the wall! The wall is death!"

The stream of protesters cut Kanto off from his hosts. He spun around. He had no way of returning to where he last saw Jhee or Mirrei. A man had taken up a position on the rim of one grand, marble Cetus fountain in the plaza.

The man pointed into the crowd. "What of you, brother? You look well kept. What's your name?"

Kanto looked around. He noticed all eyes had focused on him. "Bright Harmony."

"Veiled names. What era are you from? Is that name your family's choice, your anchor's, or yours?"

He had always imagined himself the center of attention, just not like this. "All."

"Well, aren't you a fine pet?"

Kanto wrinkled his nose. He should have known. "Feh, CARPs. I enjoy being taken care of, and I like nice things. My path isn't yours."

Core Andro Rights Proponents wouldn't be happy unless he came home stinking of the sea every day. Indeed, the plights of men who were not in such a favored circumstance as his motivated him. Men who had been forced to flee and wound up as refugees or Prospectives at Tranquility Bridge's abbey. If they were fortunate. Others wound up worked to death or as bed slaves. He'd rather his silks and colognes, instead of cassocks and the burnt flesh scent of a brand.

"THE WALL IS DEATH! All Folx unite!"

Jhee worked her way through the protesters to an eye of calm at a nearby shrine. This disruption felt like the first time in forever she had a moment alone. The journey via yacht from their former home to the capital had been long with several interesting stops along the way. While she had her own state-room on the ship and her master bedroom at the villa, Mirrei and Kanto were still a constant presence.

Ambassador Naiman's path had converged with the miners, and they had fallen into a civil conference. They were a mix of Fire and Water Folk, though identifiers other than their eye colors and Maker's Mark had been obscured by the dust of their trade. With their reddish shade, glowing eyes, and esca, they conjured images of Trench bound wisps.

The shrine Jhee occupied only contained altars for the First Makers. She placed a cypher inscribed shell on the shrine's Unknown Maker space and offered common devotions to the First Makers for Kanto and Mirrei before trying to reach them via conch.

How did Jhee proceed with the dendes' marriage arrangements? Kanto had elicited a promise from her she would not try to marry him off. Would he still be so eager to stay once they reached the capital proper? There he would be surrounded by an excess of well-appointed lords and ladies.

The idea bothered Jhee a little. A fact which surprised her. She had done her best to maintain a distance between them for just such a possibility. The business at the abbey taught her to value him and in a smaller way Mirrei as well.

Advocate Farkhande stood at the center of another group, listening intently to their concerns; more common laborers and farmers from their aprons and overalls. While Jhee hung back, Jhee listened in to their grievances. Had Jhee been called to adjudicate she likely would have found in their favor. In the Far Reaches, most everyone made their living directly from the sea. Open field farming was practically unheard of. What farming there was, took place at sea or on terraces like those surrounding their former home. Shep's family had been quite renowned for their dive farm.

For so long, it had been only Jhee and Shep. Then almost overnight it was the four of them. The dendes' energy and fresh outlook had become a welcome addition. New blood may have been just the component their household needed. It would be disappointing to see them go. She and Shep, while still short of three jubilees, had lived a fair bit. They were set in their ways and had a routine that worked for them. Kanto and Mirrei were younger and had much to anticipate in their lives. It felt like holding them back to obligate them to stay.

The travel writer had climbed an awning to capture images. Lake, at last, found a receptive audience for his combine amongst the protesters. The fisherfolk had locked arms to form a protective wall around his table as he preached about the benefits. Jhee understood the fisherfolk's lot the best. But by the time the Shield had come, her family with their dubious history and relatively new noble status had already diversified from fishing.

The Shield had changed much in the Reaches and Jhee was one of few who had a legitimate means out. Jhee knew full well the reasoning behind the commitments her new spouses and their families had made. Still, arranged marriages; she detested the practice. However, her attempt to flout it had caused so much misery and strife. Their families had reached arrangements, and for all the best reasons: giving the two a better life. At what cost, though? Jhee had been clear and upfront; they were under no obligation to stay. Should they wish to break their marriage contracts early, all they had to do was come to her. She would not pursue legal action against them or their families to force the return of dowries. She asked them at least to let her negotiate their new marriage contracts so she might benefit from their remarriage.

Jhee got a message through to her spouses. On the other side of the protests, they rendezvoused and sought transportation back to the villa.

"Stop the wall! All Folx unite!"

"Stall the wall! Stop the squall!"

Kanto plopped back into the ferry's cushions. "Let's never do that again. I had a run in with a core rights proponent, CARP, on the way here. They don't respect me any more than the ones they claim to be rescuing me from. What's so enviable about being some diving boy who showers off sea brine every day?"

"Like Shep," Mirrei said.

"I didn't mean it that way."

"People are desperate and worried. Who knows? With the way the wall has spiked food prices, being a diver could make one's fortune, and it's probably a lot safer than the mines."

"My biggest worry about the Shield is that it won't work," Kanto said. "They say the barbarians have already found a way through: cheap sailing vessels without any modern navigation equipment to be fooled by the Shield's defenses."

"Wouldn't they be dashed on the rocks?" Mirrei asked.

Jhee tensed. "Not if their ship were the right size and made of metal which they have in abundance unlike us."

Kanto frowned. "All that money and resources for a defense system that can be defeated by technology older than the Prototypes."

"On a lighter note," Jhee said, "we've been invited to a high society fundraiser. The proceeds go toward the local clinics and the Breath of the Deep Society. I'd say that splits the difference between both of your concerns."

Mirrei sighed.

"Next Startide," Kanto said as he went over the fundraiser invite. "Less than a week, way too little time for me to finish outfits for us myself. I'll compose our response at once, then work out particulars. I saw a few boutiques along the lane. I'll make inquiries with them. If this is the major event it's supposed to be, they may be swamped too."

～

The Boutique

The transport bearing Jhee, Kanto, and Mirrei came to a stop in front of a boutique on Hake Hill in Galleon City. The boutique boasted a much more modest and rustic storefront than its modern peers along the row.

"I don't see why we need to purchase new outfits for the fundraiser," Jhee said. "I much prefer your designs in both look and comfort."

Jhee also considered the expense involved.

"As much as I would like to have constructed our outfits for this event," Kanto said. "There simply is not enough time for me to design and make outfits for each of us. There was barely enough time for me to locate a boutique up to my standards who can guarantee completion in time. This should be just a quick fitting, and then we shall proceed to other activities."

"They could have at least traveled to the villa."

"No, they couldn't. This saves time."

The chauffeur helped them out of the transport. A shopper from the boutique approached them, lighted umbrella at the ready, and escorted them inside.

"Denbe," Mirrei said, "you of all of us shouldn't balk at spending more time in the city. What was the most time you've spent in a city?"

"I spent some time in a city at various intervals, such as during my final confirmation to the justiciary."

"What about when you were in the academy or during your service?"

"The Academy was outside of town. I boarded there and went home when I could much like Lady Delphine. On one of my assignments during the war, I did have to live in a small apartment. I did my best not to leave."

"You never visited the city for fun?"

"We went out on the odd night in my academy days. The Academy had an extensive library."

Kanto returned from speaking with the boutique owner bearing sea-green robes with gold and blue embroidery. Assistants brought out daises.

"Up." Kanto pointed Mirrei at the dais. She hopped to. "Of course, our denbe would prefer to spend her time with a conch to her face."

Quick as a flash, Kanto draped her in the robes and then Jhee. The owner brought over her tailoring kit and started to pin and fit their robes. Somehow Kanto now had hold of a tailoring kit and was pinning his own robes on a dais of his own.

"Once we are done here, what should we head next?" Jhee asked.

"You tell us, denbe," Mirrei said, "you're the one chatting up all the guests and street guides."

"I'm sure I don't know what you mean."

"You've been in detective mode since we got here."

"I have not."

Both Kanto and Mirrei frowned at her.

"Fine," Jhee said. "Maybe a little. Delphine's been having problems at the mines. Equipment going missing. That sort of thing. Minor problems."

"So minor she put you on the case?"

"I provided a satisfactory answer."

"But?"

"It has too many dangling threads."

"Dangling threads the scourge of both your work and mine," the boutique owner said.

Kanto chuckled. "That's our denbe: always working; always a puzzle to solve. Woe betide anyone who tries to keep her from it."

Jhee forced the conversation back on track lest the oddities at the mine take over all of her mind share. "I suggest we visit some museums. Galleon City is a city teeming in history and a blend of unique cultures."

"We only made it through half the famous Hake Hills shops our last trip, Mirrei. Care to shop the other half?"

Mirrei folded her hands. "I had another idea in mind. The clinic Vash volunteers at isn't hard to reach from here."

"Ouch!" Kanto set down a pin and tenderly poked his side. "Tailor's maxim."

"You move, you bleed," the boutique owner said. She walked over and did a quick re-pin on Kanto. He nodded approval. She whipped the robe off and then returned to Jhee and Mirrei. "Please check that the pockets are where you like them."

The pockets were precisely where Jhee liked them. "I believe we can do that. I'm very interested in seeing what sort of facilities they have. It'll give me a better idea of what sort of donation to give."

"You mean it?" Mirrei said.

"We'll see."

They finished their fitting.

"I'm going to look for some odds and todds pieces for our house. Meet you for the ride back?" Kanto pecked Jhee on the cheek. He and Mirrei gave their characteristic finger waggle goodbye.

"Hey let me go!" a child yelled.

The shopper had the Latcher girl from the beach by her collar. "Pardons my lady, this little crab-rat was trying to harass you."

"Was not. I have something important to tell the lady. She knows me. We've done devotions together. We're like this."

The Latcher girl entwined her fingers.

Jhee held up a hand. "You may let her go. I know her."

The shopper released the girl who smoothed her ragged gown. The shopper returned to holding the umbrella with a disdainful look.

"What do you have for me?"

The girl stared fish-mouthed at Mirrei for a moment. "Wave Wanderer ships have been spotted out to sea. Near the mines."

"Wave Wanderers? You mean Water Nomads?"

"So you do know some stuff after all. What's more they've been coming ashore."

Jhee paused. Water Nomads live nearly their entire lives on ships. "Any idea where or why?"

The Latcher girl cleared her throat and cupped her hands. Jhee fished out a melon candy and some shell.

"Something to do with the observatory opening. The mines have been going crazy. The crystals have been singing. It has to be their water songs."

"There's only been the one death at the site?"

"I suppose. At least not that's not normal. The mines is rough. It kills up and grinds up a lot of folk. Like my 'mere and my 'bere."

"I'm sorry to hear that. Who takes care of you now?"

"I do."

"May I ask you to keep the information flowing?"

"Sure, as long as you got the money and candy. It ain't just for me, see. It's for the other kids. They helped me get the information. They should get some reward, too."

"Would you tell me if the Water Nomads leave?"

"Sure." The girl held out her hand for another candy. Jhee gave her another one. Jhee had created a worse melon candy fiend than Kanto. "Thank you kindly, ma'am. The Maid of the Mists guide your steps."

"Why the Maid of the Mists?" Jhee asked. The usual saying was to have the Makers' Design guide one's steps.

The Latcher girl looked over Mirrei again. "Full Makers don't come near us folk. All we got is the Singers of the Sea. The Maid of the Mists keeps her eye on the nature wisps. They're her companions. You keep going in the mines, best get her on your side. If you want them to go away, it's best to ask her. You need anything else lady?"

"That will be all for now. Thank you very much for your help."

"You sure talk funny."

The little girl pressed her nose at the shopper before running away. Jhee had the transport take them to the docks where Vash's clinic was.

"What an adorable little operator," Mirrei said.

◝◞

The Clinic

The clinic's large cubic structure rose out of the water like some square behemoth. Engineers built the clinic on flotation moorings, which could raise and lower with sea levels. On the seaward side were moorings where junks and more modest river transports sailed up to deliver patients or fisherfolk stopped in for quick visits.

"Here you go." Vash handed a little girl a candied plum stick. He turned to the girl's father. "Have you been giving her the antibiotics like I prescribed?"

The man bobbed his head. "Dey. Dey. The medicine though it's not working."

"I'll write you another prescription."

"Dey. Dey. Thank you again, doctor."

"Ah Justicar, Mirrei, what an unexpected surprise," Vash said.

"I hope you don't mind," Mirrei said.

"Not at all. Quite the bit of excitement at the street fair."

"Indeed. You look a little busy. Injuries from the protests or the Miner's Lung Disease swell?"

Jhee was taken aback then remembered between Mirrei's interest in healing and being an apt pupil she would notice the signs of disease in others.

Vash nodded. "Those and a Fresh Lung Syndrome outbreak. Though there is some debate whether it's an outbreak or the result of an increase in the number of salt-to-fresh displaced persons."

"Fair assessment. Fair assessment," Mirrei said.

"Speaking of which, how is yours doing?"

"Oh, much better."

"Please allow me to show you around. We have a fully committed practitioner of the Pillarist healing who volunteers twice a long-tide as well as me and several other Academy doctors. We lost a doctor last week and had to scale back our hours from a full day cycle to dawning, day, and setting."

Jhee positioned Mirrei in between her and Vash and kept half a step or so forward.

"How many surgical facilities do you have?" Jhee asked.

"Three currently."

"I noticed the modular construction," Mirrei said. "It lets you add more as the need arises?"

"Just so. Or subtract them. We're retrofitting some moorings to full mobility.

Once that's complete, we will be able to sail at least a part of the clinic down the waterways to reach more folk, perhaps even the Wave Wanderers. The clinic design is based on Water Nomad structures."

"Tell me more about the clinic's operations."

"It's quite dull. really. Not the sort of pursuit to interest a jet-streaming heiress such as yourself. I, for one, would not hesitate to leave it behind if the right situation presented itself or should my future wife insist. I should think a proper wife would insist I devote myself to her needs and those of our family."

"What happens to the clinic then? Or your patients?"

"Who's to say? It's likely to close. Since I would no longer work there, mumsy is likely to withdraw her support. Unless perhaps I could convince my denbe to help. Some sweet, compassionate woman who truly wants to help people. Either way, it would hardly be my responsibility anymore. Let Oriel see to that. It's her job after all."

Jhee rounded the corner and saw a young man having a heated discussion with a weaselly woman in expensive but tacky clothing. She noted how the woman held her arm favoring her side, not as if with an injury but as if with a weapon.

"No more excuses. My patience is wearing thin," the weaselly woman said.

They went silent when they saw Jhee. The woman gave the man a smile, patted her flank, and then dashed off. Vash and Mirrei caught up to Jhee.

"Is there a problem here, sir?" Jhee asked. She walked forward to where the woman had been. Rust-colored powdery flakes covered the floor. A disposable napkin bearing a stylized letter Cee lay among them. The logo matched the local business who had provided linens and music equipment for the fair. Jhee picked up the napkin. Writing scrawled on the back read: Pool. Underground lake. This blight of a city consumed in a pillar of light. Mineral sands. Starry eyes.

"No, my lady. No problem at all."

"Bastian, this is the Justicar and Star Mirror. They are friends of my mother who are staying with us for a few weeks. I was just giving them a quick overview of the facilities."

"Pleased to make your acquaintance."

"Bastian here is a volunteer who donates his time to the clinic just as I do. He also volunteers technical work for the Breath of the Deep Society."

Mr. Bastian bowed slightly. "I do what I can. Excuse me miss, my lady, I couldn't help but overhear. You have FLS?"

"Why yes I do."

'Might I ask you a few questions?"

"Um sure."

"Where are you from?"

"Talasisle."

Mr. Bastian leaned in. "Lived there your whole life?"

"Just about."

"How long ago did you start showing symptoms?"

Mirrei backed a step away. "I've shown some my whole life, but much like everyone else it got worse as we journeyed inland. Here, though, it only troubles me a little."

Mr. Bastian had closed the distance again.

"Vash," Mirrei cooed then sidled over to his side, "can we finish the tour?"

Upon closer inspection, Jhee located a struck-out artifice mark, on Mr. Bastian's wrist. Was that the bloodsucker tattoo of a paid remora? "Yes, I'm sure Mr. Bastian has duties we're keeping him from."

"There are still some preparations I have to make for our upcoming joint gala."

"No worries, chum," Vash said. "Be about it."

Before Mr. Bastian responded, Ms. Oriel arrived. "Ah, my lady Justicar, lovely to see you again. I was just getting more testimonials filmed and picking up the commemorative crystals for the fundraiser. The area children made them as 'thank you' gifts to our donors. What brings you here?"

Jhee poked her chin toward where Mr. Bastian and Mirrei waited. "My dende wanted to tour the facilities."

Ms. Oriel frowned for an instant then returned to a cheery expression. "Hm, well, we shouldn't waste anymore of my lady Justicar's time. Bastian, could you bring these boxes to the vehicle, please?"

After Mr. Bastian left, Vash looked apologetic. "Our volunteers can be a bit passionate."

"I hope you like what you see here, my Lady Justicar, and we can look forward to some plump, juicy bids on our items."

With a formal touch of the heart, Ms. Oriel departed. After the tour, Jhee and Mirrei fought their way through another wave of protests to their transport where Kanto awaited them.

"Stall the Wall! Stop the Squall!"

"Fishers' rights! All Folx unite!"

A crowd of protesters blocked the road on their way back to the villa.

"My apologies, my Lady," the transport driver said. "These protests have been going on for several long-tides. It'll take me a few minutes to find a different route."

"See, I knew we should have taken the water taxi," Mirrei said.

Kanto wiggled his shoulders and adjusted in his seat. "Well, we wouldn't have missed the last ferry if someone hadn't detoured to visit a clinic."

Jhee stared out the windows at the faces as they passed by. Angry, twisted expressions met her gaze. Didn't they understand? We needed this shield. It was the only means to stop the coming war with the barbarians.

5

THE MIXER I

~

The Ride There

Contorted yelling faces again greeted the transport Jhee and Mirrei caught to the gala. Jhee stroked her chin in contemplation while they hurled slogans at them.

"Complicit! Oligarchs! The wall is death! One Folk! All Folk! Free the waves! Free the winds! Free the rains!"

"You live in your glass houses, but the wall is a lie. It's not meant to keep them out, but us in. Resist and wake up. We must stop the wall at all costs. Wake up guppies. Join the revolution. The time is now."

"How rude. They're protesting a charity event. We're trying to help," a fellow transport rider said, a low-ranking vizier judging by his badge and creme sash.

"Absolutely," a woman passenger chimed in. "There's a right way and a wrong way to protest."

A slim, brown-haired man, who wore clothes befitting the middle ranks, contrasted with the motley protesters that surrounded the gate. He barely batted an eye at the disruption but fixed Mirrei and Jhee with a long, direct stare as their water taxi passed the guard tower.

"If it weren't disruptive, it wouldn't rightly be a protest, would it?" Jhee asked.

Advocate Farkhande flipped the ends of her scarf over her shoulder. "That's always been my take on it."

Mirrei leaned back against the seat. "They want better lives. Like the refugees."

Jhee patted her hand. "Conditions will get better, once the Shield stabilizes."

"Didn't you tell me, denbe, 'Justice procrastinated is justice abdicated?'"

Jhee nodded.

Advocate Farkhande nodded too. "And patience can sometimes be deadly. More deadly than anything."

"Lobster drivel," the vizier said.

"What they were saying," Mirrei said. "'The wall is death.' What do you suppose they meant?"

"Hard to say, really," Jhee answered. "Many believe we shouldn't close ourselves off from the barbarian lands. It will lead to stagnation of the blood-lines, inbreeding. The inbreeding we had always been careful to avoid. The tampering with the weather. There's also the massive amount of male elemen-talists involved. The arcana. Many still don't know enough to know elemen-talism and cyphering are not the same."

"I'm not sure I do either. With the Shield up, the Other Folk may never get to go back and see their families again. They'll be stranded inside the Shield with us."

"In a way, that's how it's always been. It's the compact we made with the Other Folk: what washes up on our shores is ours. Even them."

"That's sad. It hardly seems right."

"They have to try hard to reach the empire. It doesn't just happen. The rules are clear: any who are not Water Folk who lay eyes on the Blessed Isles may not leave."

"Why?"

"I," Jhee started. "I don't know."

Mirrei's eyes flashed at the admission. She and Kanto always looked to Jhee for the answers. A better denbe might have had a more reassuring response to give her. It stunned Jhee too to realize she had always taken it as a given Impe-rial isle trespassers may not leave. Of all the assumptions for her not to ques-tion, why that one?

"Tell the truth, now, Justicar," Advocate Farkhande said, "because the previous policy was worse."

Jhee lapsed into silence as she had too often when it came to the treatment of the barbarians.

~

Fundraiser Arrival

Jhee and Mirrei disembarked from their water taxi. They had taken earlier transportation to the Observatory fundraiser with Lady Delphine's entourage not far behind. Yet, somehow, their large, ungainly retinue overtook them. The Delphines and Kanto had already queued up at the Foundation Members' entrance. The usher examined Jhee and Mirrei's invites and directed them to a longer queue separate from them while Advocate Farkhande and their other transport passengers joined the shorter line. Kanto furrowed his brow at them and raised his hands askance. Jhee shrugged.

Their queue barely moved. The security guards kept their heads down and focused on the invites while others thoroughly searched everyone who reached them. Jhee glanced over to the queue with the Delphines and Kanto. It had moved significantly faster. The guards were affable and mostly waved everyone through with the most cursory of searches. Kanto spared another concerned look before the guard swept his group inside where the porter announced their entrance.

"The pre-approved line," Mirrei said. She palmed her esca.

Was Jhee supposed to submit their credentials ahead of time? She smiled apologetically at Mirrei who returned her smile and took Jhee's arm so they might walk into the event together. "I think I may have erred."

"I'm sorry. The fault was mine," Mirrei said as if she had read Jhee's thoughts. "I should have sent ahead to pre-approve our credentials. Kanto explained it to me. Even reminded me twice. This will simply not do. This is one of my duties for our night and I washed out."

Jhee patted Mirrei's hand. In that, they were alike. She forgot about such details, too. "Don't fret over it. If you weren't here, I still would have forgotten it entirely and been waiting in this line anyway."

"Hence," Mirrei said, affecting a haughty accent, "why it is one of my duties and my responsibilities to see that an official such as yourself isn't seen in a queue like this. Not the most auspicious start to our introduction to courtly society and the social scene. Won't do at all and the shame is mine."

Jhee smirked. She would trust her younger spouses' judgment in this. Etiquette such as this had been part of their training. It certainly had been for Kanto, yet another reason they agreed to take him on as a husband. At least, that was one of Shep's motives. She could merely guess at the rest. They had found his role in their household, and she would honor him and let him do it. Plain and simple. Now, on the other hand, she had Mirrei.

Mirrei. The stickier issue. Jhee had returned with the young woman suddenly as Shep had unexpectedly shown up with Kanto in tow. Though, not at the same time, as Jhee had resolved to have only one additional marriage. She had already taken Kanto on months prior, but she simply could not refuse Miramar's request.

"Have you been enjoying our stay?" Jhee asked.

"It's going well. Lady Delphine and her family are very kind and generous. Her daughters are a hoot. Vash is caring and such a gentleman."

"Excellent. I'm glad to see you getting along. There is a chance her daughters will join the Military Academy."

"And me too unless I want to be conscripted?"

"Not necessarily. The shield has the conscription rules in flux. You and Kanto, being married, may no longer be under its strictures. With tightened requirements for recruitment, they no longer need to go as wide with their requests for service and fewer of us need to figure out how to serve or game the system to get them and theirs out of it."

"Leaving the poor most at risk still. I suppose my Fresh Lung Syndrome likely would have kept me out anyway."

"They find ways for those who wish to serve, to serve, even if they have a disqualifying condition."

The event organizer, Ms. Oriel, appeared at the doorway. She spoke to the guard who pointed at Jhee's queue. The woman hurried over her face a mask of distress. She unhooked the sealskin rope and walked Jhee and Mirrei over to the other entrance right past the rest of the line. "Apologies for the miscommunication, my Lady Justicar."

The barbarian porter announced Jhee's formal title in a booming, clear voice. "... Justicar of the Far Reaches, Talasisle, and sixteenth district and her escort, Star Mirror of Saphiria and Talasisle, beloved third and promised liege."

Beloved? Jhee winced. That had not been the impression she meant to give at all. The official designation should have been Bonded. Now, everyone would be under the misconception that they could not engage Mirrei directly. Jhee would have to field inquiries and act as her social secretary unless she wanted the woman to spend the whole event unapproachable.

Jhee did not even know what she was doing or what role she had intended the young woman to fill. She had not thought it through far enough. She only knew she had a debt and obligation to meet. A debt she could never repay. Mistakes she could never atone or make up for. This was barely even a down payment.

"No frowns," Mirrei said.

Jhee grunted as Lady Delphine's daughters sprinted by her, followed shortly by Vash. Kanto remained behind with Lady Delphine. He flashed his most winsome grin and gestured to the door with his wine glass. The younger Delphines and Mirrei chatted and giggled as excited and thick as coral in a cluster. A word drifted to her about the protests, the Shield, the refugees. She cast about her for someone else to converse with. She knew no one else here, save Lady Delphine. As long as Kanto accompanied her alone, Jhee had to maintain her distance according to household protocol.

Erma linked arms with Mirrei. "Our brother mentioned you have Fresh Lung Sickness. I can't imagine all this rain helps."

"It's all right," Mirrei replied. "I simply need to manage my salinity levels."

Semele quirked an eyebrow at them. "You even sound like Vash."

Jhee afforded herself of the exhibits. On display were some of the older telescopes once housed in the observatory's three domes and images of the former lead astronomers and their families. She tried not to get too far ahead and herd their assemblage along as she took in the exhibits.

The observatory itself was an architectural marvel with its multiple levels some of which were recessed into the hillside on which it sat. In the middle, a grand staircase that fluted outward in a pearlescent curve almost like the entire round hallway had been made of glowing mother of pearl inlay. Electrified glow orbs with bioluminescent light brighter than the basic honey and clam liquid variety led the way. A grand, crystal chandelier dominated the refinished dome above the great room. Depictions of the phases of the moons, the other inhabited worlds' transits across the sky, and other astronomical phenomena had been painted on the dome's surface.

The porters and attendants all wore matching fur and gilded gem uniforms. Many of them were barbarians. Occasionally the more high-ranking ones were traditional Water Folk who wore similar uniforms but just a little bit more ornate and with more insignia. They all bore the same logo and name: Inkerton Event Solutions. They provided the staff and catering for many high society events and always with barbarians dressed smartly in elegant, urbane attire. It was weird she had not really noticed that before. She also noted many of the service staff to be smaller and possibly shabbier Water Folk. Mostly male. Again, more people coming from the provinces to the capital for work. Her mind went back to Tranquility Bridge Abbey and to Mr. Pol, the widower, and the smuggling and trafficking of people and the refugees.

Kanto stepped away from Lady Delphine. As soon as she saw the opening, Jhee approached her. "Save me," she said.

Delphine laughed. "Were we ever that young?"

"Never."

The gang of four walked from exhibit to exhibit whispering and laughing. Mirrei behaved so alive and engaged. She would make a good heir for her fortunes. Jhee decided to scale back on their lessons at least while they were here. Kanto slipped back into the group once they had merged.

They heard more than one attendee remark sentiments such as, "Are those images of men cyphering? Scandalous."

"Think of the children," Erma said while smirking.

Mirrei and Semele giggled.

"It wasn't such a laughing matter not long ago," Delphine said.

A timeline wall showcased artifacts relating to arcana or the science of the Shield. Images and implements of early arcana tables, including recently dusted off illustrations related to pre-ban male artificers. A case featured a few yellowed gyration veils and sun-faded mats with protective circles, both implements meant to shield the men from harm. Several images showed rows of men practicing cyphers in formation.

"Arcana still isn't well understood," Jhee said. Jhee walked them through the timeline. "Pillarists had everyone convinced male artificers were going to break the world. The ensuing panic saw many men who practiced jailed or worse. The elimination of male practitioners shifted the arcane window and arcana in general might have died out."

One wing lead to a rotunda with an inertial pendulum and another housed an aquarium. The younger folk had lapsed into more subdued conversation by the time they had visited every great room exhibit and wing—except for one wing which remained unopened. The plaque read: The History of Galleon City.

"It's good to have this reminder of how fortunate we are and how grateful we should be," Mirrei said.

Semele took her hand and Erma's. "And how far we can go in our persecution of others."

"Don't think we just reserved our prejudices for the Other Folk," Kanto said.

"Hardly," Delphine said. "Your denbe and I were mid-toned. We would have barely passed the parchment test."

"Parchment test?" Vash asked.

Lady Delphine looked embarrassed. "A remnant of another time."

Jhee took a drink. "Rumors were you only gained access to certain social circles if you were dark enough. The débutantes took a piece of parchment paper and held it beside your face. If your complexion was lighter than the parchment, they did not let you join."

Vash blanched, and Lady Delphine rubbed his back. "Water Folk really did that to each other?" he asked.

"I saw no actual evidence of it being practiced, but the most elite were all darker toned."

Lady Delphine raised a glass. "Enough of that, this is also a celebration. As the Mechanists say: to being remade magnificent."

~

Brief Interlude

"Ah Lady Delphine, thank you so much for coming," Ms. Oriel, the event organizer, said. She graciously clasped forearms with Lady Delphine. "Erma. Semele. Vash. Great to see you."

"Oriel, this is our guest Bright Harmony. You remember the Justicar and this is her consort, Star Mirror."

"Pleasure to meet you, Ms. Oriel," Mirrei said.

A young man of similar age and dress to the event organizer came over, Mr. Bastian, the volunteer from the clinic. "My Ladies, allow me to introduce my fiancé, Bastian."

"Ladies," he said with a slight bow.

Kanto gave him the once over, gaze lingering on the wrist tattoo, and made an unusually territorial bow.

"We've met," Jhee said. "At the clinic."

"Ah, yes. Not the ideal way I wanted to make your acquaintance, my lady. I realize now how my questions must have sounded." Mr. Bastian slipped his arm into the event organizer's. He coughed. When the coughing did not stop, he covered his mouth with a handkerchief. "Excuse me, ladies."

Ms. Oriel followed him through a nearby archway. She returned a short time later.

"Pardon my sudden departure. Fresh Lung Syndrome. It was his plight which first moved me to get involved with this cause. You might say he is the reason we are all here tonight."

"Oriel, may I impose upon you to give my old friend the Justicar and her wife a private tour and allow her to see the telescope? She is a practicing artificer and big matron of heritage Mechanics."

The event organizer's eyes, and smile grew brighter upon mention of Jhee's matronage. "I'd be delighted."

The musicians started up, and the dancing began. Mirrei sipped from her fluted champagne glass while Jhee tapped her foot along and bobbed her head. Mirrei plucked another glass from the tray of a passing server. Something about the man had caught Mirrei's attention. Jhee couldn't help but notice, too. She had a more immediate concern. Jhee downed her glass of champagne in a single, long shot. She glanced at the dance floor and swallowed the lump in her throat. She held out her arms to Mirrei. "May I?" Jhee asked.

"I'd be delighted, denbe."

Mirrei stepped into Jhee's arms. Jhee swept her around the dance floor. Jhee tried not to move her lips as she counted steps. "I haven't danced so much until recently."

"You're doing great," Mirrei said.

"Even in my academy days, I didn't dance this much. Even though they had a ball almost every long-tide. Unless you're too much like me, you will love it."

Mirrei's smile was half-hearted. "I suppose. I might prefer the company of a good book while in a comfy chair."

"That's my girl. That was my preferred way to spend the evening. Tihalmec Academy's library is extensive with complete access to the ether collections housed at the other branches. Their physical volumes are available via loan unless you want something from their rare volume collection. I made more than a few trips to the other branches for just that reason."

"I can completely see you poring over volumes in your free time. You must have been over the Spheres."

"I was."

"May I?" Vash asked.

Jhee waited for Mirrei's reaction to the offer. Mirrei eagerly tapped Jhee's waist beneath the concealment of Jhee's sleeves. Jhee stepped aside and allowed Vash to take her place. Mirrei winked before Jhee went to find a place off the dance floor to stand. Ambassador Naiman and one passenger from her transport, the vizier, examined an exhibit dedicated to barbarian workers. Eldjin, the mustachioed villa guest, trailed after them doing the most obvious job of listening in she had ever seen.

Advocate Farkhande swept through dancing by herself or possibly with the wisps. The same shimmering haze Jhee noted before. Jhee's esca tingled and she felt light-headed. She decided she needed some air. A breather was not to be had. Instead, the mayor cornered her and went on at length about how Jhee should set a story in Galleon City. Eventually, Jhee excused herself.

Jhee came across the ambassador who appeared to be doing his dawned best to ignore his companion, the vizier from the transport. The expression on Ambassador Naiman's face was part beleaguered, part disgust. Eldjin appeared to have abandoned their conversation to socialize with other officials.

"What do sand slakers know about great architecture?" the vizier scoffed.

The ambassador gripped his tumbler tightly. "This may surprise you, Vizier, but the Fire Folk are civilized. We have cities with buildings, modern conveniences, and everything."

"Yes, I've heard about your building dedication ceremonies. I hear barbarians celebrate the start of work on a new building by killing and burying some unbedded fellow under the foundation."

"Alas, I think the Vizier is mistaken. That practice was only done on the spring festivals by followers of the Maye King over a hundred years ago."

Jhee interjected, "Around the same time, the Water Folk did as well. I also believe Water Folk from the Qibarei isles had similar practices. And I believe it was the The Djararo of the Far/Middle Isles, Water Folk, who were known for sacrificing people to volcanoes."

The vizier shrugged. "I suppose it's all the same in those backwater isles. With all that interbreeding."

"If I remember correctly, in the past this area had a tradition of when a powerful chieftess died, they buried her husbands alive with her."

The vizier shook his head and walked away.

"I like how he slipped in that nice two-tap with the last insult."

"I must commend you, Ambassador, not just on your patience, but on the remarkable accomplishment of keeping your hems clean."

"Oh?" The ambassador glanced down. "Yes."

"The main walkway near the transports has turned into a virtual lake. I'm not used to maneuvering in these longer robes yet. I suppose in your homeland the problem would be sand."

"This is my homeland."

"When you said you were a barbarian and with you being an ambassador, I—" Jhee gulped. "My apologies. I should know better."

"Fire Folk on my father's side. My mother, whom I never knew, appears to have been Water Folk."

"Imagine the scandal."

"What could she have been thinking?"

"You never know. She could have been in love. You know how these matters can be. A lonely isolated woman and someone offers her the gift of friendship and something more."

"That's what I've always hoped. I'd like to think there was some affection in my conception and not violence or coercion."

"Here's hoping you are right. I thank you for humoring a bigot, and I don't mean the vizier."

After the ambassador left, Kanto drifted over to Jhee with a drink. He faced away from her as he spoke.

"How are we making our way home then? Do you wish for me to ride back with you or them?"

"We shall see."

Mirrei ran over to Jhee and took her arm. "Thank you, denbe. That was such fun."

"You dance divinely."

"Vash is an expert partner." Mirrei nodded at Kanto. "Not perhaps as great as you, denye. Oh, Kanto, we are having the most marvelous time. Why did you leave?"

"I had responsibilities to attend to. I saw our denbe left to her own devices on a night when she is not supposed to be."

Mirrei dropped her gaze for a moment showing she had taken Kanto's gentle rebuke. She went back to beaming happiness once again. "Denbe, would it be all right if I made the return trip with the Delphines? There is something I wanted to discuss with them."

"Star Mirror." Kanto tightened his mouth then gave a weary sigh while mumbling something about completely inappropriate.

"*Bright Harmony*, it's not your night," Mirrei said.

Kanto looked away sheepishly. Mirrei returned her attention to Jhee. Her expression showed such excitement and expectation. Jhee sighed. "As it pleases you, dende."

"Oh, thank you so much. Denye, would you do me the favor of accompanying her back to the villa in my stead?"

Kanto bowed. "As it pleases, my denye."

Mirrei kissed Jhee's cheek then Kanto's and ran off to rejoin the Delphines.

The weaselly woman from the clinic strode into the fundraiser. She raised a glass at several folk, among them the unpleasant vizier from the transport ride. The vizier began to continually adjust his sash of rank. Jhee later observed the weaselly woman and vizier in conversation. Eldjin upon seeing them made himself scarce. Jhee thought perhaps she had uncovered a loan shark or gangster. The woman's presence at the clinic made so much more sense now.

6
———

THE MIXER II

~

Indisposed

Jhee did her best to pay attention as Kanto introduced her to another dignitary or minor official. This one the minor lord of that region. This one in charge of draining rights for the city. And this one handles building permits. While this one was the fourth cousin once removed from the emperor or empress and fiftieth in line for appointment to the Imperial Palace, yet farther outside the succession pool than Jhee. Her eyes glazed over and wanted to roll back in her head. She made small talk where she could. Often in situations such as this, his prompting proved invaluable. He, however, kept a close watch on Mirrei and the Delphines. A feat Jhee had done her level best not to do. He had failed. Eventually, they were alone. Kanto sipped his drink and stared daggers as Mirrei slipped her arm in Vash's and smiled and laughed with the Delphines.

The musicians finally began to tune up. *Thank the Makers.*

Kanto smiled and patted her hand. "You did well. You didn't look too terribly bored."

"I'm sorry. I didn't mean to be rude."

"Denbe, I say this with all due humility, most of these guests rank beneath you—to a remarkable degree. They may peer down at you because

61

you are from the Far Reaches, but put plainly, your status is higher than theirs. You should assert it more. Some of them really weren't worth your time, and for some, it may be too soon for them to know where they stand with you."

The band went into a rendition of the Dawning of the Night music and stanzas of Canon Chaisen. Jhee started tapping her feet.

"Shall we?"

Jhee nodded. "We shall."

Kanto spun her about the dance floor. Dancing was one of the many skills required of a consort such as him. His dancing was almost as good and practiced as his lute playing. Jhee was awkward. When she missed the step, he did a slight flourish which covered the gaffe. When she hesitated unable or unsure how to move, gentle guiding pressure on her back made it clear how and when to move. She only wished she made him look as good.

Jhee sneaked a few glances over at Mirrei. She danced with several individuals. Eventually, Vash swept her into his arms. He swirled and twirled her about the dance floor as expertly and deftly as Kanto swept her. Not a missed step. They seemed in perfect harmony. Jhee smiled. She had to keep herself focused on her current companion.

Kanto's embrace had tensed. Every so often he winced.

"What is it?" she asked.

"The musician's instruments. They 're out of tune or something is wrong with the musical equipment. Every few bars, the stringed instruments hit a false note with too much feedback and resonance. All this moisture might affect the acoustical properties. I hope my lutes won't be affected."

"You have such a practiced and attuned ear. Leave it to you to notice a detail like that."

"My musical ear is a skill I pride myself on."

"As well you should."

"I must excuse myself. There is only so much of this I can take. I only hope my lutes won't be affected."

"Would you like me to come with?"

"No, I'm going take a moment to refresh myself. You stay here and try not to be too bored without me."

"I make no promises."

Kanto scampered off. It might be a good time to refresh herself as well. Jhee found the facilities marked Neutral. Jhee used the screened stall, and as she washed her hands, Mirrei emerged from another one. She rinsed her hands and began to fix her make-up.

Mirrei had ceded her night to Kanto likely intending to have it to herself without Jhee hovering. Jhee contemplated saying something. It would not technically be a breach of etiquette as Kanto had excused himself and she would only spend a moment with Mirrei.

"So, you are enjoying your evening?"

"Yes. No need to worry about me. I saw both you and Kanto nearly straining your necks to watch me. Please, enjoy your evening together."

"How are you feeling?"

"Very well. No need to worry. I'll inform you if something changes."

"Be sure you do. A valid emergency is a perfectly valid excuse to violate the rules. Or a genuine change of circumstance."

"I know. See you later."

Mirrei finished up the last touches on her make-up. She swept out of the facilities. Jhee finished up the last bits of her toilet and then left too. When she emerged, Kanto was there to take her arm. "Have your poor sensitive ears been revived, dear husband?"

"Much better. I will find some way to ignore it. Once you hear it, though it is hard to unhear."

"I am that way about cases sometimes."

"Believe me, I know. I love the way your mind works. I like the way you watch and take everything in. So, did your talk with Mirrei reassure you?"

Jhee raised an eyebrow.

"I saw her come out."

Jhee nodded. "Just so. Forgive me. Please, don't feel pushed aside. I did not mean to violate your time."

"Not at all. I would have spoken to her myself too if she had let me."

"Shall we return to the great room?"

"Let's."

Jhee and Kanto danced and danced. She even pushed Mirrei out of her head for a few minutes.

"She abandoned you on your night together," Kanto said. "It's the height of rudeness. Why aren't you more upset at this?"

"Kanto, please. Allow her to enjoy herself."

"Well, aren't you going to put a stop to it? Not only is it indiscreet, but they also nearly killed her inside of a long-tide."

"Kanto, don't you feel you are being at least a bit dramatic? Perhaps we should return to the manse. We've hobnobbed enough for one evening. We should have some time alone. I thought a night out such as this would be enjoyable for you. And her. I see now it was a mistake. Our announcement. You told them to use the term beloved."

"I thought it was appropriate."

"Won't you please allow her to enjoy herself? I wanted her free to explore her options without having everyone she speaks to filtered by me." Jhee sighed and sought to redirect Kanto's focus. "This is our night now. Amuse me with the latest fashion or gossip. Who are the two most prominent officials you know who are rumored to have affairs right now?"

"Explore her options?" Kanto repeated. "I see. Our stay is multifold. I should have understood sooner. No wonder you've been encouraging us to accompany them places without you. Should the Mistress of the House herself, her daughters, or an Aunt come to call while we are here, inform them I cannot make their acquaintance. I am indisposed. I've taken ill."

Kanto set his drink down on the bar. He walked out of the front doors, and Jhee followed sparing a last glance at Mirrei and the Delphines.

"Wait, were you going? We haven't had the private tour yet."

"Bright Harmony's taken ill. Something didn't agree with him. Please have a transport brought around."

"As you wish, my Lady Justicar."

The sounds of protest carried from further down the drive. Jhee had not wanted to brave those crowds again so soon. Kanto stayed by Jhee's side in sullen silence. She wracked her brain for a way to get Kanto to change his mind. If he gave the Delphines a chance, he might grow to like them as Mirrei had.

The valet approached them. "Your pardon, my Lady Justicar. We are experiencing transport delays because of the protests. It may be another twenty minutes to half an hour before we can have any of the private shuttles brought up."

"What of a water taxi?"

"I'll call one."

"Call one? There's one parked right there." Jhee pointed to the water taxi idling nearby with its lights off. She started down the lane to the seaside pick-up. "Come along, Bright Harmony."

"Let's just wait for a transport. In the meantime, we can return to the opening."

"Weren't you the one eager to leave?"

"Not if it means traveling in some creepy, trench cab. Besides, I'm not inclined to wasting the pretty or brave the protesters again so soon. They've been known to throw gross substances on the finely dressed people. Also, I've reconsidered leaving Mirrei alone in the company of those Delphines."

The valet squinted down the lane. "I don't recognize their service mark, and they appear to be off duty. If my lady would allow me to check it out first?"

The valet overtook them. Once he had gotten halfway, the water taxi's lights came on, and it sped away.

"How rude," Kanto said. "I did not want to ride in some scummy taxi anyway. I can already imagine it. The second we got inside the doors would lock and speed us through the Hole in the World to the Unmaker's discard pile or the Trench itself."

"Such a vivid picture you paint."

"I try. You win, denbe. Back inside to the horrible music and company we go."

The Viewing

"You've returned," Ms. Oriel, the event organizer, said. "I'm glad you've changed your mind. We're just about to start a private tour for the Breath of the Deep Society donors."

"We're not members."

"Yet. I think we can make an exception. Don't tell anyone. Keep it between us, though."

Jhee smirked. The woman was persuasive, she could tell you that. The Delphines opted out. Ms. Oriel led them along to where a group of the fabulously rich gathered at the base of one of the astronomy towers. A woman in a rumpled, ill-fitting gown shuffled from foot to foot. She greeted Ms. Oriel's arrival with a look of sheer terror.

"Hello everyone. Yes. Yes. Gather round. I see you have already met Levinia. For those of you who might not already know, she is the Observatory's lead astronomer. She led the charge on all our restoration work here at the Observatory. Without her bringing me in, I suspect our beloved observatory would still linger in a state of disrepair."

A smattering of applause came from the crowd.

Ms. Oriel's conch went off. She tried to ignore it. She pulled it out to silence it, then changed her mind. "I'm sorry, I have to take this. Levinia, I turn the tour over to you."

Ms. Levinia's eyes went wide. She turned and began up the stairs. As she rattled off dry statistics about the observatory, Jhee stared up at the dizzying height of the dome. Why did it always have to be stairs? "Above you, gentlefolk, hangs the historic Planetarium Chandelier, lovingly restored to near original condition. After a cleaning, it went missing. It was thought to be lost until maintenance crews found it stashed in an observatory storage unit."

At last, they emerged from the stairwell to the telescope dome. The lead astronomer's eyes had taken on a bright sheen as she went into detail on the telescope's lens size and viewing capabilities. Jhee rested against the inner viewing chamber. She was careful not to lean against the dome which could move at any time. What she wanted now more than anything was a chair. A close second, an opportunity to look through the drenched telescope already.

"All the telescopic domes were refitted with composite materials after their metals were stripped for the space effort. With the increased light pollution of the city and the Storm Shield, the telescopes will now be used for terrestrial photography. I'm sure you are all now more than eager to take a look."

Jhee straightened in anticipation. Kanto had spent most of the time hiding chuckles. She was almost as glad his mood improved as she was for a chance to look through the telescope. She waited for all the other tour participants to go first. Finally, her turn at the viewfinder came. She squeezed one eye shut.

The rocky craters of the fourth moon came into startling view. She took in a breath and flailed for Kanto to look. She smiled when he gasped at the sight. He took hold of her hand and squeezed gently. Kanto turned back to her, eyes bright and full of wonder. He went back to the telescope again, his breathing now almost as labored as hers was from their climb.

As the tour continued, he stood closer than he had at the start. His other hand covered the one she rested on his arm.

Ms. Levinia gave a planetarium presentation and a brief description of the celestial finds that had been made by the observatory's previous astronomers.

Ms. Oriel clapped. "Rest assured. These are still astronomical telescopes.

So, no spying on the neighbors even if they are pointed landward. We can, however, see the Styr Mine or the royal game preserve."

Jhee had not noticed her return.

"The Styr Mine," Ms. Levinia said, "the Hole in the World. The civilized world's largest source of templarite, the Empire's indispensable mineral, used in everything from your conch to the Shield."

"Our best view though," Ms. Oriel said, "doesn't require the telescope and can be seen with the unaided eye. If you'll please follow me, gentlefolk."

Their tour guides led them to the roof terrace of the observatory. Two majestic clear pillars rose out of the ground a few miles away. Within each, whirled two waterspouts. Now and then a peal of thunder and flash of lightning would strike them. The waterspouts spun and twirled but did not move far from their centralized location. The bottoms where they touched the waters wandered some but not far. In between them sat the relay station so small and unassuming nestled between the two towering giants of water and electricity. This was truly a technical marvel. Further beyond them, she could just make out the shadow of the Great Tether to Heaven.

"Behold, the Double Tines, the heart of the defense grid, better known as the Storm Shield. This vantage affords the best view of them in the whole region, perhaps even on the entire continent. Each tower is named after one of the legendary double drakes thought to encircle the isles."

After a few minutes to marvel and sip champagne, Ms. Oriel started taking them back down the stair.

"Oriel, about those Breath of the Deep visitors' logs," Ms. Levinia began.

Mr. Oriel checked her timepiece. "Not now, don't you see we have an important guest? Would you mind showing the Justicar the Mechanist pieces while I finish up the tour? Please."

Before Ms. Levinia could argue, Ms. Oriel took off.

"Come with me, please," Ms. Levinia said.

Ms. Levinia led Jhee and Kanto to a climate-controlled vault. In the viewing room, she carefully arrayed a series of Wondrous Age-era astrological tools.

Jhee clasped her hands then touched them to her esca. "The First Devotions. Each piece supposedly designed and hand-crafted to exacting specifications by Parul, one of the earliest devisers of the Mechanist movement."

"They're on loan from the Imperial Collection. Would you like to examine them?"

Jhee's breath caught. "Yes, please."

To see an early set of Mechanist devotional tools up close, would be worth the donation the event organizer would likely solicit at the end of the tour. Kanto accompanied her to the viewing room where they were instructed in the handling procedures. She would have thought he'd find this incredibly boring. He somehow cut a dashing figure even in a smock and Thindril gloves.

"They must be at least a thousand years old," Jhee said. "A minuscule amount in geological time, a considerable amount of time even with our current lifespans. They use indirect methods to date them rather than risk damaging their integrity via chemical analysis. Be as gentle as you would with me while handling them."

Kanto grinned. Technicians brought in a portfolio, one of five copies of the original specifications. Jhee held her breath, clasped her hands then touched them to her esca again, as they set it in front of her. The portfolio displayed on a thin bio-film screen which had thousands of hairline cracks from age and a few creases. It ran on solar power, its cells probably depleted and at the end of even their most optimistic lifespan.

"Please, examine it closer," the astronomer said. She handed Jhee a magnifier.

Jhee waved Kanto over. "It's on a dedicated reader for confidentiality. Those creases date to its creation. They say one of Parul's first assistants made them. Stands to reason, to them confidential or not it was simply another tool. It was bound to get damaged as they ran their experiments."

They held the magnifier together, and Jhee thumbed through the portfolio gently. The screen barely produced enough light for viewing it by. She pointed out the infamous Bebhinn transposition error which was only caught after several years of it already being part of the curricula and how it was a miracle the Imperial Academy had not been blasted to the moons by then. Kanto's eyes shone with eagerness.

"So much history," he said. "No, stories. So many stories. You teach me so much, denbe. Subjects I would have never been interested in on my own."

"You do that for me."

Jhee and Kanto browsed through the portfolio more. Ms. Oriel entered. "I hate to pry you away, but I have to be there for the chandelier dedication."

"Yes. Yes. Of course," Jhee said and sighed wistfully.

7

———

THE MIXER III

~

The Mechanist

Jhee and Kanto emerged from the viewing room having divested themselves of gloves and smocks.

"I brought you in to get us funding, not to go into business for yourself. I intended this to be a community event for the underprivileged, not another private matronage affair," Ms. Levinia began.

Ms. Oriel silenced her. "I trust you enjoyed your private viewing, my lady Justicar?"

"Very much so," Jhee replied.

"Lady Delphine mentioned you were a matron of the arts."

"Yes. Indeed."

"Using templarite from the local mines, the Imperial History Museum was one of the first to restore a portfolio to operation on its own original power source. Our work with the telescopes and chandelier restoration pioneered technologies that allowed us to assist."

Ms. Levinia blushed. "I can't take all the credit. Bastian assisted me. He's insightful on technical matters. If the Justicar will excuse me."

69

The lead astronomer hurried off, leaving only Ms. Oriel to answer Jhee's questions.

"Templarite. I imagine it was quite expensive."

"Well, Justicar...."

"If I wanted to start an organization like the Fresh Lung Society, how would you recommend I go about it?"

Jhee nodded along as Ms. Oriel laid out the process in sensible and direct terms until Kanto began to fidget.

Quick as lightning, Jhee produced a code chip from her sleeve. "Here's a routing code for my charitable trust's business office. Provide them verification access for the financials of both the observatory and the clinic. Once they sign off, I'll authorize a donation."

"Right away, Justicar. And thank you. Very generous of you."

"Not at all. Consider it an audition. If I like what I see, perhaps we can work on other ventures together. What I was most interested in, Ms. Oriel, was starting a charity to help the refugees. I also wanted to investigate schools and funding streams for teaching the men cyphering."

"Cyphering. Forward-thinking. We can help the men learn other modern trades, too."

"The Shield will need people to maintain it, and well, I can't think of a more future-forward skill for the men to learn than cyphering or drawing."

"We are of similar minds."

Ms. Oriel and Jhee discussed the matter a little more before the other woman took her leave.

"That was brilliant," Kanto whispered and nuzzled her ear. "I'm almost done documenting my recordings from the abbey. Do you think a heritage foundation might like it if I donate some to their collection? Remember how I wanted to work with educational institutions? This event has given me several ideas on how to get involved in charitable causes of my own. I think I might work with organizations designed to help refugees. The serving staff seem happy. Are they the lucky ones? How many might otherwise wind up in plea- sure houses?"

Jhee released a breath she had not realized she been holding. She smiled approvingly at Kanto. "That sounds like a wonderful pursuit."

"One moment, I left my conch."

While Jhee waited for Kanto to return, Jhee paused on the mezzanine landing to admire the historic chandelier. Ms. Oriel and Mr. Bastian enjoyed cocktails at a nearby table further along the mezzanine railing. Ms. Oriel pulled out a jewelry box and presented it to him.

"Thank you. It's beautiful. She's right, you know? This is exactly the opposite of the event we wanted."

"It's events like this one that fund those."

The organizer's conch chimed, and she answered it. Her posture tensed. She gestured with more and more emphasis until at last, she shoved the conch in a concealed pocket. By the time she finished the conversation, Bastian had donned the plain but elegant lapel pin topped with an oversized crystal.

Ms. Oriel began to unclasp the pin. "You know what? We should probably put it in the security vault for now."

"Oh, I wanted to wear it the rest of the evening, you could show us both off."

Ms. Oriel leaned forward and lowered her voice, "I know what you've been up to and who with."

Before Jhee could move closer for a better listen, Kanto reemerged and hurried Jhee down to the main event.

"Step lively, Jhee. That's the vizier of building permits, the land development consortium head, and that's the vizier of mineral rights. Oh, and the mayor. You should definitely talk to them. They can help you in your dispute with the Brackfins. I'm sure if you put in a word or two, they might find in your favor."

"I've already had the displeasure of meeting the building permits vizier this evening."

"How bad?" Jhee pursed her lips. "We'll approach the consortium head then."

"You know so much about the household affairs."

"Yes, ever since you and I reached an accommodation, it's been easier. No more gleaning snippets from your paperwork or secondhand tidbits from Shep. I did my best to hide my intelligence from you."

"You didn't need to. You know I love intellectual stimulation as much as any other stimulation you might provide."

Jhee raised an eyebrow.

"I know that now. But I grew up being told that women would not want me to be smart. It was in my best interest to be a reflection or mirror of my spouses, see to their needs, and not be too intimidating."

Jhee found Mirrei once more in the crowd. "Well, no more. Remind me to have you sit in when next I discuss household practicals."

Kanto dipped his head. "As it pleases, denbe."

Jhee caught the weaselly woman from the clinic stalking at the top of the stairs to the mezzanine. "Enough stalling. You better come through or else."

"Bright Harmony, wait here a moment."

"What? Denbe, where are you going?"

The woman paused upon sight of Jhee. Her eyes widened, and she scuttled away. Jhee chanced upon Bastian on the lanai contemplating a glass of scotch on the rocks.

"About what you saw at the clinic," Mr. Bastian began.

"A clinic in an impoverished area. An attempted shakedown by a criminal element?"

"Precisely so, my lady. We try to keep them at bay as best we can."

"Not anymore I suppose."

"Hence, our drive to move the clinic."

"Say no more, Mr. Bastian. Relief may be on the next tide."

"If you say so, my lady. Do you believe in divine retribution?"

"I believe mortal retribution hits us faster."

"You're a Mechanist, Justicar," Mr. Bastian said.

"Yes, and an artificer."

"You know what is to be tasked with the conception and design of a devotional creation. Maybe you've even experienced the wondrous elation and closeness to the Makers which comes from a well-designed piece or simple yet elegant equation."

"Yes."

"What do you do when that feeling betrays you? When what you've wrought turns on you? When your beautiful equations go to pot, and they leave you with nothing but wreckage?"

"My mentor used to say, you can't always account for every eventuality. If you try, you could drive yourself to madness."

"What if a gunner had not misread a radar signature and led to a ship of pilgrims being blown out of the sky? What if the Bebhinn transposition error hadn't been corrected before the worst happened? Don't forget the Althan Astrolabe which had a tiny flaw. It was off by a mere two degrees, and it caused the Migdal disaster. Or the Trishanku serum contamination incident caused when technicians did not destroy one unsterilized batch? How do you think the architects of those disasters felt?"

"I am fortunate to have never faced a situation like that."

"Not even your mentor's final 'Dispatches from Arrow Point' case." Jhee's mouth twitched. "Don't you worry that with all your judgments you might have made a mistake? That you might have destroyed someone's life?"

"I can't let that stop me. If I'm too afraid to do my duty and render judgment, I'm no good to anyone. Least of those I might help. I must do my best to help those I can, to render a good judgment with the best available information and without caprice. I can only pray that if I am wrong, the First Makers see fit to make my mistakes known before too much damage is done."

"And if they're not?"

"I must do what I can to make amends."

"Would that were always the case. Some wounds are not so easily mended, my Lady. Please, enjoy the rest of the fundraiser."

Mr. Bastian headed inside. He remained on the mezzanine admiring the chandelier as Jhee returned downstairs.

"My lady Justicar, good to see you again," the mayor said. "Enjoying the fundraiser?"

"A lot more than the fair, so far," Jhee said.

"Oh yes, those nasty protests and strikes."

"It's only natural for folk to want to strive for better positioning in the Prime Maker's showcase."

Advocate Farkhande said, "We do not understand what sort of effects all this arcana can have on those who performed the work and on those who live near the constructions. What manner of artifice is it? The most sacred and reserved kind. With all these men cyphering."

"The loosening of restrictions on cyphering came because of the Storm Shield. I see it as a good thing. They needed the males' skills, and so it led to their liberation from useless traditions."

"At what cost?" the Ambassador said. "They may have released the men from their restrictions, but for the wrong reasons. This may be a problem, and they are as likely to put them back for the wrong reasons."

"Wise words," Advocate Farkhande said.

"Wise words to consider indeed, Ambassador." Jhee placed a finger on her esca.

"That's all I can ask."

"There are other rumors I heard from the nature wisps. There are those concerned about health effects. A massive working of this kind with all the various cyphering, drawings, weftings involved. And let alone one which affects the weather. Some say we are reaching too far. It's hubris. We are violating the Makers' realm, and they will punish us for it."

Jhee's vision refused to focus on the advocate. "It is also the First Makers' design that we create and innovate."

"My, what an interesting, auspicious gathering," Sianna said. She and her silent companion deposited half-drunk glasses of champagne and some shiny, pocket trash on a champagne server's tray and joined their conclave. "What sort of nasty rumors are you going on about, Advocate?"

"Nothing to concern you, director," the ambassador said.

"Everything to do with the mines concerns me and Inksy. Isn't that right?"

"Heh." Inksy's breath held a strong odor of cloves. She grabbed another glass of champagne. She downed it without bothering to remove the strong-flavored clove candy she sucked on. Jhee could only imagine how revolting such a combination tasted.

Sianna faced Jhee. "I thought it was a core Mechanist principle that society work like a finely tuned machine with everyone in their place, and any part that violates that was an anathema?"

"Were you eavesdropping on my conversation?" Jhee asked.

"No, of course not. But I couldn't help but overhear."

"There's room for both. The Grand Design is nothing if not expansive."

Advocate Farkhande turned toward the ambassador, "So, on another topic, I heard they hospitalized another half dozen in accidents down at the mines."

"Yes, quite terrible, really. I'll likely be representing the Fire Folk in arbitration against the mining company. Conditions in the mine have deteriorated with the increase in production and have become more dangerous than ever."

"It's a pity their labor contract prevents them from suing."

Sianna grabbed another glass of champagne and Inksy. "I get it. We'll go somewhere more welcoming."

Dye Hard

A murmuring arose from the attendees.

Jhee and the private tour attendees ran to the side of the terrace. From their vantage, they saw the outline of a figure scaling the side of the observatory dome. The climber noticed the scrutiny and gave the onlookers a cheeky wave. On the ground, security had gathered. Jhee looked at Kanto.

"What is she doing?" Mirrei asked.

"Whelm and waves," Erma said. She and Mirrei gaped at each other. Erma's color had drained. "She's crazy."

"Hold my robes," Jhee said.

"You're insane," Kanto said. "You can't honestly be thinking of going out there."

Jhee inspected the side of the building. She plotted her hand holds and foot holds. All around the Observatory she saw solid ground. No sheer drops to the ocean. She closed her eyes and steadied her nerves. If Jhee swung her leg over the railing, she might climb the face of the building towards the vandal. She respected the Makers of Heights; she did not fear them.

Jhee glanced back at Kanto's terrified expression. Instead of going over the side, the observatory offices had some nice, sensible windows from which to converse with the activist. "Hail friend."

A fresh, friendly face with golden eyes and watermark peered up at her from beneath ginger, shaggy hair tight in a bun. She had a fading cut on her forehead. "Hello, my lady."

"What do you think you're doing?"

"I thought it might be a nice night for a climb and to display this banner. It won't take a moment. You should probably wait inside. I wouldn't want you to get hurt."

The wind caused Jhee to yell to be heard. "You have no equipment."

"Neither do you."

"None needed where I stand. Care to join me?"

"Do mind, my lady. This is rather distracting. I need to focus on the climb."

"Perhaps you would let me throw you a rope?"

"Nay. I just need to concentrate."

Jhee went over the response time in her head. The security forces on the ground had moved an airbag into place underneath the activist. Not enough and too many things could go wrong with the placement. She had to hope they saw Jhee and figured out how to get to the office.

The activist continued to climb. Jhee went to the stairs and found the next flight up. As she passed by the mezzanine landing, it was now empty. She poked her head out another window.

"You sure I can't offer you some assistance?"

"My lady is too kind. I'll be right down in a jiffy. One way or another."

"That's what I'm afraid of."

The activist chuckled. A sudden gust of wind caught the banner and threatened to take flight with her. The activist flattened herself against the building murmuring and pressing her fingers into it. The building was stonework. She must have been an earth elementalist.

Jhee breathed deep to engage the Divine Mechanism and link her prime forces within to the breeze. The winds died down. She guided the winds to push the activist towards the building, a feat made difficult by the height. The wind vortices around tall buildings could be mercurial creatures. Their sudden appearance had surprised more than one wind elementalist.

"Handy trick," the activist said.

"Same." Jhee pointed her chin at the activist's climbing skills. "I'm a certified wind guider."

"I can't say as you can do lots of fancy wind motions climbing the side of a building."

"Perhaps you could come inside, and we could discuss elementalism techniques."

"No thanks. Maybe once I'm done here. My lady must be aware she is splitting my focus which will make it hard for me to deal with events should another gale like that occur."

"Many pardons." Jhee ducked back inside. By now the security team had entered the building. She heard their pounding footsteps on the stairs. She met them on the landing. "Follow me."

Jhee led them up to the roof access door where she and her tour had so recently used. They burst onto the roof deck. The activist clipped a carabiner to the side of a banner. She unfurled the banner and leaped off the side of the building.

The 'Free the Fire Folk' banner caught the winds, and she floated down from the spire beyond the observatory hill to some lower depth Jhee could not see and out of sight. By now, Erma, Kanto and Mirrei had reached the roof deck.

"Denbe, are you okay?"

"Yes," Jhee reassured them.

Erma ran to the edge. Mirrei joined her and leaned over. Too far over for Jhee's taste. "Was that not the coolest thing ever?" Mirrei said.

"Yes, that was not the coolest thing ever. Hopefully, the authorities will find her safe on the ground and not dashed upon the rocks."

Erma's ashen face showed she, at least, agreed with Jhee. She fled the roof deck.

Kanto gaped and gave Jhee back her robes. "Denbe, you might have climbed out there with her if we weren't here."

The realization she would have hit Jhee then. She shut her eyes. Dashed upon the rocks. She paused and took several breaths. When she opened them again, her younger spouses stared at her with concern. She straightened her posture and tucked her hands in her robes. She endeavored to project strength and self-assuredness. They visibly relaxed.

"Now shall we return to the festivities?"

"I can't possibly think of a thing they could do that might best that."

"Me neither," Kanto agreed.

Jhee had been about to say how the last thing she wanted was for them to try. A scream cut her off.

"Whelm and waves. What now?"

Jhee paused at the stairs contemplating yet another trip up and down them. She soldiered on. After a brief pause, she hurried down them as best as the unusual length robes would allow her. How much air could the robes catch? If she leaped over the railing, could she parachute down to the ground floor as the activist had? She would rather not find out and so confined herself to descending the stairs the healthy way.

Chants arose from the stairwell. "Stop the wall. The wall is death. Stop the wall. The wall means death. The wall means death."

"Don't they know this is not the time? This is a charity event," Kanto said.

Jhee shrugged. "I understand their frustration. Justice procrastinated is justice abdicated. 'Patience can sometimes be deadly. More deadly than anything.'"

As Jhee and her cohort emerged into the great room, the chants and commotion died down. Ocher and crimson dye clouds, colors of the protests, glimmered in the air. The sheer terror Kanto displayed at the prospect of them staining his robes eclipsed the one he displayed moments before. He stopped them from going any farther.

Eerie stillness and silence reigned. Protesters had filled the reception area. Activists swathed in the orange tabards had stormed the observatory opening with packets of colored dust. More carried banners, the same thin man who had eyed Mirrei and Jhee by the observatory gates among them. Spills of dye littered the floor. Someone coughed. Attendees batted at their clothes. They left glittering dye halos. Everyone else had frozen in place.

Few people's attention was on the activists or the be-glittered dignitaries. Jhee stepped forward. She followed their gaze upward.

Mr. Bastian's body hung from the ornate, crystal chandelier beneath the great room's skylight. A long, thin crystal shard protruded from his chest. Officials and security guards alike stood about covered in pigment, making no effort to do anything about it.

One of the chandelier's moon crystals crashed to the ground. Everyone leaped back. Some shielded their eyes from the shards. A barbarian sprang into action before Jhee and with a simple gesture redirected the shards safely.

Jhee returned her focus upward to discern anything else. The light fixture lazily twisted this way then that. Blood from Mr. Bastian's wound dripped down into the mess of dye and crystal in a spiral.

One tremulous drop at a time the blood dropped and congealed into the crystal dust. A steady drip continued with an ominous Tick-Tock, death's metronome. Glints and reflections sparkled through the skylight down on the body as if haloing Bastian in light like a divine celestial being. He had become celestial artwork with a morbid beauty to it. Now he was one with the First Makers. Perhaps he had even earned his place in the Prime Maker's showcase, part of the divine clockworks as he may have wanted.

The chandelier jerked then dropped a few feet. Another barbarian jumped to the fore. Their eyes had rolled into their heads and their hands held up straining to keep it from crashing down. Guests huddled together almost as afraid of the staff as the chandelier.

"Move back, everyone," Jhee said.

A barbarian server spoke, "My lady Justicar, we need to secure the chandelier."

"Come with me. No one disturb anything else, and security call the imperators. This may be a crime scene."

8

———

THE INVESTIGATOR

~

Detective Mode

Jhee hurried to the door porters. "Make sure no one leaves. Tell the valets. No transports brought around. Nothing. That is an official request."

Several barbarians followed Jhee to the landing where they stabilized the chandelier. Jhee examined Mr. Bastian's body in its resting place. A crystal lance pierced his body. A reddish-green powdered substance blanketed the floor in the lance's direction's likely trajectory. She pulled out her conch, careful not to disturb anything and took a visual record. One of the musician's instruments lay broken nearby.

Mr. Bastian had his whole life ahead of him. An occasion to look forward to with his impending marriage. A life full of possibility snuffed out so soon—too soon like the anonymous young ones out on the streets now dying unsung—such a waste, an utter tragic waste. Jhee clasped her palms together at angles for the First Makers' blessing and touched her hands to her esca before proceeding. May Mr. Bastian be remade magnificent. Jhee rejoined her dende on the ground floor.

"Disgraceful," Kanto said, having found three blue-gray exhibit blankets. He cloaked them with two. "Denbe, is he...?"

"Dead? Yes, it might be a murder. We are all witnesses or suspects."

He clutched his throat. "This evening is nothing if not exciting.

"I've noticed a trend. My nights with you often are."

"Flatter all you wish. I'm still terribly cross with you."

Jhee patted his hand and stroked along his ear ridge. He purred a little and snuggled against her.

"My night, my rules?"

"Always."

"Fine. My new rule for tonight is Mirrei rides home with us once we are free to leave."

Jhee stopped stroking his ear.

"Now come with me to see if she is all right."

"I will add a rule of my own then. Don't mention what you figured out to Mirrei. I don't want her to feel pressured. By either of us."

Kanto huffed. "Agreed."

Mirrei's eyes lit up when she saw them. She made a beeline for Kanto who mantled her with the remaining blanket. She pulled out her conch. "Did you take notes? I took notes. We should compare them."

And like that, Kanto's mood shifted. Kanto suppressed a giggle and they took each others' hands. "You know I don't take notes. That's more you and Jhee."

"No comparing of what you saw," Jhee said.

"Of course," Mirrei said. "I forgot. We want to capture our recollections but not compare them. We should keep our statements separate and not coordinate them, so the investigators can get as pristine a recollection of the facts as possible."

Jhee nodded. "We're potential witnesses. We have to avoid contaminating our statements."

"Our first time as witnesses," Mirrei said.

Kanto lowered his voice, "Or suspects."

"I know. Isn't it exciting?"

Jhee cleared her throat. She wanted to chide them about what a serious matter this was. Someone's death was not a cause for delight no matter who they were. She stopped short because she thought about Kanto's ordeal at the hand of the foul villain at Tranquility Bridge. He seemed none the worse for wear aside from occasional nightmares. If he could find it in him not to be reminded of his ordeal in a situation such as this, she did not want to make the connection for him. She had suspended the schedule to give him extra attention following his plight.

Jhee documented the blood pattern and inhaled, testing for unusual smells. If she had means to get an air sample, she might have been able to get Mirrei to do a chemical analysis once they returned to the villa.

"If only I had my field kit," Jhee murmured.

"Left side," Kanto said.

Jhee made a face at him.

"Check the left side of your robes." Jhee patted around and pulled out a small, whale skin case. "Mirrei, check your right side."

"A field assay kit?"

A tailor-made moment, as if the First Makers had designed it. Jhee felt a presence behind her. The mayor and several attendees craned to observe her working.

"What are you doing?" the mayor asked.

"I'm just noting the peculiarities that's all."

"Do you already have an idea about who might have done it?" one attendee asked.

Others nodded enthusiastically. "We want more than anything to know what you concluded."

It dawned on Jhee this was not her jurisdiction nor responsibility. She herded everyone including the dendes away from the evidence. "I'd rather not say. This is a matter for the local law enforcement. Perhaps later once I've spoken to the lead investigator who should be here any moment."

The mainly barbarian staff had thinned. Not good. Not with the tie between the weapon and the barbarians. Jhee approached the head porter, a Water Folk woman in a blue and beige, IES uniform.

"Excuse me."

"Why yes, ma'am. How may I help you?"

"Weren't there more staff here?"

"I'm sure the other staff are just in the kitchen, ma'am. If you need something, I might be able to get it for you."

"I asked no one to leave."

"No one told us, ma'am."

"I noticed not all your staff are barbarians."

"Yes, some are conscripts from the Outer Reaches."

"I see. With all the influx of people, good work is hard to find."

"I assure you, ma'am, this is good honest work."

"I did not mean to imply otherwise. You also employ barbarians."

"Has someone done something? Is their service not satisfactory?"

"Nothing of that sort."

The woman visibly relaxed. "We work within the guidelines of the Rabe documents, ma'am. Our staff are raised in the state-run schools for the betterment of their respective peoples, our tax and foundation dollars well-spent on those unfortunate enough to have laid eyes on the forbidden empire. If you're concerned about the drawing, don't worry, the ones who drew will be spoken to."

"I'd say they should be commended."

Another porter dressed similarly to the one Jhee spoke with approached them. The head porter held up a hand to cut her off.

"Any other questions, ma'am?"

"No. Just make sure no one else leaves."

"Of course, ma'am. Right away, ma'am."

By the time of the imperators' arrival, Jhee noted the sudden absence of most of the staffing service. Inksy approached a group of staff by the kitchens and whispered in one's ear. The stragglers set down their trays, and she walked them into the kitchens. Jhee hurried forward.

Sianna appeared in front of her. "A murder. How unexpected? Coconut cluster."

Sianna held out the confection to Jhee. Jhee waved it away and tried to sidestep her.

"I'm afraid we have a bit of situation here," Jhee said. "The facts of the crime had certain elements that may point to barbarian involvement."

"The coconut clusters really are amazing. I think it might be best if we separate out the staff. Until the imperators get here to maintain order. Shouldn't you let them handle it? Your family's waiting for you."

Jhee frowned and returned to her spouses.

Fire Folk. The barbarians. Called by some the bastard races. Their skin color differed from that of the Water Folk. Their skin lacked the bluish black hues of the Water Folk and instead tended towards tans and more temperate greens. Quite dull if you asked Jhee. Their eyes were also different. Rather than the divine pure and proper gold of the Water Folk, their eyes shone mundane blue-green, sometimes brilliantly so—a feature inherited from the exiles mixing of bloodlines.

At last, came their *escae*, the Fire Mark. Unlike the star-shaped mark of the Water Folk, theirs was pear-shaped. The teardrop shape bridged the difference between the round and marquise shape of the Air Folk and Land Folk exiles. The missing wedge on those such as the Air and barbarian males evoked a crescent shape. An incomplete shape unlike the more perfect full escae of women.

"What did you want with the staff?" asked the mayor. "Are they involved?"

The security guards dragged a protester limp and singing loudly towards her.

"We found this one hiding in the Galleon wing, Justicar."

"We did it for the cause, and we'd do it again."

"So, you confess?"

"One Folk! One Wave! One Force! One Rain! One People! For the cause," the suspect belted out.

"Your cause? Is that your excuse for murder? Enough foolishness from you. If you're so eager to confess, the imperators will be here shortly."

"Wait, murder? What do you mean?"

Jhee jammed her finger up at the chandelier.

"No. Wait. I had nothing to do with that."

"You can explain yourself to the magistrate."

"Lady, dear lady. I beg of you. No, I implore you to hear me out. I had nothing to do with this. I killed no one. We just painted a little sign on the galleon. That thing's offensive and should not be put on display. Free the Fire Folk! Solidarity now! One Wave! One Folk!"

Jhee caught movement from amongst the staff.

"I advise you to be silent. Last thing we need is another riot here."

"Please, put in a good word. Perhaps you know my mama or papa. They are good folk. It will just kill them to know I've been arrested."

"Then you should have thought of that before pulling a stunt like this or perhaps even murder. Explain yourself to the imperators or your advocate. I have no jurisdiction and can do nothing for you here. Now, do be silent."

"Best listen to the Justicar, my dear," Advocate Farkhande said.

"Yes, ma'am, if you say so, ma'am."

"And you, Justicar, mind you don't exceed your authority. By what right are you detaining everyone here?"

Jhee pursed her her lips, but she had the law on her side, "Extraordinary circumstances."

The advocate raised her eyebrows, and the corners of her mouth upturned. "I'll still be monitoring you."

~

The Inquester Arrives

A woman walked in wearing waist-length robes and a short, neat haircut. Jhee watched as she flashed her credentials to the Imperator on duty and spoke to security. Her eyes narrowed. She swept her gaze in a lengthy, slow assessment of the room and attendees. The woman paused in front of the wing entrance for the unopened Gray Galleon exhibit. She leaned in to read the plaque. Her posture stiffened. She turned sharp on her heel back to the crowd.

An Imperator and a security guard produced the suspect. "There's been a mistake," she said.

"I've been told you confessed," the woman replied.

"To the graffiti. Not to killing anybody. I'm a Makerly woman. I have no truck with body desecration or murder. We only want all Folk to be free and to see this obscenity is not displayed in our fair city. It was a lark, a bit of laugh."

"No one's laughing. Hold this one aside while I deal with the rest of the guests. And keep everyone away from this area until the criminal sciences unit gets here."

"Yes, ma'am. Very well, ma'am."

"You got to believe me. I had nothing to do with that," the activist said as she was dragged away.

"I'll try to get you a representative," Advocate Farkhande said. "Remember to say nothing else until they arrive."

"Advocate Farkhande, how unexpected to see you here," the credentialed woman said.

"Inquester Paij, I could say the same. I'm here on business. I had an injunction to deliver. If you ask me, that vessel should be melted down for slag."

The advocate gestured at the closed wing.

An imperator handed an evidence bag the other woman. "We found a discarded server's uniform in the galleon wing."

Jhee, confident she had identified the lead investigator, approached her.

The woman sent the Imperator away with a pat. "What can I do for you, Lady...?"

"Justicar of District Sixteen. Inquester, I wanted to inform you I secured the crime scene and made sure no one touched anything. Allow me to share with you what I've observed so far. I saw a powdery rose substance surrounding the body and on the mezzanine. I also saw a suspicious man at the gates, who I also think was dressed as a waiter—Inquester, shouldn't you be noting this down?"

"My Lady, I assure you your testimony statement is being duly recorded."

"Sensor suit technology?"

The inquester seemed taken aback. "You know about sensor suit technology?"

"Inquester, I am a Justicar."

"District Sixteen? 'Dispatches from Arrow Point.' I've read some of your tales. Aren't you a bit out of your jurisdiction?"

"I was attending the event as a guest. You understand I'm a trained observer, yes?"

"Ah yes. Of course. Forgive my rudeness, but it's a lot different when you are part of the story rather than a dispassionate observer."

"Your words are quite true. As I was saying. I separated the witnesses as best I could and ensured no one left."

"Thank you for your efforts, Justicar. Very conscientious of you. We will take it from here."

Jhee sighed. "Another observation. I observed a suspicious woman in rumpled robes coming down from the mezzanine after a tense exchange with Mr. Bastian. If you get a chance Inquester, I advise you to check out the victim's fiancé's clinic. I saw Mr. Bastian being shook down by this woman, a criminal element. She left behind a powdered rose substance similar to that near the victim's body."

"Thank you again. I assure you I will do that."

"Inquester, I don't have the feeling you are taking me seriously."

"I assure you, ma'am, I am. Justicar, forgive my rudeness, but you'll find we do things a bit differently on the main isles. We move slower and let the evidence dictate the course of the investigation. We try not to get ahead of it."

"I understand entirely. I underwent training beside the Imperators at the Emerald Isles Academy as you did."

Inquester Paij wrinkled her brow then held up her hand. "My class ring. How did you know who I studied with?"

"You also are practicing certain containment procedures, in particular methods favored by and taught only by the lead instructor at Emerald Isles Academy; idiosyncratic to the Sarlan's school. But yes, I take your point that amateurs should not go stumbling around. As mentioned, I'm a trained observer. I am offering you my services."

"Justicar, may I be candid?"

"This is you being oblique?"

"Please, Justicar, leave this to our division. Should my conclusions come under review, I don't have a fortune with which to pay the fines or the favors enough to squash them. I must rely on division resources which demand I follow proper procedures. I can't in good order afford to bring on a whirlpool investigator."

"In the interim, may I tell you what I observed?"

Jhee listed off some of the findings she noted. The Inquester smiled and nodded obligingly. Occasionally she rolled her eyes. She only humored Jhee.

"I realize this is awkward, Inquester. But I would ask that I be afforded at least professional courtesy."

The Inquester sighed. "Of course, ma'am. Take me through what you saw slowly."

"Before the presentation Ms. Oriel took me and my spouse on a tour of the museum. We were also allowed a private viewing of some of the rare exhibits. After, I observed Ms. Oriel and Mr. Bastian fighting and her giving him a bit of jewelry which I note is now missing. She also got a phone call on her conch that made her very upset. She excused herself, and we didn't see her again until shortly before the auction."

"What was the event organizer's demeanor?"

"She appeared upset, but not flustered. Her left sleeve was torn. It hadn't been when she left. She showed no markers of exertion. Not at all like someone who just murdered their fiancé."

"Yes, ma'am. Yet you understand, as do I, the overwhelmingly domestic nature of most killings."

"Indeed. Besides, I spoke to Mr. Bastian after that and he was very much alive. However, there are anomalies to this one that aren't factoring cleanly for me."

"I have a few questions for you, Justicar."

"Ask."

"Why exactly were you there?"

"Lady Delphine and I are friends, and she invited us as her guests. My dende and I had just attended a private artifact viewing when the nonsense started."

Inquester Paij adjusted her suit cuff. "Why would the event organizer take you, of all the dignitaries here, on a private tour and allow you to see rare artifacts?"

"I am something of a history buff and a Mechanist. I believe Ms. Oriel wanted to flatter me."

"For a donation."

"Precisely so."

The mayor beelined for them. Much like a bee sting, Jhee expected nothing pleasant coming next.

"Excellent! I see you are already hard at work on solving this horrible incident. I trust you, and the Justicar will bring it to a swift resolution. She did brief you?"

"If I may, madam, the Justicar and her family haven't been cleared."

"Piffle. You don't think one of the most prominent Justicars in a generation up and committed murder at a charity function in front of a bunch of witnesses."

"Witnesses of which, the Justicar and her family can be counted among. Should we go to trial, the testimony of a trained observer and expert as herself would be most invaluable."

"Almost as invaluable as an inspector's I would say, and they aren't prevented from testifying on cases they've worked. Two words, Paij: Gray Galleon."

The mayor left. The inquester pursed her lips at Jhee.

Jhee tucked her hands in her robes' sleeves. "I know you can't officially bring me on to the case until my family and I are cleared."

"Hang back. Say nothing."

~

Irreplaceable

Jhee and Inquester Paij went about collecting statements. Jhee did her best to be unobtrusive. While she observed the inquester at work, she kept her quiet.

Inquester Paij turned to her. "I trust everything met with your approval?"

"Inquester, you need no approval from me to do as you would."

"I know that look. But?"

"I noted that the porters' cuffs were dirty."

"Mm, I did too."

"Yet, you didn't ask about it?"

"No. Now, we just have a few more suspects to question."

"I, suggest we—you—speak with Ms. Oriel."

"As for speaking with the victim's fiancé, would you know where I could find her?"

"Now that you mention it, I haven't seen her since we discovered the body."

"Convenient that."

"Perhaps so."

They found the distraught Ms. Oriel being comforted by the lead astronomer in the latter's office.

"He was just fine a few minutes ago. We were making plans for our post-wedding retreat. He said he wanted to visit the new megaresort on isle three. Maybe even visit Tether Island. We discussed visiting the barbarian lands. I wanted to tour the Shield. The telescopes don't do it justice. I can't believe this happened."

"I know. Me too," Ms. Levinia said. "To say nothing of the damage to the Planetarium Chandelier, it's near priceless. Bastian's help had been invaluable on the chandelier restoration and telescope upgrades. That chandelier is irreplaceable."

"Bastian, too," the inquester began. "I understand this is a difficult time for you and will do my best to make this brief. Did the deceased have any enemies or anyone who might want to do him harm?"

Ms. Oriel rubbed her esca and shook her head. "No, everyone loved him, he was very unobtrusive and very quiet."

"Mind if I ask how you met?"

"He volunteered for the clinic. I was there capturing footage for Friends of the Observatory and the Breath of the Deep Society."

"Forgive me," Jhee said, "I thought you said you became involved with the Breath of the Deep Society because of Mr. Bastian."

"Oh no, well partially. I was already working on the Observatory restoration committee. They did a joint fundraiser with the Breath of the Deep Society. Many members are on both boards."

"Ah yes. Thank you."

"What about you, miss?" the inquester asked. "How did you meet the deceased?"

"Me. Oh, the same."

"Wait," Ms. Oriel said, "wasn't he your date at that investor cocktail party we held to kick off the restoration?"

"No, you must be mistaken. Oriel, will you be all right? I have to go inspect the telescopes for damage."

Ms. Oriel nodded.

"Don't go too far, miss," the inquester said. "I might have some additional questions for you."

Ms. Levinia bobbed her head before rushing off. Inquester Paij nodded at an Imperator who followed her.

"May I ask where you were during the incident?"

"I had to go to the vault for something. By the time I returned, all Trench had backed up. I couldn't find Bastian in the commotion. Then I saw his body."

"Thank you, very much," the inquester said and waved over a constable. "I may have more questions for you later. Meanwhile, this officer will take you to your office where you can rest."

Jhee waited until Ms. Oriel had gone. "I can confirm some of that."

Inquester Paij stroked her upper lip. "Bastian is a handsome and likable man much like your husband, Justicar. Did you also find him unobtrusive and quiet?"

"Inquester, what are you implying?"

"About your talk with the victim. Witnesses said they saw you and the victim on the terrace alone. Bastian was an event walker until he and the event organizer became engaged. Did you meet your husband under similar circumstances? Your husband has a similar background, I presume."

"You presume too much, Inquester."

"Simply, doing my job, my Lady."

"Mr. Bastian had a coughing fit. I was just inquiring how he was. Like my youngest consort, he suffers from Fresh Lung Syndrome."

"Which I would argue, precludes him from climbing up to the top of the rafters to vandalize the chandelier."

"Not without the aid of heavy mobility equipment such as the restoration crane."

"Restoration crane?"

"The mechanical crane the observatory has to do maintenance on the dome and clean the chandelier and skylight, and most importantly restoration on large artworks, such as the Great Galleon."

The inquester realized Jhee had taken control of the conversation and switched topics to regain it. "One of the other witnesses mentioned an incident at the clinic where Bastian seemed to show undue interest in your wife. I can't imagine the event organizer liked that too much or you."

How had she learned so much so fast? *Ah*, Jhee thought, *the sensor suit technology had real-time statement collation.*

9

THE MERGING STREAMS

〜

The Eel

Inquester Paij pushed the arrested activist out of her office ahead of her. Advocate Farkhande and Ambassador Naiman followed.

"Advocate Farkhande, I really must object to your presence here," the Ambassador said.

"She's wanted here. Not you," the activist replied. "At least the advocate's fighting for the little *guls*. You rolled over like a logging dolphin. Convinced us to agree to live near a bunch of cancerous crystal pylons. Got yourself a nice ambassadorship out of it."

"You'll be notified of your judgment date. Stay nearby and keep out of trouble," the inquester said. Farkhande walked the activist out.

"If that will be all, I'll take my leave too," the Ambassador said.

"So, she didn't do it?" Jhee asked.

"Ah, Lady...?" Inquester Paij paused. Jhee stared at her. "You and your cohort have been cleared and are free to go."

"Oh. I'd been asked to remain."

"Well, not at my request."

The mayor and Advocate Farkhande strode into the squad room. "Ah, Inspector, it was at mine," the mayor said.

Farkhande hopped on a nearby desk and swung her feet.

"Madam Mayor," the inquester said.

"I've been told the Justicar is not a suspect."

"No, but—"

The mayor smiled. "Excellent! May I inquire what your interest in this matter is, Justicar?"

"None I suppose," Jhee answered. "This matter has interesting aspects. It might be good for research."

"The Justicar hinted to me at the event she is working on a new story. Since she is not a suspect, then there should be no problem allowing her full access to your investigation, Inspector."

Inquester Paij rocked back on her heels. "Ma'am?"

"This death has indications arcana was involved, yes? The Justicar is already familiar with the case and an expert in arcana. We need to pool resources into solving this horrible mess."

Jhee's eyes widened, and she gaped at the inquester. She exaggerated her genuine shock, hoping to show she in no way asked for this.

"Mayor, I really couldn't. I'm sure the inquester here will do a great job alone. My family and I are on vacation. My spouses would prefer we get back to enjoying our holiday. They simply would not have it."

"Nonsense. I want the best and the brightest on this at once. The more of you, the better. The last thing we need is a scandal riding the tails of this other unrest. Together you should come up with a solution faster than either of you alone. I hope for a speedy and satisfactory conclusion to this mess. I mean it inspector, see the Justicar gets full access to your investigation." The mayor faced Jhee. "Try to portray me competently when you write this up in one of your Dispatches. I'll want an early copy of the story when you release it. Autographed. Now if you'll excuse me."

Jhee stood there awkwardly with the inquester and the Advocate once the mayor left.

"I had no part in that," Jhee said.

"Looks like that eel bent back on you, didn't it."

"Indeed, it did."

Advocate Farkhande, listening nearby, coughed loudly for attention. "Have you seen the way they portray local law enforcement in those?"

"Believe me, I have."

The inquester's narrowed eyes directed at Jhee made her opinion clear. Advocate Farkhande swept aside her scarf's dangling end.

"Then stop acting the fool. You of all people could use some good publicity. Maybe bilging off a media personality isn't the best idea right now?"

Paij rolled her eyes Sphere-ward. Advocate Farkhande hopped off the desk and gave Jhee a once over. Jhee remained impassive.

"I understand, Justicar, that you are versed in the new science."

"I've studied and been a practitioner many years."

"One wonders why the 'new science' is not simply called 'science,'" the inquester said.

"I have read your papers on forensic arcana. Illuminating." Advocate Farkhande paused as if listening to something. "The wisps say I should keep my eye on you. They know why you are afraid every time you peer over the edge into the depths. Deep forces have turned their gaze towards you."

The advocate left. Jhee turned to the inquester. "Should I ask?"

"I never do. She's good folk. I think. You really writing a story?"

"No."

"Of course. I heard you already met Wynne. She's one leader of our merry bunch of Mischief Makers."

"The building climber."

"Yep. Let's go have a chat with her. They hang out at Chuc's."

Chuc's turned out to be an underground cavern converted into an establishment for dancing and playing billiards. Folk scattered or melted away as the inquester's transport came into view. The suspicious reception she and the inquester received spoke volumes about the patrons who frequented the establishment, at least, during the day.

The crowd left a clear path for Jhee and the inquester to enter. Inside, they found the protesters clustered around a table.

"Wynne?" Inquester Paij asked.

The protesters were studious about not reacting. Jhee picked out the building climber and made eye contact. She nodded at Jhee, "What can I do for you, officer, my lady?"

Jhee took the lead, "I'm glad to see you made it down safely."

Wynne shrugged.

"Could we ask you a few questions?"

Wynne shrugged again. "Might as well before you get less than polite about it."

"Might I ask how you got onto the grounds?"

"Talent."

"So, you just went over the wall? No one let you in?"

"Your words, not mine."

"Perhaps your little stunt was a distraction for the murderer," Inquester Paij said.

"Distraction? Yes. Murderer? No."

"For the dye gag and defacing the galleon," Jhee said.

Wynne shrugged again.

Inquester Paij sighed. "We're wasting our time here."

"Again, your words, not mine."

Jhee nodded. "Perhaps. Our friend here isn't planning on wandering far. Correct? We can return if we have additional questions."

The pair made their way outside. The inquester spoke, "That went about like I expected. Guess where we head next."

"To have words with the other side of the crowd that evening."

The Marina

Jhee and Inquester Paij's quest for interviews led to the marina where several more prestigious fundraiser attendees had gathered to watch the regatta.

"Detective, can't you see we are terribly distraught?" the first noble asked.

"Inquester. Yes, I do. But a person lost their life, and it's my job to get to the heart of it."

"Humph." Tall and thin with olive skin and mid-back length, lank, dark brown hair, the Lady had an angry feel about her. Her alert black-gold eyes barely registered the inquester's presence. She raised her binoculars. "Come on. Come on."

Jhee invaded her field of vision. "Please, my Lady. Inquester Paij simply wants to ensure our safety. The sooner we conclude our inquiries the sooner you can get back to watching the regatta."

The noble's narrowed eyes calculated her relative rank to Jhee and if she could dismiss her. "As you wish. Ask your questions."

Jhee made introductions then allowed the inquester to lead. The nobles became more responsive once they noticed Jhee's polite deferral to the inquester while Inquester Paij bristled less and became more assertive. Though, her posture remained tense, and she fussed with her sensor suit's cuff link.

They at last went to question the vizier with whom Jhee and the Ambassador had the contentious exchange. While the inquester asked her standard questions, Jhee observed his demeanor. His perfectly pressed, fabulous clothes were slightly too big. The discolored hem of the vizier's robe also caught her attention.

"Inquester, permit me to ask a question?"

The inquester's eye color fluttered through a spectrum of exasperated hues.

"Vizier, did you go to the mezzanine?"

"I was in the great room all night."

"My, vizier, looks like you picked up a nasty stain on your hem."

"Oh, for the love of the Makers."

"Allow me. Strange, I thought I saw you slip out." Jhee had porters a locate a member of the housekeeping staff to clean the stain. She palmed the handkerchief with a sample of the stain before housekeeping left. The vizier's conversations at the fundraiser had put his prejudices and biases on full display. In her experience with those like him, showing you were like-minded exposed weaknesses in them. "Can you believe Team Nordale didn't even qualify this year? I have to say these 'social experiment' crews will get you every time. What would those Folk from the Scorched Lands know about sailing, anyway?"

"Exactly. If you must know, official-to-official, I was meeting with my bookmaker. I lost big on the qualifiers for the regatta. We met at the side entrance in the Galleon wing. I must have picked it up there."

"Name, so we can confirm this," the inquester said.

"She goes by Queenie, but don't tell her I said anything."

So, Queenie was the name of the weaselly woman from the clinic. "You have my promise," Jhee said.

"Thank you."

The inquester turned to her after they moved on. "What was that about? I had just gotten used to your blessed silence."

Jhee and Inquester Paij took their leave. "The hem of his robe. It was stained the same as at the fundraiser."

The inquester's expression was abashed. "I hadn't noticed it until you pointed it out."

Once outside, Jhee produced the handkerchief bearing the stain sampled from the vizier's robe. Its gray-green residue matched the stains the porters bore back at the fundraiser. She handed it over to Inquester Paij. "Several of us had those stains at the fundraiser. I had attributed it to wading through the lawn to reach the transport area. There was ankle-deep water all over there with no way around. Why is it still discolored now?"

"He also could have taken a skiff."

"Just so. A skiff." Jhee placed her finger alongside her nose and thought a moment. "There was also a gray-green stain on his sleeve."

"That I noticed. The same color as the corrosion on the galleon. Coincidence?"

"I think not."

"Definitely worth a follow-up. I'll have this sample analyzed." Inquester Paij fidgeted for a moment. "Thank you, Justicar. You were actually very helpful."

"My pleasure, Inquester."

~

The Crane

While Jhee and her spouses were out shopping, she received a summons from the inquester asking to meet at the observatory. Before she went inside, she went to the side of the building the activist had climbed. The wall kept her holds. She had used drawing on a manufactured structure and overcome all the resistance that imbued in a material. Manufactured walls not only bore many imprints, they often involved multiple elements. Either Wynne was an epic elementalist, or she knew cyphering.

The creaking and sweeping sounds of the sea and the haunting echoes of the gulls and sea life outside followed Jhee into the great room. The restoration crane occupied the center, and someone had raised the chandelier. No one was around. Jhee looked around a little suspicious. She heard a squeal and a bit of creaking rope and metal.

"Inquester?"

"Up here."

Dust and debris drifted down from the ceiling. Jhee shook her head as grit landed in her eye. Exactly what she needed. As if her eyes were not already bothering her enough this trip, she would be flushing them out from now until the next feast day. While she enjoyed the city, the strain on her allergies she could do without.

Once Jhee's vision cleared again, the inquester waved from the power lift platform that Jhee mentioned the restorers and others used.

"This thing is great!"

The inquester operated a joystick, and the lift moved up and down. She let out a little laugh.

"Inquester," Jhee said in a no-nonsense tone.

"Oh? Sorry."

The inquester lowered the platform. She shrugged when Jhee folded her arms.

"You could have at least waited for me," Jhee said.

The inquester smiled, and they shared a chuckle. "Care to do the honors?"

Jhee took the controls from the inquester, and she had her own fun as she hoisted them back into the sky. Meanwhile, Mirrei and Kanto lounged by their lonesome, ignored on the ground with only their conchs for amusement.

Inquester Paij said, "I gave this lift and the area a quick overlook. Anyone could come in here and use this thing. Let alone someone who might have as much access as the event organizer. But that's not all I found. Have a gander."

Inquester Paij pointed out voids in the dust on the mezzanine catwalk which would only be visible with a Height Maker's view. Jhee strained over the railing for a better look.

"Careful now, Justicar," said the inquester.

A gasp from her young spouses brought Jhee back to her senses. Below her, Kanto and Mirrei had snapped out of their disinterest. Jhee planted her feet firmly on the platform. Instead, she pulled out her conch and brought up the zoom and magnification function. Footprints, eight inches, stride, shorter than two feet, possibly the event organizer's, but there was no way to be satisfied. Estimating body size and height from stride length and shoe size was an inexact science. But more importantly, the crystalline rose substance that Jhee had been finding everywhere covered the catwalk.

Another glimpse of Kanto and Mirrei's anxious faces told Jhee this would not work. Jhee lowered the platform long enough to release them from their obligation to stay and insist they finish shopping without her. She would contact them to meet for dinner and drinks later.

Jhee fished out her forensic kit. Inquester fished out hers. They had nearly the same kit.

Inquester Paij and Jhee's minds worked alike. A deduction the inquester may have made too had she not spent such effort resenting Jhee's presence. Jhee had spent hours yesterday on a project that might extract her and the inquester from the predicament the mayor put her in and ease the way between them. She had the proper credentials. They must protect the law and the case. A murderer would not go free because the judiciary viewed her presence as a violation of procedure. To preserve the integrity of the case and for her evidence to be admissible, she needed to be authorized to be at the crime scenes and use arcana.

"Inquester, I wanted to do this by the guides. I started a formal request to work this case with you through the Central Authority and assignments clerks."

"Here I was thinking my opinion didn't matter."

Jhee presented the inquester with her formal credentials via ether. "It not about your approval. My dedication is to the law. I don't want the case integrity compromised."

The inquester read through the signets on her conch. "Neither do I."

"I hope this goes some way towards putting us back on the right footing."

Inquester Paij accepted the credentials with a nod. "Want to help me lift the prints?"

"Yes!"

Jhee nodded excitedly. She and Paij busied themselves imaging the scene. Despite Jhee's insinuations otherwise, she was only familiar with Sensor Suits in theory. She had not seen one used in the field. They compared notes and went over the evidence practically giddy and laughing. It was so good to have this meaningful dialogue with someone on her same level.

Mirrei and Kanto resumed shopping. "Let's hit some places in the Furnace District," Mirrei said.

"Let's not."

"Aren't you curious about what sorts of fabric or design ideas you could pick up from the Fire Folk?"

Mirrei waited and watched him think it over. At last, he shook his head. "No, we shouldn't stray too far without denbe."

"Too far? It's just up the road. I'll go by myself then, if you're too scared."

Kanto sighed. "Stay out of trouble and meet me back at the square by first setting."

Mirrei kissed Kanto on the cheek. "You're the best denye ever."

"Just go and don't make me regret it."

Mirrei marveled at the dizzying height and closeness of the architecture. She wondered if she could find that one food cart from the street fair again. Mirrei rewarded herself with a pat on the back and two skewers once she had. She skipped the stew.

Protesters still passed through the area around the carts but the tone was much more subdued. A group even occupied some tables at the sidewalk café, Che's, she had taken refuge in during the protests. One of them must have recognized her because they waved her over. She hesitated then approached.

"Was that your first action?" one asked.

Mirrei nodded.

"They're not usually that intense."

"I bet it was the Squids. They pay folk to agitate."

"Stick with us. We mostly sit- or lay-in."

"Your next time will be easier."

Next time, Mirrei thought. *Would there be a next time?* When she had tried to get involved at the abbey, she ended up bedridden. She was done being confined to a bed. She intended to spend her time having fun.

"No thanks," Mirrei said. She still had time to hit up a few smoke and candle shops she before getting back to the square.

~

Like Knows Like

The event organizer, Ms. Oriel, had been scarce since the murder. Grief-stricken, according to colleagues.

"This was the last thing the observatory needed. Oriel was supposed to help save it not drench it," Ms. Levinia said.

"When the Justicar left the viewing, she mentioned an argument between you and Oriel."

"It wasn't an argument."

"You mentioned something about her going into business for herself," Jhee said.

"I was just venting."

"What about Bastian?" Inquester Paij asked. "How well did you know him?"

"Not well," Ms. Levinia said.

"Really? Didn't you hire him to accompany you?"

"I'd hired Bastian as a remora, a paid companion and guard for social events. I'd had several confrontations with the protesters. He also turned out to be rather technically inclined. I assumed he worked as a remora to put himself through school. He assisted me with operating and maintaining the telescopes. He even helped troubleshoot the Planetarium Chandelier. The highlight of the event was supposed to be treating our guests to a presentation, not Oriel's auction. I originally meant the fundraiser to be a benefit for FLS/MLD sufferers. They would be the first to see the Planetarium Chandelier restored to working condition. At least, that's how Bastian and I originally planned it."

When Jhee and the inquester went to question Ms. Oriel at her apartment, they found no one there. Their next stop was the clinic.

"Have you seen Ms. Oriel recently?" Jhee asked Vash.

"Well no," Vash said. "Now that you mention it, I haven't seen her since that ghastly business at the fundraiser. Any progress on finding the killer?"

Inquester Paij continued the questioning. "Please, Sir Delphine, if you would just answer the questions and point us where she kept her things."

Vash led them to the employee locker rooms. "I'm still not sure what you are hoping to find."

"Do you have a key to this?"

"Yes."

"Open it, please."

Vash unlocked Ms. Oriel's locker. Inquester Paij recorded the original state of the locker before she poked and prodded about. She handed the camera off to Jhee as she removed the contents of the locker. At the bottom of the locker, the inquester found a pair of shoes coated in rose crystalline particles. She projected a virtual overlay of a ruler and the prints from the catwalk and compared them. "I'd say that looks the same."

Jhee noted the shoes of other sizes in the locker. She tugged at the inquester's sleeve. "Inquester."

"A misdirect. She wore oversized shoes to throw us off."

Jhee kept her counsel. That was a possibility. She had to admit she had nothing more to go on than her gut at this point. It still did not seem to add up. Why would she leave the shoes here where anyone could find them? She did not know Ms. Oriel, and the inquester's methods were sound. Everything by the guides. Nothing she would not be doing herself. Did she just not want Ms. Oriel to be guilty because she showed Jhee some priceless artifacts?

"Your reasoning is sound."

"So glad you approve. Sir Delphine, we will have to look at your records. Give us everything you got on the event organizer."

"Unfortunately, Inquester, our records are private and confidential. It will require an official writ of inquiry from the Imperial Circuit, not local. We are under the Empire's Health and Redevelopment Philanthropy division."

"As you wish."

"Perhaps, I might be of assistance. I know people on the Imperial Circuit, Inquester."

"Just what I hoped you would say. I intend to put all your fancy connections to work."

Inquester Paij and Jhee checked out Ms. Oriel's temporary office while Jhee sent messages and contacted folk. Jhee disconnected from the last one. "We can have a writ, but it might take up to a long-tide."

"Wraith and wrath," the inquester said. "Beats never, I suppose."

Jhee noticed a glint from the waste bin beside the desk. Jhee bent over and examined it. It was another shiny wrapper like she found at Lady Delphine's work site. Was Ms. Oriel connected to the vandalism and sabotage?

"Inquester." Jhee pointed out the wrapper. "I found a similar one near some vandalized equipment at Lady Delphine's. Ms. Oriel could have let the protesters in. Perhaps she had a hand in the street fair protests, too since she also organized that event, too. Whether it was for the publicity or the ideology remains to be seen."

Jhee examined the Friends of the Observatory tour itineraries. These were well outside of observatory hours. She found Advocate Farkhande's name listed several times.

"I'm no expert, but these payments don't seem like a normal event organizer's fees. What do you make of this?"

The inquester handed Jhee an inscribed branch painted in bright blue and yellow. She recognized the markings as the Failed Prototypes' work. Jhee held a late-era prayer rod. "An artifact of the Failed Prototypes. You would be correct,

Inquester. I think Ms. Oriel had been selling private tours and access to the restricted exhibits to wealthy patrons."

The inquester took the rod from Jhee. "New motive. Bastian caught the event organizer compromising the foundation."

"That is also a plausible explanation. As plausible as any we've had so far."

The inquester's eyes flashed. "What is your brilliant analysis since you keep throwing cold water on mine?"

"I don't have one yet. I'm still gathering data."

"The mayor did not seem to have a lot of patience with us gathering data. You are supposed to be speeding things up not slowing them down."

"That is not my intention, Inquester. I'm simply trying to be thorough and properly situate all bodies in the system. A person's life may depend on it."

"A person's life may depend on bringing this character in. She may well be out there stalking her next victim. We have a duty to protect the public first."

"I understand, Inquester."

"Are you sure you do? I didn't want you on this case to begin with."

"I understand that, too. Please, I am not deliberately trying to slow down your investigation. You should proceed however you feel you must."

The inquester rolled her eyes. "'Madam Mayor I've made an arrest in the case. Yes, Oriel, the event organizer.' 'Do you know how much good they have done for this community and how many feathers you will ruffle? Justicar, do you agree with her assessment of who the killer is?' To which you would say?"

The inquester pointed the rod at Jhee. Jhee winced at her indelicate handling of the ancient artifact.

Jhee took it back from her carefully. "I take your meaning. This is your investigation, Inquester. I would not gainsay or undermine you in public."

"Only in private."

"Would you like the honest answer?"

"I would like the benefit of your skills. You have good instincts and eyes. If I didn't trust in those, I would have put this to bed already. Which is why your doubts are making me doubt. If you say we should keep looking and there is more to this, I can't help but agree. It seems a little pat to me too. I, though, have to go strictly by the book. We need a plausible reason for not running with this lead."

"You collected samples for arcane and forensic toxicology tests, correct? Well, the most accurate labs and the premiere company are on the far side of the island. They are in high demand. It could take long-tides for the results to return. In the meantime, we should continue to work the evidence we have."

"Ah, I take your point, Justicar. You have a surprisingly devious mind."

"Like knows like. You are not the only one who's used to dealing with recalcitrant or entitled nobles trying to steer an investigation."

"All right, let's go over the evidence again together and see what we missed. You're not the only one whose instincts are warning them away from a quick arrest."

"Thank you, Inquester."

"Your reasonableness is infuriating, you know that?"

Jhee smiled. She knew.

10

THE WATERING HOLE AND THE DIVE BAR

~

The Watering Hole

Jhee and the inquester met up with Kanto and Mirrei at Che's, a mid-scale club. She bought the first round.

"Open us a tab, if you would?" Jhee asked the barman. "Didn't I see you at the Observatory fundraiser?"

"No, my lady. Not my sort of affair. They don't let the likes of me in except through the servants' way. If you attended the street fair, you might have seen me there."

"Perhaps that's it."

"Begging your pardon, my lady. This doesn't seem like your sort of affair either. I try to run a top-notch place, but the more dignified types like yourself pass my place by."

Jhee examined the branded napkins in the napkin holder, he set out for their drinks. The stylized letter logo matched the one on the napkin with the note written on it from the clinic. Jhee indicated her companions. "Just soaking up the local flavor. Young spouses, you know how it is?"

The barman looked dubious but let the matter pass. Jhee returned with their drinks.

Kanto wrinkled his nose and used a handkerchief to clean off his glass. "This place is quaint."

"I don't know. I think it's charming," Mirrei said.

"To the shock of no one. We should leave before anyone important sees us here."

"Learn anything else after I left the observatory or did you just continue to amuse yourself with the crane?" Jhee asked.

Paij laughed. "It's okay; I get to have a little fun now and then."

The inquester had been right. It was fun.

"Bright Harmony, Star Mirror, would you be dears and grab the inquester and me more ales?"

"Of course, denbe."

The Inquester stared too long after them and wiped ale foam from her mouth. "I must say Justicar, after working with you, I never pegged you as the sort to have trophy consorts."

Jhee frowned. A bowl of shiny candies sat on the bar. They were luxury candies meant to lend the establishment a posh air. Jhee tried one and nearly coughed it back out. Black pepper clove was one of her least favorite tastes. It reminded her of the home remedies grandmamere swore by and always fed them the instant they got a sniffle. She discreetly spit the candy back into the wrapper and had a drink to wash away the taste.

"Sore subject, I see. This doesn't seem like your sort of place, Justicar. Why are we really here? At first, I thought it was to humor your spouses, but now I'm not sure."

"I'm following a hunch. Inquester, I beg your indulgence as I humor a notion."

"I can't bring hunches or notions to the station. Sorry, but it's looking like I will have to bring Oriel in. Unless you want to clue me in on what about this place piqued your interest?"

"I thought you said you did not want to get ahead of the evidence or be part of the story, Inquester."

"Why don't you let me be the judge of that?"

"Still seems like there's more we're missing. The calibrations on this are off. Why would Ms. Oriel go through all that bother? It doesn't make much sense."

"Unfortunately, it doesn't always have to."

"Then there's this." Jhee placed the clinic napkin on the bar and slid it toward the inquester. "I found it after I saw Mr. Bastian and Queenie, the weaselly woman, the first time."

"'Pool. Underground lake. This blight of a city consumed in a pillar of light. Mineral sands. Starry eyes.' What does this mean?"

"I don't know, but I'd like to find out."

Jhee's junior spouses returned bearing more drinks. The inquester pounded hers back then slammed the mug down on the counter. "Well, once more off to the streams. I'm off to track down the event organizer. Catch you at to the station, ya?"

"At some interval, Inquester."

"Bright Harmony. Star Mirror. See you again sometime. If you'll excuse me, I've got me a suspect to go capture."

Like that, Inquester Paij was gone. Jhee brooded and monitored the other patrons.

"If you wanted to go with her," Mirrei said, "you could have. We must schedule another play date for you."

"No, I'd rather spend this time with you."

"That would be so sweet if I believed you."

"What will it take to convince you?"

Despite Kanto's gripe, Jhee and Mirrei drifted around the bar a while longer. She took pity on Kanto and sent him back to the villa, though Jhee remained, and Mirrei kept her company. They drank and danced.

To their shock, the inquester returned as they were leaving. She looked keeled. She was alone. The inquester paced, as Jhee and Mirrei hailed a water taxi.

"Well, it looks as though no one can find the event organizer. I can't think of a clearer sign of guilt than that, can you?"

"Surely there must be some explanation for this, Inquester."

"And she can explain it to me when she's in custody. I'm putting out an alert for her. Presumed dangerous."

"Inquester, please."

"Justicar, she is a person of interest, but she could very well be a killer. I have to act in the best interest of safety. Please, if you'll excuse me. Also, if you see the event organizer, call me immediately. This is no time for any of your 'Dispatches from Arrow Point' heroics."

Jhee sighed. "I assure you, Inquester, I am a creature of comfort. I do not go in for heroics."

"Creature of comfort? A creature of comfort with quick throw sleeve knives. I peeked at your service record, Justicar. I mean the parts that weren't redacted. Now off you go."

The inquester shut the taxi door after Jhee, and it sped off. She thought about the evidence they had found. Was Ms. Oriel guilty? No. It just didn't seem to add up. Jhee was missing something. She just knew it. She couldn't figure out what, but she had a duty to the law and the order of the state, city, and the Empire. If she found Ms. Oriel, she would do her duty.

When the inquester questioned Ms. Oriel, she mentioned how she had gone to the vault. She had also mentioned something about putting Mr. Bastian's lapel pin there. The Observatory was likely to have several vaults. What had Ms. Levinia said about the Planetarium Chandelier? They had found it moldering in one of the observatory's storage units. It was worth a shot.

They arrived at the villa. Mirrei exited; Jhee didn't.

Mirrei took that as her cue. "Go," she said.

Jhee's first thought was to investigate her theory alone. Though, she hoped to find Ms. Oriel before the local constabulary. The fear of bloodshed after a high-spirited chase too often proved founded. It was no longer her and Shep anymore. Jhee had to cut back on the foolishness such as looking for a killer in the middle of the night in a dark and damp cave. She had also promised to respect the inquester's jurisdiction. She took out her conch. "Inquester, I think I might know where we can find the event organizer."

~

The Dive Bar

Mirrei stood on the veranda watching as Jhee's taxi sped off. She thought about what to do with the rest of the evening. If she returned to the suite, she had a plateful of Kanto's pouting or ignoring her to look forward to. After all his yammering on about enjoying himself in a major city, Galleon City did not agree with him. Perhaps nothing short of the capital would meet his standards.

The Delphine siblings stumbled onto the veranda dressed for a night out. They exchanged cheek kisses with Mirrei. Erma leaned against a porch column and sparked up a smoke root. Semele held out her hand. Erma passed the smoke pouch to her.

"You want to douse this place and go somewhere more exciting?" Semele said. She took hold of Mirrei's hand.

"Like where?" Mirrei asked.

Erma offered Mirrei the root. "There's an underground club in some closed mine tunnels."

Mirrei declined. "Sounds touristy."

Smoke root exacerbated her Fresh Lung Syndrome. Not to mention what frolicking in a mine might entail. The last thing she needed was to contract Miner's Lung on top of FLS. She probably should have gone inside by now.

Vash answered, "Not this place. What do you say?"

The sisters and Vash regarded her with expectant, pleading expressions.

"Please, please, please," Semele said. Her necklaces clacked and her skirts bounced as she did a little stompy dance. She even used Mirrei's own eye flutter trick against her.

Mirrei bit her lip. No wonder denbe always caved. "Let's go."

They arrived at the busy club swarming with folk from every walk of life, from jet-streamers to street urchins. They didn't have to wait in line and were escorted right inside to a booth in the upper area. The Delphines introduced Mirrei to their friends Deziree and Taral.

"There are a lot of Fire Folk here," Mirrei said. She tried not to act like a gape-mouthed grouper. Tunnels led this way and that presumably off deeper into the mines.

"Miners," Wynne replied. She stepped out from the crowd. "They make the best Earth movers. The Storm Shield needs its minerals. Contracts with the 'heritage' schools allow a loophole in the wage laws. Companies can pay them even less than skilled refugees. I remember you. Your wifey had my friends arrested."

"Hey, take a dive, Wynne," Chappy said. "Hope, she didn't bother you too much, miss... Star, right?"

Mirrei nestled into the semi-circular couch, so it was to be all flattery now that he knew she might be important.

~

A Watery Hole

Jhee and the inquester slogged through dankness and night to the vault entrance. The sounds of the surf crashed against the beach in a darkness still teeming with life. Birds called. Breezes whistled through rock openings. Sometimes she found the subtle ocean scents comforting. Not now, not with her drenchable eye allergies acting up. It was like they were burning out of her sockets. This was the last thing she needed. They found the vault locked up tight.

Jhee explained why she thought Ms. Oriel had come here. "She mentioned the water storage facility that they had for rare objects and decommissioned telescopes and how they reminded her of the secret little spot she had on the beach where she and Mr. Bastian would go. It made a great hiding spot. It's also where they kept some of their observatory's rarer finds, to prevent them from being damaged and/or stolen."

Her eyes watered something fierce almost blinding her. She rubbed at them which only made it worse. She shone her flashlight in the darkness and continued to slosh through the cave and wade through the ankle-deep water. To the Trench with these allergies, the ankle-deep water, and her long city robes. How could they stand these gowns? She thought about that one official's hemline and the cuffs on the porters and service staff at the grand auction.

"I don't know, Justicar. This seems like a long shot."

"Please bear with me, Inquester Paij."

Their journey led to an unused portion of the mine beyond the vault sections. Jhee swept her glowtorch around. She laid a finger aside her nose in concentration. Her burning eyes and her allergies proved too distracting.

"Hm, I thought she would be here."

"Wep, Justicar, we gave it a tilt. But now let's leave it to the professionals."

Jhee raised an eyebrow at the woman.

"Sorry. I know you are 'the professionals' too."

Jhee rotated for a moment casting about the space. She made a quizzical sound, pondering what had she missed. They turned and started to leave the cave.

Inquester Paij tripped and fell. "Unmake me!"

The inquester fished around the water for her conch. At last, she got a hold of it, and by chance, it flashed against the wall, and she saw a half-lit shape in a fissure.

"Inquester, wait! What's that?" Jhee showed her light over what she thought she saw. Ms. Oriel hung from the wall pinned to the rock wall, like an insect in a collection. Jhee gasped.

"Drench," the inquester swore.

~

The Tadpoles

"This definitely puts a new wrinkle in things. The event organizer was our best suspect for Bastian's murder," Inquester Paij said.

The two colleagues stood on the beach as the criminal sciences unit recovered Ms. Oriel's body.

Jhee tucked her hands away within her sleeves. "I suspected something was off. But I had hoped I was wrong. I would have preferred to be wrong given the loss of life. Now, I have to figure out what perturbed me about Ms. Oriel being a suspect."

"Well, what usually bothers you when you are looking for clues?"

"Mis-calibrations. Imbalances. Something missing or something that doesn't add up. Ms. Oriel was jealous, yes, but it seemed as if more was happening there, more than mere jealousy. After Mr. Bastian was dead why would she still chase after him or this other person?"

"Maybe we should search for the other woman or man? The event organizer kills Bastian out of jealousy, and the lover kills the event organizer for revenge."

"Plausible. But still the character of the murders. They were very impersonal. I think that's what's missing. They were dramatic, overly so, meant to send a message or to shock. Neither strikes me as a crime of passion. They had a very deliberate nature about them especially with the religious staging of the bodies."

"The wall activists. Not that poor sod we arrested. She was a patsy if ever I saw one."

"I agree with you on that one," Jhee said.

"So nice of you."

Inquester Paij shrugged. "There are all the other activists like Wynne. Where do we even begin? There are so many of them in the city. Also, the lot of them who stormed in here that night. Who's to say that one was the only one got somewhere they shouldn't have?"

"That is a suspicion of mine as well. The person who displayed these bodies wanted to make a statement. 'One waters.' Why would killing Ms. Oriel forward such an agenda?"

"Killed for what she knew? New idea. The event organizer was the original target. Bastian surprises the killer and gets done in. We go chasing off after Oriel. Once the heat is off, the killer goes after their original target, Oriel."

"That sounds plausible as well. All these theories sound plausible. We might want to start by eliminating the most implausible. Who would want to kill Ms. Oriel then?"

"Someone who did not look too kindly on her mishandling indigenous artifacts or fleecing them for these charities. How much background research do you do on the charities you donate to?"

"My charitable trust performs financial checks on the various organizations I support. I have no problem giving away my fortune; I just want it to go to helping people."

"Maybe that's it. Someone finds out what wave witchery the event organizer was up to. They don't take kindly to the misuse of funds. Especially, if they could not really afford them. You told me how persuasive she could be."

"Charm the skin off a sea otter."

"Maybe she was too charming. Someone came looking to get their donation back. Stumbles upon Bastian in the dark, perforates him only to find out it wasn't the event organizer."

"I like it, but it doesn't quite track either. Perhaps if we did a walkthrough of the crime on scene to see how plausible it is to mistake the two."

"Concrete. Actionable. Now, our streams are merging."

Jhee and the inquester returned to Ms. Oriel's apartment. The door was ajar. Through the narrow crack in the door, Jhee saw the apartment's turbulent state.

The inquester made a silencing motion and drew her sidearm. She motioned for Jhee to stay back while she crept into the apartment. She spoke into the cuff of her Sensor Suit. "This is Inquester Paij at forty-four Stack Street, apartment two-oh-one, requesting assistance."

Jhee readied her siren module to enhance a disarm command and prepped a cypher. She got three uses of the module at full-strength, full-compulsion with diminishing returns thereafter. The inquester swept and cleared the apartment. She holstered her weapon.

"All clear." She raised her cuff. "Request for assistance canceled. Send a dust-up team to my location."

The inquester noted the positioning of Jhee's hands.

"Cyphering's useful and all but I haven't seen an artificer who can stop a bullet."

"True enough, Inquester. But in anything short of such a situation, which is most, it does well in a pinch. I take it your suit has kinetic displacement shielding."

"The latest and the greatest. Wep, it looks like somebody got here before us. What do you suppose they were looking for?"

"I wish I knew, Inquester. I wish I knew."

The inquester started walking through the scene. "Well, whatever it is they didn't find it."

"Can we be so sure?"

"Nope, we can't."

The inquester picked at a vase on the shelf. Chillenster. Expensive. "Being a fund raiser pays better than I thought."

"Inquester, may I have your permission to synchronate the room?"

"Can you magically tell who did it?"

"Inquester, you've seen my methods. I would think by now I'd have earned a little less suction from you. I'm eliminating options. If arcana has something to do with this, I'll get impressions. Some may even be detailed enough to know a category of arcana to pursue, but not who performed it. I have some theories on if it will ever be possible. Arcana is a lot less arcane than most think. We are only beginning to scratch the surface."

"I think I'm going to wait until the arcane forensics unit shows up. Yes, Justicar, we have one, fledgling though it may be."

"What I want to do is not much unlike the criminal sciences unit. You don't like arcana do you, Inquester?"

"Not so much. What I don't like even more is having everything become a nail to its hammer. I prefer technology. Less destructive. It's much more egalitarian. But arcana's the wave of the future isn't it?"

"Both can be devastating. As for egalitarian, that's one condition I'm hoping the Shield will fix. I hope it will show the value of allowing males to cypher and draw."

"You are quite the optimist. The Shield has brought nothing but misery to the city. Crime, murder, riots, and protests. Nobles from the Imperial isles are sheltered from it."

"Inquester, I'm from the Far Reaches. My ancestral home, our lands, are sunk beneath the waves."

"Lands? Ancestral home? The tragedy."

"Does this mean no more consultations and beer?"

"Depends. Will it involve a visit to your noble estates?"

"Yes, but with your behavior, it's liable to be the one underwater. The Reaches are sheltered from nothing. Not storms. Not raiders or pirates."

Inquester Paij held wide her hands in a gesture of surrender. "I accept my rebuke as much deserved and fairly meted. Consider my sucker shots binned."

"Now watch me work and squish it."

"Yes, my Lady Justicar."

The fledgling arcane forensic team arrived, and it was indeed fledgling. It comprised a handful of anxious techs using store-bought, stock kits. A beleaguered expression appeared to be the only one they had. They tried to set up a synchronance perimeter only to have the other forensic techs and investigators disrespect its boundaries. Two techs struggled to keep their stanchions upright, a young man and woman who looked as though they had newly graduated the academy. She had case notes older than them.

Jhee lent her aid. "How many cases have you worked?"

"Dozens. Simulated."

"How many field cases?"

"Three including this one," the young man answered.

"Arcane forensics is a new specialty at the Emerald Isles," Jhee said.

"Our shift commander was among the first graduating classes. It's an honor to meet you, my Lady Justicar. I did a paper on the role of arcana and forensics in the 'Dispatches from Arrow Point.' I practically grew up on it."

Jhee could believe it. Men were excluded from the field until the laws changed. The tech must be younger than Dispatches.

In due time, Jhee and the flustered technicians obtained an arcane map of the apartment which they could use for reconstructions at the lab.

11
____

A CHANGE OF COLOR

~

A Fitting Demonstration

"Can't this wait, Kanto?"

"I refuse to show up to court for the height of the festival season with all of us still decked out in mismatched country robes. Now that we are on solid ground, I can do something about it."

Kanto sighed and checked his conch. Jhee set her teacup down. She contemplated speaking but picked up her cup again. She glanced at her conch then took another sip of tea.

Kanto pursed his lips, his golden eyes taking on a reddish hue.

"Perhaps we should proceed without her."

"She could have at least informed us she wouldn't be here."

Jhee's first instinct was to defend Mirrei and make more excuses—Mirrei's actions had disrespected Kanto enough already. That angered Jhee more than anything. She nodded. "I'll address it with her when next we speak. She should not be so inconsiderate."

Kanto studied her, and his expression softened. She had acknowledged his injury, not minimized it, and let him know what she would do to correct it.

"Denbe, I'm sorry to be so crisp on this," he said. "I'm losing track of the fittings she's flaked out on without so much as a word or by your leave. I put a lot of thought and effort into these ensembles. They tie together with a unified house theme while taking into account our individual styles. Do you know how hard that is to pull off?"

"Why don't you explain it to me?"

Kanto carried on for a while, and Jhee did her best to follow along. The color symbolism and the motifs made the most sense.

"This bores you."

"No, actually. Color symbolism and motifs come up often in textual analysis and in more elaborate illuminated works."

Kanto smiled. "Come on. Up you go. Tell me about the case. I know that look."

Jhee mounted the dais and Kanto draped her in fabric. "We found Ms. Oriel dead. She was our prime suspect."

"Um hm," Kanto said a series of pins held between his teeth.

"I was skeptical it was her and had just come around. Now we're back at square one and I don't know where to start."

"Why were you skeptical?" Kanto mumbled.

"Her means, motive, and opportunity were weak or nonexistent."

The door to the observatory suite burst open. Mirrei bustled in with her weirs gear. She wore her play jacket with the hood pulled up over her head. "Sorry. Sorry, kin. Lost the time."

Jhee let out her breath. "No harm done. Right, Kanto?"

Kanto showed his teeth, his mouth still full of pins. Mirrei grabbed Tranquility Bridge herbal tea and cookies from the table.

"I think you owe us an apology for keeping us waiting without notice."

Kanto nodded.

"Yes. Yes." Mirrei swallowed the cookies. She clasped her hands. "Honored denbe, dearest denye, my deepest apologies for my inconsiderate behavior."

"Now, how about a sincere apology?" Mirrei still had not taken off her jacket. Jhee noted the green smudge on the hood. "Mirrei, where have you been, really? And why won't you take off your jacket?"

The young woman's eyes went as wide as tea saucers. She hunched and slipped the hood back to reveal hair dyed deep rose and light sea-green. "I used my personal palette, so it wouldn't clash with our ensemble."

The pins spilled from Kanto's mouth. Jhee moved forward. A pin stuck her in the leg. She flinched.

"Tailor's... maxim," Kanto mumbled.

"The dye is temporary," Mirrei said. "It should wash out in a few days."

"The cut," Jhee began. She cast about for an affirmative statement. "The cut is flattering."

"I thought so too. The shorter length frames my face just so. Shorter cuts are all the wave inland. What do you think, Kanto?"

His mouth hung open. Even as Mirrei helped gather the pins, he gaped. Jhee imagined the lecture brewing in Kanto's head about the scandalous cut, *"Improper, it was just improper."* Jhee pleaded with him with her eyes not to make a scene.

"It's... nice," Kanto said after regaining his power of speech. "Now, get on the dais. I need to make some... adjustments to your robe."

Relief flowed through Jhee. She hung her unfinished robe on the nearby mannequin. For a moment, she considered having a custom fitting double commissioned once they arrived at the capital. Though, the thought of standing half-naked in front of strangers for that long made her uncomfortable.

Jhee squeezed Kanto's shoulders to thank him for being civil. "I'm going to turn in early. I have an appointment at the local imperator branch tomorrow. Mirrei, we'll discuss your apology later."

⌇

"ALL RIGHT. Here allow me to show you how to position your stanchions properly for maximum coverage," Jhee said. An ASU tech held out the stanchion. Jhee brought it to one corner of the ASU lab and directed other techs to do likewise. "We want to put them at the corners of the room and hopefully the winds will have been right. This should maximize the coverage. What we are after is the direction of effect and its target. Which would likely be inside the room and the perimeter, so if someone cyphered into this room, we'll catch it. It carries some risk that the artificer may have cyphered from the ceiling or through the floor but if there's an artificer who can levitate or dematerialize, we have much bigger problems."

That got a little chuckle from them.

The ASU's shift commander addressed the untrained onlookers who had begun to gathered, "Arcana leaves behind echoes much like how every material contact leaves a trace. Arcane forensics looks for signs of drawing and cyphering. Elemental drawing disturbs the natural flows of elements. So, you look for elementals out of 'alignment.' And more complex drawings involving cyphers leave 'Makers' marks' on the elements in the area."

Jhee joined the shift commander at the control panel. "We activate the grid to get a pre-cyphering reference level. You put in your credentials so you'll be in the exclusion list."

The arcane crime scene techs gave a backward glance. Jhee smiled, donned safety goggles, and nodded her approval. They tried with drawing to recreate patterns from the textbooks. "Arcana does not always require arcana or technology to detect. Direct observation is the first and simplest way to determine if arcana has been used."

Jhee demonstrated draws and cyphers and had them compare it to some non-arcane types of fire and water damage.

"Now, our first victim was hurled into the chandelier by a crystal projectile from the balcony, approximately here," the shift commander said. She went to the approximate location where Jhee had found the red dust trail the night of the fundraiser."

Jhee rolled up her sleeves and then clapped her hands together. She clapped them together again. She hummed and started thinking about the sound of the ocean. Think and be the wind and the air. Air and the wood specialty of Earth were common to concealment formulations. She hummed and focused her mind. She reached out to the high waters, the fluid prime forces that flowed beneath existence, the motions of the Divine Mechanism which connected all things. As she shifted through the arcane reconstruction for residues of arcana use, she found no sign anyone had been here to go over the scene and hide evidence. No one had used arcana in that apartment recently.

By the end of the synchronance, a small crowd had gathered to watch her work.

The inquester gave her a bit of mocking applause. "You had everyone spellbound. What were you saying about you not being a whirlpool investigator?"

"Not a whirlpool. I love to teach or lecture as the spouses might say."

The shift commander clasped Jhee's forearms. "Many thanks. I've tried for months to get the rest of the department to attend a primer."

A uniformed imperator rapped on the glass. The inquester spoke with them for a moment then returned looking dour.

"Inquester, a development with the case?"

"Your wife has been arrested for disturbing civic peace."

Jhee pinched the bridge of her nose. "Whelm and waves. Where?"

"Near the Styr Mine project. They arrested dozens. There was a clash between One Waters or Folx United kooks and the miners. I know the detention facility they'll have gone to and the bull who runs it."

~

The Jail

As the jailer on duty led them down to the confinement chambers, Jhee still pinched the bridge of her nose. Her naïve, sheltered Mirrei arrested. The jail's air tasted of body odor and bleach with a vomit chaser. The cold and the smell caused moisture to build in the corner of her eyes. By the time the jailer brought Jhee and the inquester to the end of the hallway of cells filled with protesters and activists and other sorts of criminals, Jhee wiped moisture away every few moments. Lest they think she was crying.

"Over here. I put them in their own cell as a professional courtesy," the jailer said.

They came to a cell where Mirrei and Semele sat alone. They stood as Jhee and the inquester accompanied by the jailer on duty came into view. She would not meet Jhee's eyes as the jailer unlocked the cell door.

"Star Mirror? Semele? What is the meaning of this?" Jhee asked.

"Justicar, it was all my idea," Semele said.

"Somehow, I doubt that. I've informed your mother. And she will deal with you later. Star Mirror can speak for herself," Jhee said.

"Can I?" Mirrei asked. Her face flashed with anger. Jhee braced. "We were at the protests because the wall is wrong."

"You're young. You don't understand."

"Don't I? What don't I understand? That we are destroying people's homes and burning out their children because we're so scared of the big bad 'barbarians' who are kicking our butts? Well, maybe our butts need to be kicked. We tried to conquer them and the other inhabited worlds. Then there was that galleon. Ghastly. They packed in there like cattle to be shipped to a hostile, strange environment rather than stay."

Jhee let Mirrei's words sink in. She had never heard the young woman talk so passionately about anything. How had she missed this? "I'm bailing you out. We'll discuss this further once we're at home."

"I'm staying right here."

"Surely you don't mean that, Star Mirror? This is no place for someone with your condition."

"I'm staying as long as everyone else is here."

Mirrei folded her arms over her chest and sat down defiantly. Jhee turned to the jailer on duty. "Forgive me for disrespecting your house," she said.

She formed her fingers and did a simple cypher. When she was done, there was a dent in one wall.

"There," Jhee said. She held out her wrists to the jailer on duty so she could be restrained.

The jailer's eyes turned molten gold. She fixed Jhee and the inquester with a death glare before sighing. The inquester mimed the gestures for wiping her hands and out to sea. "Under the statutes on the destruction of Imperial property, I am taking you into custody. It is your right to contact an advocate unless you waive your right to do so. Any word or deed from you from this point on will affect your defense at your judgment date until you assert either right. Do you understand?"

"Understood."

"All right, let's get you up to the front for processing."

After booking, the jailer deposited Jhee in the cell opposite Mirrei and Semele. "Behave."

Jhee rubbed at her stinging eyes once her hands were free again.

"When was the last time you took your allergy medication?"

"A few days ago. This isn't about me. When was the last time you took your saline?"

"I'd been feeling so good lately. It slipped my mind." Mirrei folded her arms. She glanced at the wall dent. "Why would you do that?"

"To end up precisely where I am now. They can't put me in jail for nothing. Requests for voluntary remand require several long-tides to approve. Property damage and disruption are minor offenses which don't involve assault upon the good persons of this jail. The best I could come up with given the time-sensitive situation."

Semele laughed. "Your anchor is insane. I love it."

"Is she right, denbe? Are you insane?"

"Simply concerned. Also, this is important to you, and somehow, I missed it. Even once you changed your hair, I wasn't listening, but I'm listening now."

"I only watched the protests. I stopped to help the wounded after the fight broke out, then the Imps showed up. You were right at the abbey. Kanto and I were being misery tourists. I wanted to do something. There's so much I didn't know about, that I have never seen. All the suffering. I just wanted to do something. Other than throw a few shell at a charity. Kanto is a man of many waters: music, clothing, drawing. Shep makes food to die for and is good in a fight. You are this great, warrior detective. And what can I do? Swoon. I can't fight or take up arms, but I can do this."

Whirlpool investigator? Warrior detective? Why was everyone under the impression Jhee committed so much violence? Given her druthers, she would be the first to run from a fight. She spent most of her time diffusing fights and violence. Many conflated her mentor's background with her own, due in part to her writings. But even Jeja's exploits she had embellished to make the stories more exciting.

Jhee gave a bittersweet smile. "I remember those days. Star Mirror, I forget how sheltered you've been. How you want to have a mind and life of your own, while I keep trying to fit you into my mold. You are still discovering who you are and so am I. You want to know one thing you can do that we can't?"

Mirrei stared up at her with those young innocent amber eyes expectedly.

"Heal people."

Mirrei laughed a little. Sometime later the jailer on duty arrived and unlocked their cell doors.

"You three have been bailed out and are free to go." Mirrei started to protest. "Arrangements are being made for the other protesters as we speak. Now. Get. Out. Of. My. Jail!"

Kanto and Lady Delphine waited at exit processing. He sniffed. "By the names and countenances of all the Makers, what have you two done? Vandalism. Disturbing civic peace. I have half a mind to leave you both here overnight."

"Then you should leave because we are of a mind to stay here overnight."

"Nonsense. You are both coming home with me this instant. If either of you does anything to get yourselves arrested again before we leave, I shan't forgive either of you."

Jhee deferred to Mirrei. Mirrei swallowed. A jailer with a group of detainees crowded them out of exit processing. Behind them, more awaited. "We can go."

Jhee's conch shook.

-She likes port. It better be the best you can find. I'm partial to stouts.

Kanto held his peace until they reached their rooms in the villa. "Never pull anything like that again. Promise me."

"I promise," Mirrei said. She and Kanto pressed their escae together and embraced.

"Jhee?"

"Would you want me to lie?"

"What am I going to do with you?" He frowned. They touched escae then their lips. He sighed after the kiss ended. "I see now why Shep grayed so young."

Jhee's sheltered, fragile Mirrei. Mirrei had been more than that for a while now. If she had ever been. She always chafed when Jhee babied her; Jhee had just not seen it. She was too caught up in her own emotions.

Jhee glanced at Mirrei and could not help but be reminded of Miramar and the wages of their families' feud.

～

Talk and Collapse

Jhee went to Mirrei's room later that evening. "Mirrei, may we talk?"

"If you are here to read me, Kanto already did."

"No, not that. I want to talk about us and our family situation."

"Go ahead."

"Are you happy here?"

"I'm very grateful to you, denbe, for taking me and mum in and for making me part of your family."

"That's not what I asked. I asked are you happy?"

"I'm as happy as can be under the circumstances. One look around this city and its people, shows me how lucky I am to have found such a caring and generous denbe as you. Children and lesser spouses talk. Kanto and I lucked out with you. Both you and Shep are considerate and involved in our lives."

"You are still avoiding the question."

"I'm trying to be happy."

"You are young, Mirrei, and I am getting older. I would like to see you established with a good situation should the worst happen. Our agreement stands. If you want to be released from our marriage contract, I won't stand in your way."

"It's not that. I'm just not feeling fulfilled, I guess. Like how Kanto is with his charitable work."

"Why don't you do what Kanto is doing with the refugees and education? We'll meet with our charitable trust director and identify some charities and programs you can work with to help people."

"I don't throw myself into healing the way he does into fashion. It can't be my entire world. Not like fashion and parties are with him. You're hard to keep up with and approach sometimes. You're always so noble and do the right things. It's hard to relate."

Noble? Her? She had to look no further than the wreckage of three families to know the lie of that. "I'm as flawed as anyone. I want you to feel you can talk to me. What you see now isn't always who I was. It was a process, a journey. I have to remember you weren't there to see the falls and the stumbles. Perhaps we could go over options for your future. Maybe a stint at the Imperial Academy. Now that we are near the capital, you could enroll in the ether academy. I'll fund everything. That way you could become a doctor or anything."

"Anything?"

"Anything except arctic studies. You'd freeze your snout off. It's viewed as a punishment. Although at least one graduate in my class was genuinely excited to go. It's viewed as a bilge assignment. The program you put your children or spouse in if you want to get rid of them or have them out of sight, out of mind."

"Do you want me out of sight, out of mind or do you think I'm an embarrassment?"

"Absolutely not. I couldn't be prouder of you if you were my own blood or your accomplishments mine. It is a good thing you know your own mind. It will serve you well, especially if life turns out not to be exactly what you hoped. Besides, it would be hard to put you out of sight with that hair."

"You don't like it."

"It's an adjustment. Though, I meant what I said about the cut."

Mirrei chuckled then her expression sobered.

"This holiday has a familiar feel to it. Like my first stays at your home when we were 'courting.'"

"When did you figure out why I wanted you to get to know them?"

"The crab roast. You don't flirt with me, you flirt with the others. You flirt with the inquester. But not me."

"I'm not flirting."

"Engage in playful banter with underlying sexual tension. Now, who's avoiding the question?"

"I want you to know what options you might have."

"I'm aware. Thank you. I'm going to spend the rest of my night in my room. Meet you for family breakfast."

"It's a date."

Jhee left and gently closed the door after her.

Jhee picked up her conch. She composed an apology for the jailer along with a delivery of a case of Imperial Isles Signature port. She also sent a "thank you" message to the inquester. A cheeky message arrived from her financial manager shortly thereafter. She almost ignored it. Jhee pinched the bridge of her nose upon seeing the remits which had the manager in an uproar. Jhee's funds had bailed out the whole jail.

KANTO MET Jhee at her door the next morning and escorted her to the dining room to meet Mirrei for breakfast. Mirrei sat, her head propped up on her fist. She absently poked at her kreel and porridge with her spoon.

"Morning, wife," Jhee said and kissed her on the cheek. It felt a little warm. Kanto likewise gave her a quick muzz on the forehead.

"Morning, kin."

"You look tired, Mirrei. Did you not sleep well?"

"I spent most of the night thinking."

"You know what?" Kanto asked. "Let me go get you some orange tea. That should perk you right up."

"Thank you," Mirrei said as he ran off.

"Is this about the Shield?"

"I can't stop thinking about it. And how we need to do more."

Jhee took hold of her hand. It was a little warm too. "Are you sure you are all right? You don't look well. With all your running about did you take your saline dosage?"

"I don't recall. I'll go do it now. Then I think I'll retire to our rooms for a bit."

Mirrei stood and swayed. Jhee caught her before she completely collapsed. They took Mirrei back to her room and called Vash.

"It seems like just another Fresh Lung Sickness flare-up," Vash declared. "Get plenty of rest for the next few days and keep up with your saline regimen."

Jhee slipped her hands into her robes and paced. She continued even after Vash had left.

"You can say it," Mirrei said. "You were right. The jail was no place for someone in my condition."

"I can't see what would be gained by me scolding you. You are a grown woman."

"Nevertheless, you were right, and I was wrong."

Jhee sat down on the edge of the bed. "I don't care about that. I care about you. Mirrei, I want you to take care of yourself. You are blossoming and becoming so independent. Once you leave us behind, I don't want to worry about you."

"I would never do that."

"Never say never. I'll let you get some rest."

Jhee rose then noticed Mirrei's slippers. The bottoms were stained rose. The clothes she wore yesterday were also covered in rose dust and smelled of the smudging stick.

"Your clothes reek of the smudging stick. Have you been smoking?"

"I can't get anything passed you, can I?"

"Smoke root plus your extra exertion might explain your collapse."

"Not me, I swear. Erma and her friends do, though," Mirrei said then cocked her head. "You have that look."

"What's this stain on your shoes?"

"I don't know. I must have got it while we were running around somewhere?"

"Somewhere? Like where? It's important."

"I don't know. We covered a lot of ground during our march. Why? What is it?"

Jhee furrowed her brow. "It's nothing. Just rest."

Jhee excused herself. She called the inquester on her conch. "Hello, Inquester, do you have footage of the arrests from yesterday? I also need to know where they arrested Star Mirror and her friends."

12

THE DEEP DIVE

~

The Lament Cypher

Mr. Bastian's apartment was freakishly bare and neat except for a houseplant with brown leaves dying from neglect. It appeared he did not spend much time here. Movement drew Inquester Paij to the window. When she opened it, a domestic sea-lynx hopped inside.

The sea-lynx hissed and flared its head crest when the inquester reached for it. Jhee enabled the animal protocol on her siren module.

"Come here, little one," Jhee said spending one use to sooth the creature. The sea-lynx purred and Jhee stroked its crest. The animal protocol did not require filling out forms after using it. She found more of the rose crystalline powder. "What's this you are covered in?"

A key reading 'Sandoval' hung from its signet collar. Jhee and the inquester turned the apartment over from stem to stern. While they scoured the bedroom, the apartment door opened. Someone began rummaging around the apartment. The sea-lynx screeched. Jhee flicked on the light. The intruder froze, the hissing sea-lynx held at arm's length.

"It seems your luck still has not changed for the better, Mr. Eldjin," Jhee said.

"Justicar?"

"Unlike your bad run at gaming, this is an actual crime. Why are you burglarizing this apartment?"

"I wasn't burglarizing. I was investigating. Like you."

"Investigating what?"

Mr. Eldjin released the hissing ball of reptilian fury. It ran into the bedroom. "The competition. The bid which won the Shield contract was the lowest. Way lower than it feasibly could be. It means somewhere along the way someone had to cut corners. To a dangerous degree."

Jhee frowned at this less fanciful implication of the dangers of the Shield. "Ah, Eldjin-X, the losing contractor for the Shield. You would say that."

"You are right. But tell me this. Why has no one been allowed to see the contracts or the specs for the Shield? The labor receipts? I may have a harpoon to hurl, but it doesn't mean I'm wrong. The mortal toll; they have to be grinding up and burning out practitioners at an alarming rate. Also, what of the physical tolls. It has to be maintained around the clock until it can sustain itself. My bid was so high because I tried to do right by the workers and their families. My estimate included the costs of care, pensions, dependent care and survivors' benefits for spouses and family. There is no way the winning bid took that into account."

"So, you are doing this out of the goodness your heart?"

"Hardly. His design used synthetic crystals made from compressed dust."

"His design? Mr. Bastian's?"

"Vilmar. The winning contractor. Compressed dust is a fraction of the cost of whole crystals of those sizes, but the dust is toxic and leads to respiratory illness in miners. To get Blue Waters certification, his contract then needed to provide extra pension and medical benefits for the miners and their family. Someone waived the provision. I just want to find out who it was. Those provisions were part of the reqs for the contract. If their bid didn't include them, how did their bid get approval? Someone had to waive that requirement. I think the Delphines called in a favor and got Vilmar awarded the contract."

For years, Jhee had swam in a sea of conspiracies surrounding it. This felt different. Mr. Eldjin might have inside knowledge. Her frown deepened. Jhee thought about Mr. Bastian's remora mark. Was she wrong about what it represented? "And Mr. Bastian?"

"A technician with some company in charge of the project. He said he wanted to help me. He needed my credentials to the bid system. We were looking for the proof templarite mining was unsafe, and the government covered it up. He said he had research data. Oriel hid it. We just don't know where. My competitor must have silenced them both. Maybe even the mining supervisor, but I heard Lethys was more of a stranger at her gaming table than mine. What are you going to do?"

"I'll look into it."

"That it?"

"I'll look into it. That's a promise." Jhee yelled over her shoulder, "Inquester Paij, I trust you'll see to this matter."

"Yes, my lady. And you, Eldjin, you will go with me for detention. You were trespassing."

"Wait, you were there this whole time?"

Inquester Paij escorted Mr. Eldjin out. Jhee would have to investigate his accusation further. This did not bode well for Lady Delphine. Jhee wandered about the room. Lady Delphine had been on the council that decided the contracts. Other officials Kanto had introduced her to at the charity may have had a hand in the decision. Was there a connection there? In the bedroom, she came to a stop in front of a wall mural.

A depiction of the cataclysm that destroyed the Failed Prototypes' civilization, Findar-beneath-the-Waves, hung on one wall. It had sunk beneath the waves amidst a torrent of godspark and ash allegedly because of hubris. Her foot contacted a valise overflowing with paperwork. Jhee pulled the valise from under the edge of the bed. More paperwork trailed with it. She was still organizing it by the time Inquester Paij returned. "Over there."

Jhee pointed at a shoe box of medical bills she had placed near the lamp. "On top, you'll find a recent transcode message."

"'We regret to inform you your fourth stage aggressive Miners' Lung dementia has progressed to a terminal stage.'"

Jhee found receipts for wigs, many water taxi trips, and hair dye in the closet. What were you up to, Mr. Bastian?

"With his advanced Miners' Lung Syndrome, he couldn't be running around the exhibits. He would need to enlist someone else for that. The activists?"

"Could be Ms. Levinia."

Jhee pulled a disposable conch from the bottom of the valise. When she turned it on, a video played. It was motion-activated security film of Mr. Bastian talking to someone off-screen. "Careful with that. Look around us. One mistake in calibration and you could start a chain reaction that would set the whole thing off."

"Inquester, look at this footage. What do you see?" Jhee pointed to the standing lamp. "Look at the way the shadow falls, that's not right."

"That's not this apartment."

Jhee crawled over to the financial papers. She flipped through them on her hands and knees until she found a lease. She flicked it with her finger then shoved the lease at the inquester. "A-ha."

The inquester rocked back and forth on her heels. She took the paper with a hooded glance at Jhee. Jhee realized how she must appear knelt amidst a storm of papers framed by a painting of a world-ending squall. She rose, dusted herself off, and tucked her hands in her robe.

"It's not for this apartment or Ms. Oriel's."

"Sandoval's long-term vault storage."

It took two more uses of the siren module on the sea-lynx to tranquilize it enough to get the key off its collar. Each time the effect diminished. A fourth use might not work or do irreparable harm.

The key from the sea-lynx's collar unlocked a storage unit down on the mine docks. The vault workshop was not so modestly appointed as the apartment. Antiquities, knick-knacks, rare books had been pushed aside and piled in dusty heaps. Engineering books though had been arranged on the shelves with great care. An entire wall of the apartment was covered in bio-film filled with equations and schematics. Mr. Bastian must be more than a technician, an engineer perhaps. Whose lie was it? Mr. Eldjin's or Mr. Bastian's? Jhee filed the tidbit away for later. Over the top of the brainstorm wall were written the words, "This was to be my hymn to the Makers."

Articles and clippings about the Shield and the protests occupied one wall section. Another had geological surveys. While another displayed refraction indexes; half-lives: exposure rates. Each one had other words or phrases scrawled over them. "Not right." "It doesn't add up." "Complicit." "Liars."

"Who would want to kill a dying engineer?"

"He looked as though he did not have long for the world, anyway. You see, Justicar, everyone has something to hide."

"That goes without saying, Inquester."

Jhee and the inquester explored the squatter's workshop. The designs for devices, including one Mr. Bastian labeled a synchronator, screamed unhinged as if conjured and written straight from the depths of the Unmaker's Trench.

Some were lightly penciled in, some traced over and over again. Frequency equations and more frequency equations accompanied numerous charts about body types, weights, and sizes. "Not right. Not right" was scrawled all over images. Mr. Bastian sought an answer only his disturbed mind could fathom.

This reminded her of one of her academy mates. Doli Monkfin had a breakdown third year. She had gotten into numerology arcana, and became obsessed with number patterns, formulas, and something called the Lament Cypher: a derivation so intricate and detailed that if you attempted to solve it, you went mad.

It appeared as though Mr. Bastian had found his own Lament Cypher. But what was it about?

Bits and bobs of tech sat on the workshop in various stages of construction along with signs of his Mechanist devotions. A hardware equation deriver which if properly designed and calibrated could do a thousand times more calculations than software worked continuously. There were frequency textbooks thrown about with treatises on toxins. A book on the bed, on the table, tons on the workshop's table beside stacks of periodicals. Passages had been marked ranging from catering, food prep, food-borne illnesses to home brewing and bottling.

The living area, though, contained little other than an unassuming chair, table, and cot. Everything there was basic and functional, reminiscent of a prison cell—a prison of his own mind and Make. The disordered signs of a disordered mind. Was Mr. Bastian always this obsessed or was it something that happened to him because of his advanced Miners' Lung condition?

Scale models of the Shield tines, pylons, and the relay station rested on one table. 'Free the Fire Folk' had been scrawled on the surfaces. Jhee touched it. Still wet. This must have been done recently. Mr. Bastian was a wall activist. Something or someone had accelerated his descent into madness. Had Mr. Bastian been planning to poison them all, or something else? It seems they had dodged a lance.

~

The Weirs Court

A knock at the suite door interrupted Kanto's sketching. He recognized Vash's knock pattern by now. His was better. He set aside his sketchbook and headed for the door. Mirrei hopped by him, still putting on her shoe while managing her weirs bag.

"Weirs. Must go. Bye."

"Weirs? In your condition?"

"What exactly is my condition, Kanto?"

"Didn't you just have a 'health scare'?"

Mirrei horn glared him. "Suck silt."

"Bottom feed, you little faker."

"Which you were fine with when it gave you an opportunity to spend more time with denbe because you thought you could use it to usurp Shep."

"You're not my denbe or denme."

"Well, you sure as water are trying to act like mine."

"Someone must."

"It doesn't have to be you, Kanto. You're allowed some irresponsibility. I'm going. You can come with if you're that concerned. You might even enjoy yourself."

"Fine. I will."

"Fine."

"Oh, so the weirs courts are underground now?" Kanto said after they stepped inside Chapman's Underground Club. This was leagues worse than that horrid little bar they met the inquester at.

After they entered the hangout, everyone cheered. "There's our hero of the day. Healer, our failed banner hanger, and bail provider."

Mirrei took the drink the man behind the bar offered and kissed him. "I can't take all the credit. My denye's the one who bailed everyone out."

Kanto grimaced.

"Fine, then, all hail...."

"Bright Harmony."

"Your wife doesn't even let you use your own name in public. Has she kept you bred or bled, so you never have time to pursue your own interests?"

Another drench CARP. "Denbe is very supportive. If she weren't, Star Mirror wouldn't be hanging out here, and you Trouble Makers would still be jailed."

"Star Mirror?" the man behind the bar asked. He chuckled. "Any denye of *Star Mirror* is welcome here, too."

Mirrei pinched Kanto's arm. He gave her an offended look. Why pinch him and not laughing boy? Two jet-stream setters with red-tinted eyes and a flask in hand abandoned their card game and wandered over to them.

"Oo, Star's brother-groom," the woman said. "I'm Deziree and this is Taral. We've heard nothing about you. Means we get to figure it all out ourselves."

The man who accompanied her wore a bespoke vest and a dapper waved coiffure. He gave Kanto a once over. "Exquisite fabric, golden thread, black pearls in the embroidery."

As the pair assessed him, they passed the flask back and forth.

Deziree nodded. "Tailored beautifully. Don't recognize the designer. Oo, but maybe that's the point. A trendsetter."

Kanto refused when they offered him the flask. "I only drink champagne."

They giggled and went back to their card playing.

"These are my friends. Don't embarrass me," Mirrei said. He gave her a sidelong glance. Embarrass her?

After taking a seat away from the bar, they treated Kanto to the uncomfortable sight of Mirrei snogging Semele and the barkeep, Chapman. Kanto continued to sit there; he played with his cuffs, unsure of what else to do. This far underground his conch did not work. He saw a bio-film periodical sitting on the bar. It took a few pages for him to realize its erotic nature.

"You look sad sitting over there all by your lonesome. Wouldn't you be more comfortable over here with us?" Taral asked.

"I'm fine where I am," Kanto said.

Erma patted the stool beside her. "Don't worry, sweetie. You're safe with me. Alas, so too with your lovely sister-wife. I say personal companions are much like driving transports: best when they confine themselves to a single lane."

"Don't you find that view limits your ability to find a situation outside your mother's household?"

"Plenty of such situations exist. Mumsy is quite aware of my interest in those with more mammaries than fewer."

Semele came over to the bar to grab a drink. "Mumsy's greater disappointment is their financial accounts don't have at least as many digits. Vash is the hope of our family in that regard."

"Her biggest disappointment is our association with those who protest her livelihood."

Deziree sat beside Kanto. She smiled then leaned in to kiss him.

"I'm married," he exclaimed, "and so is Star Mirror. Get your things. We're leaving."

Mirrei rolled her eyes. "You can leave if you wish. I'm enjoying myself for once."

Kanto walked towards the door but thought better of leaving Mirrei here with these reprobates. He stormed onto the balcony that overlooked the rest of the underground club. The club had not opened for the evening yet, but a few staffers were there to make last-minute preparations.

Vash joined him. "I'm sorry if what you saw in there made you uncomfortable."

"We should go. This is all very improper."

Vash moved closer to Kanto. "Winsome Bright Harmony, every aspect of your appearance designed to entice. Yet, in which direction? Do you seek to lure more to your house or to be lured away?"

Kanto attempted a coy remark, "As my anchor wishes, so shall it be."

"Tell me of them. Should you or Mirrei find a place here, they would seek to fill their household numbers?"

Vash laid his hand over Kanto's and leaned in. "Envision an alliance between us. A united front against any other suitors, perhaps, should it come to it, we might even force out an unwanted one."

An offer to usurp Shep and be co-anchors was sure to follow. How long before he would seek to be anchor himself? Or bring in another to force him out. Kanto considered the offer. How Jhee looked at Shep even now? Their relationship was better since the abbey, but nothing like the longing looks or easy touches she shared with Shep. How long, if ever, might it be before they shared that rapport? Sooner, if Shep were not there. Vash didn't want Jhee. He would be no threat.

Vash watched him with an open, expectant leer as if he knew the options Kanto weighed in his mind. Vash it seemed was more interested in a wifely benefactor rather than a wifely companion. The cold, mercenary nature of it rankled Kanto. He did not want to be a family with this man in any capacity. He did not want to expose Jhee to his fickleness or be a part of his treachery.

Kanto yanked his hand away and swept back into the main room. "Star Mirror, are you ready to go?"

What offended him more about Vash's behavior? The very act of it or its crude mockery of how Kanto often found himself obligated to behave.

Mirrei stomped over to Kanto. "Why are you being so impossible? I invited you along, so you could have some fun."

"Our definitions of fun differ."

"I thought being turned away from denbe's bed less often would make you less insufferable not more." Mirrei sighed and grabbed her coat. They hailed a water taxi outside. Kanto paced. "I thought you of all people would want to try new things."

"Not infidelity."

"I see, which is why you constantly try to nose in on days with denbe that aren't yours."

"What? I do not."

"I can't remember the last day she had with Shep or me where you weren't hovering trying to get her attention."

"As well I should, given how quickly you strayed."

"Run, tell denbe all about it then. It will provide you the perfect opportunity to spend more time with her. I realized how smitten you were with her despite your complaints. I thought with time I too would develop the same affection for her as you and Shep did."

"Revered Makers, look at your hair. It's like I don't even know you anymore."

Mirrei grabbed her bag from coat check, popped a clove candy, and waved a smudging stick over herself. "As if you ever knew me to begin with."

"You're shaming our denbe. We have an enviable situation with Jhee. Why are you trying to ruin it?"

"So, it's 'Jhee' now?"

"You could call her Jhee, too."

"It wouldn't feel right. I don't think we're there yet. Even you have to see what she's doing."

"Even me?"

"You know what I meant."

"Yes, I know precisely what you meant."

"I'm sorry."

"Jhee needs time. I don't think she really wants us to go. If she were serious about this, she'd hire a professional arranger."

"I don't want to sit around a mansion for the rest of my life embroidering. Being kept like two pond fish."

"Learning to sew was for me. I did it for the enjoyment, the craft, and the achievement; a matter of pride. While we weren't poor, it was the only way I might get to wear some of the latest fashions from inland. I like being the one taken care of for a change. I like that Jhee spoils us."

Mirrei scoffed. "Being told what to do. What to eat. How to dress."

"Not being the one who must decide what another eats, having to dress them."

"Being mothered all the time."

"Yes. Not having it always fall on you to take care of someone else. She's our denbe. We must respect her."

"I do. While I complain about denbe, she's always been kind and understanding. I just wish she wouldn't smother me so much."

"If she hovered half as much over me as she did over you, I'd be ecstatic."

Mirrei sighed and took Kanto's hand. "I told you about my mother. You know what she was like. In her way, denbe's just as bad."

"I don't like being left to my own devices so much. She's running around town with that investigator. You're off who knows where. I swear to the Makers I will put a tracker on you both if you don't check in more. I never thought I'd miss Shep's presence. Once, I thought it'd be great to be somewhere so lively. Now, I find it's the loneliest thing ever."

"Have you spoken to denbe about children?"

Kanto's hand went to his chastity tattoo. "The time never seems right. We're still getting to know each other. We're still getting used to the way everything changed since the abbey."

Mirrei degenerated into one of her signature coughing fits. At first, Kanto ignored her. He hesitated a moment. The deep gasping and wetness of phlegm which accompanied the coughing marked this one as authentic. He rushed over and put an arm around her. He was one of the few who could distinguish the two.

"You didn't fake your collapse, did you?"

"I'm fine."

"How long have you had this cough?"

"The protest action and the arrest proved more taxing than I expected. Don't tell her about any of this. Keep all this amongst us," Mirrei said. "Please."

Kanto grudgingly agreed.

13

A PRACTICED EYE

~

Ill Fitting

"The length of these robes. I'm not sure I like it. They feel too long," Jhee said.

"They wear their robes longer inland," Kanto replied. "Presumably, because it's drier."

"I don't imagine they do a lot of wading like back home."

"Yet, somehow you managed it. Also, please, don't give them away this time."

Jhee looked in the mirror at her gorgeous robes, and she looked at Mirrei's robe sitting on another chair unused.

"Don't worry," Jhee said, "she'll be here. I'll talk to her."

"Don't. Don't. Let her have her fun. You're right. I'm being selfish. She never got out much; she has a right to live it up a little. Like I always thought we would once we got to the city."

"I thought you wanted to attend the festivals and galas."

"I did. And I do. Just not alone. I wanted us to attend together as a family. Denbe, I know you were just flattering me at the observatory. I want to introduce you to new experiences, so you can appreciate them like I do. Think of our lessons, how you taught me about how to recognize the feel and movements of the different elements."

"Tell you what? Why don't I attend one of these with you?"

"Jhee, you'd hate it. It's gossip and schmoozing. You barely made it through the fundraiser."

"Maybe I'm not looking at it properly. I like to people watch and figure out the relationships between people. So, I'll go to people watch."

"Thank you, Jhee."

Kanto started pinning the robes. Jhee thought through the case out loud. "We've got one murdered fiancé. Possibly having an affair and who is caught or at least suspected by one dead event organizer. The inquester thinks it's possible it was a case of mistaken identity. The Gray Galleon project was very controversial, and there is also evidence Ms. Oriel was misusing Findari, the Failed Prototypes, antiquities. Maybe someone killed her and strung her up to find out which unauthorized people she let see them."

"It sounds plausible. Struck over the head in the dark. They have similar body types."

"That is my assessment as well. Make the pockets higher. Conchs are getting bigger and heavier. They pull down and hang too low."

"I'm proud of you, Jhee. Old you would have simply dealt with it. Also, we must fix it, so it doesn't distort the lines and designs of the robes. I can't have you looking like some marine rustic. I would never live down the shame. My denbe will be the most stylish well-appointed official at court, or else the Trench will have more residents. I'll put my mind to the length dilemma later. What is it you say Mr. Bastian did for a living?"

"An engineer. Though, more recently, he offered his services as an event walker until he met Ms. Oriel. He may have also found some work as a sire."

"Unsurprising."

"You knew."

"Suspected. Body language. His positioning regarding her. Always ready with an arm when she entered or exited a room."

"You positioned yourself similar to him. There's also your seahorse tattoo."

"If you want to know something, Jhee, ask."

"Would that be proper? Only if you wish to discuss it."

"Grandmamere always wanted me to have options. I had private instruction. It wouldn't do for me to be seen attending the training. I also needed to know who to look out for. Men who make the leap from remora to mister are not uncommon. I had my gentleman's surgery at a young age. Then I undertook limited engagements to have resources for my independence kit. I have friends there, which is how I found out about Shep's inquiries. He looked so out of his depth during his interviews. Being sired, I could already be counted upon to have an impeccable pedigree. To be honest, Grandmere or I could have told Shep anything, and he would have believed it. Mr. Bastian didn't show the markers of formal training. Strictly amateur."

"How do you know?"

"How do you know who trained an investigator? His lanced-out tattoo for one."

"The astronomer also called him a guard."

"Ah, that explains the shoes." Kanto sighed. "His footwear. A formally trained remora is an accessory counseled strongly on all aspects of appearance. His shoes were sensible and very worn. Unsuitable for a society event. An upper-class remora has no such considerations. If they have occasion to go anywhere which required shoes like that, an advance team has already cleared and made a proper place for them to walk. They may buy them or wear them to appear humble or relatable, but not enough to show signs of wear. Again, at least not without the deliberate efforts of servants."

"They have their servants make their clothes appear worn?"

"For 'authenticity' and 'character.' You can't merely look like some aristocrat who bought cheap or modest clothing to appear poor, you must look like you wear them."

"I'm glad I have you to explain these matters because that would never occur to me. Now tell me more about these pre-frayed shirts and garments."

"I preferred to do it myself. Collars with just the right amount of fraying. Creases in just the right place."

"Why does that not surprise me?"

"You were born to be a denbe, Jhee. You think you understand what it means being groomed as a dende because you pretend interest in our pastimes. It's obvious when a conversation or subject is of no interest to you. The trick of it, the art, is for your denbe to not know it. You must sell them on your interest. Any but the most self-absorbed denbes will suspect, but you must allow them enough doubt to assuage their guilt. True denbes are deferred to. They take a certain amount of agreement for granted."

"I'm sorry."

"No need to apologize. Our accommodation must go both ways. I accept it's your nature. It's who you are. Certain details will always be beneath your notice. This is because of Mirrei, isn't it? Despite our agreement, you still may want to get rid of me. Is that why you insist I hang out with those awful Delphines? Vash is the worst. He tried to kiss me."

Jhee flinched and got stuck again.

Kanto looked aghast. "I hadn't meant to blurt that out."

"My apologies. I didn't know."

"No reason you should. I suppose he could write it off as trying to get my approval. You do not understand half of the tricks denmes try when approving minor spouses."

"I don't suppose I do."

"Some can be quite bold. More than one grabbed my rear. They try to take other liberties, too. One husband thought his approval warranted dropping his robes right in the middle of grandmamere's receiving room."

Jhee thought about minor spouses and some of the behavior they got up to. She knew it was a common tactic of minor spouses to ingratiate themselves with spouses other than those they married to secure their position.

"What Mr. Bastian did had an honest integrity to it. On the other hand, Vash, with his clean looks and good breeding, will leech off some prominent spouse until they tire of him. He's a chum."

"A chum?"

"They call everyone 'chum' or 'kin' and are drawn to status or riches like sharks. Isn't that what you thought of me, of us? What's worse, Mirrei's started acting like a chum too. Stop trying to sell us off."

"I'll quit pressuring you to mingle with them."

"So, you and the inquester are like whales in a pod?"

"Not quite. I empathize with her plight, being tugged in so many directions. She has a tough job, but she is a more than competent investigator."

"If you say so. Just so you know, I'll outfit her as expertly as I outfit you."

Jhee glanced down. Kanto raised an eyebrow.

~

A New Tack

The inquester and Jhee broke out the case files in the former's office. While they reviewed their findings, the inquester's conch clacked. She answered.

Inquester Paij put away her conch. "Nothing mysterious about this cause of death, Justicar. Good old-fashioned projectiles to the chest. Not mind bullets. Tangible objects fired from a traditional firearm."

"Interesting you say mind bullets. Some elementalists have been able to enhance the speed and accuracy of gunshots."

"Must you scuttle all my theories? Am I allowed no comforting certainties?"

"May I review the findings?"

"Knock yourself out, mayor's friend who must be allowed complete access to my files."

"You need to come up with new material."

"No can do. My humor is all middle- and low-class. Since we can't afford to keep buying new jokes, we reuse ours until they wear out."

"The rest of us suffer in the meantime."

"Speak for yourself, Justicar. I'm a laugh riot. Okay, what are we looking at here?"

"One possibly jealous event organizer and a fiancé possibly having an affair. We've got a bunch of Findari artifacts. And some choppy record keeping."

"Certainly adds up to motive. What about means? The last anyone saw of Oriel that night was shortly before she left you to go prepare for the auction. Enough time to sneak up to the mezzanine and confront Bastian. They struggle and argue. She stabs him."

"Then drags his body up to the chandelier with no one seeing her. Even with the crane that seems a hard ask."

"True." The inquester made a shooting gesture. "Blasts them over there with air drawing. No need for the crane. Oriel may have known how to cypher. Though, to hang them from the chandelier and make that tableau. How much arcane strength and hard work does that take?"

"A minor wind charm can give one strength enough to lift the body. A skilled drawer could even draw the body up there. Air makes it more likely to be a woman. Did the ASU find any evidence of cyphering or drawing?"

"Everywhere. The whole area tested positive for arcana."

"Yes, the restoration projects would lead to confusing positives. They would need earth drawers to maintain the integrity of the vessel and the chandelier crystals." Jhee touched her chin and mulled it over. "Maybe it was one massive blast that propelled them from the balcony to the chandelier. Not of air, but of earth. It would explain the crystal dust. They needed to form the lance out of something. The noise downstairs would cover any sound. An earth drawer that powerful lends itself to a male drawer. Arcana is distinguished by the sexes."

"But with men being forbidden from cyphering and drawing, it's my understanding that women also had to learn earth and water if only as their tertiaries."

"True. Water and earth are not my strongest elements, but I have some skill with them. I might conjure something up even with my limited skills."

"So far our suspects-other-than-Oriel list has been narrowed down to nearly anyone."

"We need to go back to first principles then: means, motive, opportunity. I might want to cross-check the personal records just to be sure. One matter is for certain though. If they used air, the killer is unlikely to be male. Even with the loosening restrictions on cyphering, the highest demand for male artificers is water and earth. There remain serious superstitions about men being taught to draw air or fire. Heavy restrictions remain on those. And some forms of cyphering are likewise off-limits."

"So, empty nets again. What other woman then would have a motive to kill Bastian?"

"Ms. Levinia. I'd know that longing look anywhere. Perhaps this other woman whoever she is?"

"You don't think she is the other woman?"

"Perhaps. The 'longing' aspect suggests something one-sided."

"Are we so sure it's a woman? All we know is Oriel suspected Bastian of being unfaithful. There's nothing that says who she suspected it was with."

"Inquester, remember when I told you, I saw a criminal element hanging around the clinic. Perhaps that is it. Mr. Bastian could have been killed as a warning to Vash and Ms. Oriel. She still did not get the message, and the criminal element kills her."

"I could see that."

"Did the forensic accounting come back on Ms. Oriel?"

"Yes. It seems the only things of the event organizer's that was not a complete mess was the charity finances. She was conscientious about that at least. The clinic on the other hand. That's a different story."

"May I see the records?"

"Please do."

"Here. What's this?" Jhee held up an out-of-place invoice for a medical supply distributer. "There was a suspicious character hanging around the clinic the day Mirrei and I went to visit. I overheard them arguing. They may have been shaking the clinic down for medicine or supplies."

"That tracks. What if Oriel began to refuse? First, they kill her fiancé then Oriel?"

Jhee put her hand over her mouth. "I had a more horrible thought. What if the lesson wasn't for Ms. Oriel? What if it was for Vash? I think we need to speak to him again."

"I'm thinking you are right."

The inquester keyed her conch. Jhee folded her hands inside her robes. She did not even know how she would explain this to Mirrei. She was so fond of Vash. Would Mirrei think the accusations malicious or made of jealousy? Would she believe Jhee is acting out like Kanto? She could not think about that right now. They had a suspect to question.

Jhee browsed through the case files a few more times trying to find out what it was she was missing. It all looked cut and dried. The evidence pointed to one suspect and then another. If Ms. Oriel had not turned up dead, she would have still been their prime suspect.

"Only one of the clinic trio is left to shine sunlight on the matter," the inquester said.

Jhee nodded. "Vash."

~

The Ink

After Vash and his advocate arrived, Inquester Paij escorted them to the interview suites.

Inquester Paij sat across from them and rested her elbows on the table. "You're comfortable, aren't you? You don't need a drink or anything?"

Jhee watched the interrogation from the other side of one-way glass. She did not want her presence to be a distraction. She wanted this to be legitimate and by the guides. An outburst from her would not be the act to scuttle the case. A keen advocate might even argue she unduly influenced Vash.

"Inquester, to what do I owe the pleasure?" Vash asked.

"Oriel has been murdered."

Vash played with his signet ring. "My word. How did it happen?"

"we found her pinned to a cavern wall near the templarite mines. The cause of death is still indeterminate."

"What can we do for you, investigator?" Vash's advocate asked.

"We just wanted to give your client a chance to mention something now which if he relies on it later might harm his defense."

"I don't know what you are talking about, Inquester," Vash said.

His advocate put a hand on his arm. "Inquester, precisely what are you hinting at?"

"It has come to our attention that certain unsavory types have been hanging around your clinic. I'm saying this is your client's opportunity to come clean about anything which may concern him about the goings-on there. Perhaps someone who comes around frequently making demands."

Vash leaned over and whispered in his advocate's ear.

The advocate turned to the inquester. "My client has something he needs to tell you."

"It was an inherited problem. Almost from the moment we opened the clinic, they started hanging around. Equipment started to go missing. We had several break-ins. It continued that way until someone showed up in person. She made it clear many of the problems were her doing. She could stop them in exchange for a favor or two now and then. Maybe some medication. Perhaps treat a few of her personnel. We agreed."

The inquester sat back in her chair. "Then what happened?"

"With all the influx of new patients and then our funding went south, we weren't getting as many resources as before, and we had to make them last more. She came back and said she could put us in contact with another supplier who could give us supplies for a discount. We had no other choice, don't you see? Then that's when we noticed why the drugs and supplies were so cheap. They watered them down. The supplier had cut the medications with something and was selling the excess to others, double billing for the same amount of supply. We wanted to stop. We begged to go back to our old supplier, but by then we were in too deep."

The advocate touched Vash's arm. "Inquester, my client is a victim in all this."

"Did Oriel know?" the inquester asked.

Vash nodded. "Though, it didn't sit right with her. Eventually, we stopped paying. She had even written up a new contract with our old supplier. Even though we weren't paying anymore, all the intimidation had stopped dead calm. I assumed she had made some other arrangements with them until... We hadn't made our order for weeks when 'our friend' showed up to ask why. She and Oriel had it out. She threatened Oriel."

"Why didn't you come forward before now?"

"When Bastian was killed, I didn't make the connection. Afterward, she paid us a visit at the clinic again. But now that you've found Oriel's body, I put it together. I waited because I'm afraid for myself and my family and my friends." Vash glanced at the one-way glass. "Justicar, are you back there? I just wanted to protect Star. She threatened our families."

Jhee folded her arms. She did not look forward to telling Mirrei about this, not one bit.

"We'll check your story out. You are free to go for now. Don't go far. We may have follow-up questions for you."

Vash hunched. "Where would I go? This is all I know."

He and his advocate stood and left. The inquester joined Jhee in the observation room.

"So, do you believe him?"

"It tracks with what I saw. One of his patients complained that their medicine was not working effectively."

Vash and his advocate stumbled back into the interrogation room. Sianna and Inksy close behind them.

"What is that?" the advocate asked.

Inksy answered. "An imperial writ which allows us to hold you as long as we want until the imperial guard comes to take you into custody."

Vash's advocate leaned back, "My client has been nothing but cooperative. This is outrageous—"

Sianna cut him off, "Then you won't mind taking the time to cooperate with us. You're dismissed, Inquester. And please clear the observation room on your way out."

"Well, we've done all the interrogations they will let us do today."

Jhee and the inquester headed to Paij's desk. "There's rude, and then there is those two."

"You've never been privy to the delight that is working with the Squids."

"Not since my days working as a Military Police Magistrate." Jhee thought for a moment. "Since Vash and the Inkertons are tied up for the time being, we could go check on Ms. Oriel's files at the clinic."

"You're such a bad influence on me."

"Like knows like."

~

The Makerly Steward

At the health clinic, Jhee and the inquester accessed the clinic's terminal via her sensor suit's link.

"I hope you meant what you said about the writ," Inquester Paij said.

"Why?"

"I copied the signet from the Ink's writ to gain records' access. Here, can you make sense of these?"

"Salinity tables. Wind dispersal patterns. Charts of the currents and waterways. Maps of the Fresh and Miners' Lung outbreaks."

"Makes sense, tracking the outbreak of a health crisis. Do you think they were looking for a patient zero?"

"It is a possibility."

"Let's have another gander at those lockers."

While they made another pass on Ms. Oriel's and Mr. Bastian's lockers, a steward grunted and pushed a squealing cart into the employee locker room.

"Oi, what you doing here?"

The inquester tapped her lapel insignia. "Galleon City Imperators. We're investigating—"

"All the dead folk. You won't find nothing there. That volunteer, at least, kept his things elsewhere. What you need to be investigating is who stole my uniform?"

"Someone stole your uniform?" Jhee asked.

"That's what I said, didn't I? At least, the other supplies that went missing made sense. Squishies could sell those."

"So, you had a lot of break-ins and thefts?"

"Not as much anymore. Shame about the passionfish though. They was a cute couple. Just when this ship had righted itself again."

"I heard they were a dedicated pair," the inquester said.

The steward shrugged. "Ain't Makerly to gossip, mind, and that volunteer and the money lady worked hard to keep this place going. But something odd about them."

"Odd, how?"

The steward motioned them closer. Jhee and the inquester leaned in.

The steward continued in hushed tones, "Times the man acted more the doctor than the doctors. Other times he acted more a squishy than the squishies, if you know what I mean. I also wondered if maybe he was the squishy behind the thefts, what with all the places I found him where he ought not be. But I ain't one to gossip."

Jhee nodded. "Of course."

"I caught him at the incinerators once, hiding stuff in the medical waste."

Jhee cast her eyes from side to side. "Do you know why?"

The steward smiled. "No, but I think I know where he kept his things. I told his fiancée, the money lady. I don't know if she claimed them or not."

"Would you show us?" the inquester asked.

The steward lead them to a locker hidden in the storage room. Jhee said, "Thank you. We'll let you get back to work."

"Let me know if you find my uniform in there."

Inquester Paij proved to be a deft hand at picking the mechanical lock. In the hidden locker, they found various reagents and cannisters of powders, including a cache of templarite dust. They also found a log with dates, patient names, with what looked like various templarite dilutions, and results. Among the entries, they discovered the mining supervisor.

They gathered the new evidence and went back to the inquester's office. A cross-check of the patients' names with public records produced a disturbing result: most had died. The cause of death most frequently listed was Miners' Lung Disease. In addition, Mr. Bastian's results bore notations about mouth sensations and detectability. His secret workshop had contained treatises on toxins and catering. He had experimented with ways to hide the taste of templarite. A liquid solution with high alcohol content proved least noticeable.

"The bad squelch," Jhee said aloud.

"What's that?" the inquester asked.

"Have you had large incidents of food poisonings?"

"We've been having problems with a bad batch of squelch going around. We've had trouble tracking down the makers."

"I think I know why."

Jhee slid Mr. Bastian's notes toward the inquester who read over them quickly then captured them with her sleeve recorder.

"Why would Bastian or Oriel poison miners? To drum up business for the clinic?"

"To slow down work at the mines?"

"If they were in on the sabotage together, then they may have planned something for the event." Inquester Paij plopped the arrests records for that night on her desk. "That is until the merry dusters pulled their stunt."

"To the contrary," Jhee said, "it would have made them perfect pseudopods."

"Then why didn't they go through with it?"

"Maybe they argued, and Mr. Bastian wound up dead. The event organizer did not strike me as particularly tech-savvy. She might not have been able to pull it off without Mr. Bastian's expertise."

"Then she goes looking for someone to replace him and gets a bullet for her trouble."

~

Tailor's Maxim

Jhee dwelt on how narrowly her household avoided both Mr. Bastian's schemes. Then her thoughts flowed into what Kanto had said about the inquester during their last fitting. She laid a finger aside her nose. A pin stuck her in the side. She flinched.

"Tailor's maxim," Kanto said in a scolding tone.

"You know I have no designs on getting another spouse."

"What if Mirrei's stay with the Delphines goes as well as you hope? She will be happy. She will have found her bit of belonging. But what about you? I know you need a form of intellectual stimulation you won't get from Shep or me."

Jhee stilled Kanto's hands from his pinning. "No. I will just focus my attention the two of you if Mirrei leaves. I won't just run out and try to acquire another. That is not me."

"If it's so easy for you to get rid of her, would it be so easy for you to get rid of me?"

"You're not going anywhere unless you want to. I've said it before, I'll repeat it. I'll say it a thousand times until you believe me."

Jhee put a finger under Kanto's chin and raised his face. He pressed his muzzle against hers.

"Jhee," he said. "You and this family mean so much to me. I want nothing to happen to our family. You three are my world. You, Mirrei, and Shep are my household, and I want no others. She is irreplaceable as are you."

"I understand. You must leave off Mirrei and the Delphines. You must let her make her own decision on this, agreed?"

"All right, denbe."

Kanto and Jhee embraced, and he clung to her. "It means a lot you try. I don't know if I say that often enough."

"Will it always be enough?" Jhee asked.

"What do you mean?"

"Will it ever wear on you I must try or be forced? Will it bother you to have a spouse not as enamored of a pursuit as you are? Who can't find the same joy in an activity you do?"

"Does it bother you? Why are you asking this? Are you still wondering if I want to be elsewhere? If I did, I wouldn't choose the Delphines. You're better appointed than Lady Delphine. Your holdings are worth three times hers, and her family's influence has faded. There's little for you to gain via spousal price. I don't know why you considered the match in the first place."

"You truly were humoring me all those first moons."

Kanto winked. "You enjoyed teaching me, so I let you."

"Fine, Maker Foz, then you have to help me with ledgers."

Jhee hopped from the dais. She whipped off the fabric and handed it to Kanto. He should learn this. She needed to adjust to the idea Mirrei might not be there to help her with the accounts. She had always figured Kanto would be the first one to leave.

"Most expensive vacation ever. Look at this charge here. Thousands for bail. The whole jail, Kanto?"

"I wanted you freed. They were being obstinate. Apparently, you and Mirrei roiled their oceans. I'd call those her charges or yours."

"You made a good case. Settled." Jhee produced a list she had compiled of every judicial caseworker she knew. "However, you need to help me make calls to these folks. Ensuring most of those bailed out return for their judgment dates is our only means to recoup some of the expense."

After they called a quarter of the list, Jhee and Kanto returned to the accounts.

"Ms. Oriel wasted no time cashing my donations." Jhee grimaced. "Whelm and waves, these charges for spa treatments cost how much?"

Jhee examined the charges closer. These weren't household charges. The

Fresh Lung Clinic's records had somehow gotten mixed in with hers. "If three thousand shell is what the clinic charges for services, they should never want for funds."

"May I see that, Jhee? Spa treatments are my area of expertise."

"I defer to the master."

Kanto chewed on his lip. "These charges make little sense. For instance, see here this charge for three thousand shell for a massage. An all-day session with Mr. Andre one of the best in the known worlds, booked moons in advance, referral only, costs fifteen hundred. And look how often these charges are. Anyone this high in the demand doesn't have time to meet with anyone except his regulars or most valued patrons this often."

"Maybe Vash is one of his most valued patrons because he's paying him three thousand shell."

"Fine. The price I mentioned is for a full day. Now look here at Vash's clinic appointment schedule. A spa visit and then he's seeing patients less than an hour afterward. Paying this amount for less than a full day is preposterous. He only uses it for a half-hour at most. What would be the point? Here, compare the charity, clinic, and the Delphines' finances."

Kanto confronted her with a conch displaying financial transactions.

"Kanto. How did you get access to these?"

"While I tidied up for our fitting, I noticed them amongst the documents you left about."

Jhee shook her head. She had to take better care with evidence now that it was no longer her and Shep.

"No. Please, hear me out. The additional clinic records, I asked your charitable trust director to request. The Delphines have some huge liabilities. There is no way they could have afforded such a huge donation. I went looking, and I found a series of suspicious donations to the charities account and mysterious deposits to Vash's clinic in matching amounts. Vash may be embezzling from the clinic. I thought Vash was just a cad. What if he's a killer?"

"Even should all this prove to be true, we may have compromised the means to prevent him from doing more harm. I can't go to Inquester Paij with this."

"Can't you handle this yourself?"

"This is not my jurisdiction."

"Can't you handle it some other way? Mirrei may be in danger. Why won't you protect her like you protected me?"

"I hope you are not implying what I think you are. Your disrespect for the law shows disrespect for me. And this obsession with undermining the Delphines shows a disrespect for Mirrei."

"Like the respect you had for the law at the abbey that nearly got me killed or the means with which you dealt with the culprit? Like the way you treat Mirrei as some wilting weed. If only you knew."

"Knew what?"

"Nothing, Jhee. Nothing. Handle it as you see fit. I pray Mirrei does not pay the price for your self-righteousness."

"Enough, Kanto. I think we need to draw tonight to a conclusion. You should return to your room."

"But—"

"Fine. Stay if you wish. I'm going for a walk, and I don't intend to return until you're asleep."

"Please, Jhee, just look."

Always a step back for every step forward with him. Jhee took the records from Kanto. She furrowed her brow. These were indeed worrying. Weird liabilities. Weird assets. Deposits. All highly confidential. If he had poked into Imperially protected records, though.... She backtracked the document custody chain to compile her account of the mishandled evidence. On closer examination, these weren't records she obtained working with Inquester Paij. Of course. Her requests for authorization before she donated. They did not need an Imperial Writ. Ms. Oriel had handed their records over.

Jhee hopped to her feet.

Kanto who had hovered over her shoulder jerked back in surprise. "Ow! What? I think I stabbed myself in my chastity mark with the pen. Not quite a Tailor's Maxim, but close enough."

"'You move. You bleed,'" Jhee repeated. "Not a bloodsucker. That's it, Kanto. That's it!"

Jhee reached for her conch.

"Jhee, where are you going?"

"I've got to go see an expert about a tattoo."

"You're getting another tattoo?"

She pressed her esca to Kanto's.

"What was that for?"

"Being you. Also, send my charitable trust director, no everyone at the trust, a nice gift. My financial adviser too."

14

STINGRAY

~

The Stingray

A place the size of Galleon City likely hosted a branch of the Manray Society gentlewoman's club with its attendant Whisper Room. Jhee met the inquester for brunch outside of one such place, the Stingray Club. The inquester fidgeted and looked uncomfortable. "Members only. They don't give my kind membership."

"You're my guest. Where I go, you can go."

Jhee and the inquester walked inside. The concierge greeted her with a smile. She turned a large bio-film ledger her way. "Sign in please."

"Thank you. I've brought a guest for brunch."

"Very well. Sign in, Miss. Would you like me to go over the Stingray Club rules?"

"Would you."

"All visitors are expected to adhere to the decorum standards as befits a gentlewoman. Male visitors and young children are only permitted during special events or through prior arrangement. Full conch use is only allowed in the dining hall. Only in quiet mode. Absolutely no imaging anywhere on the premises. Beyond the dining hall, device disablers are employed, and only basic communication services will be available. In the event of an emergency, additional services will be allowed, but only at the discretion of management."

They took a small table in the solar overlooking a small cove. Jhee was distracted and unable to eat her steak and sea quail eggs and whale milk with a light bit of watercress and cured maye sausage. The inquester, however, had a big healthy appetite.

The inquester gestured at Jhee's plate with her fork. "You going to eat that? Mind if I?"

"Go right ahead, Inquester."

"Thanks." The inquester speared the food from Jhee's plate. "A separate person has to have killed Oriel."

"What would be the motive?"

"Revenge for the Bastian killing. There're also all those barbarians around. One of them might have gotten it in their head to take revenge for the Gray Galleon."

"Fire Folk."

The inquester raised an eyebrow. "Yeah, Fire Folk. It's one thing to know such a practice existed in abstract. It's another to see it up close and personal like that."

"That sounds plausible."

"What's your theory?"

"I'm still trying to work that out. I think the same person killed both. We just have to figure out the hidden reason."

"Other than their being engaged. You are like a tyro, a newling. There always has to be a greater mystery than the obvious. Start simple. Go cautious."

"First principles my mentor used to say. I like for details to add up."

"A holdover from your arcane training no doubt. People and the real world are messy. Spells and potions aren't."

"Spoken like someone who has never dealt with many equations. Some simple cyphers made me long for third-year chemistry."

The inquester grimaced. "That bad?"

"Worse."

The inquester sopped up the last bit of egg yolk with a roll. "Grain bread. If I get to eat like this, you can have access to my case files anytime."

Jhee raised an eyebrow.

"Just a joke. You don't think much of me do you, Justicar?"

"I'm sorry if I gave you that impression."

The inquester waved off her response. "You are much more polite about it than most. You are one of those proper types who believes discourtesy is the greatest sin you can commit. Although you do and think many discourteous things. Fire Folk you call them now, but you think of them as barbarians. And you and me, we can pal around and go gull over investigation techniques, but at the end of the day you are grandly named, and I'm plainly named. Part of you believes in your inherent advantage to me or else you'd renounce your titles and land."

"I believe in the comfort and protection title and lands can provide."

"Fair enough. In a district where people live far away from each other, and there is not a lot of oversight, you can make logical leaps you can't back up. In a district like this where everyone's brushing fins and living gill to gill all the time, and I've got fifty bosses, simple and cautious is the best way to proceed. Everyone thinks they are my boss. Everyone second guesses my conclusions. I'm not empowered to render judgment as you are, and I have to walk many people through my evidence chain and my thought process."

"Every isle."

"Come again?"

"Are you familiar with the Fair-Weather statutes, Inquester?"

"Yeah, folk law."

"It's a fancy way of saying every isle has its own rules. Usually determined by its ruling family."

"You're not in the boonies anymore, Justicar, where you have sole authority. We have a centralized legal process here. I don't just have to convince myself. I have to bring my evidence to a tribunal and a bench of justices." Inquester Paij took a sip of kolal. "Under your tenure, I noticed an uptick in the number of bodies lost at sea in your home district, even before the wall."

"The corrupt are cunning. Poison was the preferred method of murder in the Far Reaches. With corrupt Justicars and personal security forces, they often labeled deaths without obvious signs of trauma or which took place in private spaces natural or accidental. A central authority with which to report deaths did not exist. Coroners, medical examiners, and appointed magistrars could often be convinced to look the other way. With help from the previous governess, I had implemented mandatory autopsies on all deaths."

"Unintended consequences."

"Just so. If those were the crimes I'd be forced to investigate, perhaps it's just as well they summoned me to serve at the capital. The Reach families need to get used to not being the final authority on everything. I need to get used to it, too. Even justicars will go away soon as law enforcement and arbitration are standardized under the Central Authority. I didn't mean to overstep. I'll do better."

Jhee looked around at those staffing the Stingray Club. They did not have the Inkerton Event Services logo, but that of another company Jhee knew was similar. She could not help but think of what had got them here. What indignities had they suffered to be allowed to interact with the rich? She bet it was sold as some manner of honor. Some staff were the sons or daughters of minor houses getting in a little extra work or networking in before they could get memberships themselves. If one could not be a member, the next best thing was to work here.

The inquester looked at Jhee and noted where her eyes went. "You are finally starting to get it. I think there is hope for you yet, Justicar. Perhaps I am being a little harsh. Therein lies the rub. Fire Folk. It doesn't quite roll off your tongue yet, does it? Many still call them Stipples or Dapples, not in polite company so much anymore. This is what I have to deal with. I have to deal with them as they are. Are they abused and exploited? Yes. But you also have to deal with what that does to them as a population. Bleakness, hopelessness. Many are trapped between two bad options: the police or the smugglers and gangs. Call them barbarians or call them Fire Folk but it won't change their lot in life. The only thing that can do that is action."

"Where do you stand on the Shield, Inquester?"

"I have no opinion on it really despite how it might seem. I understand the impetus for it entirely. But like so many things, it is a double-sworded fish. For every problem it seeks to stop, it creates another. One I have to address."

"Thank you for your candor."

"Thanks for introducing me to these sausages. Makers, I don't know what I did without them in my life. So, Justicar, what exactly are we doing here?"

"Waiting."

The inquester speared another sausage. She motioned at the waiter. "Orange juice. Thanks."

"Also, would you bring a selection of periodicals from the bear's den." Jhee picked more at her food. "Bastian's shoes. Kanto said his shoes did not match his professed occupation."

"That's an interesting theory."

"What if it's true?"

"We already know Bastian was leading some dual life. The question remains why?"

"Why indeed?"

The inquester's conch clacked. Other diners gave them dirty looks before she silenced it. "More results from the lab. It's confirmed, cause of death was slugs to the chest. You may find this interesting though. The slugs were magicked."

Jhee turned towards the inquester. "That is indeed interesting, Inquester. I'll want to examine them immediately if you'll permit it."

"Do I have much choice?"

"We all have choices."

"Ain't that the truth. However, they aren't always good ones, are they?"

"No, Inquester, I don't suppose they are."

"Might I ask you a question, Justicar?"

"Of course, Inquester."

"How did you become a Justicar?"

"The person who preceded me had to resign in disgrace. Oddly enough they meant my appointment to Justicar as a fluff assignment. It was meant to be relaxing to appease my family and berth me out of the way." And to keep her out of the trouble Jhee was liable to get in by coming to the Stingray.

Perhaps Paij's scenario where Ms. Oriel was the intended victim and Mr. Bastian's death mistaken identity bore reexamination. In which case, Jhee might do well to stop poking into his background. "Ms. Oriel and Bastian were of a similar height and build. A matched set we used to call them in my youth. Their offspring would be as well."

Inquester Paij shrugged. "Topic change accepted. Some like the same. Some like different."

"What about you, Inquester? Are you married?"

The inquester raised an eyebrow. "One mister, though he says I'm married to my job. I don't know how you manage it. I've had trouble enough maintaining one relationship over the years."

"It was just Shep and me for a long time. Now, we're just finding a way. They have reduced my duties. I will now be an official of the court at the capital. It will not require so much travel as my old duties did and I can dedicate more of my time to my household. Even now, a policing system like that here in the city will be rolled out in some fashion to all districts and regions. Especially given the amount of power a person in my position has the potential to wield. Which is part of what caught up my predecessor. He was like a textbook case of the numerous capricious and petty ways the holder of the office could wield their power. I expect the Justicar system to be abolished in not too many more years particularly with the population being concentrated more in large cities."

"I can see that. You said your family wanted to dry dock you?"

"There was a political matter that affected my ability to be assigned any rank in the capital. This was a compromise. Meant to place me somewhere, I would be mostly unobtrusive. My family needed something to do with me. I had some small skill with judging matters and getting to the truth of things. When I returned from the academy, I had done well in my civil service boards, and I had done my time in the service. I had developed something of a reputation though in my early years. I had a keen mind for sorting out the truth of disputes, except when it came to personal matters."

"Why does that not surprise me? So, you were observing and deciding things from when you were a wee little thing, huh?"

"Yes, indeed, Inquester. I wasn't supposed to inherit. I had several siblings older than I and more beloved. However, most of them were killed in warring and fighting. I was not smartest or bravest. I just paid more attention than most and made the logical connections others often had trouble making."

"Do you mind if we keep the questioning going?"

"For now."

"Is that how you learned arcana? Making the connections no one else would? You have such a traditional mind. It seems odd to me you would go for arcana."

"I learned most of my cyphering and drawing in the service."

"Oh, those classified missions I'm not allowed to read."

Jhee made her face impassive.

"Ah, gotcha. Did you learn as part of your normal service or as part of your super-secret spy training?"

Again, Jhee made no expression and did not change her body language.

"So intriguing. I almost learned. I mean I know a few crude cyphers. They require us to learn some things in the academy."

"I had learned some drawing and cyphering before my academy days. Most of it crude and of limited use, for farming and the like. One of the few reasons I have at least some expertise with water even if only as a tertiary focus."

"That seems par for the course. Myself, I'm fire. Such as it is. I can't do much more than snuff a candle flame."

"Sometimes that's all you need. A spark on a bit of kindling or underbrush and whoosh! Up everything goes."

"Like the city. You are correct, Justicar. I used to do parlor tricks with it, not much more. You got any more tips on how to use next to nonexistent drawing?"

"I'm full of them. A puff of air to clear something off or move something aside. Even as little as a breath. Then there is earth drawing. That one proves to be trickier. It is one of the more difficult of the elements to master. Any obstruction whatsoever can disrupt control. It also seems to be the most location dependent. Some people have trouble controlling soil from different regions. Sterile soil with few contaminants is the easiest to manipulate. Unlike fire and water though, carrying around a bucket of soil sticks out and draws attention to itself."

"I guess it's just as well the menfolk are best at it. With all the bulk of theirs to carry it with and crevices to hide dirt."

Jhee cracked a smile.

"Finally. I was beginning to worry, Justicar. I talk a good game, but I pride myself on my humor."

"In my later years, I've never been much of one for frivolities. I apologize. Your humor is quite amusing at times. It's just it might be much funnier if I weren't the brunt of it."

"Ah, okay, but you know I have to bust your pouch."

"Yes, as a test of what kind of person I am. Can I give as good as I get? Will I shrink away? Will I blow it out of proportion? I've often thought of doing a paper on hazing rituals."

"What a way to kill the mood."

Jhee laughed. "I got you."

The inquester wrinkled her snout. "That wasn't funny."

"Not even a little? Just a wee bit."

"Not funny."

"A scoche. An iota."

The inquester shook her head, but the corners of her mouth were upturned. "We're going have to go soon. Let's settle up and get back to the station."

Jhee stopped the inquester when she reached for her conch. "My treat, Inquester."

"I will be so spoiled once this is over. It's back to boiled squid and fruit chutney."

Jhee grimaced. "How ghastly."

The waiter returned with a selection of bio-film publications on a polished, silver tray. Jhee leafed through them until she saw one with a clipped corner. "This one. Thank you."

"Would the lady like to read it in the Whisper Room?"

"Yes. Thank you."

"Follow me if you would, ladies."

The waiter strode towards the far arch of the dining hall without regard to if they followed. Jhee left. The inquester downed the dregs of her juice and wolfed the last bit of sausage before she hurried after them. The waiter continued down a curved stair. Once the waiter reached an onyx black door, she paused for them to catch up. An attendant in white robes and black gloves stood as they approached. The waiter departed. Jhee and the inquester's conchs sounded to let them know they had lost signal. The attendant held out her hand for their conchs.

"Sustained silence is the rule of the Whisper Room," Jhee said.

Jhee set her conch to quiet and motioned for the inquester to do the same. She tucked the periodical under her arm. The attendant paused, looked her and the inquester over before she dropped her hand. She inclined her head and led them inside. She indicated two empty chairs by the fireplace.

A couch in the far corner was occupied and a settee by the window.

Jhee pretended to read the real estate brochure for a few moments before setting it down on the table beside her chair. A woman in a short robe and pants switched out the magazine for hers as she passed by without so much as a look. The inquester caught Jhee's gaze and leaned forward to ask if they should follow. Jhee lifted one finger from the armrest to indicate they needed to wait. She fanned through the pages of the replacement periodical. No inserts. The inquester gave her another glance.

The room attendant reappeared. Outside, Jhee saw movement from an alcove with a milky white glass door. Jhee made the slightest head motion towards the milky door. The attendant kept her focus elsewhere as Jhee and the inquester turned away from the stairs.

The woman in short robes sat on a bench toking on a cheap smoke root. "He's a ghost. Not surprising with all the people moving in from the Outreaches."

"Unofficially?" Jhee asked.

"He worked for MANTEL, all right, as a line engineer."

"Why would they wipe the records of a line engineer?"

The woman stubbed out her root in a caramel colored clay dish. "They wouldn't. I wanted to warn you in person, though. They pushed back. Your activities have not gone unnoticed. I'm bowing out. Good luck."

She left. Jhee walked to the dish and picked up the smoke root. She rolled it between her fingers. Too springy. Jhee tapped out a small rolled bit of bio-film. She slipped the roll in her pocket and lit up the root.

"MANTEL? Did she say MAN-flipping-TEL?"

"Keep your voice down. You've heard of them?"

"Of course I have, but not officially."

The inquester took the root from Jhee and puffed on it. They left out the smokers' entrance the opposite of the way the woman had gone. "My aunt used to talk about places like this. Tell me again you were some desk jockey in the war."

"Tell me more about your aunt."

"Story for another time."

"The same."

"The mister is going to kill me, for more reasons than one," the inquester said. She had one more delighted toke on the smoke root before her attention alighted on the pocket where Jhee had placed the roll. "Line engineer?"

Jhee stared at the Shield in the distance. If Mr. Bastian worked for MANTEL, the struck through sigil on his wrist was not a sucker or a spider as she originally thought. It must have been an octopus and that meant he had been part of the Octopus Inkworks research groups. "Lead engineer. I think there may be some catastrophic flaw with the Shield."

"Storm Child's rage," the inquester swore.

15

THE ACTIVIST

~

Mine Chase

Mirrei walked into the game room at Chuc's with Vash's arm loosely about her waist. Erma and Deziree sat at a table playing cards while Taral and Semele lazed about on a windowsill.

"I've brought your 'weirs' partner," Vash said.

Mirrei gave him a "thank you" muzz to the cheek.

"See you in a few hours. Try to stay out of trouble this time, chums."

As much as Mirrei liked his work at the clinic, Vash had quickly become a bore full of constant questions about denbe's holdings and homes. As soon as he found himself a proper wife, he intended to quit work at the clinic and devote himself full time to her. Talk of the clinic made him uncomfortable. Whenever she tried to talk about the clinic and the work he did for the community, he quickly changed the subject to her wealth or denbe's. He seemed particularly interested in denbe's.

How Vash spoke during Mirrei's first to the clinic proved most telling. Any interest Mirrei had in Vash soured the moment he sought to use the clinic as a bargaining stone in courtship and a sweetener to predispose her to his suit. "I, *for one, would not hesitate to leave it behind if the right situation presented itself or should my future wife insist.... Either way, it would hardly be my responsibility anymore. Let Oriel see to that. It's her job after all."*

"Did you hear about what happened?" Deziree said.

"What this time?" Mirrei asked.

"Another food riot down at the docks," Taral said.

"We need to plan another action," Semele said.

"We need to lie low. Mamere and babere threatened to enroll me in Arctic studies at the Imperial Academy," Deziree said.

"Mine threatened to put me out to sire," Taral said.

"So, we sit around on our anchors like a bunch of frightened brats, is that it?" Mirrei asked.

A sniff of disdain escaped Deziree. "We don't all have powerful and indulgent shell mommies like you do, Star."

Mirrei coughed. "She is not my mother and doesn't control me."

"I didn't mean anything by it, Star."

"I hear there's a sit-in at one of the wall's broadcast pylons," Semele said.

Taral nodded. "Yeah, we can go there."

Chappy picked up a glass and started polishing. "And do what?"

"I don't know. Amplify their voices."

Mirrei pursed her lips. Chappy smirked. "He's right. How about we do something else? We make a splash. We make a banner and hang it from the top of the substation?"

Chappy set down the glass and fixed her with an unwavering stare. "The last time someone did that your wifey got them arrested for murder."

"They were stupid. We'll be smart. Unless one of you is planning to murder someone, we should be fine. What do you propose?"

Chappy shrugged. "I'm just a lowly barman. You're the great activists."

After a few more minutes of debate and apathy, Mirrei took a water taxi to a substation protest check-in without them. It was just a game to them. They were dabblers who could walk away once the going got a little rough. But not her, she was truly committed. Next to the signage table, Mirrei found the first aid tent and volunteered to help. While she organized medical supplies, she watched signs parade by. "Stall the wall." "Death wall." "Tear down the wall." "Free the winds." "Freedom for the Fire Folk." "Solidarity now." "One waters."

Shortly after midday, the march leaders had them head out.

"Star!"

Erma, Semele, Deziree, and Taral waved at her, signs in hand. She smiled. They ran over and joined her.

"You were right. We need to do this."

"We're with you. All the way."

They marched from the park to the up-link substation's front gates. They added their voices to the crowd and did what they could. Mirrei had a coughing fit. She found a place off to the side where she used her saline monitor to check her salt levels. She took a couple saline lozenges.

"You don't look so good, Star."

"I'm fine. So, are we going to do this or what?"

They rejoined the protesters.

Mirrei looked out at the faces of the counter-protesters and curiosity seekers. So many folk just stood by watching. They could add their voices to hers. She still felt a little light-headed.

A member of the onlookers caught her attention. Why had her mind singled him out? His stance. Shep's primer on body language and violence. His posture was rigid and his face impassive. No hate. No curiosity. Unlike those around him. What else? Denbe's lectures on how to observe bubbled to the surface. His clothes were all wrong for the setting. Oversized and too warm for this weather. The rain had stopped. His arm was held oddly stiff at his side. What was that in his hand?

Mirrei dropped her sign. She ran forward. One constable stopped her.

"That's as far as you go, Miss."

"Imperator, please. Get everyone out of here."

"So, now you are concerned about protests?"

"No. That person." Mirrei scanned the crowd. She found the person again. She pointed at him. He noticed her and began to flee. "Stop him."

"He has as much right to be here as you. Unlike you, he's minding his own business."

"You don't understand. I think he's here to do violence."

"Sure. Sure. I recognize you. Didn't we arrest you and your friends last long-tide?"

"Yeah, then you should know who I am. My wife is a Justicar. She's friends with the mayor and Inquester Paij. She'll vouch for me, but please we detain that person."

"Fine, I will call her. To come down here and get you before you get yourself arrested again."

Shouting interrupted the imperator. A fight had broken out between a group of Water and Fire Folk in mining gear and another in makeshift armor with their faces covered by scarves. The imperators moved to separate the folks striking each other. Their interference became a conflagration amongst the original combatants, giving them a common target. And like a fire, the fighting spread.

A surge of protesters rushed the gate. Armored amateur militia tried to hold them back. The constable rushed to intervene. Mirrei dove through the crowd to find her friends.

"Hey, come back here."

The constable swore as they dodged a bottle. Mirrei located her compatriots. Via looks and gestures, they coordinated to pull the injured from the melee. Within minutes they had formed a small, sheltered area for the wounded.

She caught sight of the man from earlier taking advantage of the fracas to slip inside the substation. She took off after him.

"Star, where are you going?" Deziree yelled.

Mirrei slipped past the chaos into the substation, applying the secret lessons on shadowing from Bax. The man had reached the central power room. He laid out a parchment and attached a data shell to the console. He pressed buttons attempting some procedure on the controls. Mirrei spotted an alarm on the wall and hit it.

The would-be saboteur spotted her. He snatched the parchment and data shell then bolted. Quickly he ducked through a bank of power regulators, disappearing.

Mirrei squeezed through after him. She found herself in access tunnels. She listened then chased the suspect as he ran. Her head was positively swimming by now. The tunnels gave way to unfinished rock. She doubled over to catch her breath. Her breathing resonated throughout the cavern and filled her ears. So many crisscrossing catwalks. She held her breath while she listened closer. Only distortions from drips and the struggle outside reached her.

Each step became an agony. Each breath became a chore. Her extreme vulnerability and isolation hit her then. Old mine tracks led off into unlit, unused passages. The tunnel walls changed from the smoother walls of the heavily used tourist section to rougher hewn surfaces made with pickaxes.

They were no longer in the substation, but a mine. How far down had she gone? If something happened to her, would anyone be able to find her, or would she just wind up another lost soul the likes of Kanto told stories about as cautionary tales?

Mirrei turned to leave. She spotted the suspect at the other end of the catwalk. He hid his face. Yet, Mirrei wanted a clear description for denbe. She struggled forward, and the figure backed away. She stumbled forward arm outstretched. If only she could just get a look. Spots swam before Mirrei's eyes.

Star, the name she used with the activists, echoed from shadows. Was she imagining them calling for her?

Mirrei blinked her eyes. One moment, she leaned against the shaft wall, hoping the light-headedness would pass. The next moment she had slid to the floor. A fuzzy blob loomed over her then ran off. Her wheezing filled the shaft. She could not get more than a sip of air at a time. She was still wheezing when rescuers found her. Her eyes fluttered closed.

The Hospitalization

"Justicar, it's Mirrei," Inquester Paij said.

Jhee rolled her eyes. "She got herself arrested again so soon?"

"Mirrei's been taken to the hospital. She and her 'weirs' club are in the hospital. There was some kind of incident at the substation. She and her friends were injured. We're still trying to figure out the details. They found them passed out in the back room at Chuc's; a known hangout for the more violent radicals."

The inquester's tone was somber her words carefully chosen.

"Thank you very much, Inquester," Jhee whispered.

"Justicar—"

Jhee disconnected. The conch slipped from her loose grasp. She sat down with a long exhale. She had to go see her. Jhee had disconnected from the inquester before she learned to which hospital they had taken Mirrei. What had the inquester said? They found them at the dive bar. That area was poor and underserved. Lifesavers would have taken them to the clinic if they were poorer. With their families means and influence, however, they would get private expedited transport to a top medical center. The nearest to that area was Makers' Care. Another center might better serve more specialized trauma. Jhee stilled her shaking hands. It would be Makers' Care; no other choice fit the givens.

Her conch sounded as if on cue. Sure enough, it was Makers' Care. The doctor she spoke to was very matter of fact that Mirrei's family should come at once. She called for a water taxi. She tucked her hands in her robes and went to Kanto's room to inform him what had happened. He smiled upon seeing her at first. His eyes narrowed, and he began to frown.

"Mirrei has been hospitalized." Kanto flinched. "A water taxi will be here soon. Come to think of it we should pack a day bag for her and us. Would you mind gathering anything of hers you think she might want or need?"

He studied her. His frown deepened. "Jhee, sit."

"I can't. I need to see to a few matters before we depart. Among them, inform Shep. He would want to know."

"No. Sit."

Jhee sat as he instructed. He touched his esca to hers. He gripped one of her hands tightly. "I'll contact Shep and pack us a day bag. You sit here until the water taxi comes."

Jhee closed her eyes and sighed. She felt almost as if in a dream while they rode to the hospital. She only felt awake again once the physician explained the extent of Mirrei's condition.

"This is probably one of the most aggressive cases of Fresh Lung Syndrome I've ever seen. You said someone examined her a few days ago?" Dr. Pike said.

Kanto gasped.

Jhee put an arm around him. "She had a fainting spell. The house physician at the villa, Vash, examined her and said it was nothing to worry about. That she had just overextended herself. We increased her saline regimen, monitored her, and everything seemed fine. I thought she was getting better. It was her first relapse in some time. The journey here she had been feeling poorly. However, once we arrived, she seemed to perk right up. Mirrei was getting her color back. She was very active in sports and humanitarian work. She really seemed to come alive here," Jhee's voice trailed off.

"Well, this condition has proved unpredictable. Not to mention the spontaneous occurrence in her friends. All from the main isles, you said?"

"Vash, Erma, and Semele are, yes. They're from right here on the cape. The others I don't know."

Mirrei's Confession

"I'd asked the First Makers for you not to get yourself arrested again," Jhee said. She took Mirrei's hand.

"What a way for them to implement your design."

"Precisely my thoughts. You keep reaping a harvest for seeds of misery you've never sown."

"By that, you mean the repercussions of your feud with mamere."

Mirrei lapsed into silence. Her mouth twitched as if wanting to say more. "What is it, Mirrei?" Jhee asked.

"As our house took on more and more water, she would see yours on the hill and talk about all the things your family had taken from ours. After they were kind enough to take you in. Every time our travels took us within sight of your home, she would point up at the house on the hill and say, 'There. There lives the fiend who ruined our lives.'

"When mamere and I stayed at your home the first time, I was trembling. Here we were at the spawning bed of the monster, the evil, Trench-hearted villains who had tried to destroy our family. I expected giants or creatures resembling leviathans from the deep. Horrible blood-stained fangs and claws. We announced ourselves. You opened the door yourself in a dressing gown and slippers with a shark-skinned volume tucked under your arm. You were soft-spoken. I almost mistook you for a servant. And I thought this, this is the woman who mamere cursed nightly so vehemently.

"My mother, nay the whole reaches, painted you as some fiendish cross between a seductress and an ogre who'd destroyed our family out of jealousy, and Shep as a disloyal lech. You were small. Almost pathetic. That's when the seed was sown that it was all small. And pathetic. This grudge which threatened to engulf both our families, our isles. I soon realized I wanted no part in perpetuating it."

Jhee supposed it was progress that everyone thought her a seductress now. Initially, no one but Miramar thought she seduced Shep. Perhaps Miramar had seen something between them that no one else had. It hurt that the first thought on everyone's mind was Shep had tricked her. Maybe he had.

Jhee reached into an inner pocket and extracted Miramar's somewhat rumpled letter. She read from it as she had so many times since Mirrei came to live with them. "... protect and honor my daughter," Jhee finished. She left off the last part as she usually did.

"You owe me, Jhee."

"Mamere's letter. You never read all of it aloud, especially the last part."

"Because when I share it with you, I want it to be about her love for you and not whatever transpired between us."

"'She owes us.' That's the way mamere always put it. What did you owe her?"

"The short version: I stole her fiancé and bankrupted, nay crushed, your family. I had to break my betrothal to do it, which gave your family an unlikely ally in the merchant kings and queens of Crag Hall."

"You, denbe? Hard to believe."

"Which part? That Shep might desire me more than your mother or my fortune is the result of others' misery?"

"I didn't mean it that way."

"Of course not."

"The problems in our home weren't about resources. Life at Crag Hall was never as full of privation as she made it out to be. They made a decent living as merchants. We just weren't rich like you. That's what bothered her the most, I think."

Jhee kept her own council. Almost every shred of her wealth was geld minted from the weakness of others. Even she had gotten her strikes in. The Mitsus and Crag Halls would never have been able to force Miramar and Mirrei from one home after the other without Jhee's machinations from long ago.

Mirrei took Jhee's hand. "Don't blame yourself. You've never struck me as vindictive. It seems petty, cruel, beneath you."

"It was. I can be both cowardly and cruel. You've just never seen that side of me. I was young and stupid. We all were."

"You've always been so gracious to me. I'm not sure if I deserve it."

Mirrei looked pained.

"Do you want me to fetch the doctor?" Jhee asked.

"I kissed Shep. When we first came to your house, I tried to seduce Shep. We weren't engaged yet. It was before I knew him, before I knew you."

"During my nights with Kanto, Shep took abrupt efforts not to share a bed with you alone. Which meant he had concerns, if not about his behavior, then yours. Even if he hadn't told me, I would have guessed on my own. And the fact you may have oversold how frail you were."

"You knew yet you said nothing. Why?"

"Not the whole time, but I caught on soon enough. Who am I to judge? Mai—Miramar, your mother could be intense. You wouldn't have been the first to embellish the truth for a little relief from her. Also, when you first became part of our household, you may have felt you needed to do it to get extra attention. An impulse I understand too well. Until you came along and stole my thunder, I was a world-class hypochondriac."

"Like knows like."

Jhee flashed back to young adulthood and her home and the silence, the disinterested parents who wanted nothing more than to lose themselves in memories. Was that what it was like growing up with a bitter, obsessed Miramar? How much of the hardship of her upbringing laid at Jhee's feet? "I can only imagine what it was like living with her like that for all those years."

"Please, denbe, tell me what happened between you."

"I was jealous of Mai. I always was. She was popular, and had a loving, if demanding, family."

"Don't. You don't have to play the villain to protect my mother's memory. I know who she was. You never badmouthed her. You've been very gracious. Mamere was jealous of the life you and Shep had together. The life she could have had with you, together. If she had stood up to her family."

"I wish my turn as the villain had only been play. Everyone had to pick a side and my family crushed anyone who chose wrong. Families who had been our friends for years. Families who had risked their lives in the search for my missing sisters. And families who had lost children just like my parents had. The worst part was, it was the most alive, the most united, I had seen my parents in years which is why I reveled in it too. So, if your mother hated us, hated me, she had good cause. For I am indeed the engineer of her misery and likely yours as well."

"If you hated each other so much, why did I also see you and she kiss that night?"

"Your mother and I were friends, more than. I was enamored of her and Shep or the idea of them. I wanted that for myself, and I took it. It was petty. It was vindictive. And we're all still paying the price for it. Well, she's dead now and no need to speak ill of her."

Mirrei winced. "Neither she nor I deserve your gracious words."

"Nonsense. You are probably the only true innocent in all this."

"That's the last thing I am. The obsession with the past went both ways. She said I reminded her of you. And you both tried to mold me into a shape not quite mine. You think you were the only one obsessed? You need to stop trying to make me into your very own little nerd. My mother already tried that, to turn me into a cutting of you so she could punish me in your place."

"Enough old pain for now, only some sweet dreams. Good night, Mirrei."

16
____

THE SQUELCH MAKER

~

The New Arrival

Jhee and Kanto continued to sit with Mirrei. Two days later, Jhee returned to Mirrei's room where Kanto lovingly brushed her hair as usual.

"You won't believe the latest gossip," he said to her. "The Damsels over on Isle Quiescence are in a feud with the Makos of Presque Isle. They had this long-standing marriage pact who knows how many years ago. But the youngest son you see decides he wants to be a whale rider to impress his fiancée. He had gotten it into his head or had heard her parents talking about how they no longer considered him a suitable match. Although I heard that she told him flat out she thought he was beneath her. Anyway, her family has a whale preserve. He and two friends get drunk and sneak into the whale pens with nets and riding hooks. I suppose they fancied themselves the remaking of Whale Rider. They climb into the water with the whales. The whales panic. One of them leaps up into the air, spins, and flops back down right on top of the son who had managed to rope and ride one of the other whales. He was severely crushed, and they injured both the whales. He has no breeding potential anymore. They are out two prize whales. Now the families are arguing back and forth over whose fault it was."

Jhee leaned against the door frame and smiled. Mirrei turned her head towards Jhee and gave a wan smile. She watched quietly as Kanto told her more stories. Every now and then Mirrei giggled a little, but a coughing fit shortly followed it. Jhee walked up behind Kanto. She put her hands on his shoulders and squeezed them gently. He touched her hand.

They took turns reading to her, Kanto from the gossip sheets and Jhee from the latest academic and forensic journals.

They heard footfalls at the door and turned. Shep stood there. He opened his arms, and Jhee ran to them. Kanto approached them quietly and respectfully. She composed herself and brushed away her tears.

Shep crouched beside Mirrei's bedside. "Hey, Sprite, how you doing?"

Mirrei's head turned towards his voice. "Been better," she mumbled through the haze of medication.

"You know there are better ways to get me to hurry back," Shep continued. "Wait to see the new house. You won't believe it. It should meet even Kanto's high standards."

"Is it our fault Mirrei and I are the only ones in this household with a decent sense of fashion and style?"

Shep shrugged. "Hey, Sprite, do you mind if I sit here with you for a while and give Tunes and Puzzler a rest?"

Mirrei moved her head the barest amount up and down. Shep gave them a single nod that said they could rest assured. He would be there. In the hallway, Jhee placed an arm around Kanto's shoulders as he shook and cried.

"It was that drench Vash! She was supposed to be with him. He said he would take care of her. Now, look at her. You just simply can't let her marry him. He'll kill her just like he did Ms. Oriel and Mr. Bastian. I went on one of those 'weirs' dates with them. It was nothing but debauchery. I told them I wanted no part of it. She, she made me promise not to tell you. Denbe, I'm sorry I didn't tell you. I'm sorry. I'm sorry."

Jhee rubbed Kanto's back. "This isn't your fault. You think I hadn't surmised they weren't playing weirs, anymore? Especially once she got herself arrested. You have nothing to be sorry for."

Shep approached them. "Go. Get some rest the both of you."

Jhee opened her mouth to speak.

"I demand it. It's my day today."

Jhee nodded. Shep procured them a transport, and they headed for the villa. The driver of the transport navigated past all the roadblocks and protests.

Jhee's thoughts threatened to overwhelm her. She had to find stillness, so she could help her household.

"Driver, pull over please."

"My lady?"

"Pull over, please. Ground level."

"What's wrong?" Kanto asked.

The driver maneuvered to a pull off on the side of the transport lane.

"Nothing. I want to walk the rest of the way."

"What ever for?"

"Driver, bring him to the villa." Jhee smiled for Kanto's benefit. "Don't trouble yourself. I'll be there soon."

"If you insist."

Jhee squeezed his hand. She grabbed a lighted umbrella to protect herself from the light drizzle before hopping out. The transport merged back into the transport lane and sailed off. As she walked, Jhee gazed at the rich green trees lining the hills. Sometimes they gave way abruptly to a sharp drop. She cleared, centered, and directed her thought to the Wave Makers. The Wave Makers had claimed their due from her family and more. She took a step closer to the edge. For a few moments, she opened herself up and merely listened. The sounds of the sea called to her. Did she hear her siblings and her parents laughing in the surf? Jhee opened her eyes and returned to a safe distance from the waves.

Back at the villa, Jhee could not sleep. She crept to the boathouse Lady Delphine allowed them to use for a workshop. She pored over journals and sheets, then her healing derivations. Finally, everything she had learned about the curative properties of Tranquility Bridge's golden nectar. She had uncovered actual healing benefits to it, though she was no chemist or epidemiologist. That was more Mirrei's bailiwick.

Jhee hesitated in front of Mirrei's portion of the workshop they shared. If Jhee disturbed anything, Mirrei was likely to feel her privacy violated. Not much matched the feeling of returning to find one's belongings not where you left them.

If circumstances had kept going as they were, Jhee would be freed of worrying about Mirrei's space. That's what Jhee planned. Mirrei would be married to someone more suitable whose age and interests better complemented her own. She would lead or build a robust, thriving household that would one day return House Mitsu to its former glory.

None of that would happen if Jhee selfishly clung to the poor girl like a needy lover. She must let Mirrei thrive and flourish in whatever manner she saw fit. This was not her choice.

Along with casks of Tranquility Gold and samples of the wild yeast cultures, Mirrei's section contained glass jugs stoppered with corks. Tubes in the corks led to another lower set of jugs. Jhee took a whiff. She recognized that smell from the academy days. The only ailment that cured was boredom. She examined Mirrei's makeshift lab or should she call it a still.

Squelch. Mirrei's work? Jhee took a sip. She screwed up her face. If her eyes now resembled swirling fireworks after a swig, she would not have been surprised. Then the buzz arrived. Strong, but tasty. Better than anything Jhee and her classmates whipped up in her day. It tasted much like the refujuice the refugees had served her on Torilsisle but went down much smoother. Was that where Mirrei got the idea? She had gotten sick like this after she and Kanto sneaked off to visit their camps near the Shield. Was it because of the squelch?

Jhee set the jug down. She would bring a sample to the hospital just in case. As Jhee gathered a sample, she found another foil wrapper in the trash.

Jhee did not want to go to bed, but was there anything more she could do tonight? Jhee just stopped at a loss for something else to do.

The idleness became too much. Jhee wrote a series of prayer letters then sought the shrine. She waved the letters through incense smoke to scent them before burning. She summoned happy memories of Mirrei and Mai so that she could complete proper tribute to Pascoe and Lashae.

For Mai, she thought of their swim team days. Miramar and Shep competed on the school team while Jhee managed.

For Mirrei, the times they spent in their home library. Jhee had taken an instant liking to the young woman. Cultured and well read. Simple clothing. After a few months of dealing with Kanto's pretensions and hectoring, it was nice to have someone around who had nothing to say about her clothes or hair or image. With whom she could discuss the classics and philosophy. Jhee gave the Makers her laughter and letters.

Chimes answered from somewhere in the distance. Jhee turned her attention to Futou, his effigy forever poised in the process of ecstatic drumbeating.

Kanto would be devastated if Mirrei left them. But Jhee could not let that sway her, she must do what was best for Mirrei.

Jhee was not oblivious to what was happening with him. The two had grown so close so fast. Jhee tossed geld and hummed until she could be alone with her thoughts no more.

Jhee had to learn more about the true Mirrei. She had an idea where to start. The wrapper in the trash: she had seen many in a dish at Che's.

The Dive Bar Revisited

Che's had been a dead end, but the same man owned both, a man named Chappy. Chappy, the man who had rescued Mirrei and her friends, hovered while Jhee poked about the dive club, the infamous game room at Chuc's. Cigarettes, joints, booze, and a snooker table occupied the space. Not all that different from Stingray Club with the same manner of doings as the older set it would appear. Their very own junior Stingray Club.

"I wanted to thank you for bringing Mirrei and her friends to safety."

"No need."

"They're lucky you were there. I figured you for one who stays behind the bar."

Chappy tucked his hands into his trouser pockets and kicked at the floor. "She was here right before it happened. Giving everyone what-for for turtle shelling. Don't worry, m'lady. She's feisty, a fighter. She'll come through just fine."

"The First Makers' Design be done. May I look around?"

"Uh, sure."

One part of the dive club stood on its own, a giant wall painted with slogans. "Miners Unite." "Free the Fire Folk. The Wall is Death." "Free the Waters." "One Waters. Fishers. Miners." Protest signs and that ridiculous banner they tried to hang over the plants lay crumpled. Were they insane? Why would they do such an act again so soon? She taught Mirrei better than that. Perhaps the repeat action was her lot's idea. Mirrei understood better how not to get caught or at least she should have. Repetition was a sure-fire way to get caught. Mirrei needed to vary her methods. That way no one got too used to one tactic and could counter it. One must do the unexpected. This would keep the imperators on their toes. Jhee smiled at the irony of her thinking about ways to teach Mirrei to flout the law. Ironic.

Jhee examined their materials and propaganda; hiding among them was a

shiny wrapper for black pepper clove candy, but no dish of the candies themselves. Mirrei had hit it off with the Delphines as she hoped. They had practically accepted her into their family. Jhee wouldn't be surprised if, within a few
years of marriage, Mirrei would run the entire household from offspring to
dame. She might expect no less of a woman who learned from both her and
Miramar. A woman. Jhee, at last, thought of Mirrei as a woman. Some part of
her had always thought of her as a girl.—the girl she may have had with
Miramar or the one they all might have had together. Jhee owed Miramar so
much. This plan had worked out too well.

The apparatus in the corner caught Jhee's attention. The equipment much
like what occupied the work shed she and Mirrei kept at the villa. Jhee realized
she wasn't alone. Wynne, the activist who escaped at the observatory, sat at the
bar. She looked like fifty knots of rough seas.

"Nice still. Star's?" Jhee asked.

"Only in the loosest sense. She has a secret ingredient. Everyone loves it. All
efforts to reproduce it, not so much. Her squelch recipe pulled the Fire Folk
and other miners in like the tide. It reminds them of what they drank back
home. You're Star's denbe."

Wynne gave Jhee a slight chin jut of recognition and challenge. Her face
was heavily bruised and bandages wrapped her head.

"I'm here to help Star and wanted to thank Chappy again. I understand he
was the one who got Star and her friends to safety."

A flash of anger reddened Wynne's eyes followed by a wince of pain.
"Chappy? It was Vash who saved them. Chappy was LAS. He only turned up
after everything was over, apparently to take the credit."

Lost at sea. Chappy had lied. "You were present for the attack on the substation? Did you hear about what happened to her and her club friends?"

"I'm sorry to hear she's sick. She was good folk."

"Is. I don't suppose you want to help me save her?"

"Sure. Sure. What can I do?"

"Walk me through everything that happened at the substation protest."

"I saw her run off, but I was in the middle of a scrap with some scuttle
miners Styrling hired to cross the labor lines. Some say she went into the
substation. She'd passed out in the mine maybe trying to run away from the
Imps and Squids. We found her before they did. Then the gas got deployed.
They brought her and a bunch of other folk feeling fog-headed and woozy
back to the med tent. I wound up at crit care on the crag getting patched back

together after of bunch of scuttles with gas masks, who didn't look much like miners, jumped me. They found a group here passed out after they came here to regroup. We've been maced and gassed before. Some milk and a few hours and most folk are okay. Not this time. I'm not sure gas was the only thing they hit us with."

"They're escalating."

She clutched her side and grunted. "Well, we're not going to take it lying down, I guarantee you that."

To get a proper sense of the arrangement of all bodies in the system, Jhee needed to visit the substation.

At the substation, guards challenged Jhee. She flashed her credentials. They made her wait while they called it in but eventually allowed her on the premises. The fence which normally surrounded the substation had been knocked down in places.

Guards shadowed her as Jhee paced out the perimeter to get a sense of the size of the lot. She engaged the gears within and synchronated the area with an arcanum trace. The presence of the templarite dust and deposits caused a tricky-to-account-for reverberation. With the aid of onlookers, Jhee proceeded with due care and deliberation in a grid across the yard and noted the levels on her conch. This felt good. This was a finite, measurable action she could perform; a part of the Divine Mechanism she could know.

Emanations consistent with the Shield readings covered the middle of the space the protesters had occupied. That made sense given the proximity to the substation. Jhee studied the grid more. This level in the center was significantly higher than the residual in the rest of the area. The tract of land had been irradiated. The characteristics matched the trace radiation from the substation. She sought to discover the source. The faint trail did not lead toward the substation. As Jhee walked the affected area, the surface under Jhee's feet felt buckled. She bent and placed her hand against the shell concrete. Hardened, concentric ripples scarred the surface texture as if a pebble had been tossed into it only for the oscillations to freeze in place. The perimeter of the disturbance matched the concentration spikes. Their path dropped in from the sky.

First Makers, Styrling was escalating. The substation fell under the extreme trespass statutes. According to law, once the protesters had gained access to their property, they were within their rights to use enhanced force from gases to sonics, as long as it was "non-lethal." Had the crowd control measure Styrling used almost killed Mirrei?

Sianna and Inksy awaited Jhee at the villa. "Have a nice chat with Wynne and visit to the substation?"

On a mental boil because of the substation, Jhee's patience evaporated. She stomped over and spun Sianna's bar seat towards her. "Enough with the veiled barbs. Out with it."

Inksy stepped forward. Sianna waved her off and pushed several images toward Jhee.

"What are these?"

"Images of your wife in the company of a known Folx United radical."

Jhee recognized the person in the images as Wynne.

"Here she is entering the substation. I understand her prints were also found in the control room along with some sabotage tools."

Jhee pushed them back. "Fine. Threat made. I swear if Star Mirror dies because of whatever you deployed on the protesters, I'll dedicate myself to dismantling both your worlds. Your careers. Your reputations. Your well-being. Nothing of yours will remain safe from me. Just ask the Reaches. I'll save you the trouble of spying on me. I'm retiring for the evening. We've got an early day tomorrow."

17
_____

QUESTIONS

~

Awakenings

When Jhee entered Mirrei's room, she found several orderlies trying to restrain her. "Mamere, mamere, is that you? Mamere, mamere, come back, please. I'm sorry. I'm sorry."

At last, Mirrei collapsed back on the bed. Jhee brushed damp hair away from her esca.

Mirrei swallowed. "Did you see her, denbe? Mamere was here. She was here."

Jhee pulled the parchment from her pocket and unfolded it. "You remember this don't you?"

Jhee began to read from Miramar's letter. Mirrei reached out and grasped Jhee's hand. "There's something else I need to confide...."

The feeble gesture caused Jhee to stifle a sob. There was almost no strength in the grip. "Whatever it is, can wait until you're better."

"If I'm going to die—"

"You're not going to die."

"If I'm going to die, I want to die as myself without so many lies between us. You'll never know how grateful I am to you or how much I don't deserve it. I lied, denbe, about my mother's last words. She didn't want you to take care of me or see me safely anywhere. I only said that to get you to take me in. With her not there, I couldn't remain at that house anymore even. I had nowhere else to go, and you had been so kind to me when we stayed with you. You were the last place she wanted me to go."

"The letter?"

"Fake."

Jhee crumpled the letter and chucked the letter over her shoulder. "Thank the First Makers."

Mirrei furrowed her brow then chuckled. A moment later, she winced in pain. "Don't make me laugh."

"My pardon."

"You're relieved?"

"I suspected it to be a last attempt by Mai to manipulate me from beneath the waves. I didn't want to sour your memories of her, though."

"No chance of that. I wanted to tell you every time you read from it to give me a pep talk. I thought you needed to believe it was real more than I did."

"Perhaps I did at first, the more I read it though, the more it felt wrong."

"I composed it based on old love letters she wrote."

"To Shep. That explains much. I wrote those. Your mother was accomplished at many things. Expressing herself through words was not one of them."

"The letters I found weren't to Shep. They were to you."

Jhee gaped in stunned silence.

"Her feelings towards you were a lot more complicated than you know."

"I'm beginning to see that."

Mirrei coughed. "Some part of me can't help but feel I deserve this. That it's punishment, divine justice, for exaggerating the extent of my illness all these years. I wasn't always sick as a child. I had a persistent state of mild, ill health which came and went. They fought often. I got sick once, and for once they stopped and were kind to each other. Mamere wasn't always the most engaged. When I got sick, she was so attentive. The talk of divorce stopped. Next I knew, I was sick a lot more. The magnitude of that sickness grew whenever divorce was mentioned. Not by my design mind you, but as I would learn later, my father's. Though, false doctor's visits became my father's and my own little secret. Once he passed, I found it to my advantage to keep the ruse going. I think she realized eventually and turned it to her advantage when dealing with her adversaries."

"So, and the fainting and ill health when you visited, were mere theatrics?"

"Mostly. Though, I found, when we stayed with you, a pall lifted. I genuinely felt lighter and more at ease. I blamed our home. At your house, I suspected what a toxic environment my home was. When the opportunity came to leave it, I ran."

A mausoleum out in the shoals was an apt way to describe what Jhee's home in the Far Reaches became. For Mirrei to see it as a refuge, buoyed Jhee's burdens. "After everything I've done to your family, I'm glad I enriched your life too."

A nurse came in and administered a sedative.

"No, babere, no more medicine, please," Mirrei murmured.

Jhee held the young woman's hand. Mirrei smiled and drifted to sleep. She remained asleep as the hours passed and they put her on a respirator. Jhee switched seats with Kanto and held up several bio-film periodicals. With the additional equipment, conch use was now restricted.

"Look what I brought. Frontiers in Forensics and Historian Daily. It's like you told me when we met, 'The least you can do is keep your mind sharp.' Not as exciting as Kanto's fashion books. A few pages of this and you'll hop right up out of that bed and flee screaming."

The inquester cleared her throat. Jhee let go of Mirrei's hand and set down the trade journal she had been reading to her.

"How is she?" the inquester asked.

"She is on an extreme replenishment course and requires a lot of rest. Her Maker within has been running on reserves for who knows how long."

"I'm sorry to hear that, and even sorrier to disturb you at a time like this."

"I need to do something tangible right now." Jhee paused at the echo of Mirrei's words from the jail cell. She shook her head. "What is it?"

"I was going to interview her friends. One of them woke up and is talking. I wanted to know if you wanted to come with."

The inquester stepped outside.

"One moment. Kanto."

"Jhee, no," Kanto said.

"It won't take long I swear."

"What if...? What if...? We might need you. I'd never forgive you if... You'd never forgive yourself."

"I must go. What if this provides the key to why she became so sick? I need to find out what happened to her. I need to see this through."

"Go. Shep and I will take care of our sister-wife while you go run off chasing villains."

Kanto broke away and returned to Mirrei's bedside.

Jhee stared at him for a moment, but he had already turned away. She took a shaky breath and joined Inquester Paij. The inquester handed her the case files.

"It seems one imperator had a run in with Mirrei at a rally right before she fell ill. She said she saw someone suspicious. Someone she thought would do violence. The imperators thought she was just causing more trouble. Then later on after the rally, the cleaning crews at the substation found this."

Inquester Paij handed Jhee a bricker, a programmable electromagnetic and incendiary mechanism. She used to plant similar units on comm towers in the war. This one was lighter and shaped more like a puck.

"A sabotage device. Do you think it belongs to the killer?""Possibly. Maybe he recognized Star Mirror and tried to finish her and her friends off. They saw something they shouldn't have. Maybe they can identify the killer."

Jhee wiped at her eyes. She composed herself as best she could. This was indeed good news.

"I ran down the leads you told me about and looked into those items you found at their dive club. It turns out the stuff on their clothes is a match to the substance we found at both murders. It's templarite. The mineral used in the Shield. I have to tell you, Justicar, it doesn't look good for Mirrei and her friends. This evidence—it might be the motive. It might tie them to the murders."

"Mirrei is a hero. She may have saved many lives."

"Or...." the inquester trailed off. "Star Mirror trained in medicine and chemistry, didn't you say?"

"They were just making homemade squelch." The inquester made a face. "What is it?"

"The prevailing theory on what felled the protesters is a bad batch of squelch like at the mine."

"One: the mine poisoning happened before our arrival. Two: Mirrei—Star Mirror did not chase a punch bowl into the substation. She chased a person. Three: I've sampled her squelch, and I'm not ill."

"You admit though she has the skills and training."

"Where is this coming from Inquester? Don't answer. Allow me to guess, someone showed you images of her talking to Wynne."

The inquester rocked back on her heels. "You understand, Justicar, I have to examine every possibility no matter where it leads."

"My wife is not a murderer or mass poisoner, Inquester, and neither are those nitwits she fell in with. None of them except her has the imagination to stage the scenarios we've seen, and frankly she wouldn't be so stupid as to leave incriminating evidence lying around."

"Fair enough. One other is awake. Would you like to go interview them?"

Jhee squared her shoulders. The law. She had to respect the law. The law was finite. It was definite. It was fallible, but it was the duty of those like her and the inquester to help it obtain the divine state of perfection they knew it was capable of. Trust in the First Maker's Grand Design.

"Let's go."

~

Questioning

"My lady, how is Star doing?" Erma said.

"The truth is not good. She's slipped into a coma. Erma, Semele, I will need you to tell me the truth. What were you up to?"

"We weren't up to anything, we swear. We had all had a good think and reconsidered what we were about after getting arrested. Not Star, though, she was just as committed as ever. More so."

"That sounds like her. Stubborn like her mother."

"Yeah," Semele said, "rather than give up she doubled down. She shamed us into going to the next rally. We were there with her when she ran off. She was complaining of feeling light-headed. She said it was nothing, and she slipped off to adjust her saline drip. Next thing we know, she's running around saying people are in danger. We didn't know what she was about. When she was gone for too long, we went after. That's when we found her."

"Later after the action, we went back to our dive club. We had a few drinks and a smoke or two. But not Star, she only had a little now and then. We were feeling a little soggy and next thing we know, we wake up in the hospital."

Jhee thought about it. That sounds like her Mirrei. She was taking after Jhee. Maybe too much and it might have gotten her killed.

"Erma, Semele, this is very important—did you see or notice anything unusual once you got back to the hangout? Something that should be there that wasn't. Or something out of place."

"I don't know. Wait, the door. The door wasn't how we left it. I thought nothing of it at the time. The dive club is a public space, and we aren't the only ones who come through there. Most people know it's where we like to hang out. So, they don't mess with anything. We have had none of our things tampered with in a while."

"And where was Wynne?" the inquester asked.

Erma's eyes flashed red. "She was getting her head bashed in by Imps and Squids. They took her to Crag Critical Care. She can't afford a place like Makers' Care."

"Erma, you recognized her while she was climbing," Jhee said. "Your concern also seemed profound. You and Wynne?"

"The perfect choice for a rebellious daughter. It's been over-not-over for some time."

Inquester Paij fiddled with her sensor suit cuff. "Was it you who sneaked the Folx Uniters into the fundraiser?"

"It was me," Semele said.

"But I knew. They didn't inform us about the base jumping and defacing the galleon."

The inquester and Jhee left and went to the room across the hall. Deziree, another of the Dive Club miscreants, proved less helpful. She gave them nothing but Maker Foz worthy rejoinders and retorts. Jhee recited cyphers to restrain herself from activating her siren module and compelling the girl to tell them what they wanted to know.

Jhee yanked the pillow from under Deziree's head. "I have scant patience and time so I can't abide with your lies and disseminations. You will answer truthfully, or I'll have Dawn Wolf dissect you while you are still alive."

The inquester pulled Jhee into the hallway. "Justicar, I think you need a break. I invited you along as a courtesy, but I can only give you so much leeway."

"I'll pay the drench fine."

"Not on my case you won't. Take a walk. Now."

Jhee went outside for a constitutional around the hospital. With measured breaths, she focused her siren module's calming abilities on herself. As wound up as she was, accidentally making herself docile might have been an improvement. Those foolish children. What have they gotten themselves involved with? What had they gotten her naïve Mirrei involved with? Her naïve Mirrei? More like her drinking, smoking, homemade drug making, know several ways to sneak in and out of a building Mirrei. She must not do this. She must not infantilize Mirrei.

The rose substance. Mirrei's merry band of mischief Makers could easily alibi each other, and that was the problem. It was a hit to all their credibility. If means could be proved for one, it could be proved for all. Mirrei though had not left Jhee's sight for most of the evening, though. Or Kanto's. Even if she had, Mirrei would not have been a party to murder. But Jhee did not put it beyond her to cover for the others, though.

It was sloppy and most of all stupid—the last word she would apply to Mirrei.

Jhee found Inquester Paij with the last of Mirrei's club Taral. The inquester gave Jhee an inquiring once over. Jhee put her hands together to show she had composed herself.

"Star wasn't there. I mean we hadn't seen her for a while by the time they hit us with the wobble ray. When we found her later, we assumed she'd got hit with it, too."

"Assumed?" Jhee asked. "So, you didn't see her get bombarded?"

"No, ma'am."

"I've heard enough," Jhee said. "For now. I'm sure the inquester will have more question for you later."

Questions of a Queen

Jhee returned to Mirrei's room with a much calmer head. Shep kept watch over Kanto and Mirrei while they slept. Inquester Paij motioned to Jhee from outside the observation windows, and Jhee joined her in the corridor.

"We're tracking Bastian's conch. Someone turned it on."

"Great news, Inquester."

"We're about to close in on the location. Justicar, I could use your help."

"I'm sure you have it all taken care of and are more than capable of handling it yourself."

"I think I might require more unusual help."

"Ah, my cyphering expertise. I thought you disliked arcana."

"I dislike my team and me getting shot more."

"As you so eloquently stated before arcana can't stop bullets. Very well, inquester. Keep in mind though I'm not a gun on a stick. I'm not a super weapon, just another hand in a fight. My offensive powers are even more constrained by line of sight than my detecting powers."

"Fair enough. I'll get you some protective gear."

"That'll be peachy."

Shep regarded Jhee with a sigh. "A firefight. You are heading into a firefight now? Possibly gunplay. Now?"

"Please, Shep."

He spoke in almost a whisper, "I've lived through this before when we were in the service. Kanto hasn't. Mirrei hasn't. They need you. What happens if she wakes up? Is that the first thing I will tell her when she asks for you? 'She got her fool self shot trying to avenge you.'"

"I'll be behind the others. Watching their backs."

"You, bring up the rear? I'll believe it when I see it."

"Please, just keep them calm and watch over them while I do this."

Shep sighed and nodded. Jhee took a last look at Mirrei before she left. Kanto caught her gaze. He scowled and showed her his back.

Jhee needed to do this. In the end, she could count on the law. Always. Always. This was her calling.

The inquester led Jhee to the trace team's transport. The location of the signal had stopped.

"Any more movement?" Jhee asked.

The inquester nodded to the trace team member to let her know it was appropriate to answer.

"Not yet. It's been in the same spot for about an hour now."

"Okay. Everyone suit up and move out. We're going in. Whoever this is may be armed and dangerous. They have already killed two people that we know of."

Jhee put on a displacement vest. She drew a pure rune on it. For protection. No rune stopped a bullet though. Arcana was not a cure-all. She also drew some runes on her hands.

As they closed in on the conch location, they heard yelling and breached the door. Queenie, the weaselly woman from the clinic, was there shaking the depths out of Ms. Levinia. She let go of Ms. Levinia and held out wide her hands when she saw them.

Jhee checked Ms. Levinia. "Are you all right?"

Ms. Levinia rubbed her neck and nodded. Inquester Paij snapped the restraints on Queenie then warned her against self-incrimination. Despite that, Queenie proved cooperative. The savvy, career criminal wanted no part of high-profile capital murder charges.

The woman had a mid-sea accent so thick you could smear it on bread double. "The Queen had nothing to do with these nasty, nasty murders. She does not kill. Corpses can't pay. Accidents are another story. The Queen got an invitation to meet one of her clients there. He had a small personal loan payment to make. Several did in fact and so the Queen figured she would collect them all at once and make a delivery."

"Vash said you threatened his family and that the same thing that happened to Mr. Bastian and Ms. Oriel would happen to him."

"It was puffery. Once folk assumed the Queen was responsible, a lot of slow payers got quick. However, it came with other drawbacks."

"Did Mr. Bastian owe you money?"

"He owed the Queen something much more valuable. He offered, amongst other things, a device to bypass the Shield. And He also promised a weapon that would bloodlessly and instantly incapacitate someone."

"What did he want in return?"

"For us to stop leaning on his girlfriend and at first, just templarite dust, later several large flawless templarite crystals. Those caused the Queen approach other parties, who are displeased her side of the bargain has not been fulfilled. Their connection at the mines fell down a shaft. Your mining supervisor owed folks much less pleasant than the Queen. She hopes not to find herself at the bottom of the shaft with her."

"The aforementioned other drawbacks."

Queenie raised an eyebrow and gave a coy quirk of her mouth.

18

NOT TODAY

~

Interrogation and Workshop

"Vash, if you are in any way involved with what happened to Star Mirror, you need to tell me now."

"I swear to you, my lady, I had nothing to do with it. I went to Bastian and Oriel's apartments looking for something else."

"What?"

"Bastian had images of me and someone."

"A lover?"

Vash twisted his signet ring. "Yes."

Jhee narrowed her eyes. "Please, Vash, I have no time for games."

"The ambassador."

"Why would you go through all this nonsense for an image of you and the ambassador?"

"I won't say any more."

"Vash, Star Mirror's life is at stake because she fell in with you and your family. I thought you would protect her. I trusted you and thought she would be happy with you. Now I don't know what I was thinking. You need to tell me what you know so I can save her life."

"I'm sorry, Justicar. It's not my secret to tell. I just can't."

Jhee stood up in frustration. She stormed outside to the roof. She stood face to the sky, feeling the gentle mist on her face. Jhee recited statutes and cyphers. Vash's terseness was a blow. What could he possibly be hiding? It wasn't a lover. She knew that from his body language. But what? What could be or who's that important he would not tell her?

Bastian and Vash primarily knew each other through the former's volunteer work at the clinic. Did the secret pertain to the clinic? Other than Queenie's extortion, that is. Jhee examined the prospectuses and other promotional materials for the Friends of the Observatory and Breath of the Deep charities. The clinic is also how Bastian and Oriel met. Maybe Jhee could view the connection from this angle.

Vash featured prominently in the clinic's welcome footage. Toward the end, Vash and a handful of community leaders, including Ambassador Naiman, posed with individual children thanking prospective donors. Jhee found no trace of Bastian in any of the shots. The promo terminated with a wide group shot of VIPs and children. Ambassador Naiman and Vash framed opposite sides of the shot in a similar stance.

Even at opposite ends of the room, tension and avoidance radiated from the pair. Vash might have told part of the truth. Jhee had seen him and the ambassador arguing. They weren't lovers. The body language had been all wrong. They had also avoided each other since then.

Ambassador Naiman's awkward final waves to the camera matched. Jhee switched back and forth between Vash and the ambassador's 'thank you' segments. Now, she saw the resemblance, as if they were a set, but in different palettes.

Family. Vash was dedicated to his family. Jhee thought back to the altercation on the beach. The few words she caught. *"Why you?" "Stay away."*

Other aspects of Vash and the Ambassador Naiman's features tickled at Jhee's recollection. Then Jhee thought about what the ambassador had said about his heritage. Half barbarian. On his father's side. Jhee performed a quick calculation of the ambassador's age. Ambassador Naiman like Vash had to be born about the time Jhee and Delphine left the academy. A scholarship student who worked the grounds had Delphine's eye. She tried to hide it. Jhee knew about them, one of the few.

Jhee went back inside and daubed the moisture off her face. She confronted Vash. "He's your brother."

Vash looked aghast. "How did you? Yes, ma'am. Bastian, much like you, thought it was romantic."

"Because you had tried to kiss him much like you had Bright Harmony."

Vash twisted his signet ring more. "Yes, ma'am. It wasn't. The ambassador came to me and told me who he was and how he had been forced to get involved in the Shield negotiations because of our parents. He wanted to come clean. I tried everything to convince him not to."

Jhee loomed over him. "Vash, now no more lies."

"I wasn't only after the images. I'm not a credentialed doctor. Mumsy had always been reluctant to let me marry. The arrangements always fell through for one reason or another. When Naiman came to me and told me who my father was, I understood why she found fault with so many of the offers. It all made sense. I dropped out of the medical academy."

Vash pressed his hands flat on the table and Jhee seated herself.

"Bastian had obtained copies of my transcripts showing I hadn't completed all my coursework. I trashed the event organizer's apartment. I thought they might be there. Then I tried Bastian's apartment. They weren't there either. Then my sisters told me they had seen Bastian drifting around Chappy's Underground. I found a trail that led to his storage container. But the proof he claimed to have wasn't there. I found something else. He had all these weird designs and photos."

Jhee returned to Mirrei's workshop. She rubbed her eyes. It had been such a long day between Vash's betrayals and lies and her shattered vision. She had hoped to find Mirrei a place where she fit in and could be happy. Much like Kanto though, she knew it would not be with the Delphines. How far would she go? Once Mirrei recovered, Jhee would have to grapple with whether she would give her blessing if Mirrei wanted anything to do with these cads. Would she force the issue? She could sue Mirrei to remain married. Something she had promised not to do. She had promised to respect Mirrei's desires. And if she still desired to join the Delphines household? What would she do then?

If Mirrei recovered. Jhee sat down at Mirrei's work area. She looked over her set-up. Mirrei specialized in potions and healing draughts and chemical analysis. They had been putting her through the correspondence courses to get her chemistry degree and possibly a medical license. Jhee had the image of her helping her with cases. Once properly certified, Mirrei's findings could be used as testimony in court. As is, Mirrei's help was mostly unofficial.

From the looks of that dive club, Mirrei had other plans and found alternate uses for her skills.

Jhee held two such different visions of her relationship with Mirrei in her head. In one future, Mirrei and all of them were part of a crime-solving family who dedicated themselves to the law and justice, each with their own little niche. In the other, it was back to just her and Shep while Kanto and Mirrei were off somewhere else living their lives happy. Could she and Shep go back to how they were before those two came into their lives?

Mirrei's first love was medicine similar to how Jhee's was the law. Understandable given her condition and how much of her life she spent "sick" and cooped up with books and knowledge.

Jhee spied a little cask of Tranquility Gold. She drank a little to settle her nerves. The sip tickled all the proper keys. Smooth, fragrant, and peachy unlike whatever Mirrei had whipped up at the dive club.

After Jhee moved papers around Mirrei's desktop, she found notes and derivations Mirrei had worked on for Tranquility Bridge's nectar. Was Mirrei trying to replicate that as she had the refugee's squelch?

Jhee continued to sip her wine as she thumbed through Mirrei's research. Thorough research it was. Mirrei had been documenting the properties of the nectar. The famed curative effects may have not been merely a placebo. The fermenting element gave you a mood boost. Meanwhile other factors increased immune response.

"Jhee?"

"Ah, Delphine, I believe I've solved your glitch mite problem."

"I'm sure it can wait. How is Mirrei?"

"In a coma. The haunted mines were nothing more than youngsters partying. Apparently, mines have become pop-up nightspots popular with the miners, activists, and the jet-stream set."

"Good to hear it's not Makers' feedback for my sins."

"It may yet be, but that's not for me to judge. You must have noticed the similarity between Vash and Naiman. Tell me about their father. Geology student who also worked the grounds?"

"Vulcanology and mining studies. Scholarship student. Even back then Vilmar thought big. He designed an early defense grid prototype based on pyroclastic clouds. Brilliant. Vash resembles him more than Naiman does, aside from the obvious."

"You kept the socially acceptable child and sent the other away."

"You're a fine one to judge me. I wasn't the only one in an illicit relationship. Which attracted you more? Your family's likely disapproval? Or stealing him away from Miramar?"

"It wasn't like that. Entirely. Do you know how much damage you caused by not keeping mum?"

"You caused. It was your lie and your broken promise."

"I had been waiting until the right waters."

"Tell yourself that if you must. I vowed never to regret my decision especially after witnessing what happened in the Far Reaches when you followed your heart."

Jhee pinched the bridge of her nose. If only that business had been as noble and romantic as it must have seemed from the outside. "It may not have happened in that manner if you hadn't breached the levee about my marriage to Shep."

"I hadn't meant to, for what it's worth."

No one else knew they had eloped. Only Delphine, her roommate, who was there when Shep showed up at academy to whisk her away. Was it a preemptive strike? Delphine had outed her and Shep before she could tell anyone about Delphine and the handyman. It all made so much sense now.

"You'd worried I caught on to you and Mr. Vilmar. You wanted to neutralize me and have me kicked out."

"I'm sorry. I hadn't realized that you had left the grounds as some grand elopement. The sweep team spotted me with Vilmar later, so we told them we were searching for you to divert suspicion. That night changed us, too. Your scandalous marriage put many ideas into Vilmar's head about our future. Mine, as well. They clashed. I guess I'm just not as strong as you. I couldn't put my family through that. First, I maintained Vash was sired. Then I arranged siring for Erma and Semele as well to maintain the pretense."

"Appears you looked forward to marrying into the Portshires as much as I did the Crag Halls."

"Less. He was a Portshire-Crag Hall."

"Endless talk of furniture supply chains instead of fabric."

"And wood importation. You must not forget the wood importation."

Jhee and Delphine laughed.

~

Researchers

Jhee awoke the next morning rubbing her aching neck. She had fallen asleep in the workshop. The scent of Kanto's favorite cologne rose from the blanket which had been thrown over her during the night. She gathered the research on Tranquility Bridge's nectar. She would consult with Mirrei's doctors about using the nectar as a treatment—as long as it did not hurt. Mirrei loved it so much. A little orange tea and nectar surely would not hurt her. Yes, she would ask the doctors if they could bring Mirrei her favorite tea.

First, though, Jhee made a stop at the main villa. She brandished Mirrei's notes in Vash's face as he ate his morning shrimp. "Did you help Mirrei with these?"

"My lady—"

"Did you help Mirrei with this research?"

"We made a sterilization series and tried it on some cultures at the clinic. The clinic isn't outfitted for research though. Is it appropriate for us to speak?"

"I'm a guest at your resort, and you're the in-house physician, or so we were all led to believe. How could you have missed it? How could you have missed the signs she was so ill? Fraud. Charlatan."

"I didn't miss it."

Jhee threw the research at Vash. She tucked her hands in her robes as she visualized cyphers and statutes. Vash gathered up the mess and set her down in the solar. "Forgive my outburst, Vash."

"I didn't miss it. There was nothing to miss. It also doesn't explain my sisters and the others. I dragged them out of there. I'm not a total incompetent as a doctor, my lady. Fresh Lung Syndrome is a catch-all term, a lazy diagnosis for a group of ailments being suffered by those coming from the Outer Reaches or a holdover from the deep ages of medicine when they had vague ailments for the gentry as well. Chronic wasting sickness. I was gathering the data. Fresh Lung Syndrome is just an immune response. Their immune systems were failing. The doctors were blinded by the fact the victims were poor and from places with atrocious health care. So, they would just write it off as Fresh Lung or exaggeration or depression because you know the poor are always sick."

"That's incredible. Why did no one tell us?"

"Snobbery. Incompetence. Even the rich doctors didn't know. To them, it might have resulted from bad food. They saw you were from the Outer Reaches and that was it. Problem solved: she had Fresh Lung Syndrome. I wanted to help people. I had come around. Often, I, too, misdiagnosed it. I also thought the outbreak came from so many migrants, but it made little sense. The variety of symptoms did. I thought it was just because of being over-diagnosed and as a catch-all. Then I noticed there seemed to be a pattern with the symptoms. All the various diseases being attributed to Fresh Lung could have one underlying cause. Immune system breakdown. Fresh Lung was not a disease itself but a state of compromised health. The patient got it and then could be fine unless an opportunistic infection came along. At which point, their body could not defend itself and thus all the different things called Fresh Lung."

"That's amazing. But then what do we do about it. That means the nectar could help. It's an immune booster. Vash, come with me. I want to take another look at the dive club."

"But?"

"Do you want to help Mirrei and your sisters or not?"

"Yes."

"Then behave like it. You've taken up enough time already. Now, come on, and no more of your foolishness. Fussing about after you has already cost me enough time away from my household."

Jhee and Vash headed to Chuc's place. Vash brought them in via the private entrance. Chappy hurried away from two passed out patrons at the bar.

"My lady, what time is it?" Chappy asked.

"Early. Late. Depending on your perspective," Jhee answered.

Jhee browsed the drugs and paraphernalia on the table. "Grab these items. We need to test each one. One of these might be it."

What else was Jhee missing? While they were at the dive club, she pulled out her conch. She played the footage she had taken at Mr. Bastian's. How had Mirrei gotten sick? She suspected the Inkerton's crowd suppression ray. But in case she was wrong, Jhee should test out other possibilities. All the talk of murder, suspects, and going on a wild wisp chase after Vash had consumed her.

As Jhee approached the sleeping pair near the still, Chappy hurried over and blocked her. "Now wait a moment, Justicar, you have no cause to take that without a writ. I'm not responsible for what my patrons—"

Vash held up a hand. "Public health matter. Anything we take will be confidential."

Jhee cleaned out a bottle and gathered a sample from the still. They brought their collected samples to the hospital.

"Doctor, are you familiar with Tranquility Gold nectar wine?" Jhee asked.

"Why yes."

"I was wondering if we could administer some to Mirrei."

"I don't think it's a good idea to be giving home remedies to someone in her state. Her system is so weak. Any shock might prove too much."

"The curative benefits may not be a fish wives' tale. There's been legitimate research into it. Mirrei's own experiments and studies by the Imperial Academy have proved its genuine health benefits. A pharmaceutical company had already been making overtures to the abbey's clerics. Here, examine the data."

Jhee shoved the bio-slips and bio-film papers into the doctor's arms. "I'll take a look. But Tranquility Bridge's nectar is rare and expensive."

"We have a supply. Mirrei uses it in her orange tea and home healing draughts."

"We'd need a more sterile form."

Jhee held up another bio-film. "I found this article on how to produce a sterile sample of fermented nectar. We also have wild yeast culture samples."

Dr. Pike cast a glance at Vash for rescue. He delivered a summary of his findings.

"Yes. Yes. I'll read through the data," the doctor said.

"Thank you, doctor. Thank you."

~

The Trap

Jhee and the inquester sat in the darkened transport waiting for their quarry to arrive.

"So, do you think this will work?"

"I have full confidence this will work. In the excitement, I nearly forgot about how I first got involved in this matter, the mining supervisors death, the sickened miners, and the glitch mites. The key to catching the murderer is to also catch the mine saboteur. The incidents are linked by a desire to disrupt mining and wall operations. I think they were going to try another dry run at the street fair, but the riots canceled that. Their next chance was at the fundraiser. They may have sought to try again at the substation. If the data shell figures into that at all, they'll come back for it."

They had laid a trap by feeding a story to their major suspects.

"The inquester and I attempted to catch the killer when they tried to sabotage the telescope controls yesterday. They got away. However, they left a data shell in the console they used to hack into it. I have a sample of other incriminating code on another data shell from the substation. Once it arrives, I'll be able to compare the two and find out who amongst you was the last to use the satellite repositioning terminal to target the worksite with the EMP signal."

Jhee picked up her beef and goat cheese sandwich and took an enormous bite. She was eating so unhealthy without the others to scold her. Kanto would talk about if she gained weight it would ruin the lines of all his carefully made robes. Shep would say how she needed to slow down and pace herself and take the time to enjoy what she had already accomplished. What was the point of the comfortable life of mental exercise and fitness she put herself through if she would simply fail to do the work when it came to her body? Mirrei would weigh in on her choice of meat. Jhee had to let their opinions slide off her. She needed comfort food more than their approval now.

Around midnight, their waiting paid off. A slight, black-clad figure crept up to the observatory waving a conch light. An experienced burglar this wasn't. As the would-be burglar struggled loudly with the lock, Jhee and Inquester Paij opened the transport doors and crouched behind them. The inquester lined up her shot before she flipped on the transport headlights.

Ms. Levinia gasped when she saw them. "I can explain."

Inquester Paij closed the distance and subdued the woman with minimal fuss. "Spare us. I'm putting you under arrest for the murders of Oriel and Bastian."

"Wait, I had no reason to kill either of them."

"Why is that?" Ms. Levinia bit her lip. The inquester pushed her toward the transport. "Fine, say it to your advocate after a night of Imperial hospitality."

Ms. Levinia's eyes purpled with fear. "Ow, the restraints are too tight. Jail? I can't go to jail."

Jhee adjusted Ms. Levinia's restraints, so they were more comfortable. Jhee said in strategic sympathetic voice, "It's that or tell us everything this instant."

Ms. Levinia crouched toward Jhee. "Fine."

Inksy strode up with another meddlesome imperial writ held high. "We'll take it from here, locals."

Jhee snatched it and read it over. Everything seemed in order. Inquester Paij reluctantly released Ms. Levinia to the Squids' custody. More Inkertons rushed past them to secure the scene. She raised her face to the sky and contemplated the Grand Design and Divine Mechanism to calm her thoughts. They had been so close.

"Well, it was a game plan, Justicar. But if it's not Levinia, I don't think they're going to show now that storm Styrling's made landfall."

"Just give it a little more time, Inquester."

"Sorry. I'm calling it a night."

Jhee folded her hands inside her robes. What had she missed? She knew the murders and the worksite problems were connected. What had she overlooked?

"Unmake me," Jhee cursed. They walked out to the curb.

Perhaps she should head back to the hospital. Do as Kanto suggested: pray and spend what time remained with Mirrei while she could. Jhee opened her eyes when a nearby transport door slammed. She barely made out a figure cast in shadow by a water taxi's front lights paying from the curb. How fortuitous. The figure froze as she approached perhaps concerned Jhee meant harm. She squinted past the lights and held a hand to hail the taxi driver. A perturbation in the system struck Jhee, a misalignment she could not quite name.

Jhee walked toward the water taxi. A moment later, the gears of the Divine Mechanism aligned in her thoughts. Who would taxi here at this time of night? Jhee quickened her pace.

The figure at the taxicab fled. Drench. Jhee gave chase.

"Justicar!" the inquester yelled after her.

"It's them!"

Jhee continued without knowing if the inquester followed. The figure raced down the street towards the Stones footbridge. If they made it there, they could cut across to the plaza and get lost in the crowd.

The suspect sprinted up the iconic Fairgull Steps. Jhee cursed loudly. More stairs. Why did it always have to be stairs? This drench city. So busy was she lamenting the stairs, she did not realize the suspect had taken a different turn. Not towards the Stones and its bustling street and pub scene, but away from it and towards the bluffs.

They reached a chasm. The suspect leaped. Jhee went right up to the edge to gauge the distance. One look down made her head swim. The gap dropped to rocks and white surf. Jhee wheezed, grabbed her chest, and staggered back.

Try as she might she could not force herself to approach the edge. In the distance, the object of her pursuit rapidly receded. She backed away and attempted to make the leap blind. She stopped short of the edge again.

Storm Child. Storm Child. Not today. Not today.

The inquester caught up to her. Jhee remained there trembling. Somewhere as if through distant fog and waves, she heard Paij's voice.

"I'll see if I can figure out what taxi company that was and question the driver."

Jhee raised her face to the sky again. *Storm Child. Storm Child. Not today.*

19

THE RENT VEIL

~

More Questioning

Jhee sniffed and rubbed her eyes.

"Are you sure you are up to this?" the inquester asked.

"It's allergies. I'm sharp. I can do this."

"Maybe you should—"

"Inquester, I'm fine. Now, what are the facts? We have a disgraced engineer trying to redeem himself for his part in the Shield debacle. A contractor who knew something was amiss but couldn't prove it. A contractor who covered it up to hide his use of blackmail to get the contract. The ambassador with blackmail material of his own. Who had cause to kill both Ms. Oriel and Mr. Bastian? We have Mr. Bastian's as yet unidentified partner."

"Do you think Bastian knew what the partner had planned?"

"Perhaps. His obsession was such I'm not sure if he would have cared. We also have three key pieces of evidence. The proof of Vash meeting with the ambassador. The data Vash and Ms. Oriel were gathering which showed the locations of the Fresh Lung outbreaks and the connection to the substation. Mr. Bastian's filter design prototype and a map showing the substation locations."

It had become clear to Jhee there was some link between FLS and Miners' Lung. Mirrei had already hallucinated. Was a descent like Mr. Bastian's something Mirrei had to look forward to? Jhee had read all the literature she could. She trusted the arts of science, medicine, and arcana. Their confusion on the malady had her worried. She believed in that and the law to find proper solutions to people's problems and as long as they trusted and worked the system properly. Their virtual ignorance on a topic which turned out to be so close to her and relevant to her interests had her shaken.

Inquester Paij rocked back in her chair. "I think it's about time we get some of these folks back in for follow-ups. We have enough to see if it might shake something loose."

Jhee wasted no time once the first callback, Chapman, arrived, "What about you, Chapman? I knew I'd seen you at the fundraiser. You helped cater the event, so you could easily grab a uniform and pick up a tray. No one would even look twice at you."

"You're right I was there. The activists had to get in somehow."

"As someone in food service, you'd know about food handling and food-borne illnesses."

"I make killer crab puffs, but not the way you're thinking. The instant I saw the body, I ditched my uniform and left. I knew the Imps and Squids would look to blame fighters for the cause."

"That leaves you plenty of time before that to kill Mr. Bastian."

"But I didn't. Ask the serving staff. Ask their handlers. They do regular headcounts and staff searches. During one, they looked closer at my identification. They held me aside so IES agents could question me. I slipped away while they were otherwise occupied by damage control."

After a few more questions, they sent Chapman off, but told him to stay close. The shift chiefs confirmed some of his story.

"The Styrling duo could corroborate or disprove the rest, but Lethys's luck getting them to come in for questioning," Jhee said.

Inquester Paij leaned back and smiled. "I don't know. Let me worry about that."

They spoke with Ambassador Naiman next.

"Ambassador, you had motive because Mr. Bastian had linked you to the improper contract to build the Shield."

"I could care less about the wall. Or the coward who claims to be my mother. Her and that family. My concern is the workers being exploited by both the state and companies such as Styrling Staffing. It's a travesty. Men like my father who are stripped away from their homes and forced to serve vain, careless women like Lady Delphine. Do you really believe that nonsense about the staff being prisoners who saw the forbidden isles? You know how hard this place is to reach from the other continents."

"It was plenty easy for the barbarians to get here when they wanted to raid and destroy."

"Do you buy that swarms of Fire Folk are braving the ocean just to come harass us? They are not coming to us. We are going to them. That is the truth of it. The inquester knows, don't you? The Galleon's a drenched tomb, a testament not of faith or resilience but hate like the wall."

Jhee rubbed her eyes. "Please, Ambassador, you must tell me what you know at once. My understanding and my patience are at an end. I'm about to get not so nice. I understand your grievance against Lady Delphine. Believe me, I do. But bribery, blackmail? Is that any way for a man of the waves to behave? You should set the example for others not flouting it."

"Like the example the noble Water Folk set."

Jhee tucked her hands in her sleeves. "It is within the Makers' Design for us to strive to improve ourselves and others or else be remade."

"In the Water Folk's image, via conquest. We are not an example. If anything, we proved their point. We cast out the Air Folk and Land Folk, for being too violent. Look at us, we are press-ganging their children into service. Are we any better? Look at 'disasters' like the Gray Galleon. Is that noble, and decent of us? Is that behavior worthy of the Makers' Criterions as we like to call ourselves?"

"Folk have a right to protect the sovereignty of their lands by any means necessary. We do it, the Fire Folk do it, even the Other folk."

Weariness then resolve played across Ambassador Naiman's features. "By any means necessary? Do you hear yourself? To what end? Total control over the Water Folk. It helps them control you not the Fire Folk. Don't be so naïve, Justicar."

A resolve of Jhee's own overtook her. "What do you want me to say, Ambassador? We're hypocritical bigots, me included? Fine, we are. What now?"

"That's always the question. I wish everyone would admit it as easily as you did."

"Then what? How do we move forward? Don't you think I wish I could take a pill or discover a cypher that would make all my conflicted feelings about

Fire Folk go away or undo the horrible acts I countenanced as a Water Folk because of them. Tell me what to do, and I'll do it."

With the admission from Jhee, the ambassador's posture relaxed. "I wish I had the answers for you. I initially took up the wave coif searching for answers of my own."

Jhee re-centered with silent prayer and concealed finger-cyphering exercises. She had lost control of the conversation. In the process, she had created an opening with which she could draw more information from Ambassador Naiman.

"The off-world expeditions were misguided, wrong. But separating ourselves from the Other Folk via the Shield is different," Jhee said and pivoted to the immediate matter. "Time is scarce. I need to know why were you in the closed wing."

The ambassador acknowledged the impasse and accepted the topic shift with a calm response, "Because I was working with Advocate Farkhande to help the Fire Folk escape their contracts. They're made to sign onerous agreements tantamount to indenture. They charge them for food and lodging. And get them so far in debt they can never get out. Workers then often will send money to other relatives. I know because me and my father did everything we could to not wind up like that. Before I took the coif, I've worked as a cleaner, drove a taxi, and did cooking and maintenance. They will never see the end of service to Styrling. You should look over some of their contracts. It's a virtual prison sentence."

"I will, Ambassador. I will."

Jhee hung her head. She thought about the staff at the observatory fundraiser and the galleon. She suspected as much, and she had turned the other way. Jhee would do so no longer. "I still have to ask you for corroboration of your whereabouts and who you were with."

"I was meeting with my folk smuggling contact. They may not back me up, given their line of work and their cultural traditions."

"You book them passage with Water Nomads."

Ambassador Naiman nodded.

Jhee took down the details. She and the inquester proceeded with their follow-up interviews. They were soon treated to another visit from Sianna and Inksy.

"Right on time," the inquester said. "I'd figure this would get their attention."

Jhee admired the inquester's ploy. If she had tried to call in Sianna and Inksy directly, they likely would have refused or stalled.

"Inksy and Sianna, you keep two floating to the top like dead fish. What were you doing at the mine site?"

"Same as you, investigating. Styrling Mining had leased it from Lady Delphine. But we've been plagued by accidents and equipment failures."

"The same for Ms. Oriel's offices at the clinic and the observatory?"

Sianna looked taken aback. "Styrling Mines is known for its great philanthropic contributions to many causes. As you can attest, she could charm the skin off a sea otter."

Jhee frowned, while Sianna looked smug.

A Sympathetic Ear

The Styrling pair substantiated Chapman's claim, which also explained their movements. They claimed not to have enough time to debunk his disguise but provided no other helpful details. The inquester motioned Jhee aside.

"I arranged for Levinia to be kept in temporary holding. I'll keep our friends here."

"While I go have a chat with her."

The inquester nodded and slipped Jhee an earpiece. After having let Ms. Levinia contemplate her accommodations for a few hours, she appeared on the verge of mania. Again, she huddled against Jhee for support.

"You said you had no reason to kill Ms. Oriel or Mr. Bastian. You need to tell us the full details of why you and Ms. Oriel were arguing."

"We resolved it."

"That's not what witnesses said. They said you and she parted loudly and angrily."

"Oriel caught up to me later, and she said I was right. The restoration project was mine. She had found an even grander use for her talents. She said she would credit me for the restoration as long as I kept quiet about her sideline."

"Then why were you skulking about?"

"Because I knew you'd find my fingerprints all over the chandelier winch and data shell with the backdoor program I implanted. I wanted to remove the traces of my break-in before anyone found out I did it."

"Why implant it at all?"

"To gather intel for the exposure piece. Bastian and I whipped up a means to spy on Oriel. Before Oriel and I had calmed our waters, I thought publicizing the Friends of the Observatory and the Breath of the Deep impropriety was my only means to finally get the recognition I deserved. The journalist had started to get impatient. Xe suspected I had perhaps oversold how big the scandal was and what I knew. Bastian used my credentials, and we installed a means to monitor the observatory's restricted feeds from a remote location."

"You wanted to embarrass or discredit her. Why not just kick her out?"

"The foundations most influential members viewed her like unto a Miracle Maker. She turned the benefit Bastian and I planned into a fundraiser associated with the Gray Galleon which drew the protesters and remade it into a spectacle. Oriel was taking credit for the restoration projects, selling exclusive access. I located the original chandelier in storage and spent years getting the funding together to restore it and the observatory. I worked and slaved over it. Oriel was just supposed to be the mistress of ceremonies. Instead, she swoops in at the last moment to take the accolades and line her pockets. I wanted to find some proof. I just wanted her to share credit like she promised she would. But I swear I didn't kill her or Bastian. I did go to her office to gather data. Then I heard them on the landing. They argued. It was about a woman I think then Oriel left. Before she did, she said something like 'I know what you've been up to and who with.' I thought she had learned about me and Bastian. When they left, I exited as fast as I could. Next I know, they find Bastian dead hanging from my life's work."

"I witnessed the exchange. There's no way you could have heard what they discussed."

Ms. Levinia hunched and gave a sheepish expression. "Arcane eavesdropping."

Jhee pursed her lips. "Do you have any corroboration of your whereabouts?"

"Afterward, I got drunk and went to record voice-overs for the observatory tours. I may have left an unflattering drawing on the board complaining about the restoration and recorded a few sarcastic messages. They may have a time stamp. I'd also started complaining to a journalist. Xe told me xe was a covert exposure journalist working on a shocking scandal. Xe's interviewed me several times about the observatory. I used to meet hir at a boathouse at the Delphines."

"Where is xe?"

"I don't know. After I spilled my guts in more ways than one, I woke up in the boathouse. I haven't seen hir since."

Jhee slipped back to the interrogations. She tapped her ear and nodded to confirm she recorded her exchange with Ms. Levinia. The inquester had moved on with questioning.

"I object to their presence here." Advocate Farkhande pointed at Sianna and Inksy. "I have a matter before the courts in which they are explicitly named. We wouldn't want this case or that tainted by impropriety or allegations of intimidation."

Sianna ran her tongue along the inside of her mouth. "Of course."

Sianna and Inksy bundled out.

"That includes watching from the side room or accessing the footage," the advocate called. "My team and I will be second-checking."

Jhee and the inquester did their best to appear disinterested.

Advocate Farkhande grinned at them. "Tell me you haven't always wanted to do that. You may proceed."

"Tell me, Advocate, how do you explain your name on these 'after hours' itineraries?" Jhee asked.

"I was there but only acting as an intermediary on behalf of those who wished to see the artifacts."

"Can you tell us who?" the inquester asked.

"Confidentiality oaths apply. Since you have the itineraries, I'm surprised you haven't deduced who on your own."

"Our records showed you called Oriel just before Bastian's murder."

"Making sure we were on the same sea about the Galleon Wing. Even for private viewings."

"And the green corrosion on your robe?" Jhee asked.

"I saw that detestable vizier sneak in the Galleon Wing. I thought perhaps Oriel had ignored our understanding. It turned out to be him and that quirky Queenie woman."

"Did you overhear their conversation?"

"Something about building permits."

"Are you sure?"

"How could I be wrong about something so banal when the wisps have so much more interesting things to say?" Advocate Farkhande paused as if listening. "The eye of the drake knows. The wisps have something they want you to see. All you have to do is open your eyes and look."

"Farkhande, enough with the wisps already," Paij said.

"Fine. Let us speak of more relevant details, perhaps of cures hiding in the wrong hands. Curing people who weren't sick is hardly profitable."

"No, it isn't. Curing sick people on the other hand."

Advocate Farkhande gave a bittersweet smile at Jhee's realization. "Now, the coverings are falling from your eyes, Justicar. When it's the wretched and destitute being hurt, no one cares as much. If it is as you say Justicar, how much would it have cost to implement the fix once they found out? How long did they know how to fix it? Someone had been too cheap or callous to implement the solution, while all those people were sick or dying."

Jhee finished for her, "On the other hand, make the right people ill, and they'll be clamoring for the cure."

"What if Styrling or MANTEL wanted to hoard the cure?"

The inquester scoffed. "It's the oldest conspiracy theory in the book that the powerful have the cure for a bunch of diseases and are just keeping it for themselves."

"Is it?" the advocate asked. "I can't tell you anymore. Either charge me or let me go."

"You can go, but—"

"Don't go far. Justicar, the wisps want you to keep going. Balance the scales. Close the circle."

The advocate left humming. The shimmer remained a moment after her. Jhee's esca and arm sigil tingled.

"Justicar, I don't know. Everyone's stories pass inspection," the inquester said, her voice breaking Jhee's fascination with whatever forces followed the advocate.

Jhee swore and touched her chin. Another dead end and she was nowhere near finding the murderer or helping Mirrei. What to do now? Where else did she turn? "Think. Think. Who else had reason to do so and why?"

"Perhaps you need to wind it back a bit."

"I'll wind it back once I've found the killer and Mirrei is cured." Jhee scowled at the inquester. The inquester's look of affront said it all. Jhee sighed. "I apologize, Inquester. This case has gotten too personal for me."

"Which is why I think you need to go back and see your family. Spend some time with them and get your head on straight."

"Yes. Yes," Jhee said. She rubbed at her burning, irritated eyes. First, she should go back to the villa and clean herself up and get some eye drops. It would not do for the others to see her in such a state. She had to project strength for them. They needed her. If she panicked, they would panic.

The Fallen Scales

"The eye of the drake knows. The wisps have something they want you to see. All you have to do is open your eyes and look.... Balance the scales. Close the circle."

Jhee went back to the villa and took a shower and put on a fresh change of clothes. She picked up a few things for Kanto and Shep as well. Advocate Farkhande's cryptic words nagged at her all the way back to the hospital.

Not quietly enough, Jhee stole into Mirrei's room. Shep awoke. His one good eye bright gold and the other much dimmer watched her in the dark. Kanto slept in a chair beside him. Jhee placed a finger to her lips. Shep went to her, and they embraced.

"Any change?" Jhee whispered.

Shep shook his head. Kanto's cherished, recently restored music box rested lightly in his lap. Jhee moved it to Mirrei's bedside table as a precaution. Kanto stirred. He gestured for her to wind it. She opened and cranked it back into working condition. The simple tinny song played in the darkened room, as the three of them watched eerily still Mirrei. The music box's melody drowned out the machines monitoring Mirrei's vital signs. Kanto took Jhee's hand and gave it a squeeze.

Jhee awoke to find Mirrei's doctor standing over her. With her head, she signaled Jhee should join her out in the hall. Vash stood by quietly.

The doctor cleared her throat. "Vash walked me through the clinic's research and what you showed me. Her immune system is compromised. You also said it involves another device."

"A standalone synchronator that doesn't need an artificer or stanchions."

"If we could get the device to examine it and figure out what frequency it's operating on, we might develop something that might help Mirrei without too much risk. Her research was thorough."

"I know. She was a conscientious and proper student. I expected nothing less from her work."

"Our experiments on cultures in the lab showed promise. However, when we administered the treatment to her. It barely made a difference. She responded well enough at first to the nectar treatment, but it's like her immune system is under assault and the nectar can't keep up. The most optimistic thing I could say about the nectar is that it doesn't hurt."

Back in the room, Kanto and Shep had awakened and pulled over the wheeled table with a turtle hidden-image puzzle over to Mirrei's bedside. Kanto also had the gossip sites open on his conch. "You see that? That's why siring should be done by contract. Official and legally binding. Good contracts make good sires. The norms and standards are you stay away unless contracted again, but you get the unscrupulous sire or dame who attempts to profit after they have rendered their services," Kanto finished.

The puzzle comprised a turtle painted on a tray and a colored see-through shell broken up into pieces. Jhee picked up a piece and searched for where it fit. As participants assembled the colored lens, the shell revealed a new image. She tried to wrap her head around what they had created. It wasn't until she rotated the puzzle did it make sense. She had been looking at it all wrong. Like everyone did with Mr. Bastian. Somehow, she was not seeing the whole image of the man.

Jhee located Vash in one lab desperately working on a cure. As a major donor to the hospital, Lady Delphine had him granted temporary privileges as a lab assistant. So long as he had the supervision of a credentialed doctor and did not treat or get directly involved with any patients' care, he could use their facilities.

"Any progress?"

Vash shook his head. "The poisoned squelch theory is consistent with our findings, though. We've been testing every sample we could get our hands on."

"What if we're looking at this all wrong?"

The doctor helping Vash chimed in, "How do you mean?"

"What if Mr. Bastian wanted redemption, not revenge? What if he wasn't trying to poison the miners? Maybe he wasn't trying to harm the mine personnel but help them by inoculating them against MLD."

"We've already concluded the squelch might have been him testing delivery methods," Vash said.

The doctor nodded. "Either their immune systems were too far gone. Or, if the solution meant to respond to the radiation with a counter wave. If the wave was out of phase, instead of making it better it made it worse."

"The other mystery though was why were all these people's immune systems compromised. There was no rhyme or reason. Oriel and I started tracking their connections and various contacts. We started tracking where everyone was from. Our data was on those data shells. A pattern started to emerge. Yes, it's true most Fresh Lung Sufferers came from the Outer Reaches. But not all of them came from regions with saltier water. We overlaid the map of the Fresh Lung outbreaks and the water salinity tables. They did not match up. When we reached a dead end on our own, Oriel threw herself into the fund raising. She wanted to surprise Bastian. Instead of a party, what if she got extra funding for cure research? Bastian had similar renderings at his place. Except he had a map of all the Shield substations and pylons. Those corresponded with the Fresh Lung outbreaks on a nearly one-to-one basis."

"The Shield—the wall is causing Fresh Lung Syndrome," Jhee said

"The Shield is compromising people's immune systems."

The Rending of the Curtain

The Storm Shield, the wall, was the death wall its detractors had proclaimed.

Jhee needed to sit. The previous governess, an aggressive proponent and strong supporter of the Shield, spent a large amount of time touring and inspecting the facilities and construction sites. She had also died of FLS.

Jhee thought about Mirrei's family home. It had been right by the Shield. Jhee's family lived not only at higher elevations but more inland. The lavish homes on the beach her family had eschewed as the sea took its due. That was the key. Mirrei had grown up right next to the Shield. It also explained why she did seem to get better when she stayed at Jhee's house. She had also started getting better when they headed for the capital. She suspected Miramar had been doing something to the poor girl, or it was just pure happiness at being free.

Then Jhee had the yacht captain sail closer to the wall, and Mirrei took ill once again. Also, after Kanto and Mirrei had sneaked off to the refugee camps on Torilsisle.

Mirrei got better once again here in Galleon City about as far away from the wall as one could get. Except for the substation. The substation.

How close was too close to the substation? Only Mirrei was inside for any length of time. What had happened in the meantime to fell them all at once? The crowd dispersion device. There was still something Jhee was missing, some key to the puzzle.

Jhee concentrated on the recordings of Mr. Bastian's properties while dissecting aspects of their extended conversation at the fundraiser. He was the engineer who screwed up the Shield. He was obsessed with redeeming himself and waking people up. The synchronator would show them what the Shield did. No, not reveal what the Shield did. Mr. Bastian wanted redemption. Olipo, the name of a Lesser Maker recognized by Mechanism, was scrawled in block letters across one schematic. Olipo sometimes went by the title "The Tinkerer" or "Fixer." The Fix. A cure.

Surely curing people who weren't sick wouldn't do anything. No, it wouldn't. Curing sick people would. The synchronator. It could not just heal people but make them sick. The synchronator could have stopped the Fresh Lung Syndrome. Someone had been too cheap or careless to buy the fix, and all those people were sick or dying. She was weary of the fight with the Other Folk. If the authorities had only told them, Jhee might have gladly accepted the risks. Many of them were. Many of them would.

They could have protected themselves. Moved themselves away from the pylons and the barrier itself. Correction: those with enough means, like her, could have. For as many refugees as there were, how many had stayed behind? Because they would not or could not leave.

Jhee met with Mirrei's doctor and hid her hands in her robes as she spoke her speculation aloud. "Doctor, is it possible she is being bombarded with radiation?"

"Well, we shielded her from most forms of radiation and electromagnetics, and it helped. She responded very well to the isolated environment. However, we have yet to identify the specific frequencies doing the most damage. If this is indeed caused by the Shield or substation like you say it is, they are putting out powerful, broad-spectrum signals designed to penetrate through everything. Nothing we have here can counteract it for long without knowing specifically which frequencies to block."

"It's not enough to block the signal you need to send the counter wave."

Doctor Pike nodded. "You said you saw plans for a device? It would help if we had access to that device or the Shield technology itself. We may be able to synthesize something from the nectar and the device."

"The synchronator? That's what I dubbed it."

"We need to do tests. We can buy some time by leaving Mirrei in a medically induced coma. I don't want to try an unproven treatment on her without a minimum of testing. For that though, I will need the inducement device to test cures against."

"The Shield tech is classified, state secret."

"Without it, I don't think we can treat her. Keep in mind however, the hospital has legal obligations and cannot be found in possession of or use any restricted devices or any improperly acquired equipment."

Jhee folded her hands inside her robes. Mr. Bastian's Shield technology synchronator might fulfill those requirements. He had developed it on his own while volunteering at the clinic. "Don't worry, doctor. I will get you what you need. With Mr. Bastian's schematics, I can commission a new synchronator or build the drenched device myself if I must."

"We may not have that kind of time."

"Also, we run the risk he may have modified the designs in the meantime. We need the working prototype."

Jhee returned to find Ambassador Naiman saying devotions with Kanto and Shep. The ambassador excused himself. She cast her eyes to the floor. "I have to leave again. I'm on the trail of something that could help Mirrei."

"Jhee," Shep said. His pale, gold eye trained on her.

Kanto pursed his lips, tears streaming down his face.

Jhee rushed to head off their objections. "I know what you're going to say, 'What if it doesn't? What if you are wasting precious moments you could spend with her?' It's a possible treatment. It might cure her. I have to try."

Jhee turned to leave.

"Are we allowed no say before you leave?" Kanto asked. He cranked the music box. "Do you know how this got broken?"

Jhee held her tongue. He faced Mirrei and set it on the bedside stand.

"I used to play this for my mamere. One day she lashed out at me and struck it from my hands. She dashed it to smithereens. Every craftsman said it was irreparable. But you, Jhee, you fixed it. I don't care what it is, Jhee, or what you must do to get it. If there is a cure for Mirrei, find it."

"I will."

Kanto spoke without turning, "You won't come back without it?"

"No."

Shep put an arm about Kanto's shoulders. "Do what you must, Jhee. In the meantime, Kanto and I will address our pleas to other powers."

He and Shep knelt by Mirrei's bedside and raised their hands in supplication.

"I swear," Jhee said.

20

RACE FOR TIME

~

A New Search

Jhee pounded on the door at Lady Delphine's house. The servant answered.

"Justicar, how may I help you?"

"I need to speak to Vash. Is he here?"

"One moment, mum."

A groggy Vash descended the stairs, rubbing his eyes. "My lady, what's happened?"

"I need to access the clinic's patient records." As she spoke to Vash, she thumbed through the various crime scene images on her conch. Vash stared at her. "Examine the patient records from the clinic."

"Justicar, you know I can't. The medical ethics oaths I swore—"

"Apply to a valid doctor, not you. I don't need personal or specific information. I just need you to check your records. It's important. It might save Mirrei's life."

"As you said, I'm not a valid doctor. I've been suspended and no longer have access to the clinic's records."

"But you have personal records, don't you? Also, if I understand it correctly, you're suspended pending medical review and have limited access to aid in your defense."

Vash pulled out his conch. "The best I can do is check the records myself. But it will be the most basic information and no patient identifying information."

"That's fine. That should be all I need."

"What am I looking for?"

"Any case of Fresh Lung remission." Shock anchored Vash to the spot. "Now, please. Yav-yav."

Jhee took her time on each image. The suspicion she had seen the synchronator prototype when they searched Mr. Bastian's storage workshop had a hold to her. Sometimes the best way to hide something was in plain sight. Where might one hide a large data crystal? Among other crystals. The observatory's mineral rock collection or the chandelier, the mines.

Vash ran a few searches. "That's right. We had a few cases. Especially recently, we thought we had misdiagnosed them. I remember this one in particular."

Jhee tried to seize the conch. Vash pulled away. "Forgive me. Who was the volunteer who worked with them when they came in?"

"Allow me to check the shift logs." Vash did more searching and scrolling. "Bastian was on duty or had some contact with all of them. My lady, what's this about?"

"I think Mr. Bastian had discovered a way to treat or cure Fresh Lung Syndrome and he was using your clinic to test it out on patients."

"My word."

"If we could find the treatment he was using, we might use it to treat Mirrei."

While Vash continued his search, Jhee scoured her record of Mr. Bastian's experiment notes for hints about his treatment methods. He referred to the silver or sparkling eyes. It may have been a code in case his notes fell into the wrong hands. Was it mechanical or a substance? At last, she found references to a silver eye housing. She viewed the images of Mr. Bastian's apartment walls full of not only formulas, but schematics. If sabotage was not his goal, then what were the schematics? The treatment must be based around a device.

Jhee compared the footage of the apartment, the workshop. What was it? There was something here. She did not know for sure what she sought, an item out of place, a commonality between the two locations. An object missing which should be there would be the hardest to notice.

Because of Jhee's captures not being the highest quality, the process was slow going and headache-inducing. If Mr. Bastian had come up with apparatus to arrest the effects of the Shield, then what was he doing at the Observatory? What was he up to? Jhee pored over Mr. Bastian's obsessive scribblings. Now, she saw it; several references to some device called a synchronator. Jhee needed to examine the originals. She contacted the inquester. "The last time you and I checked the clinic records we'd been looking for deaths. Don't you see? We had it backwards. Do you still have the evidence we collected from the hidden storage unit in the evidence room?"

"Justicar, I hate to tell you this. Inkertons showed up with an Imperial writ."

Jhee felt punched. She hoped the inquester was not about to say what she thought she would say.

"They've confiscated Bastian's research equipment and his notes."

Jhee expelled a breath and collapsed down hard on the desk. Mirrei's cure. Their last, best hope for one.

Blessed be the First Makers. They who created the waters. Know the waters. Trust the waters.

The Race

Jhee recited several litanies to the First Makers and Lesser Makers. Then she switched to listing statues to calm her Maker within.

"Justicar? You still there?"

"A list," Jhee said. "They needed to have provided a detailed confiscation writ. Do you have it?"

"I can get it. Hold on. Transmitting."

As she read through the confiscation log, she paced. Nothing matched what she sought. The clicking her thought processes did to show a misalignment in the system began.

"Meet me at the warehouse."

The clicking continued as she and Paij met at the warehouse. "Something's not adding up and my Maker within is screaming at me. May I see an inventory of the workshop or do you have sensor suit footage I can view?"

"I can do both. I'll collate the lists. You review the footage." Paij operated her sleeve controls then pulled a microcrystal from her sensor suit collar and handed it to Jhee.

Jhee attached the microcrystal to her conch and they both delved into their assigned tasks.

"Got it," Paij said after a moment.

"I may have as well. Here. Look." Jhee squinted at the controls and scrubbed the scene backward. "What's that on the worktable?"

"Don't know. Nothing like that is on either list. Let me access that footage we found on the scene."

Jhee played the footage Bastian took alongside the footage of her and Paij collecting evidence.

"There. You see it?"

"Yep," the inquester said. "The lists of confiscated evidence don't match ours either."

"Someone else got there before Inkerton did."

"It must have been the killer."

"But why would the killer take all that stuff? It's of no use to them."

"No use if you want to make a profit, but what else could they use the data for?"

"Access to the substation. Our friends are chasing wisps into whirlpools."

The inquester rocked back on her heels. "Bastian found a way to transmit his fix and his cure to the Shield substations via an access terminal or pylon. But his discovery could just as easily transmit malicious code to all the substations and bring down the wall. I suspect Bastian had been duped by his accomplice."

"Ms. Oriel suspected Mr. Bastian of having an affair and followed him and found the storage locker."

"Or realized he had been using the clinic patients as test beds. Remember what Oriel said, 'I know what you've been up to and who with.' Either way, she located the storage locker. After Bastian's death, she puts two and two together with the map and shift logs and returns to the storage locker. She may have surprised the killer."

"They kill her and hear someone coming and have to get rid of the body quick. They leave the data behind to dispose of the body. Before they can come back, we've found it and sealed it off."

"Precisely. The killer though still has a mission to complete."

"Bring down the Shield."

"This may be their last chance before the security exploits are fixed."

"We find the killer. We find Mirrei's cure."

"Let's go. I'll drive," the inquester said.

Later at a lot overlooking the substation, Jhee regarded the impressive panorama with detachment. She attempted to marshal the Prime Forces within her while Paij had an animated conversation on her conch. Paij. When had Jhee began to regard the woman so informally?

The inquester slammed her conch down on the dashboard. "Inkerton Enforcement Services and their lawyers are stonewalling. They'll be no help."

"Did you tell them we suspect someone might try to sabotage the Shield?"

"I told them. They just don't care. They say they'll handle it."

"Of all the times to be playing politics! Don't they know people's lives are at stake?"

"Maybe you should sit this one out, Justicar. I can handle this. You go be with your family."

"I'm of more use here. I can't do anything for Mirrei in the hospital. But this, this might be her cure."

"If you say so."

"Where would they go?"

"Their real aim."

"The substation."

"I'm on it. I'll contact the courts for Imperial entrance orders."

"And I'll see what I can do as well, Inquester. I'll inquire if any of my judicial contacts will issue us one as well."

Jhee and Inquester grabbed their conchs. Jhee soon reached the end of her most likely prospects. Now, she had to use her favor lists if she wanted that order.

The inquester gripped her conch. Her clenched teeth spoke of her weighing if she should hurl it. "Looks like we must go rogue on this one. Inkerton Enforcement's lawyers filed an emergency injunction preventing us entry into the substation or within a hundred feet."

"I'll call in a few favors."

"Maybe we don't have to enter. Maybe we can do it from here."

"What do you mean, Inquester?"

"I mean we have you. You're an artificer. All the relay station is, is just that: a relay station. You say you can do magic detection or whatever. Can't you just whip up something like the ASU team has? We wouldn't even have to enter the substation. We set up a perimeter and triangulate."

"Not at this scale. That's not how arcana works...." Jhee took in the view before her again. They had a whole city full of stanchions in the form of the defense grid pylons. Jhee began going over possibilities. Could she combine a method like her eavesdropping formulation with a synchronance perimeter made from the pylons? "You might have the right of it. But I won't be able to pinpoint an exact location."

"We don't need one. We just need to get close enough and do it the mundane way. The imperators will set up a perimeter. Then we can trap this murderer."

~

The Gyro

"Inquester do you have a light flight vehicle, preferably a stealthy one?"

"I have something better. Come on."

Back at the evidence warehouse, Inquester Paij brought her to vehicle depot next door.

"You'll love this," the inquester said and slammed the button to open the hangar doors.

The doors revealed a small, three impeller, wind arcana gyrocopter.

"Blessed be the First Makers," Jhee said.

"We seized it in a raid," Inquester Paij said. "Can you make it work?"

"Can I ever." Jhee rushed over. As she ran her fingers over smooth, white composite material, she familiarized herself with its design, controls, and operations.

Despite its name, the gyro maneuvered as smooth as silk. Jhee barely had to spend any mind share fighting the internal stabilizers, unlike the models she had flown in the service. They approached the tines like the quiet before the storm. Thunder and lightning surrounded the clear waterspout towers. Between them, the deadly, relay station presented itself as so benign and innocuous. Once, Jhee had been so proud and amazed by the heart of the defense grid as a display of Water Folk cleverness and ingenuity. Now, what amazed her were the costs and the untold victims of their arrogance and hubris. Jhee turned away and thought of Mirrei and Shep. He was the real reason she had such high hopes for the Shield. Everything that had happened to him during his service to the empire. All to protect themselves from the Fire Folk. She had been so eager. She had hoped for something, anything to prevent that kind of carnage again. But was the wall so much better? Not that she could tell. Had they just traded one evil for another?

Jhee and the inquester touched down outside the injunction's radius at a good vantage point with which to cast their data net. If the killer so much as gave a cross look to the data stream, they would know. They had to bide their time and wait. Jhee thought about Mirrei lying there in that bed. What was she thinking? Was she dreaming? Jhee's scientific training said she wasn't. A coma was unconsciousness, a state where no conscious activity took place or activities such as dreams. Jhee did not like Mirrei just lying there surrounded by darkness in an abyss or nether realm from which there was no escape. She needed to get this cure. She wanted to see Mirrei laugh and embroider and do all the things a young woman her age should even if it was without her.

Jhee shook loose the morbid thoughts. There would be time enough for that later once Mirrei was back on her feet. She could already see her bright, smiling face. Beaming full of joy. That's the way she wanted to think of Mirrei. That's the way she wanted to think of Mai. Not as some cold bloated corpse beneath the sea.

"What happened back there at the Fairgull chasm?" Inquester Paij asked. "You let them get away."

"The redactions to my service record aren't what you think. My family had enough influence to have certain embarrassing aspects hidden. I was in the intelligence pool because they couldn't trust me on a ship. Vizier Jeja, on the other hand, was an even larger force of nature than I depicted. In 'Dispatches from Arrow Point,' portraying myself as on par with my mentor was wishful thinking on my part. Much of those stories were."

"Fish flakes," the inquester sad. "I told you I know what a place like your gentlewoman's club is. I also know they're not in the habit of welcoming military disgraces. Couldn't trust you on a ship, but your flying was calm pool. You don't want to tell me that's fine, but don't feed me a load of fish food."

"Nevertheless, I assure you, Inquester—"

Jhee's skin tingled then her makeshift detector pinged. Jhee straightened up. Something had disturbed the relay network. She engaged the gears of arcana within her. She became a conduit for the prime forces of the Divine

Mechanism to work through her. Like the pieces of a magnificent clockwork, she traced a pathway through the system to achieve her goal.

The inquester set down her kolal. "That's it?"

"Someone's tampering with the tower security. It'll take me a few minutes to triangulate." Jhee would have preferred a full grid. But with the time and resources at her disposal, she had had to settle for a basic triangulation system which only allowed her to be so accurate regarding the location of the saboteur.

Jhee closed her eyes and stroked the waves of air and the waters coming at her. She circled to divine the direction where the signal was the strongest. She continued to spin around.

Jhee and the inspector hopped out of their aircraft. Jhee pointed her conch in the direction and watched the beeping on her screen. Someone was definitely trying to access the relay station's terminal. It might take a while if they were not skilled with programming. Mr. Bastian had done the programming and may not have been able to walk the accomplice entirely through the process of how to use and upload the code to the substation's systems. So, they would have extra time to track the person attempting to do the sabotage.

"Thank you for how understanding you've been, Inquester."

"Let only those whose feet have never been wet lecture someone else on how to keep theirs dry."

"Wet feet. Wet hem. Clean hems."

"We've assumed everyone has been getting the rose dust from somewhere they've been. What if it's from how they got there?"

"The water taxi."

The inquester palmed her esca. "Who else would have an excuse to know and meet with all the players."

"They could also have brought people like the ambassador to someplace dry."

"So, it has to be in a cab. What cab company?"

"Do we have Mr. Bastian's financial records still? Remember he had all those charges from the same water taxi service. Can we get an emergency order to look into the ambassador's finances?"

"I might. If you've got any favors left, I'd call them in too."

Jhee wracked her brain for details about the encounter at the observatory with the taxi and the killer. The odd water taxi at the fundraiser sprung to mind, followed by the taxi at the sight of their first trap again. The door. Its window had been open. The patron had been reaching inside for something from the front seat. Though the taxi had been lit and running, the driver's seat was empty.

Jhee went over the events at the fundraiser again. She did not want a repeat of the myopia at Tranquility Bridge which put her family in danger.

The murderer had already tried their sabotage at the observatory and the substation. Those places would have heightened security. Additionally, as she constructed her detector, she learned not every pylon had active access terminals. That left limited places for them to go for another attempt. What else was part of the defense grid and not on total lockdown?

They left their vantage to head in the direction the detector pointed. After a while the signal switched from one active pylon to the next. Then another. By the fourth, Jhee deduced where the path of pylons led. She gazed at the structures towering over the city and staring right at her.

The inquester traced her eyeline. "Oh, no. You know we can't go anywhere near—"

"You know this is our only chance. We have to get the killer before Styrling does."

They took an underground shortcut to head their quarry off.

All that remained now was to wait. Exhausted, Jhee found a darkened vantage near the bank of switches and dozed off. A rustling awoke her sometime later. A technician tried his access signet against the maintenance hatch.

Jhee hit the activator for the safety lockdown. The set of blast doors between the tines sealed shut as Jhee and the inquester sprung their trap. Jhee squinted into the dim light as recognition dawned—recognition, but not surprise. "You can do away with that ridiculous disguise. It's over."

21

THE RACE CONTINUED

~

Runway

Ambassador Naiman paused and removed his wig and cap. "How did you know?"

"Clean hems," Jhee said. "The skiff way was soaked because a mix-up triggered the lawn sprinklers. Everyone's hems got dirty."

"Except mine."

"You must have arrived via a different way. My mind also kept coming back to how did the killer know we were going back to the secret workshop to get there ahead of us and Inkerton."

The ambassador nodded and lowered the zipper on his coveralls. "Drench. I'm sorry."

"You were there to provide comfort to my family. Bright Harmony invited you."

"I did not mean to abuse my authority. I was there to help and comfort you and yours. After I had gone for kolal, and when I came back, I saw you consulting with Vash and a doctor. I'd also seen you and the investigator talking."

"So, you hid and listened in."

"Just so. How are you doing, Justicar?"

"To be honest, Ambassador, not well. It could have something to do with my spouse being about to die because of your foolishness."

"Sorry, I did not mean to expose her or any of them. Maybe Chappy. I've had to live my whole life with the activists thinking they are better than me, questioning my loyalty because I want our people to have a decent education and jobs."

"My wife is dying. Do you understand that? She's *dying*, and that device you stole might be the only option that can cure her. I don't intend to stand by and watch that happen without first going through you to prevent it."

The ambassador raised a conch and pressed an icon. The passageway doors opened. He dashed through then re-activated the blast door system. He progressed several airlocks ahead of Jhee and the inquester before they closed the bulkheads again. "I'm afraid I can't return it, Justicar. I'm trying to prevent a hundred, a thousand Star Mirrors. So, I must stop the wall. I must bring it down."

Inquester Paij placed the cuff of her Sensor Suit against the panel. "The override function will take time to counter. Keep him talking if you can."

Jhee moved next to the door. "I'm afraid I care about only one Star Mirror right now. I'm thin on patience and tolerance about now. The inquester here will arrest you. But first, I need you to turn over Mr. Bastian's prototype synchronator right now."

The bulkhead opened. Jhee drew air to burst herself through before the system locked them again. Likewise, the ambassador had advanced another chamber. The inquester gritted her teeth from a chamber behind Jhee before going to work with the Sensor Suit again.

"Please, Justicar, I'm appealing to your sense of All Folk solidarity. We need to stop this wall. You've seen the costs. If it's allowed to stabilize, there's no telling the amount of devastation it can wreak."

"It's wreaking plenty of havoc in its unfinished state. What of all those poor people near the relay station who are already suffering? The device you have can allow it to fix the victims. Many of whose lives you tried to improve in other ways."

The bulkhead opened again. Jhee narrowed the chamber gap between her and the ambassador, but Inquester Paij remained stuck another chamber farther behind.

"You sound like Bastian. He couldn't see the bigger picture just like you. It's not about fixing the wall. The wall can't be fixed. It has to be blown apart wind by wind and drop by drop. Didn't that galleon tell you it's folly for the Water Folk to recapture the past? The Other Folk are here to stay now. We should welcome them and make our peace with them."

"Some of us have tried and perhaps we will once they are ready and are civilized."

"Like my mother? I had to see her. I stayed under her roof. Watched her with her family. All without letting on who I was. You sound like her. She slummed it and slept with a barbarian, but she couldn't keep me. Not with eyes this color or the markings on my skin. Unlike Vash. The whirlpool of fate spun out a random biological collection of eyes and markings such that Vash is *Vash*, and I am *me*. It made it so some were born inland and others outland. I do this as much for the Water Folk as the Fire Folk. Look at the cost to the people, some of them from your own home district. We need to accept defeat and embrace the Other Folk. Do you see, Justicar? The wall is evil."

"Why would we want open transportation between the two realms? So more of the Other Folk can become stranded on our shores and be raised in the imperial run schools to be servants. Would you have more children like yourself stuck between two worlds? With parents unable to express their love for each other? I met your father. He was the caretaker's son. They stayed on the grounds. Your mother and he used to talk all the time. They were inseparable."

"So inseparable she turned him and me away."

"You don't know what it was like back then. She had to, but I'm sure she didn't want to. I'm sure she thought about you every day."

"Justicar, you are such a terrible liar. But I appreciate your attempts to make me feel better. Do you know how I found out who my mother was?"

"Please, tell me about it."

"He wanted the wall contract. He looked into who was in charge and who knew who. Well lo and behold it was his old sweetheart. In the end, I became a bargain stone to him. He used me to convince her to assign him the contact. Then he botches the project. It was typical of him. He made his fortune just by being good enough and cutting corners on the rest. All those people, poisoned. He should never have been awarded that contract. He might not have if not for my participation. It was then I realized how much like him I was.

"I had just concluded my part in the galleon deal. They got me to sign off on the retrieval by promising me money for a clinic and schools, but it all goes to a shell company. The various tribes are fighting over the money. They're excommunicating and disenfranchising those whom they disagreed with to get a bigger portion for themselves. It turned into a nightmare.

"I tried to make something good out of the wall, but it all turned to slush like everything the wall touches. It can't be fixed. It can't be redeemed. It just has to be torn apart. We can't make amends, Justicar. That's what I learned. We can't undo the bad we've done. All we can do is resolve to make the current life as best as possible now. If I can do my part in making that happen for others by destroying this wall, then that is what I must do. Tell Bright Harmony I'm sorry and to keep faith. You are not abandoned by the Makers. Tell Dawn Wolf there was nothing he could do about it either. And you, Justicar, I want you to forgive yourself. You were young and foolish. It was something small that spiraled out of control. It took all of you to make into the mess it became. You were nothing more than children, and the adults around you let you down. How were you to know they would not calm down and act no better than children themselves?"

"Ambassador, please, stay and let's talk about this."

"The dead cannot be improved only remade. The time for talking is done. Time for remaking has come. Once we put our plan in motion, I didn't want anyone to stop it."

"So, you killed the only person you knew could lift the lockout. What you didn't know was he was working off code Ms. Levinia designed."

"You're lying."

Inquester Paij opened the blast doors again.

Ambassador Naiman barreled down the passageway. He hit a button to re-trigger the lockdown sequence. Jhee sped through the closing doors. She was only one airlock chamber behind the ambassador now. She drew the winds to give her an air-propelled burst of speed. The ambassador made it to next chamber. Jhee barely slipped into the chamber behind Naiman. Inquester Paij was stuck another two chambers behind her.

"The wall went right through the Water Nomads' sacred waters. You needed to accelerate the timeline especially once Advocate Farkhande's injunction against the wall went down in defeat," Jhee said.

"We only got one tilt at this. We could have wasted it on the off chance it cured everyone. Or we could use it on the certainty it would stop the wall. Bastian, however, still thought the plan was to fix the wall and cure the sick. Bastian wanted to run more trials. He did not much like going down in history as the man who poisoned a generation. He viewed fixing the wall as his redemption. But you and I both know, Justicar, there are some actions you just can't repair."

Jhee activated her siren module. "I know that. I do. Please, Ambassador, I am begging you. For the life of Star Mirror, I'm begging you. Tell me where the prototype is."

The ambassador considered it.

An alarm warning about the pressure and air levels blared out of the address system. The swear she said at the top of her lungs had been just as drowned out as the ambassador's response. Jhee became short of breath as the ventilation system depressurized the compartment. The ambassador snapped out of her influence. That was one use down.

The doors opened. The ambassador bolted to the next chamber and re-started the lockdown. "Or you'll do what Justicar? You respect the law. Even if you don't always play by its rules. You will not harm me, a man of the coif. Not a devout woman like you. It's almost over now. You should go. There's nothing more you can do here."

"What about Ms. Oriel?"

"Oriel was what the mining company might deem an acceptable loss. She came back and found the secret workshop. She also accidentally caught footage of me meeting with Bastian and our underworld contact at the clinic."

"Ms. Oriel caught you and him together and assumed you were having an affair."

"At first. Oriel caught on and realized Bastian had found a cure. Ever the glory grabber until the end, she tried to extort me into licensing it and putting her name on it. In the beginning, she was an integral part of the plan. I intro-duced them, you know? I told him to get close to her like Levinia so we could get access to her credentials and use the clinic as a staging area. But I didn't realize Bastian would use it as a testing ground."

The inquester signaled Jhee. They were almost through the lockout. Just a few more minutes.

"What I don't know is was the mining supervisor you or Bastian?" Jhee asked.

"Bastian. According to him, that was an accident," Ambassador Naiman said.

"Her fondness for drinking on the job. If she caught him supplying the miners, or he caught her stealing sips, she'd want more."

"He didn't give me the details."

"Again more time pressure."

The ambassador held up his conch triumphantly.

"It doesn't have to end this way," Jhee yelled.

He pressed the send button. The conch he held emitted the no signal noise. The next door slid open. Ambassador Naiman slung himself to the companion tine's shaft, using a mix of air and earth drawing to outrun her. Jhee slipped into the chamber behind the ambassador. Jhee gaped as she caught her breath. Not only had he used interfering elements, but on manufactured metal. Jhee ran forward before it closed again. It slid closed again trapping the inquester only a room behind her. The inquester began working on the next override.

He pressed send again over and over. "What did you do?"

Jhee gathered her breath, "Take me to where you hid the prototype."

Ambassador Naiman winced and grimaced. He gazed at the tines. His body shaking.

"You think the miners will thank you for destroying their livelihood?"

"They'll be free of the mines and Styrling. If they won't thank me, maybe the communities devastated by the wall and the pylons might."

This was her last chance. Jhee increased the attenuation on the siren module. "You know their hearts better than I. Will they see it that way? Communities who view templarite deposits as blessings given them by the Makers as much as we in the Reaches view marine life."

The ambassador turned away from the tines and took a confused step toward her. Jhee held her breath. He shook his head and turned back toward the tine's base. She had used it too many times in succession on him. If she upped the attenuation to overcome his growing resistance, she risked turning him into a blathering idiot. She swore.

"Ambassador, why did you become a man of the coif?"

"To help people."

"Then be a helper and not the man who left my wife to die in a cavern or killed two people. Let your desire to help conquer your desire to punish Delphine and the system. What you are doing will hurt so many more people. You are not stopping anything. You stop this wall, and they will just build another. Meet me halfway. Work with me, and we will do our best to make a good world for the Water Folk and the Other Folk. We will build bridges instead of make swords."

Ambassador Naiman hurled the useless conch at the tine's base.

"I would love to believe you. I've taken that bait before, but not this time.

The hole in the world isn't the mine, Justicar. The hole in the world isn't out there, it's within. Though we can build bridges, more often than not we make swords. I'm sorry, Justicar. Star Mirror seems like she cares about the plight of the Fire Folk. I may not have been able to plant the code via the substation, but I found an alternate way to still stop the wall and help the miners and those affected by the pylons. You are a clever and smart investigator, and if you took me in you could get me to talk and tell you where I hid the synchronator. Goodbye, Justicar."

Ambassador Naiman spread his feet and arms apart. Particles coalesced from the air and accumulated on his hands. He turned his hands as if winding a giant clock key. A burst cypher, a self-destructive arcane technique pioneered by Doombringers designed to inflict maximum damage to arcanists and environment alike.

Jhee dropped into stance for the counter. She exhaled strongly and turned her hands opposite his. His face strained. His body shook. More particles streamed out of the air. Jhee's legs wobbled. She drew upon the prime forces within to replenish what he took. Her body burned like she was being scoured with electrified acid.

A sniper round went through the ambassador's head. His body fell to the ground. Jhee collapsed to her knees.

~

Outside of Bounds

"No," Jhee said. "No. No. No."

The inquester overrode the last door and entered the column with Jhee and the ambassador's body.

"Justicar, are you okay?"

"Who? Why? He hadn't told me where the synchronator was."

"We'll figure it out, but for now, we better get out of here."

Jhee stared at the ambassador's body. They still had no idea where to find the synchronator, and time was running out for Mirrei. Jhee had to think. Where would the ambassador have hidden it? He hinted he had another endgame in mind. What was it he said? He found an alternative way.

"Wait. Wait." Jhee pondered then addressed to the inquester, "I don't quite think this is over. The ambassador, I think he may have discovered another way to destroy the defense grid."

"Makers, no."

"There has to be a clue where he's been and what he did with the proto-type." She examined the soles of his shoes a combination of dirt and plant matter and more templarite dust. She began checking the ambassador's clothes and body.

As Jhee tried to order her thoughts about where the ambassador may have hidden the rest of the crystals and the synchronator, a loud bang sounded. Alarms went off. Armed Squid troopers wearing tact gear burst into the chamber.

Two Squids approached with a digital parchment held high. Jhee tensed in anticipation of the now familiar refrain. Forge her patience in flames, she prac-tically knew their script by rote.

"Pursuant to this imperial order and the imperial seizure act, Inkerton Enforcement Services has been authorized on behalf of the empire to take over this matter. I'm afraid Justicar and Inquester we must ask you to leave," Sianna said.

"You can't. You don't understand," Jhee said. Jhee started to fight and protest. "We haven't found every device, and the ambassador may have been planning another attack."

"We'll take it from here. I assure you the matter will be thoroughly investi-gated, and any additional devices found in due time."

"In due time? My wife is dying now."

"Just be glad we're overlooking your violation of the injunction considering your assistance stopping the radical."

"This passage is one hundred-twenty feet away from the nearest substation."

"Justicar," the inquester said. "This looks official. Let's leave them to it. Come along, Justicar. I'll take you home to your villa."

The inquester grabbed Jhee and started to drag her out. Jhee began to protest. The inquester caught her eye and shook her head. The inquester brought Jhee out to the gyro. Jhee climbed in the seat morose and somber. The inquester slipped into the driver seat.

"Why didn't the conch work?" Jhee asked.

"I copied the Stingray Club's jamming signal."

They flew away from the perimeter via the gyro's backup motion drive and a stomach dropping series of hops. The inquester thankfully brought the gyro to the ground on a nearby outcropping. She pulled out a conch. The inquester extended a tray from the console and placed the conch on it. "I took this while they weren't looking. It's encrypted so we won't be able to look at the data, however. But we can get its unique signet without an imperial access order. The prototype isn't on him. So, where is it?"

"Good question. I must think. Where would he put it? How else could he destroy the grid? He was not the tech-savvy one. That was Mr. Bastian."

The inquester hrmled. "Okay. The ambassador didn't have much time to hide the synchronator since we stopped him at the observatory. He also needed to be at the hospital in order to not raise suspicions."

"Let's just hope he did a poor job of securing his conch."

Jhee took out her quick unlocker. The inquester waved it away and touched the sensor suit's cuff to the ambassador's conch. Jhee watched the lights and characters spin. And spin. Her heart began to sink. They would have to bring it to the techs to have them unlock it.

There had been more templarite on the ambassador's shoes. It couldn't have been from the workshop, because they had that place sewn up tight.

"Where are the source crystals for the pylons mined?" Jhee asked.

"I don't know. Maybe in the Rose Hills."

"Too far. Where did the templarite dust originate if not there? Everyone else with it on their shoes and clothing, got it from being in the water taxi."

"Or did they? They were also at the clinic and Chuc's. Could it be that simple?"

"Would the ambassador have gone back there with us crawling all over it?"

"We can go look."

"But if we're wrong, we've wasted more valuable time. I need to make a better educated guess." Jhee took a beat, so impatience would not in fact cost them more time. "You said we could get the unique signet? If the ambassador used the location services at all, we might track his movements. Conch only use a handful of methods for location tracking. We can figure out the conch's unique signet and the services he used. We track him via the infrastructure without having to crack the conch."

"The data the Imperium doesn't track and isn't supposed to keep a record of."

"Correction, Inquester, doesn't track or keep record of after a long-tide. We won't be able to know where the ambassador has been past a long-tide, but all we need is the last couple of days since he eluded us at the observatory."

"Precisely. Exactly. However, no doubt it'll involve violation of the privacy protocols and use of infrastructure controlled by the Imperium and by extension our Styrling prickle fish. If there are any favors you have left, call them in. Also, what about his room at the villa? There might be a clue there."

"Good thinking. Likely our friends already searched it, but they didn't know what they were looking for then."

"Show me the evidence manifest again." Jhee stared at the list again for the hundredth time: receipts, disposable conch, workshop footage. What did she expect to see now that she hadn't before? She remembered the disposable conch's footage of Bastian and presumably Ambassador Naiman speaking in his workshop.

"Careful with that. Look around us. One mistake in calibration and you could start a chain reaction that would set the whole thing off."

"The synchronator is like radiation shielding. It can still bring the Shield down. The ambassador wasn't the technical one, so it had to be a solution he figured out from a layman's knowledge. They made it from an unstable crystal. The substation needed to be run by the crystal. Without the crystal, the Shield would break down. A chain reaction. Destroy the crystal mines. The synchronator was a resonating device. It shielded. What happened if you overloaded it? It was still tuned to the same frequency as the Shield. The synchronator prototype could be reprogrammed to send out a feedback signal without much trouble. All you had to do was put it near the signal boost, and you could create a feedback loop.

"The hole in the world. The Styr Mine. I think that's where he planted the synchronator. He was going to stop the power sources. While without Mr. Bastian's access to the substation and code he can't shut down the Shield digitally, he can destroy its fuel source. With a chain reaction created by resonant vibrations from the synchronator, the templarite will start a cascade explosion."

"An explosion like that could take out half the drench isle, Water Folk and Fire Folk alike."

"It's even worse than that I'm afraid. That same mineral is used in many of our screens from conchs to viewers. The chain reaction could spread far beyond to the pylons and the tines."

"If the tines and the pylons keep the Storm Shield in place, what happens if something destroys them?"

"The storm gets to wander where it will. Years of captured storms suddenly freed. Utter devastation."

"Merciful Makers, was he insane?"

"Not insane. Bitter and desperate perhaps. It's even more imperative we find the synchronator now. Every moment that goes by means more than Mirrei having less and less chance of waking up. We can't wait for the formal investigation."

"The scene integrity."

"The ambassador is dead, and this may never go to trial. Preserve life first. Make the case second. The case always comes second to someone's life, Inquester. That's the way I was taught."

22

WAITING

〜

Sterling Eyes

Jhee and Paij could not remain in the gyro on the outcropping overlooking the tines forever. Jhee contacted Shep via conch. "Shep, where are you now?"

"I'm back at the villa. Taking a rest. Kanto is at the hospital still with Mirrei."

"I need you to search the first floor harborside suite. It's Ambassador Naiman's."

"On it."

"Company may arrive soon."

"Understood." Shep's image shook and his quick footfalls carried through the conch's microphone. The image became blurry. The tune and hiss of a lock sounded before his face came back into view. "What am I looking for?"

Jhee pulled up Mr. Bastian's designs. "We are looking for any sign of where he's been over the past few days or any piece of technology that looks out of place or a rectangular enclosure thirty by fifteen centimeters on a side housing an eight-centimeter diameter crystal—."

"Small box, large crystal. Got it."

Shep began to scour the ambassador's room. Meanwhile, the inquester's console retrieved the conch's signet code. None of Jhee's judicial contacts answered her calls. Jhee considered who really owed her. Zeloach, whose son had been falsely convicted by the last District Sixteen magistrate, was not part of the judiciary. However, she would not need a writ.

"I may know of a tracking method that does not require an imperial order," Jhee said to the inquester.

The Imperium controlled the skies and the towers; they were much laxer about the sea and the ground. The Zeloach family had been tinkers who maintained the heavy machinery in the Outer Reaches. They had kept everyone's equipment, running from the farmer and fisherfolk to miners and shippers. It had afforded them service contracts with many houses. Still did. As times had changed, they had branched out into communication infrastructure. With the airways unsafe and most air travel grounded, they had the only means of running communication lines under the ground or along the sea floor.

Jhee contacted Zeloach, her contact with access to the imperial location grid, and she was all too eager to help. "Do you still have the waypoint grid system in case the broadcast power goes down?"

"Yes."

"Can you track a conch if I gave you its signet code?"

"I can, but our system is less accurate than the air track grid used above ground."

"What if I also had a time and location I know it was present?"

"That is a fur of a different stripe. With that info we can narrow down where it's been to within"—Zeloach paused, and the clack of keys came across the sound channel—"say ten to twenty meters at any point after."

"Accurate enough. Do it, please. Also, thank you."

"Don't consider this a favor sunk. I'll always be on your lists."

One of the first things Jhee had done when she took over the justicarship was review the old cases. It had not been her intention, but so many had come to her. If she thought the previous Justicar was corrupt, she did not know the half of it when she began looking into his so-called judgments. If he had not already bankrupted his house, what she uncovered would have done it. She had sometimes even paid for some appeals out of her own pocket for the more impoverished families. First Makers knew she needed the goodwill after how her family had behaved.

She had restored justice and order to District Sixteen and then came the Shield. Many of the families she had grew up with had moved their homes inland. Winter or seasonal homes closer to the capital had now being retrofitted to become permanent residences. And as residences changed so did jobs and expertise. Lesser houses who once made their livings from spawning beds and kelp farms now had to adapt. Many had taken up positions within the government infrastructure which had grown to accommodate the centralization of power into large population centers.

"Jhee," came Shep's voice. "I haven't found a device like what you described. I did, however, find a lot of notes about mirrors, crystal stars and silver eyes and a list of suppliers."

Jhee went through her finger-cyphering exercises to calm her mind and steady her nerves. She tucked her hands into her robes to stop herself. Mirrei's plight had thrown her off.

"I think company's arrived, Jhee."

"All right, Shep, get out of there. Did you remember to cover your tracks?"

"I'll do my best."

Shep disconnected. Jhee needed to cease her reckless, unordered behavior and use the wits the Singers of the Seas had given her. Mirrei's life depended on it.

"I've got it, Justicar. The location data is coming in," the inquester said.

Jhee examined the incoming data. The ambassador had visited the templarite mines and a custom crystal, lens, and mirror supply company which was consistent with what Shep found. The ambassador had remained committed to the last to completing his mission: destroying the Shield. So, what would visiting those locations have to do with bringing it down? Power source. And where would he leave Mr. Bastian's shielding synchronator?

"That's it," Jhee exclaimed.

"Uh oh," the inquester said. "Shep isn't the only one with company."

The inquester pointed and engaged the gyro's motion drive. The Ink's troopers had spotted them. Some ran toward them. Others hopped into transports. The inquester sped off. "I guess they figured out I have the conch. Without you at the helm, we won't be able to outrun them in this contraption. The motion drive is no match for their pursuit cruisers."

"Don't outrun them. Hide. I know a place."

The Root

Jhee directed them to the Maid of the Mists grotto. The grotto provided just enough concealment to house their transportation. Jhee hopped out.

"All right, Inquester. This is where I leave you."

"I'll buy you what time I can. Where will you go? Wait! don't tell me. The less I know, the better. That way I can't tell them what I don't know."

"Thank you, Inquester."

The inquester tapped her temple and sped off. Shortly, Jhee heard the Galleon City Imperators' sirens and saw the weak, distant reflection of alternating emergency lights.

Jhee searched around in her robes for one of Kanto's infamous hidden pockets. She found one tucked under the armpit. This time with a bandanna and a bit of concealing make-up and facial hair in it. She slipped off her robes and flipped them inside out. He thought of everything. He must have taken the story of her disguising herself at the refugee camps to heart. Maybe he wasn't so bored by her work. She had never given him enough credit for his cleverness. Her mind popped back to the night of Mr. Bastian's murder and how she and her two younger spouses had worked as a well-crafted machine.

Jhee stared at the Inkerton Enforcement Services security sticker on the building with its unblinking eye atop a watchtower design. IES. Eyes.

"All you have to do is open your eyes and look."

What had Advocate Farkhande been trying to tell her?

Something about the clinic's financial records and Mr. Bastian's receipts nagged at her. His workshop was also close to here. The Sandoval Storage business address matched that of one of the shell and dummy companies Vash had used to hide his transactions with the clinic. She had seen it somewhere else. The catering company who Ms. Oriel had used to pilfer her money from selling access also gave a similar address. The addresses were all postal rentals.

Jhee traced the physical location to a small ocean-side storefront near where they found Ms. Oriel's body and right next to where the observatory stored their decommissioned equipment.

The Delphines' old mining operations were right around the corner. Jhee took off for the worksite. She examined the underwater storage tanks and found nothing. What else was nearby?

The subsistence mines. The mines other than those leased by the Delphines to Styrling were exhausted. They did not produce commercial-grade crystals anymore. Individuals mined enough crystal dust to eke out a living with, if not the Delphines' blessing, then their forbearance.

A sound behind Jhee startled her. The Latcher girl stared at her.

"Quickest way to the main shafts?" Jhee asked.

"Transport bins." The girl brought her to a motorized vehicle attached to carts on a track. She pulled the pin to separate the mine carts. "You can tell me, you're a Singer of the Sea, right? The lady with you at the shop was the Maid of the Mists? Tell her I did my devotions proper."

Jhee sped to the mine entrance near Lady Delphine's. Amongst some miners having a drink, she found Wynne, who asked, "What are you doing here? And dressed like that?"

"I need your help. It's urgent. Ambassador Naiman implanted a device to blow up the mines. I need help to find it. Crystal stars. Does that jog any memories or have anything to do with the Shield or the One Waters movement, Folx United?"

The activist eyed Jhee.

"Please, my only concern now is saving lives. I have no time for anything else."

"Okay but only to help Star. We uncovered one of the smaller companies who helped build the wall. They were only a two-person den, with a small ocean-side storefront and a bunch of rental boxes. Not worth the time to protest. We needed to make a big splash and take our fight to the heart of the big corporations. Not harass little guls."

"Thank you, thank you so much." Small fries, little guys her behind. That company was a front, one of the various places nobles like Vash and the others laundered their money through.

"Everyone fan out."

"I need the device intact. Will that be a problem?"

"Trench yes, but we'll try, anyway. The last time a member of your household yelled about imminent danger they turned out to be right."

"You know these mines better than anybody. Where would he plant it for maximum destructive effect?"

"Deep underground. As deep as you can."

"Does it have anything to do with this?"

Jhee showed Wynne an image of the number and message on the back of the napkin from Che's. Pool. Underground lake. This blight of a city consumed in a pillar of light. Mineral sands. Starry eyes.

Wynne passed the image along. When it got to an old timer, the color drained from her face. "Merciful Makers, the mnemonic we use to locate the root crystal."

Wynne looked ill. At Jhee's desperate look, she explained further, "The entire city rests on crystal beds, the root or mother crystal. This must be its frequency signature."

Jhee's stomach sank to the depths. "Without support, reinforcement, the literal foundations of the city would be pulverized, turned to dust. Millions perhaps more would die. The land might be made uninhabitable in a way the Pillarist Doombringers could have only imagined."

"Yeah, well, welcome to Galleon City, a monument to short-sightedness, bad decisions, small-picture thinking, and heinous choices."

"A disaster that size with us trapped inside the storm wall could cripple the empire. It would be equivalent to a volcanic eruption. Monhar-before-the-light and Findar-beneath the-Waves all over again."

"Never thought he had it in him."

"You sound impressed, almost like you admire him."

"It's dedication I grant you, but not if it blows our people to the high heavens. Becoming a shared fine mist of cremains is not the sort of oneness I'm after."

"I need a direction toward the root of the crystal, can you guide me?"

Two older miners brought Jhee to a larger tunnel. They took a sitting position on either side of the tunnel. Placing their hands on the ground at their sides, they hummed. Their hum resonated in the ground at her feet.

"Follow the beat to the heart."

Jhee took off into the darkness following the pulsing beat.

Jhee dove through the mine tunnels. She blocked out the echoes of the beat coming from down the side tunnels and simply focused on the resonance at her feet.

As she got deeper, a beeping echoed from down the tunnel. That must have been it.

Jhee covered her ears as the ringing got louder. The synchronator must already be powering up.

She kept charging down. The narrow tunnels opened up into a large chamber. A massive crystal formation supported the chamber. At the top of the formation was a small machine wired in. That must be the synchronator. Luckily it wasn't a bomb, so it shouldn't be hard to shut—

The synchronator finished beeping and whirred to terrible life. A vibration began to echo throughout the chamber. Was Jhee too late? The crystal began to tremor and spark. Jhee reflexively covered herself to block the falling shards.

The tremors subsided. Had the synchronator failed? No, Jhee felt its external pressure. Its pulse was being canceled by another, the pulsing beat she followed here. She could only conclude it came from the miners. The miners were countering the vibration. They had given her a chance; she couldn't waste it.

She climbed up to the synchronator. The controls' intuitiveness matched what one expected of an engineer. She hoped she could get this device shut down before the Squids started pulling the miners away from their suppression.

She started fiddling with the controls. Sequences she had studied backwards and forwards from Mr. Bastian's sprang to mind. None of them worked.

Two sets of footsteps approached. Squids? The miners were still holding the synchronator back. Jhee began to rush through the shutdown. All the time preparing to defend herself. The air was thick with the crystal dust, heavy to draw. Gathering up enough to use was a laborious process.

Two miners entered the room. The two large Fire Folk wielded pickaxes. Whether they agreed with the ambassador or the Doombringers, Jhee must work faster. The pair began to clamber up the crystal root. Jhee unleashed an air burst to push them back. Charged with crystal, it came out much more violently than expected. The pair reeled back into the cavern tunnel.

The reprieve gave Jhee time to finish the shutdown sequence, but she still needed to disconnect the synchronator and escape. When the pair returned, she used the siren module and gave the command to "Flee!"

Feedback surged through her siren module. One turned and ran, but the other continued to climb. She swayed and scrabbled at the crystal.

Jhee arrested her fall but had slid within reach of the remaining miner. Jhee kicked down and got her in the face a few times before she caught Jhee's foot. The miner was much stronger than Jhee and held her grip. She swung her pickaxe at Jhee, who pushed herself back to avoid it.

Jhee struggled to gather another air burst. At this range, it might be enough. The miner pulled herself up to the top of the crystal and raised her pickaxe. Jhee seized upon the opening. She unleashed the small burst she gathered right at the miner's stomach. The miner fell backward off the crystal root, slamming into the ground below.

Jhee disconnected the synchronator. The synchronator comprised a fist-sized crystal housed in an electronic lattice much like an inverse of the bricker left at the substation. Her siren module still rang. The ringing brought her to her knees. A trickle of blood ran from her nose. *Close the circle. Fill the void. Until all are one.* She forced herself to her feet and fled past the writhing body of the fallen miner.

~

The Vigil

Jhee burst into the hospital emergency room. She roamed the hallways seeking Mirrei's doctor. The people regarded her with caution. The sight she must have made, wild-eyed and frantic.

"Doctor Pike?"

Mirrei's doctor came out and stared at her in bewilderment. Jhee's slovenly make-up used for disguise remained as did her wrong sided robes.

"Doctor Pike, I have it. I have the device which can treat Mirrei."

The doctor gave her the once over. Jhee took out the shielding synchronator and placed it in her hands. The doctor waved over an orderly. "What is it? How does it work?"

"It's a frequency jammer. You said you put Mirrei in an isolation chamber. This has the right frequency. It should stop the assault on her system." Jhee pulled out a data shell. "Here is the data. Someone used them to successfully treat the sufferers of Fresh Lung Syndrome and Miners' Lung Disease. Please, doctor, hurry."

"I'll get this to the lab."

The doctor took the data shell from Jhee.

Jhee entered the isolation ward. Kanto sat outside the polymer tent, a fashion book in his lap. He gently fiddled with a grooming kit. He rose when she entered. The beep of the meridian rate monitor was steady but slow. Jhee hugged him tight.

"Is it over?" he asked.

"Yes. It's over," she said. "I won't leave again."

Kanto hugged her tight then regarded her appearance. "You look a fright."

"I feel a fright. Any word from Shep?"

"He said he was on his way back from the villa. He said you were on the trail of something that might help her. Did you find it?"

Jhee put her arms around him. "I did."

"Will it work?"

"I hope to the Singers of the Sea it will."

Kanto cranked the music box. "I see you found the surprises I left for you in your robe."

"They were very helpful. Pivotal in fact. The disguise bought me the time I needed to find Mirrei's cure."

"You should go refresh yourself. I can't take care of you right now. I don't have the energy to fix you up too." He toyed with the brush from the grooming kit then stared away from her. "When mamere took ill, I cared for her every day. I bathed her, groomed her fur, and did her hair. She would have made quite the image on the social scene. She always took great pains with her appearance. I used to groom her after she had her stroke, sing, and play my lute for her. They won't let me groom Mirrei. When I play, I'm not sure she can hear it anymore."

Jhee had heard the story from Lady Kaydence, Kanto's grandmamere, when she gave her the music box. After his mother got sick, he would sit beside her bed, brushing her hair, reading to her. Just before he would take his leave for the night, he would play the music box for her. One night in her anger, she lashed out and knocked it from his hands shattering it to many pieces. He could not bring himself to throw them out. Instead he collected the pieces and kept them in an old box where Lady Kaydence found it.

"You were a good son." His hand tightened on the brush. Jhee covered it with hers. Kanto shook his head.

"Sit." Kanto offered her his seat. Once she made herself as comfortable as possible, he undid her hasty bun. He gently stroked the brush through her tangled hair. "You were right, Jhee. I had it backward. Vash wasn't embezzling money from the clinic for his independence kit. He was propping up the clinic with it. Someone else was draining the accounts. In my desperation, I wanted it to be him."

"I should have been more skeptical. Kanto, I owe you an apology on many things. I viewed you as the irresponsible one, the one who instigated the trouble you and Mirrei found yourselves in. Mirrei was the instigator. You went along to keep an eye on her."

"Sometimes. This mischief-making we did could be fun, and it was always interesting." He rested his chin on her head. She grasped the arms he slipped around her in a reverse hug. Shep arrived. They acknowledged Shep's arrival and continued to watch Mirrei's tent. Shep laid his hands on them to let them know he was there. "I love this family, Jhee and I love you and even dour Shep. Even if he doesn't quite know how to run a comb through his mane on the regular."

Jhee smiled weakly. "She will be fine."

"My denbe, the Mechanist who always wants to find a way to fix matters. Jhee, when you say it, I can almost believe you."

"You took good care of Mirrei in my absence. You've always taken the best care of her. Thank you. Now, allow me."

Jhee squeezed Kanto's arms again. She took hold of Mirrei's hand, so much slighter and the fur drier and much more brittle than she remembered.

The doctor returned shortly to transfer Mirrei to the isolation chamber. Jhee put an arm around Kanto. Shep stood behind them with a hand on each of their shoulders while the doctors began the treatment. She pecked Shep's hand and held Kanto tighter.

23

THE FIRST MAKERS' DESIGN BE DONE

~

A Slow Recovery

Mirrei was in and out of treatment for long-tides. She seemed to make a remarkable recovery. She was still not at peak efficiency. After a long-tide or two of treatments, she could visit the grounds. Jhee entered the sea garden courtyard. Mirrei and Shep sat at a table playing tiles and laughing while Kanto did sewing nearby. Mirrei perked up and smiled at her. A nice kettle of orange tea and Tranquility Bridge's nectar next to them. Jhee sat down and poured herself a cup. She studied it and contemplated all she had learned.

"Drink up," Mirrei said. "This stuff will give you life."

Jhee grinned. "Don't I know it. Well, aren't you looking quite the picture."

"I know. Isn't it wonderful?" Kanto said.

"I feel great. Better than I have in a long time. Kanto was just filling us in on the latest celebrity gossip."

"Was he now? So, who did what to whom?"

"Well, the third Earl of Ylush from the Summer Isles had her husband moved out of the whole household and took up with a fisherman. They were trying to foster children, and it turned out the husband had certain predilections. She claimed. She found out about it and filed for divorce to protect her children, she said. The scuttlebutt though is it was because he could not give her children and the offspring she fostered are in fact hers by said fisherman."

"My word, that sounds scandalous."

"I know, doesn't it?"

Mirrei slammed down the last tile. "I win, Pup."

"Well, I'll be," Shep said.

"I told you not to play her," Kanto said. "I tell you never to play her."

Mirrei grinned. "You and I both know he lets me win."

"I do nothing of the sort, Sprite. Those are one of the ironclad rules. That violates the rules of all sportsmanship. Good or bad, you do not throw tiles. Always play fair."

Mirrei quirked the side of her mouth.

"Honest. I never throw a game of tiles. It's a hard and fast rule."

"Denbe, join us for a game?" Mirrei asked.

Shep moved aside, and they mixed up the tiles again and made space for Jhee. Jhee and her household played tiles, and she explained what had happened.

"So, the murderer wasn't Vash?" Kanto asked.

Jhee played her tile. "It was the ambassador. Mr. Bastian was the engineer whose muck-up caused all this. He had made a mistake in calibrating the Shield to use synthetic instead of natural crystals. The crystal dust caused excess radiation leakage because of refraction. Not only was the radiation orders of magnitude stronger than predicted, the safety zone around the Shield was much greater. As a result, the wall radiation eroded the immune system. Mirrei had grew up too close to the wall because her mother refused to leave her home and move inland like most others. When she came to live with us, she began to get better. Mr. Bastian had found a cure for the Fresh Lung Syndrome and was experimenting on the patients at the clinic."

Kanto capped it. "Perhaps I should apologize. I was so convinced."

"You wanted it to be true. Vash was just an unwilling dupe. Mr. Bastian and the ambassador played him to get access to the clinic. Vash is not entirely off the hook. His medical credentials are incomplete. And there is the mess that is the clinic's finances. It may take long-tides or even moons to find out."

Mirrei's tile placement hemmed Jhee in again. "It's a shame. The clinic was helping people. With a few adjustments and a proper doctor, it could be a great help to people up and down the waterways."

"I know, but the scandal. I don't know how it will survive."

Kanto nodded. "I'm sorry, Mirrei."

"You should be. Not the least of which because I'm about to wipe the tiles with you." Mirrei tapped her tile against her chin. "The clinic's needed now more than ever. What happens to the patients in the meantime?"

Jhee placed a rescue tile to divert Mirrei from Kanto.

"Mistake," Shep taunted.

Jhee pursed her lips as she tried to think her way out of the trap the other three had laid for her. "Unfortunately, they will have to rely on public or faith hospitals."

"Who put up all sort of conditions on their care," Mirrei said.

Jhee at last broke her pieces free. "Unfortunately, unless they can find someone with credentials to take over. They will have to close the clinic. Vash will likely land on his feet for his work on the FLS cure."

Mirrei gave an extended sigh. "My cure."

"The cure worked."

"What if it hadn't? How do we know all the people Mr. Bastian tested it on are really okay? Or won't have unintended side effects? The later patients are fine. What of the early ones? Before he perfected it. Look what happened when he tried it on the miners. A cure tested on the disadvantaged without their consent just like the wall's effects. The contractor? Styrling Mining gets away with poisoning all those people?"

The headlines held misleading news of the sabotage plot. However, a blind item proclaimed how they had found a minor error with the wall, and they were retrofitting some of the pylons. Also, the minor flu outbreak among the miners had burned itself out.

"In a shocking turn, the recent terrorist attempt to sabotage the Storm Shield uncovered a potentially hazardous flaw. The authorities are taking steps to correct the flaw which may have caused potentially hundreds of people to get sick."

"In other news, the opening of the controversial Gray Galleon exhibit has been pushed back again because of a court injunction and continued protests..."

With resignation, Jhee nodded. "For the most part. The Imperial Courts will impose fines in lieu of confinement. It likely will include a trust to treat Fresh Lung sufferers and provisions for the pensions and death benefits they should have included as part of their original contract bid. However, having to pay after the fact still has netted them large savings as it will require some expertise to determine who is eligible. They might stall for some time, and many may die without them having to pay out a dime for their treatment. For what it's worth, thanks to the efforts of the activists and people like you who supported them, their gambit will cost them more than it saved."

Mirrei frowned. "If those such as ourselves hadn't gotten sick how long would it have taken before the problem was addressed? The shield company only needed to put a couple million shell worth of extra dampeners on the pylons, but they didn't. Then we get a disaster that makes Trishanku a pygmy sea drake beside the shell drake. Companies like Styrling take those chances with our tacit approval."

Silence reigned for a time as they played.

This time, Shep blocked Jhee's tile break out. Jhee squinted at him. He raised an eyebrow. "I'm just happy you're still here to beat me at tiles, Sprite."

"Breach, Pup," Mirrei said.

Jhee chortled.

"So very happy," Shep mumbled. He studied the board as if trying to puzzle out his defeat. "Someday, Sprite. Someday."

"What of the Planetarium Chandelier and the Gray Galleon?" Kanto asked.

Jhee folded her hands. "Well, it looks like the Imperial Historical society will take over the observatory and do a thorough accounting of the assets. They'll go over Ms. Oriel's finances with a fine-tooth comb to find out who paid her and for what."

Mirrei breached Kanto's tile stronghold. "Such a shame. It's the Findari's history. It belongs to them. How selfish of her not to respect their privacy."

"What will happen to the Mechanist Devotions?" Kanto said. Freed from his obligation to play by his sound defeat, he had taken out his sketchbook.

"The Imperial Historical society will see they're returned to the Imperial Collection. They will spend some time unwinding the finances of the charity. I had my accountant looking into it already when I was looking to donate."

"Overrun, denbe," Mirrei said and dispatched Jhee, as well.

Recriminations

Shep, Kanto, and Jhee read to Mirrei and kept her abreast of the latest goings-on. Mirrei rested her head on her hands as Kanto went over the latest gossip. She smiled and nodded. Jhee noticed though she no longer paid as rapt attention as she once did. Mirrei turned more and more inward.

The Delphines visited, Erma and Semele at first.

"It's nice to see you looking so well. You'll be back in the fight in no time."

"Or kicking our butts at weirs."

Mirrei giggled.

Lady Delphine spoke to Jhee off to the side, "I suppose I owe you a thank you. You got to the bottom of the harassment."

"I don't feel as if I did you a particular favor with that. Thank you for squashing any lingering issues and clearing the roadblocks with the prototype."

"I figured it was the least I could do for all your family suffered at the hands of mine. I'm sorry. All the grief he caused your family. The many people he harmed."

"Have they made arrangements for his body?"

"His father is handling all that. He refuses to give me any of the details which I suppose is only proper. If I cared while he was alive, I would have made the effort."

"I can't imagine what it was like or how hard it was to make such a decision."

"I wonder what might have happened had I chosen to raise him and defied my family. If I wouldn't have put him and his father out to begin with so many years ago. But after witnessing what happened in the Far Reaches...."

Jhee shrugged. "Some part of me still wonders if it was all worth it."

"I wouldn't trade my children for anything. I shouldn't have traded Naiman. But Vilmar knew the only way for them to stay was as servants or else risk having our secret exposed."

"It's best not to be too obsessed with past mistakes or it may consume you as it did Mr. Bastian and Naiman. Consider, for the damage he did, his efforts encouraged Mr. Bastian to find the cure. One which might never have been discovered without him."

"The error might never have been made without him. Vilmar's shoddy work caused this mess. A contract he would not have gotten if it weren't for me. He said I owed them."

Sentiments Miramar had expressed to Jhee often enough in person she had not questioned the faked letter. "The question though remains what are you going to do about it. Lady Delphine, you are smart and resilient. You will find a way out of it for you and your family."

"The same old Jhee. Always so affirming. Thank you for all your work."

"Flog yourself over if and maybe elsewhere. You'll find my sympathy strained to its limits. Thank us by using your remaining influence to save the clinic."

"Mumsy," Erma said, "what's this we hear about you and the Justicar being the sort who spent their time reading instead of attending the dances?"

Jhee and Delphine rejoined their charges. Delphine poured them the several glasses of melon drink. "Is that what she told you? Even though your denbe and I barely passed the parchment skin color test I told you about, they knew better than to invite two Trouble Makers like us. We spiked a punch bowl once. This one was quite the Trench Trawler. The way I remember it we didn't attend many of the dances because we were deep drunk in the graveyard from drinking bathtub squelch while reciting bad poetry."

Eventually, Vash showed up.

"You are looking well, Mirrei," he said.

"No thanks to you," Kanto retorted.

"I deserve that."

Kanto sniffed.

"May I have a word in private with Mirrei?"

Kanto opened his mouth, but Mirrei preempted him, "Whatever you have to say to me you can say in front of my household."

"First, Kanto, I wanted to apologize about my forward behavior. The revelation of my parentage knocked into me hard. All the lies, the betrayal. I simply wanted to see myself out of my mother's house and influence. I thought my mixed breeding might hamper my ability to find a situation elsewhere."

"So, you thought to 'ingratiate' yourself through junior spouses in order to join another family."

"Mirrei, Star, I just wanted to apologize to you for not being the man you thought I was."

"Would you give me more credit than that, please? I knew the man you were after our first walk with all your talk of finding a wife and abandoning the clinic. I needed someone to help me sneak away from denbe, and you served that purpose. Who you should apologize to are your patients and the community."

"I didn't think my lack of credentials should matter. It was only one or two courses. I was fully qualified. They were getting better care than they could have afforded otherwise. I thought what could it hurt?"

"It hurt. You hurt many people. Least of all me. I'll live, Vash. I'm rich, and

I'll get the best care. What about your patients though? What are they going to do now? How can they ever trust anyone to help them again? Your foolishness and your stupidity nearly cost those people their lives. As if they don't have enough to deal with already. Did you even think about how this would affect them?"

"I know, Star. I know."

"Go, Vash. Don't come back here again. I don't want to see you anymore. Your sisters are welcome, but not you."

"Star."

Kanto rose and laid a hand on Vash's arm. "You heard her. She would like you to leave."

Vash turned on his way out. "It was selfish, I know. But I had to view lives like his up close. I had to know what my life may have been like if it had been me instead of him. I also thought I could help in the meantime."

Mirrei faced him. "Thank you for getting me and the others to safety. Thank you for your work on the cure, but I still need time."

Vash bowed and left.

Kanto reached out and touched Mirrei's hand. "You okay, Mirrei? I know that must have been hard for you."

"Spare the shark's tears, Kanto. You never liked him from the beginning."

Kanto recoiled then nodded. "Nevertheless, you did. The last outcome I want is to see you hurt."

Mirrei backed her mobility chair up and rolled out of the sea gardens leaving Kanto there to stare after her.

Jhee placed a hand on his shoulder. "She'll be fine. She'll come around. Mirrei needs some time."

"She's right. I should have been happy for her."

"You were right about him. Partially."

"That seems so unimportant now. I would be wrong if it meant she had one less moment of pain and distress over this."

Jhee pressed her esca to his. "This is what makes you such a good co-spouse."

The Sea Garden

In the mornings, Jhee had taken to doing her devotion in motion exercises in the hospital's sea gardens before visiting time. Occasionally, her husbands joined her. Though, she was alone when Inquester Paij arrived. They sat down for some morning tea.

"The mayor sent me to remind you she wants an autographed copy of your next 'Dispatches.' She also said make sure you portray her realistically and not as some clueless bureaucrat. To the mayor's point, have you considered writing up your more recent cases? How about 'Dispatches from Galleon City' where you'll follow the cases of a savvy, beautiful investigator?"

"You and she can't have it both ways."

The inquester chuckled. Jhee slid an engraved envelope across the table to Inquester Paij. "What's this?"

"A probationary club membership. You must wait a year and get another sponsor for full membership, but I'll know you'll manage it."

"What I would love is access to that quiet room. Does it come with that?"

"No, but I'm sure you'll manage that as well."

"Thank you. Though, 'Dispatches from Galleon City' has a nice ring to it."

"I have a suggestion, Inquester. Why don't you write up your own adventures?"

"I'm not a writer."

"Neither was I according to my critics. And from the feedback I get on those old stories, I never was or will be. One last matter, there's a group of children known as the Latchers who hang out by the arriving ferries. You'd be doing me a favor if you kept an eye on them. For a little candy and some change, they can be quite helpful."

Jhee and Paij had a pleasant tea where they spoke of everything except work. As their conversation wound down, Advocate Farkhande arrived.

"You shouldn't receive any flow back about the synchronator provided it's turned over once you're done with it. Ask your friend Lady Delphine to exert influence on your behalf if need be."

"There's much more beneath the surface with you, Advocate Farkhande."

"I'm just a well-meaning crank. Just like you're a harmless, bumbling, rural magistrate."

"On whose behalf were you acting as an intermediary with the observatory artifacts?"

"The only ones with a true right to see them. I have friends who enjoy the sea more than you."

Jhee held back a retort about that being a lower bar than Advocate Farkhande might reckon. "Water nomads. If your head scarf were removed, what Makers' Mark would I find?"

"Not the one you're expecting, but good guess. And if I were to inquire about the scar on your neck or sigil on your arm?"

"Understood." Advocate Farkhande played with the ends of her scarf, but did not leave. "Was there something else?"

"I might need your intercession on another matter. The labor negotiations with Styrling have stalled. An arbitration is scheduled for later today to see if we can break the impasse."

"You wish me to use my influence with Lady Delphine on your behalf as well."

"Only if you feel comfortable doing so. Another quick, legal mind for support is appreciated."

"What if I side against you?"

Advocate Farkhande listened to the air. "The wisps say I can trust you."

Jhee scratched her esca which had itched. "The wisps, huh?"

Advocate Farkhande shrugged. The arbitration proceedings were already at full pressure when Jhee arrived. Nix and the mining pods were there along with Sianna, Inksy, Lady Delphine, and Folx United. The various sides yelled over each other. Delphine brightened at Jhee's presence and torpedoed towards her.

Wynne hobbled over on crutches. Her assistance in the mine had exacerbated her injuries. Jhee's expression changed to concerned. "This is just a scratch. I'll be back to jumping off buildings in no time. They're closing down the mine to cover up the incident."

Sianna and Inksy joined them. "Advocate Farkhande got her wish. The Styr Mine will be closed indefinitely."

"Are you two happy now?" Nix asked. "This is your doing Wynne. You and all your agitating, If your mother and father were here...."

"They'd be coughing their lungs out," Wynne finished.

Delphine clutched Jhee's arm. "The mining families that worked there and called our isle home for generations will be out of work. The mine closing is liable to hurt my family just as much. I can't survive just off the resort."

Sianna swept a hand at Wynne's side of the room. "All those mining families you claim to care about, out of work. Their communities gutted."

"We'll be alive and healthier," Wynne said.

Nix balled up her soft cap in her fist. "You think they'll see it that way. Your problem is you never think things through."

Sianna nodded along. "How do they work now? How do they feed themselves and their families?"

Jhee said, "Spare us your shark's tears for the miners routine. How long before you replaced them with strip mining and heavy equipment? You'd have done it already if you could. No one can stop the progress of the Divine Mechanism no matter how much they try. It'll grind us all up eventually, you, me, the miners."

Wynne stomped her crutch on the ground. "You'd do better to bring the miners to the table than to spend so much energy on lies and intimidation aimed at holding back the tides of change."

Sianna narrowed her eyes. "I could say the same of you. Well, I'd say that just about concludes our business here. Thank you, Lady Delphine. Those melon drinks were quite refreshing."

24

STAR

~

The Shattered Image

Kanto held the door as Mirrei piloted her mobility chair into the villa. "Don't worry. I got this," he said.

Mirrei focused her gaze forward.

"Shep went back to oversee the last bits of getting our house ready. He's sure you will love it. The design already included assistance ramps and easy open doors to account for the mobility chair. So, even if you still require one by the time we leave, you should still be able to navigate around like an expert."

"That was very nice of him. But—"

"But what? I can't wait to see our new rooms. Aren't you excited to see yours?"

"Sure," Mirrei said.

Jhee brought Mirrei into the common room.

Mirrei lifted herself out of her mobility chair. Jhee and Kanto rushed to help her to the nearby chaise lounge. Kanto fluffed her pillow and made sure she was comfortable. He flitted around then said, "I'll return shortly."

Kanto went into the small kitchenette. Mirrei's gaze swept slowly over the suite, her expression neutral. Jhee's heart tightened. "On second thought, I'd like to spend some time on the patio."

"Of course," Jhee replied.

By the time Jhee had taken Mirrei out to the patio, Kanto returned with three glass dishes and the tiles set. "Look what I got? Iced fruit and cream. I thought it might make a nice treat for when you got home. Don't you like it?"

"Yes, but."

"Don't worry. I cleared it with your doctors."

"Thank you."

Kanto scooped the dessert into their dishes. They ate their iced fruit in cream and played tiles with Mirrei immersed in an uncanny silence. Kanto continued to chat, but he would catch Jhee's eye with a concerned expression. However, whenever he spoke or faced Mirrei his face was always the image of cheerfulness. Mirrei's wasn't.

Mirrei tapped her utensil against the empty glass dish. She hummed a bit.

"It'll be about a long-tide before we head to our new home for good," Kanto said.

"That's nice."

"Mirrei, what is it?" Jhee asked.

"I don't." Mirrei placed her spoon down. "I won't be going with you."

Jhee took a deep breath. There it was.

"What do you mean you won't be going with us?" Kanto asked. "The doctors said you were fine to travel."

"I am fine to travel. That's not it. I—"

Mirrei looked at Jhee for support. Jhee just nodded her head.

"I won't be moving to the capital with you."

Kanto's smile froze in place. The corners of his muzzle twitched. "You're talking nonsense. Sleep on it. This is nonsense. You are talking crazy. A night's rest and you'll reconsider. You are still a little tired and unused to being out of the hospital."

"Kanto, listen to me."

"I am listening and what you're saying is preposterous."

"No, Kanto. I've thought about this for a while now. I don't want to move into the capital house. I just need some time to myself to think about what I want to do with my life."

"You can do that at the capital in our new home. Jhee, tell her."

"Kanto," Jhee said. "Don't."

"Tell her. Tell her to stop this foolishness, right now."

"Please, Kanto," Mirrei said, "this is already hard enough as it is."

"But why? I mean aren't you happy with us. I thought you were."

"I've been looking into the requirements for Imperial Academy of Medicine. They have a program, an internship."

Jhee caught her breath and tucked her hands inside her robes. This had been some time in coming, but still, she was not prepared for how much it affected her. Kanto stared at her. The plea for her to make it better, make it not true in his gaze. Jhee felt compelled to say something.

"We talked about you attending the Imperial Medical school in the past," Jhee said. "Our new home in the city is right by the Imperial Academy. There's a branch within easy travel. I mean you can go to the capital and enroll in the Imperial Academy. You can finish medical classes there and still come home to see us."

"I've been thinking about the clinic and all those people who will be without care. They fixed the mobility devices on the clinic. It can become a teaching hospital. They found another doctor to staff it. The new staff will take it up and down the waterways to treat the Fresh Lung sufferers who can't come to the city. They will bring the cure to them. I want to help them."

Kanto seized at the thread of hope. "You can help them in the capital."

"To what end? I've been cooped up and kept for so long. I was so scared of striking out on my own, but now I want to do something else. I want to see more of the world now that I'm cured."

"Don't worry. We can find another assistant willing to take it over. It doesn't have to be your responsibility."

"I want it to be my responsibility. The Imperial Academy has a study abroad program. The coursework I've already completed meets the requirements. I can take classes via conch like I've already been doing. We'll provide medical treatment, and while we do, I will pursue my medical credentials. My work on the clinic will count towards my residency requirements and practical experience credits. In the meantime, I'll be able to help people—help them in a way I never could before."

Jhee could not face Mirrei. She did not want her to think Jhee questioned her judgment. But she needed to at least try to preserve their family. "Are you sure this is what you want?"

"I don't want to be stuck at home again. Mamere kept me locked up in that dank, old house. I used to think, 'Of course, I'm sick cooped up in that house.' It was as if the sickness was in the walls. I wondered if it were cursed. I was glad when it started to sink, and we had to leave. I was so grateful to be gone from there. Once the gratitude wore off, I started to wonder is this all there is?

"I thought I could make this work, but I can't just move from her cage to yours. You can't imagine what a relief it is to know what was wrong with me has a name and more so could be cured. For the first time, I get to travel and see more of the world."

It dawned on Jhee she felt the same about her childhood home. For many years the richest and most prestigious families built their residences on the low-lying isles with plenty of beaches and shoreline; in a few places, even on Folk-built islands raised from the sea by mortal hands. That had been the Maker's Mark among the newly rich. Higher, rockier homes like her family's 'summer home' had been sniggered at and called ghastly, garish, gothic. Then came the Shield. In happier times before the feud, their family had acquired another home on one of those trendy mortal made isles. It was underwater now too. She now identified the emotion she felt the last time she had seen her family's waterlogged seaside manor: relief.

"Tell her she can't go, Jhee. Tell her." Kanto clenched the tile. He punctuated his words by jabbing it against the table as he continued. "Tell her, as her denbe, you order her to stay here with us."

Jhee faced Mirrei. Jaw clenched, eyes fiery orange and defiant, Mirrei dared her to do so; dared her to forbid Mirrei and to have Mirrei never forgive her thereby perpetuating the cycle. *"...she turned in time to see the towering wave bearing down on her. Defiantly, she faced it as it crashed upon our dock. That was the last I saw of her."*

The account of Miramar standing on the shore the raging ocean behind her savage winds whipping her hair about her had sold Jhee on the letter. It's how she wanted to imagine Miramar had died, defiant and as large as life to the end. Jhee had made a promise to her memory in the name of that image. Even if Mirrei had lied about that, Jhee owed Miramar, nonetheless. No. Jhee would not let her regrets rule her choices forever and continue to ruin Mirrei's life. The image of Miramar shattered in her mind to reveal only Mirrei before her. Jhee broke eye contact.

Mirrei nodded.

She piloted her mobility chair down the patio ramp to the garden. Kanto stared down the incline where she had left then turned to Jhee. His lower lip trembled. Kanto glared, hurled the tile down on the table, and stormed back into the suite.

The Sponge

"Would you mind another visitor?" Jhee asked after she poked her head into Mirrei's room at the villa.

"More geld for the Merry Maker," Mirrei said.

Jhee and Erma piloted Wynne into the suite. The building climber still bore bruises, cuts, and other lingering injuries from her beating at the substation. Jhee left them alone to talk. Soon after, Mirrei summoned her back.

"Come with us, denbe. We need you to help us conclude an investigation."

Not long after, Jhee and Mirrei entered the game room at Chappy's Underground Club. Mirrei had spent the whole ride on her conch, inviting all her activist contacts to meet her there. Quite a crowd had gathered to meet them. While Mirrei received warm greetings, Jhee's reception was much icier. A few fled. Most though fixed Jhee with horn glares or tried to crowd her. Jhee decided to just follow the young woman's lead. But despite the paperwork, Jhee readied to use her siren module just in case.

"Well, if it isn't the guppy and wife," Chappy said.

"Well, if it isn't the tattlefish," Mirrei responded.

"I presume you'll be swimming along upstream soon. Have you come to tell me the secret ingredient for your squelch? All my efforts have resulted in a brew affectionately likened to bilgewater."

"And let you continue to leech off the accomplishments of those better than you?" Mirrei addressed the miners and Weirs' Club. "Ask yourselves who knew where we would be that day? Who else knew the miners were meeting there that day? The Imps and Squids were waiting for us. Also, didn't it seem to you like we were targeted? Of all those who got arrested or got away, why us? They had opportunities to arrest others. They let them go to chase after us."

The Folx Uniter who had been suspected of murder at the fundraiser stood. "But the protest at the observatory fundraiser? He pretended to serve drinks to sneak us in."

"He convinced Semele to help. He was there dressed as a waiter not to help protesters but to meet with his handler, the mining rep. It was a trap to sell out the leaders. Whoever he let inside; he did to cover his exit."

"He rescued your group from the Squids," another remarked.

"Vash did that. It's what Chappy does best: misdirect."

"You're not going to believe this guppy, are you? She'll be here and gone with the tides. You know me. I'm part of this community. We're the ones who did the work, and no one is calling us heroes. How do we know it wasn't her?"

"On cue." Mirrei pitched her voice to the crowd again. "Did you see how deftly he did that? The substation protest wasn't the first time the Imps and Squids were a step ahead of you. Who was present every time your groups met? Who so generously offered his establishment for your use? He's a fake; a phony who filches others' accolades; a traitor to the cause."

"'The cause?' Are you the Justicar now? You're not unique. I've seen women like you before. Guppies like you are a pittance per school. You're a tourist who wants to be a great liberator; a faux activist. In a month, you'll be at the capital living the ether life having forgot all about the plight of the poor miners, the refugees, and the Fire Folk. Once you move on, the rest of the fish have to figure out have to survive your wake."

"He's right. I arrived yesterday and will be gone tomorrow. I can walk away anytime, but this is your lives. It's up to you what happens from here. I'll step back and follow your lead."

Click. Click. The gathering had gone silent. The activists parted. Erma assisted Wynne to the fore, her crutches clicking on the back room's floor. "Keep going, Star. You're doing fine. I saw you, Chappy, with the Styrling Mines duo, twice. Once, while I was sabotaging the loader. The second was at the substation protest action. I thought they didn't see me. Next thing I know, I'm getting jumped at our next action."

The crowd fell in behind Wynne. This merely confirmed what Jhee already suspected about the link between Chappy and Styrling. His establishments were the only ones that carried those clove candies. It also explained how he "slipped through their fingers" at the fundraiser.

Chappy hunched his shoulders. "The Ink's bounty was money too good to pass up. It beats shaking down small fish to have protests of their business stopped."

"Would you like to do the honors, dende?" Jhee asked.

Mirrei smiled. "With pleasure. Inquester, did you get all that?"

"Every word." Inquester Paij emerged from the crowd. "Chappy, you're under arrest."

"For what?"

"For extortion and squelching."

Lake, the fishing combine representative, and the travel writer burst into the club. "Imperators, arrest that man."

"He's already under arrest," Inquester Paij said. "Wynne, expect a visit from me later."

Wynne waved farewell with her crutch. "Looking forward to it, Inquester."

"Thank the Makers," Lake said.

"I can't believe we missed it," the travel writer said.

"You will still mention the fishing combines in your exposure piece, though?"

"Why did you want him arrested?" Jhee asked.

"Kidnapping and assault. The bar owner kept us locked up for days because we uncovered his involvement in misdeeds at the observatory. Levinia gave me the scoop, and we went on the quiet to ask around."

"Not quite quiet enough," Lake said.

"Wait, you were passed out at the bar when I dropped by a few days ago," Jhee said.

"Not passed out. Drugged," the travel writer said. "We must have gotten too close. This story will be just the break I need to stop writing travelogues and break into exposure journalism."

Lake took the travel writer's arm. "You said the combine's involvement in uncovering a scandal would get our work out there. You told me you already were an exposure journalist. That's the only reason I went with you."

The travel writer cleared hir throat, "I'm quite sure I didn't. I'm not responsible for what you inferred. Lake, didn't you have a proposal you wanted to bring to the Justicar and the miners?"

Lake screwed up his mouth then turned his attention toward Jhee.

"We heard about the mine closing. Well, one way you can save the mines... ask Lady Delphine to cancel her lease with Styrling and lease it to the miners instead. Make a mining combine like I'm trying to do with the fishers."

Erma shook her head, "Styrling would sue us both into oblivion. Wouldn't they?"

Jhee tapped a finger aside her nose. "Let me and Farkhande look at your lease agreement. I bet we can break it if they don't intend to mine. We can make a good case that they broke the lease by closing down the mine."

Miners clapped Lake on the shoulder. "Explain how these combine things work?"

Lake and the miners wandered off. The travel writer chased after them with hir recorder. Wynne chuckled.

Mirrei muzzed Jhee on the cheek. "You were right, denbe. That was fun."

Jhee offered her arm. "It's a classic and one of my favorite tricks. Wynne, that was brave of you. If you require help with any fines or fees related to your law-breaking, I'm sure Mirrei will step up. I'm sure her allowance can cover it."

Mirrei went wide-eyed.

"Don't bother," Wynne said. "I don't think anyone will press charges against me, and if they do, I got the fees covered."

At Mirrei's confused look, Jhee offered, "How do you think she's been getting access to the work site?"

Mirrei rolled her eyes. "Erma and Semele."

Wynne and Erma caught each other's gaze then looked away. "And you thought I was just using you for after hours access to the work sites?"

"Well, you were, weren't you?" Erma asked.

Wynne grinned, her eyes tinging pink.

⌒

Under Wraps

On the ride back to the villa, Mirrei was thoughtful. She gave Jhee a few hesitant glances before speaking.

"Denbe, you're very level and fair about things. Why do Fire Folk keel you off so much? Why are you so invested in the wall?"

"I fought the Fire Folk for many years, either in combat or stopping raiders, so did many in the Reaches. I've killed them. Befriended them." Jhee pulled back the sleeve of her robe to reveal several tattoos along with the command sigil on her arm. "It's hard to turn that off."

"We started it."

Jhee shoved her hands into her sleeves and pressed her palms together tightly. "Regardless of who started it, the situation is complicated. If it weren't for our navy and now the barrier, we'd be the ones serving them food and cleaning their houses. Maybe those of us left behind in their lands do just that. Maybe there, we wear the funny uniforms and are housed by the state. Or maybe they treat us with the compassion and dignity we can't quite manage for those left behind here. I'm not unsympathetic to their plight. They took their due. They hold the other continents. They carried off my family members. They took back their lands and then some. It is best for both our people to stay away from each other to the extent we can. We've earned our peace and I want no part of anything that disrupts that. I earned it with Shep's scars and mine and the lives of my sisters."

"I'm sorry."

"Don't be. Believe me, I also know the raiding went both ways, as did the trade. I don't know if they've stolen as many of our children as we did of theirs. It's different for the younger set I suppose. The wall's been up in some form most of your lives."

Mirrei bit her lip. "It's not just that. The distance, the respite from fighting has forced people to re-evaluate. So much about the past is coming to light and no longer sublimated. The Galleon City reconciliation project has all these records. Water Folk call ourselves the Makers' Criterions, but some of the things we did... Advocate Farkhande hinted that the previous policy regarding those Fire Folk who came here was worse. Was she was right?"

"They still call Other Folk who land or wash up on the shore driftwood. In gram-gram's day, there was a standing Imperial order to kill them on sight. And all Water Folk who traveled to their lands 'should henceforth consider themselves banished.' Those who sought return should likewise be killed."

Mirrei gasped.

"The policy had more lip service than enactment paid to it. Trade was the true concern of the policy, to limit the financial resources of rivals to the Dual Sovereign's rule."

"We were so cruel and then we were beaten."

"You wonder if maybe the Other Folk know something we don't. They're the winners. We're the losers. It's natural to want to emulate them."

Mirrei nodded.

"I never believed in the Pillarist Soothbringers' Ten Thousand Temples vision, a network of sacred spaces across the inhabited worlds dedicated to the Makers or the Seven Underwater Temples either. Enlisting is just what you did as your duty to the Empire and to show your pride at being Water Folk. Serving is also how you made a name for yourself. My family, especially had something to prove, not far removed as we were from gram-gram's piracy and gran's monogamist preaching. We had to wash the stink of disreputableness off our name."

Mirrei slipped over and hugged Jhee tightly.

Jhee ended the hug and patted her hand. "That's enough of that now. I just want the fighting to stop. And I don't know how we do that with both sides as bitter and dug in as they are. Maybe the Pillarists and their universal adoption of penance have the right of it. Neither side can make it right, but maybe we can make a new way. A new way to bring equilibrium to the system, if you are an example of our future."

Mirrei's eyes took on a shade between the pinking of embarrassment and brassiness of pride.

The transport pulled up to the villa. Inksy opened the door for them.

"We need to talk," Sianna said.

Mirrei paused and eyed the two mining company troubleshooters.

"It's all right," Jhee said. "Go inside. I'll be along shortly."

"Follow us."

"No, you follow me. We'll speak in the boathouse." In the boathouse, the pair looked around. "I assumed you've already searched here, and you have found no more data about the defense grid."

"We had to be thorough," Sianna said.

"I know. I saw your thoroughness all over the news and my shoes along with the ambassador's brains."

"We kept it quiet because of the panic. People wouldn't believe the problem was just some math error or shielding. Not to mention a male engineer made the 'error.' They would blame the use of male arcana. People's minds would go back to the Middle Pillarists. We couldn't take the chance of another Doombringer Uprising, once it got out that a male engineer no less, made the error."

Inksy crunched into her clove candy. "You stumbled onto something, Justicar, that few people are supposed to know about. The existence of MANTEL is a state secret, let alone any of the shareholders. As an officer of the court and a former intelligence officer, I can't impress upon you enough that it remain that way."

"I told you I can't stand the smell of those candies. Spit them out. Get rid of them," Sianna said.

Jhee waved them off. "May we skip the threats and flattery? How soon will 'the error' be repaired?"

"Almost immediately. You have our word. Eldjin-X just received a loan to buy out Vilmar's company. The Shield maintenance and any additional work will be done by Eldjin-X using a hybrid design."

"There is another matter we should discuss: how you weaponized Mr. Bastian's mistake. You deployed an experimental crowd control device on protesters, my wife amongst them; one based on the Shield's design flaw. It nearly killed her because she was already weakened by Shield exposure. It might risk the health of many Fresh Lung or Miners' Lung sufferers."

"Extreme measures on our part were justified. A mining supervisor was killed. We didn't know if it was miners or activists," Inksy said.

"The mining supervisor's death may have happened in multiple ways. Between her drinking, stealing, and gambling, she was on a self-destructive spiral. Bastian's notes had her listed as suffering from MLD, too."

Sianna interrupted Inksy's reply, "We can consider that 'experiment' a failure in exchange for your discretion."

Jhee had to accept it at that. She had pushed as much as she dared. Anything else she might do could cause a visit from the Abyssal Constabulary.

Before the pair left, Inksy pulled out a pocketful of wrappers and tossed them in the bin. A few of the foil wrappers escaped on the breeze. Jhee kept it to herself how the wrappers had marked places they had visited. She might need that advantage if the Path Maker crossed their streams again.

A NEW LETTER

~

The Cuttlefish

Mirrei was waiting for Jhee when she entered the suite. "So, how did it go?" she asked.

Jhee began changing into her night garments. "They're satisfied. I also got them to depth charge whatever they used on the crowd at the substation. For the moment."

Jhee flopped on the bed. "I think I'm going to clamshell up with a good book for the next day, then visit every gallery and museum I can before we leave."

It hit Jhee that the "we" no longer included Mirrei. Now she just felt awkward.

"I'm still getting used to it, too," Mirrei said.

"I take it you have no interest in visiting them with me before you leave."

"We can if you want."

"But, you really wouldn't enjoy it. Not like I would."

"But I would enjoy it, nonetheless. The same way I enjoy everything I share with a member of this household. Clothes and creative works to die for; soul nurturing food; arcane and legal brilliance; you even have a master thief.

Everything this household does is excellent and comes from such a genuine place. All your caring does, every one of you. It didn't feel like an angle or that I was being wielded against another. I gave you each what you wanted. For you, a bookish companion and ingenue. I gave Kanto what he wanted: a sister and model. Shep, I could never quite figure out if what he wanted was you or my mother."

"Bluer skies were never seen. Have I ever seen the real you?"

"More often than you might believe. That's how it works denbe, I find and amplify in myself the parts I think the person I'm with most wants to see. Do they want the party girl? The student? The sibling they never had? You were all so honest and genuine from the moment I first arrived. I began to feel sorry for taking advantage of you and intimidated. Then the fear and dread set in. Would you accept me if you knew? Ironic, as I didn't really know who I was myself. I had been playing a role for my whole life."

"That I understand too well."

Mirrei flopped on the bed beside Jhee.

Jhee propped herself up on her elbows. "Bookish companion? I guess your herbal knowledge didn't come about from texts and a keen interest in healing."

"Most of it. I read a lot as a child. There was scant else to do when they kept me trapped in that house or while waiting for my next doctor's visit. The rest, I had to pass the time somehow."

They shared a chuckle. Then a kiss, then a night in each other's arms.

THE DAY CAME for them to see Mirrei off and Kanto had still not come down. Shep glanced at his conch and then at Jhee. He had hurried back once they informed him about the course correction Mirrei extracted from the Path Maker.

"We'll give him a few more minutes," Mirrei said.

Shep pursed his lips. They waited a few more minutes. "I'll go see what's keeping him."

"No, I'll go," Jhee said.

Jhee and Mirrei found Kanto in his makeshift sewing room ironing fabric.

"Mirrei has to leave, Kanto," Jhee said. "Don't you want to see her off?"

"No."

He drew his heated iron back and forth over the robes putting a crease in them so sharp you could cut steak with it. Mirrei entered the sewing room behind Jhee. She walked over and admired his work.

"I wanted to see you once more."

"If I had known it would be for a three-part look rather than four, I would have cut these differently and spent less time matching colors and prints."

"I see you've been working on a new set of robes."

"They were for you. The hems and sleeves required your detail work. I designed these pieces to complement your embroidery. Which much as I hate to admit, had just the right character to put them over the top."

"When I find somewhere new to settle, you can send them to me there."

Kanto stopped ironing. He picked up the robes. He looked her dead in the eyes and tore them. "These robes are for family. You're a stranger and thus entitled to none of the benefits of my work."

"Kanto, please."

"I had just gotten her to stop trying to send us away. Then you leave. I seem to be the only one trying to hold this family together. Am I the only one who likes the family we made?"

Mirrei stood defiant. "This isn't about you, Kanto. It's about me and what I need. I have to live my Make."

She grabbed his chin. "You and Jhee see me similarly: as a doll. For her, I'm delicate earthware, fragile, a legacy she has to protect. To you, I'm more of a mannequin for you to dress up as the sisters you never got to know. Is it too much to ask that you of all people be happy for me?"

Kanto picked up another robe and started ironing.

"I give up. What can I say, Kanto? I can't be your doll. I can't be the sister you never had. I can't be the friend denbe never reconciled with. I'm just me, the cuttlefish, the sponge."

Mirrei turned on her heel and left the sewing room. Kanto bent his head over the ironing board. A sob shook his body. Jhee walked over and lifted his face.

"I'll miss her too. We shouldn't keep her here if she doesn't want to stay."

He pulled away.

"We shouldn't make it easy either. She has to know you care. Fight for her. She's testing you to see if you'll fight for her and you're failing her."

"Mirrei is not you, Kanto. She's had a foot on land ever since the start. A fact I would have known before if I had listened to her. It'll be best for you to let her go with joy."

"I don't accept this. I won't. Is this about what's best for me, or your redemption?"

"Please, Kanto, you may only alienate her further. Read this, please. Mirrei wrote this while convalescing."

Jhee removed a letter from her inner gown pocket and rested it on the ironing board. A genuine letter written to replace the fake.

"'I'm a sponge. I'm a cuttlefish. Kanto wants a sister. I'm a sister. Shep wants a wounded creature to tend. I'm a sickling. You want a pupil. I'm a pupil. You two want a child. I am a child. My mother wanted revenge. I am revenge. I'm the healer. I'm the one down for the cause. I'm the pretentious heiress. I am the cuttlefish. I am the sponge. Forever changing myself to suit my surroundings. Soaking up everyone's expectations.'"

Kanto flattened it. After he gave it a once over, he returned to ironing. "Perhaps you should go as well and leave me to my work."

~

Strange Goodbyes

Jhee, Shep, and Mirrei transported her and a few belongings to the clinic. The rest of her belongings they packed for transport to their mansion in the city.

"Maybe you should donate them. I know many people who would love to have some Kanto originals."

"We'll hold on to your possessions just in case."

Shep hopped on board the clinic. He went over it from stem to stern. Its actual crew looked at him quizzically as he attempted to help them with the cast-off. Mirrei grinned.

"It'll do," Shep said. "I just wanted to make sure these dry landers knew what they were about. I also checked your quarters. I left you an emergency kit. And a waterproof instruction list from the Prepared Watchmen. It has some survival tips just in case you get caught or stuck somewhere. That way if something comes up, you'll have what you need to handle it."

"I also wrote some notes for cyphering exercises to keep your skills up," Jhee said and handed her two sheets of bio-film. "They should work in close quarters. You should practice for a minimum of half an hour a day. That should be enough to keep your skills up. The second sheet... A donation in your name to a refugee center, the Fresh Lung Research Foundation, and the

Miners' Health Fund. I wasn't sure which was your favorite, so I donated to all three. I was going to buy a necklace or other trinket, but I figured you might enjoy this more instead."

"Thank you both for everything."

Mirrei hugged Shep. She stepped in front of Jhee and then pressed their escae together. "Goodbye, denbe."

"Goodbye, dende."

"I'll never forget what you've done for me."

"Don't make it sound so final. We're not divorced yet."

"If I need that to change, you'll be the first to know."

"Good. I intend to drive a hard bargain. And don't get complacent just because you are on a floating hospital. Monitor your salinity levels and keep up with your saline regimen. Who knows what the composition of the water will be like wherever you make port."

"Don't worry. I will."

Yelling came from behind them. Kanto stood at the edge of a pier. A water taxi sped off behind him. He waved, a box under his arm. With a disdainful look and wrinkled nose spared for the dock, he took a step forward. He took a deep breath, hitched up his robes then rushed down the crowded pier.

"Star. Star." Kanto stopped short in front of them. "Star. Star. I was afraid I missed you."

"You almost did."

Kanto gazed around the dock. "I guess you are serious about this, aren't you?"

"Very."

"If this is what you say will make you happy, I have to accept that. To be honest, I resented you a little when you first arrived. I had just married Jhee, and now she had another spouse who took away my time. I didn't want a denye at first. But then I got to know you. I never knew how much I wanted a denye until I had one."

"Like whales in a pod. Bonding over questionable mothers and a new wife uncertain of our new roles and our position in the household."

"I know. I was a clown fish. I'm sorry. You forgive me?"

"I don't know. What's in the box?"

"Star, you will love this."

"You don't have to call me Star. I think I'm done with that phase for now. Mirrei is fine."

"I didn't want you to leave without giving you this, Mirrei."

Kanto presented her with the box.

Mirrei opened it. It was the robe he had torn. He had patched it with more practical fabric.

"I turned it into something more suitable for your new role. It has detachable sleeves and a convertible hemline and extra pockets. Someone who doesn't know how to take care of her hems inspired it. All this fuss about clean hems, dirty hems. And vents under the arms for better airflow and temperature control. At least you can be the most well-dressed doctor or intern on this floating tub."

"Thank you."

"And you better call me, you hear? Every night. I intend to bend your ear every night. You may not live in the capital, but by the Lords of the Sea, you will hear every juicy bit of gossip I offer. And you dare not say a word about it."

Jhee laughed. Mirrei did too. Shep gave a curt nod which caused the two to break out into hysterics.

"I also wanted to let you know about a few charity events. They will provide supplemental funding for the clinic. You know what else, I've decided you are not the only one who can help people. Besides starting my charity for refugees and an activist bail fund. I will inquire into commissioning more of these tubs. That is if yours works out. So, you better make it work. Who knows how many other countless lives are depending on it?"

"No pressure."

"No pressure."

Kanto hugged her and whispered, "I'll miss you."

"I'll miss you too."

"Live your Make, dende."

"Always."

Mirrei gave a last look to Jhee as if waiting.

Shep gave Jhee a gentle shove. "Drenchit, Jhee if there is something you want to say. It's now or never. You might never get another chance."

Jhee tucked her hands in her robes at first. "What if I lied as well?"

"About?" Mirrei asked.

"Releasing you with joy."

"Tough."

"I don't know if I'm supposed to fight for you or let you go, but it matters to me you're leaving." Jhee hesitated then held out her arms. Mirrei fluttered her eye color through a spectrum of ambers. Jhee dropped her arms. "Not fair."

Mirrei touched her esca to Jhee's. "Jhee, your timing sucks. Maybe we'll discuss it when I get back."

Jhee smiled. "Maybe?"

"Maybe. That's all I can promise, for now, Jhee."

Jhee kissed Mirrei's slim hand. "Yes, my dear."

"That time I think you actually meant it."

The four embraced one last time.

Mirrei remained on the stern of the barge-like clinic. It lurched, and the crew with long poles pushed it away from the deck. The engines kicked in and began to froth the waters. The three waved at her from the pier. Even when she had left the stern, they waved and waved. She grinned and waved back at them. Mirrei oriented toward the horizon with a look of hopeful determination on her face.

The End

Leave a review!

WANT MORE JUSTICAR JHEE?

WANT MORE JUSTICAR JHEE?

Thank you for reading JUSTICAR JHEE AND THE HOLE IN THE WORLD! Please check out these other Justicar Jhee mysteries and read about Jhee and her cohort's other adventures.

JOIN THE SWIFTNESSE COMMUNITY to get a free copy of **Justicar Jhee and the Spectral Armada**, receive special offers, and hear about future books!

http://swiftnesse.com/spectral/

Other Books in this series:

Justicar Jhee and the Cursed Abbey: https://books2read.com/cursedabbey

Justicar Jhee and the House of Sorrows: https://books2read.com/sorrows

(Continue on to read an excerpt.)

EXCERPT: THE HOUSE OF SORROWS

Please enjoy this excerpt from Justicar Jhee Book 3…

Justicar Jhee and her spouses have settled into life in the capital, and for once, things seem peaceful. After Jhee's old Captain invites them to an Imperial retreat, he tells them that a war buddy of theirs has gone missing. Jhee is concerned about her friend as the woman had not been herself when they last met. When her husband mentions that one of his friend's is also missing, Jhee's suspicions are raised further.

Chapter 1

A seaweed-paper planner with several dates circled and a note reading "Pick one" awaited Jhee in her favorite chair. Jhee placed the planner on the end table and plopped into the cozy chair by the fireplace of their townhouse. The note had been written in Kanto's precise ornate hand. Both note and planner bore matching amethyst scalloped designs. The dates, Jhee presumed, were for counseling sessions. Kanto had been getting treatment for the lingering effects of his ordeal at the abbey. The process had prompted him to get on Shep and Jhee about their own neglected mental health and hygiene. Jhee admitted with a veteran's service center so nearby she had no excuse not to avail herself of her earned aid. But she had so much work to do between the academy, the law clinic, and consultant work.

Shep settled into the cushioned chair beside hers. He plopped a similar planner on the end table with hers.

"Where did he leave yours?" Jhee asked.

"On my exercise equipment. I have to give him points for persistence and knowing his targets."

"Could he be right? Perhaps we need to talk more about our experiences during the Flower Wars."

"Or how close we came to losing Mirrei."

"I'm not sure if I need the extra stress at the moment."

"Right or wrong, we agreed to be more open about our service, among other things."

Jhee rubbed the bridge of her nose. "I know. We should have just said 'no' if we didn't want to do it. Part of me wants to do it."

"And part of you wants to let the Trench swallow the anchors of the past."

"Yes."

Jhee and Shep brushed *escae,* the four-pointed, iridescent Makers' mark Water Folk bore in the center of their forehead. She briefly touched the scar that ran through Shep's right eye, which made it dimmer than the other. They nestled back into their chairs.

Between counseling and the reconciliation and living history projects, Jhee and Shep had over-committed on a topic they rarely spoke of in-depth: their service. Had keeping their experiences to themselves been proper or had doing so made it worse? Jhee extended her hand into the space between their chairs. Shep clasped it and stroked her knuckles with his thumb. Not long after, humming announced Kanto's return.

"*Denme,*" Kanto said and squeezed Shep's shoulder. Then he planted a kiss on Jhee's lips. "*Denbe.* I see you both got my little reminders."

Kanto draped himself in his fireside seat opposite theirs. The embroidery on his amethyst and citrine robes echoed the decoration of the planner and note.

"Subtle," Shep said.

"Never," Kanto said. "So?"

"Give us a moment, we're still coming up with excuses to put it off."

Kanto grinned and shook his head, then hopped to his feet. "You two are incorrigible. Dearest wife, dearest brother-groom, when you come back from your night out, I expect the most amazing tale ever of why two are breaking your promise to me."

Shep grimaced. Jhee took a breath. Kanto knew how to hit them where it mattered. Shep and Jhee seized their respective calendars, circled their dates with finger quills Kanto provided, and handed them in to him.

Kanto peered at the calendars and nodded. "Excellent. Enjoy your evening out."

Once Kanto left, Shep and Jhee turned to each other.

"Drench, he's good," Shep said and raised an eyebrow.

They laughed.

For their night out, Jhee and Shep chose a gourmet restaurant a short transport ride away.

"Elaborate about what we ordered," Jhee said.

"Green beans almondine with a light caramelized butter glaze served alongside pan-seared whale-auroch with water chestnuts in oyster sauce with just a hint of truffle oil."

"Land meat? Are you sure about this?" Jhee asked.

"Trust me," Shep, her senior spouse, said. "The chef gives it a quick sear to seal in the flavor, then covers it just slightly with juices and simmers it in a covered pan."

The waiter arrived with their meals in short order. Shep took the eating utensils—knife and nail pike—sliced a piece of the red meat, and used his index finger to spear it with his nail pike. His teeth clinked on the pike as he slid the juicy morsel into his mouth. Jhee tensed and held her breath. As she watched for signs of an involuntary shift, her fingers hovered over the failsafe sigil on her arm. It remained cold and inert.

Shep swallowed. "Delicious."

He sliced another piece, then held it out to her. As she took a bite, they held each other's gaze. The tender whale-auroch had just the right amount of sear and seasoning.

Jhee had not had meat this rare in so long. She had indulged when she could during her stay in Galleon City, but Mirrei's ethical concerns put the damper on any enjoyment from the experience. Jhee found it hard to savor the meat while her youngest spouse watched with mild distaste.

"The trick to the perfect plate is not dissimilar to the trick to a perfect pour." Shep shimmered his amber, glowing eyes at Jhee. "Then there is the pairing of a wine to complement a brilliant meal. They have a lovely tasting selection for each course. They also have an exclusive house red I wanted to sample."

After the meal and several glasses of excellent wine were consumed without incident, Jhee's worries had dissipated. Despite the location, she and Shep indulged in hand-holding and a few kisses. Mere months ago, as a field Justicar in a rural district, she would have been scandalized to publicly carry on in such a way. In the capital as an academic, though, no one batted an eye at her behavior.

A few doors down, they visited a family-run zoba tea place crammed next to a darkened shop offering tailoring and shoe repair. Their introduction to the tart and tangy beverage was easily one of their best discoveries since moving here to the capital. The capital rarely seemed to sleep. Even now, pedestrians and transports moved by them often. This activity and closeness was a contrast to the ocean expanses of their former home in the Far Reaches. Though, when a Storm Wall fueled gale hit the Reaches, it made even full-sun's bustle appear tame.

Jhee swirled the zoba berries at the bottom of her lidded, clear tea bottle. "How fortunate I am to be surrounded by such experts with respect to food and drink."

"Want to know another aspect of the perfect meal?"

She passed the bottle over to Shep, so he might have the last sip. "What?"

"The right companion." The smoldering tint to Shep's amber eyes suggested they should pay and make their way home. On the sidewalk, Shep swept Jhee into his arms and planted a kiss on her in full view of Makers and masses alike.

A man with a messenger bag and delivery logo on his jacket jostled them as he passed.

"Oi, sorry fel," the messenger said and patted Shep's robe a couple times.

As the man walked on, Shep immediately checked for his wallet, keys, and digital conch communicator. Jhee and Shep both recognized the old pickpocketing ploy. Shep removed his hand from his inner pocket and gazed at a glinting object in his palm. The command sigil on Jhee's arm switched from normal to burning hot.

Shep bounded after the messenger then grabbed him by the lapels and pinned him against the building, all with frightening speed. "What is this? Who sent you?"

"A *gul* just paid me to plant it on you as a gag."

"Who?"

"A gul. I don't know—an older lady with graying hair, maybe a little nervous."

"Shep, enough. Let him go."

Jhee got Shep to release the messenger. Shep held up his hands and backed away a few steps. While he paced like a caged animal, Jhee checked the messenger for injuries. The messenger had sustained some slight scratches and a bump on the head. Jhee apologized and also slipped the messenger a twenty-shell note.

The messenger rolled his head from side-to-side while rubbing his neck. He whispered to Jhee, "Your mister's got quite a temper there. Maybe he should see someone about that."

Shep fixed his good eye on the messenger to let him know Shep had heard that. The young man swallowed and scurried off. Jhee waited until the tempo of Shep's pacing slowed.

"Mind telling me what that was about?" Jhee asked.

Shep opened his palm to reveal a miniature representation of a kalacha war club, the preferred weapon of the berserker regiments. "Someone has a poor sense of humor."

"The berserker corps regiment pin. Who would send that to you?"

"I don't know." Shep's nostrils flared, and his eyes narrowed at something over Jhee's head, but he did not go on full alert. "Someone's there. The scent seems familiar."

Jhee turned. "Who's there? Show yourself."

"Hey, *guls*, I see you got my message," a hesitant voice said. The figure of their old war buddy Ursula emerged from a shadowed doorway. She wore her hair in a slick ponytail. While her jacket was too baggy and loose-fitting, her other clothes appeared well-fitted, new, and clean, unlike the last time Jhee saw her some years ago. Overall, Ursula came across less frantic than their previous meeting. However, her gaze never settled in one place for long.

"Ursula!" Shep swept her up in a big hug and spun her around. "Urlibird! You old sneak."

"Sorry if my message upset you."

"You could have delivered it yourself."

Ursula shrugged and kept her gaze on a constant move. "Too many people. I'm not doing good with crowds these days."

"Understood."

"You two, though, are looking good."

"It's all surface waves, we assure you," Jhee said. She and Ursula hugged. "How are you doing?"

"You know. Hanging in there."

"Come on. Let's all go for a walk. We can catch up."

"Sure."

They grabbed another round of zoba teas then went for a stroll through the park along the lakebed. Few people would be there this time of night. They reminisced. Several times Ursula paused as if she wanted to say more.

"I owe you, Urli," Shep said. "What's going on? Why did you have a regiment pin planted on me?"

"I had to see your reaction. It was stupid. I didn't mean to upset you."

"Forgiven. I can't count the number of times you saved my skin over the years."

"Or you mine," Ursula answered. "So much has happened since we last spoke. I wouldn't even know where to start."

"Whatever you need, ask," Shep said.

Shep handed Ursula back the regiment pin, but she refused it.

"Keep it as a reminder," Ursula said.

Shep glanced back at Jhee. He frowned. That sounded like "goodbye" to him as well.

Ursula stopped to give them a long once over. "I still can't get over how good, how together, you two look," she said.

"You know how it is," Jhee replied, "the cozy life of an academic and civil servant. What are you doing for work these days?"

"A little this. A little that. I'm in a similar line as you were, Sniffer, private inspector work, and the like."

"My field work isn't so far in the past. Is there anything else we can do for you? Do you need a place to stay?"

Ursula smiled. "No, I got that covered. That's just it. For the first time in a long time, I can see a way through. I'm here to check in on you two. Thanks for the offer, though."

Shep pulled up his collar. "We're good."

"I guess that means you found your way through, too. The last of the unit, except Cap. It's been so long since more than two of us have been in the same place together."

Their walking slowed. Jhee allowed them to get a half a step ahead. Jhee had been their unit's liaison and wasn't a berserker, a war-trained full skin slipper, like Shep, Ursula, and the others. She accounted it an honor they viewed her as part of their unit if only partially.

Ursula glanced around her. "I have to get going."

"Make for Make," Shep said, invoking the tradition of hospitality in exchange for the berserker pin. "Take our private c-cards. Contact us if you need anything. Please."

Jhee handed over a numbered credential card to Shep, which he put together with his and a hand-carved shark's tooth. He touched them to his *esca*, Makers' mark, before presenting them to Ursula.

Ursula took the pin back long enough to touch it to her esca then stuffed Shep's offering in her coat. She turned to Jhee and pulled an object from the devotional pouch at her waist, likely Maker geld. Jhee dug out a geld coin she had stamped with the gear emblem of Jhee's path, Mechanism, which she brought to her forehead. Perhaps the Prime Maker's design would guide Ursula to the other side of her difficulties unscathed.

After Jhee and Ursula exchanged coins, Ursula seized her in an embrace.

"The Makers have blessed you. Don't forget that." Ursula refused to release Jhee immediately. "You enjoy the rest of your evening," Ursula said.

At last, Ursula released her. Jhee examined the small, smooth object she had been given. It turned out to be a circular, hardwood disc carved with the batfish or maye. While Jhee did not remember which specific Makers Ursula honored, she knew it wasn't the Maye King or Queen. The maye, though, was Ursula's preferred berserker form.

"Urli?" Jhee began.

Ursula had already slipped away. Jhee and Shep tried to locate her but lost her tracks by the lake along with her scent.

At home, Jhee and Shep concluded the evening in her bedchamber. Before turning in, Shep went downstairs to grab them some iced sweet-berries and cream. Jhee tidied up their discarded clothes along with others she had strewn about while getting ready for dinner. A shiny, jet black data shell clattered to the ground. It may have been one of hers or her students from the legal clinic. She threw it in her valise for later. Jhee took out Ursula's hardwood disc with the maye and wondered.

~

Days later, Jhee still puzzled over Ursula's visit and hardwood disc carved with the maye. The batfish or batwing maye was a sizable cartilaginous fish similar to a shark. Ursula used to leave this symbol to mark trails when scouting. Ursula had marked a trail for her, but to what? A few long-tides—weeks— passed, and Jhee all but forgot about it. She settled back into her regular routine of lecturing, advising the Academy's legal clinic, and giving arcane forensic seminars.

"We conclude from these records that the person was murdered," Jhee said. "Or more precisely, there is a high likelihood of their having been poisoned. And that concludes our virtual autopsy. Questions?"

Jhee signaled her teaching assistant to increase the lecture hall's lighting. Several hands in the arcane forensic seminar raised. Nevis, her colleague from the local Justicar's office who had been sent to evaluate the symposium, gave a grudging nod from the front row then scribbled on her evaluation sheet.

After the seminar, Jhee checked the time and gathered up her materials and slides. Plenty of time remained for her consult with the imperators and then refresh herself before tonight's evening out with Shep. In her haste, Jhee knocked over her valise and lecture materials. As she gathered up her fallen valise contents and slides, the jet black data shell she found the other day caught her eye. Following several failed attempts to decrypt it at home, Jhee thought to have someone at the office or clinic try. She stooped to pick it up. A floorboard creaked on the other side of the lecture bench.

Jhee grabbed the data shell and straightened up. A Water Folk individual standing by the lecture bench leaped back. She eyed Jhee and waited, hat clutched in her hands, looking sheepish. "Begging your pardon, Magistrate."

"Did you have questions about the seminar?" Jhee asked.

"Nay." Jhee gave the stranger a once over. Her clothes were threadbare. She continually twisted and worried the brim of the hat she held around in a circle. A sharp breath of the sea wafted from them. This was not a typical student or attendee. "This ain't about tome learning. You sees, a mutual friend gave me this card. She reckoned you might could help me."

The slight accent and pale body hair were peculiar to longshoremen and sailors from the Dales nicknamed sea dogs. The old sailor handed Jhee a credential card. After a quick inspection, Jhee realized the sequential number matched the one she had given Ursula.

"I have to head to my legal clinic. Walk with me." Jhee grabbed her valise, and she headed across the quad with the sailor. "What can I help you with?"

"I suspect this sea dog what I know be a med divisioner," she said using the sea dog dialect.

"I see," Jhee said cautiously. By "med divisioner," she meant a member of the Medical Protectorate. Between renewed interest in the Flower Wars and Medical Protectorate's recently uncovered unethical experiments, an obsession with war criminals had wormed its way into the popular consciousness. Folk had begun seeing them in every flower bed and suspecting every reclusive neighbor. "Have you brought your suspicions to the imperators?"

The sea dog handed her a copy of the complaint. "They laugh me off. I wants be sure before me goes back. I follow't along with your arcane detecting talks and be read your 'Dispatches from Arrow Point' adventures. Might I use some cypher or whatnot to prove me true?"

Jhee wrangled a few more details out of the sailor, but nothing that rose above the level of general war criminal hysteria. They arrived at the legal clinic where Jhee's grad students were sorting the files the Inquesters had brought with them. Consulting with Inquesters, the investigative ranks of law enforcement, comprised the other part of her new Justicar duties in the capital. At first sight of the Inquesters' insignia, her walking companion stopped short.

"Well, mum, many thanks for your time," the sea dog said and turned tail.

Had it been a generalized distrust of law enforcement officers that sent the sailor fleeing, or did she have more specific cause to avoid them? Hopefully, Jhee hadn't handled the card or incident report too much to get usable prints from them. Jhee tapped a finger aside her nose and proceeded to her consultation. A grad student handed her a stack of case files, and she went to work.

"There could be no denying it," Jhee said after examining a few reports. She peered through her magnifier at the images. Because of the lividity and bluish lip pallor shown in the images, Jhee suspected poison. Several victims' skin and body hair also bore pinkish blotches. This pattern seemed familiar. Jhee consulted the diagnostic tip sheet she had compiled over the years and compared it to the victims. Once she determined the cause of death to be poison, she had reached the end of her official mandate as consultant. All that remained was to turn her findings over to the local constabulary.

"Not all of these folk died of natural causes. You may be looking at a Maker of Death situation here. The calibrations and the alignments are key. Calibration: no common industrial link prior to their hospitalization. Alignment: all these victims show exposure to a rare pesticide present nowhere in their environment. This is a pattern I've seen before as a field Justicar in the Far Reaches."

"Folk can be so predictable. They always think they are so clever and have committed the perfect crime. They think they will be the ones to get away with it," the investigator said.

"Quite right," Jhee agreed. She tidied the bio-parchment printouts and handed the files back to the grateful investigators along with the clinic's and her grad students' findings.

"Thank you, Justicar. With your help, hopefully, we have enough to put this gutter guppy away," said the partner.

"My pleasure, Inquesters. Drop by anytime you need my help."

Later, Jhee might ask Shep what he thought. She had no doubt of her conclusion but missed talking through cases with him. Jhee pulled out her conch and recorded a summary of her notes. She double-checked her determination for good measure. Her notes concluded with the recommendation that a full murder inquiry be undertaken at once.

The Inquesters thanked her again before they left. Jhee basked in the sense of accomplishment.

Another conclusion expertly reached, but the job still felt half done. The urge to do more than make a determination had Jhee drumming her fingers on the case folder. She snatched up the folder again. Why give them the cause of death when Jhee could also give them the murderer? Jhee started running down the local suppliers of said pesticide. Only a few manufacturers produced it, but it had been prevalent amongst the older families. The pesticide mimicked the symptoms of a heart attack and was hard to detect. Until Jhee had helped discover additional markers that differentiated the pesticide-induced heart failure from a more typical one. With their favorite means to hide their crimes less effective, many in her home district switched to some form of direct violence. While the pesticide had a commercial use, it was an artifact being kept alive mostly via the Trench market by murderers. Had she single-handedly put a whole industry out of work? The Wolphin family from her home district might think so.

Unintended consequences. An interesting conundrum for another time. Jhee paused for humility's sake. This was not about her patting herself on the back; it was about getting justice for those who had no one to speak for them but her.

According to the wall-mounted clockworks, she had some time before she had to meet Shep for dinner. Jhee laid out the data shell, the card, and incident report. She plugged the data shell in and started another decryption protocol on it. While it worked, Jhee played with Ursula's disc.

Jhee continued to go through her files and review death records. A banded bruise on a body with the cause of death marked as accidental made her pause. Banded bruises like these often came from fingers. She projected the autopsy images and notes on the wall. She re-checked the cause of death and the findings on post-mortem lividity. With this heavy bruising and these injury patterns, how could someone have called this an accident? This person was badly beaten.

The coroner who called this an accident or natural causes had to be blind or corrupt. Some coroner late for a dinner or event took the word of a family member or authority figure. Jhee grabbed her conch to query the coroner. She noted the time. A few minutes and she might be able to tell which one this particular coroner was, and then she could hurry to meet Shep with time to spare.

Jhee now took her time and carefully went over the autopsy findings. She pored through reports from the time the body was found until autopsy. As she did so, she recalled Jeja's lessons on first principles and smiled. *Don't assume. Let the evidence lead.*

Sometimes the mortuary staff mishandled bodies, and without due diligence, post-mortem damage could be confused for pre-mortem. The logs showed no discrepancy. No mentions of anyone dropping the body. No gaps in the timeline. If the marks didn't come from post-mortem mishandling, that made it more unlikely this man died from an accident.

Jhee brought up full-dimensional images of the victim's body. Blunt force trauma to the head, contusions: she examined each injury's characteristics. Other bones showed evidence of old breaks and fractures, not all of which had set properly. From the depressed knuckles and metacarpal fractures, she determined this man might have been a pugilist of some sort.

A check of the fighter's lists, public records, and footage proved him not an extremely good or popular one. From his record, a minor one. He had a few low-level bouts, which he had all lost. He acted as a meat bag for up-and-coming fighters and a sparring partner. No fortune and glory for this one, his story ended in some dirty alley, and the injustice of his death may have gone unnoticed without her due diligence.

Jhee dictated her findings. *Should she investigate this one herself?* She checked his records for family. None. The matter had kept this long, and no one was breaking down the door to solve it.

This was not Jhee's mandate, and she was not a field Justicar anymore, she told herself. Her duty was in the lecture hall or lab like she had always wanted or to consult as the Empire required. She had gone from the assistant of the intrepid Jeja of Marpele to a bureaucrat and academic. This had always been the Path Maker's plan: the original course for her life, a position in academia. She slipped off her fingernail ink reservoir and laid a finger along her muzzle. Jhee missed the old days when she solved the crimes and judged them by her lonesome, but her life had changed. She longed to see a whole case through and not just review others' findings. This had to suffice. She had a household, a family to consider. Though, she might ask Shep, with his greater anatomical knowledge, his opinion on the autopsy injuries.

Family. Shep. Jhee viewed the time with horror. Her conch chimed, and she answered.

"Jhee, where are you?" Shep asked.

"At the legal clinic. I lost the time."

"Get moving. They won't hold our reservation much longer."

She grabbed her valise and dashed out the door.

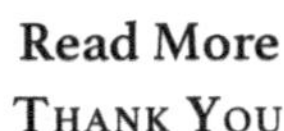

Read More

Thank You

Thank you for reading this THE HOUSE OF SORROWS excerpt! If you would like to read more, you can pick up your copy today! Buy THE HOUSE OF SORROWS!

ACKNOWLEDGMENTS

Adam C., Anne K., Elizabeth Frenette., Mark S., Val A.

ABOUT THE AUTHOR

TREVOL SWIFT is a sometimes-sassy author of fantasy who grew up in Connecticut. She graduated from WIT with a BS in Computer Engineering Technology and now lives in Eastern Massachusetts. In her spare time Trevol enjoys gaming of all styles, cosplay, reading, writing and dancing. She also likes to relax by getting creative, with drawing and storytelling among her favorite pastimes.

Follow her on BookBub to get notifications of new book releases and sales:
bookbub.com/authors/trevol-swift

You can also contact Trevol Swift at:

Website: swiftnesse.com

facebook.com/swiftnesse

pinterest.com/swiftnesse

twitter.com/Swiftnesse

instagram.com/swiftnesseauthor

www.ingramcontent.com/pod-product-compliance
Lightning Source LLC
Chambersburg PA
CBHW032108180726
48284CB00002B/502